Finders

Irish Studies
Kathleen Costello-Sullivan, *Series Editor*

For a full list of titles in this series,
visit https://press.syr.edu/supressbook-series/irish-studies/.

Finders

JUSTICE, FAITH, AND IDENTITY IN IRISH CRIME FICTION

ANJILI BABBAR

Syracuse University Press

Copyright © 2023 by Syracuse University Press
Syracuse, New York 13244-5290

All Rights Reserved

First Edition 2023

23 24 25 26 27 28   6 5 4 3 2 1

∞ The paper used in this publication meets the minimum requirements
of the American National Standard for Information Sciences—Permanence of Paper
for Printed Library Materials, ANSI Z39.48-1992.

For a listing of books published and distributed by Syracuse University Press,
visit https://press.syr.edu.

ISBN: 978-0-8156-3791-2 (hardcover)
       978-0-8156-1157-8 (paperback)
       978-0-8156-5588-6 (e-book)

LCCN: 2022041726

Manufactured in the United States of America

This book is dedicated to Colin Dexter,
for the kindness, encouragement, and tea,
and to my dad, who always read everything I wrote

Contents

Acknowledgments

I wish to thank the incredible team at Syracuse University Press, and particularly my brilliant and patient editor, Deborah Manion: it has been an honor and a privilege to work with her. I am also indebted to all of the authors in this study, and especially to the people who generously dedicated their time for interviews or permissions, or both: Adrian McKinty, Gerard Brennan, Eoin McNamee, Brian Mc-Gilloway, Steve Cavanagh, Claire McGowan, John Connolly, Jeremy Dexter, Jay Stringer, and Ellen Clair Lamb. Adrian and Gerard also offered invaluable feedback, as did Brian Cliff, Elizabeth Mannion, Thomas C. Foster, Frederic Svoboda, and S. A. Cosby, for which I am extremely grateful. For the images, I am indebted to photographer Jaytee Van Stean, sculptor Ewald Böggemann, and editor Tim Harris. Finally, I would like to thank the colleagues, friends, and family who provided critical support and encouragement: Andrew, Tracey, Sarah, Myron, Gemma, Jean, Leslie, Leila, my parents, Moriarty, and Pomme.

Ewald Böggemann, statue of Saint Anthony at the Oxford Oratory, 2014. Carved based on photographs and remains of the original statue, which was damaged by fire. Photograph by Anjili Babbar, 2021. https://www .oxfordoratory.org.uk/news.php?newid=3363.

Finders

Introduction

Tony, Tony, come around, something's lost and can't be found.
—Prayer to Saint Anthony of Padua

The most iconic Irish hard-boiled detective insists that he isn't a detective at all. "There are no private eyes in Ireland," explains Ken Bruen's reluctant protagonist, Jack Taylor, in his first appearance in *The Guards* (2001): "The Irish wouldn't wear it. The concept brushes perilously close to the hated 'informer.' You can get away with most anything except 'telling.'" The dismissal is, at once, a distancing from the fundamental signifiers of hard-boiled vocabulary and from the traditional symbolism of detective-character tropes. It defines the novel both in relation to and as contrary to expectations of its genre and leaves Taylor scrambling for a vague, noncommittal explanation of his occupation: "What I began to do was find things." Eventually settling on the title of "finder," a reference to Saint Anthony of Padua, the patron saint of lost articles and missing persons, Taylor uses similar distancing language to both emphasize the religious connotation of the word and deny that such a connotation is important: "I didn't come to one morning and shout, 'God wants me to be a finder!' He could care less. There's God and there's the Irish version. This allows Him to be feckless. Not that he doesn't take an interest, but He couldn't be bothered."[1]

Taylor frames his rejection of divine influence on human behavior as disaffectedness rather than nihilism: a disappointment with God that is, however ironically, reliant on a presumption of God's existence. His stance is remarkable for a protagonist in a genre of

1

fiction whose inception is inextricably linked with secularization and the situation of reason above spirituality in the restoration of order; generally speaking, in detective fiction, "the certainties expounded by the Church are reenacted through the figure of the rational investigator whose perspicacity never fails to uncover the perpetrator and return the world to its pre-lapsarian tranquillity."[2] Indeed, a suspicion of organized religion is so paramount in the genre that faith is rarely introduced except as a clue to the insincerity of a suspect. Such an approach is, of course, dependent on transference of the trust conferred on religion in the past to secular systems of legal justice; while the detective may place himself above the law or question the competence, morals, and reliability of individual members of the criminal justice system, his ethics must correspond, more or less, to those espoused by his society, as the essence of his job is to bring perpetrators who have acted against these standards to justice. In this sense, despite any qualms or protests he might have, the detective is a caricatured embodiment of the legal norms of his society and a tool to enforce them.

Taylor is certainly not the first fictional detective to look back to religion as a possible, if imperfect, alternative to legal order; Ian Rankin's Inspector Rebus, for example, examines a variety of religions in hopes of finding one that he can reconcile with his rational nature. What is noteworthy about Taylor's consideration is that, notwithstanding the expected aversion to corrupt manifestations of spirituality and inability to resolve what he perceives as a dissonance between faith and reason, he never ultimately rejects religion as a vehicle of justice. On the contrary, by insisting that he is a "finder" rather than a detective or an investigator, Taylor suggests that he is more comfortable aligning himself with spiritual ethics than with legal ones. He unabashedly proclaims his envy toward those who are able to embrace religion fully—"people . . . going to confession . . . how I wished I could seek such a cleansing"—and even flirts with the notion of a religious life, upon encountering a Franciscan who is "[his] age, without a line in his face."[3]

This flirtation is short-lived, however. When he inquires whether the friar enjoys his work, Taylor is met with a rebuke: the work of a friar is "God's work" and not his own. As appealing as the apparent comfort and certainties of the religious life are, Taylor is too much a product of secular rationalism to absorb its ideology, let alone embrace it as a lifestyle. He finds a middle ground in Anthony, to whom he prays for assistance with an investigation, even as he chastises himself for considering requesting intervention on his own behalf: "At the abbey, I went in and lit a candle to St Anthony, the finder of lost things. It crossed my mind to ask him to find *myself*, but it seemed too theatrical."[4]

Taylor's metaphoric application of Anthony's skills is neither obtuse nor ironic. Anthony's association with lost things and people stems from an anecdote in which an apathetic novice decides to leave the order, taking Anthony's valuable book of psalms along with him.[5] For Anthony, the theft is less material than intellectual: he regrets the loss of the notes he has painstakingly scrawled in the psalter's margins and prays for its return.[6] The novice, affected by the prayer, restores the book—but, more important, his faith is restored to him, and he returns to the order from which he has strayed.[7] Thus, with one prayer, Anthony reclaims not only a lost object but also lost knowledge, a lost person, and a lost soul. In this sense, one might well understand why he represents, to Taylor, an idealized embodiment of his profession, in which the furtherance of education and the restoration of personal well-being—reason and ethics—are the natural results of an application of justice.

But Anthony has much else to recommend himself as a model for Taylor. By welcoming the prodigal novice upon his return and refusing to punish him for his theft, he establishes a paradigm of forgiveness, rather than castigation, in the reinstatement of order. He becomes known in Padua for promoting ethics so convincingly that criminals make restitution of their own accord and lawmakers are inspired to liberate repentant prisoners.[8] Significantly, in terms of Taylor's acute awareness of the history behind his culture's mistrust in the criminal justice system, Anthony devotes much of his energy to promoting an understanding of the way in which disenfranchisement inevitably leads to lawbreaking and to decriminalizing actions taken out of necessity rather than malice. He risks his own safety to confront the tyrant Ezzelino da Romano to demand the release of prisoners,[9] rails against a system that effectively criminalizes poverty, and induces the magistrates of Padua to pardon those individuals who have been arrested for their debts.[10]

Anthony's legacy is not, however, one of absolute adherence to the practices of the church. On the contrary, he resents the hierarchical, exclusionary structure of the church, which he views as a mirror of an unjust socioeconomic system, and insists on delivering his sermons in marketplaces and public squares, rather than cathedrals, to increase accessibility for anyone, of any social class, who wishes to attend. He also risks the censure of Francis himself through his emphasis on literacy and education—things that Francis is suspicious might "quench the spirit of holy prayer and devotion according to our Rule."[11]

Anthony's rebelliousness, his envisioning of a justice purer than that which is provided by either the law or the church, and his dedication to breaking down the dissociation of class and education allow for the possibility that respect for him or attempts to fashion oneself in his image might not necessitate the sort of unquestioning religious devotion that Taylor finds so difficult to attain. In fact, while Taylor has, at least, an admiration for the theoretical promise of faith, Bruen's appropriation of Anthony is actually an intertextual reference to a more traditionally atheistic detective, Colin Dexter's Inspector Morse. Having shunned religion as irreconcilable with his passion for logic throughout his career, as he approaches retirement, Morse nevertheless finds himself drawn to the Oxford Oratory, "a building he'd seldom paid attention to before, although he must have walked past it so many, many times." Like Taylor, he finds the atmosphere "seductive" and regards a faithful parishioner with jealousy: "Morse envied her, for she looked so much at home there: looked as if she knew herself and her Lord so well, and was wholly familiar with all the trappings of prayer and the promises of forgiveness." His ultimate approach of Saint Anthony is less wholehearted than Taylor's—he is distracted and wonders from "whence had sprung that oddly intrusive 'h'" in Anthony's name—but he finds himself lured, by a text describing Anthony's miracles "for those who almost had sufficient faith," into lighting a candle. Lacking Taylor's Catholic upbringing, Morse isn't sure how to proceed from here: he knows he is supposed to ask for miraculous intervention but "[isn't] at all sure what miracle he [wants]." Nevertheless, he is acutely aware of his comfort and his feeling of communion with Anthony: "The elegant, elongated candle was of importance to him; and on some semi-irrational impulse he took a second candle and placed it beside the first. Together, side by side, they seemed to give a much stronger light than both of them separate." A confirmed and compulsive alcoholic, Morse is nevertheless convinced, as he makes his donation for the candles, that the visit is worth the price of "a whole pint"; the time has passed quickly and peacefully, despite the fact that he has "no faith in the Almighty and even less in miracles." Nihilism aside, when his usual self-neglect later results in a precarious situation—his blood sugar has fallen dangerously and he has little food in the house—he credits and blesses Anthony for the uncharacteristically early arrival of the milkman.[12]

Morse's quest for solace in Anthony's companionship comes at a pivotal point in his life and career. His poor health and emotional exhaustion have left him with little choice but to abandon the occupation onto which he has transferred all of his yearnings for personal fulfillment, and a reopened cold case brings a past decision to prioritize compassion over legal considerations into full focus. Determined to stand by this decision, he faces unwarranted suspicion and is forced to finally confront his long-standing impressions about the distinction between ethics and law. Lacking a caretaker or confidant in the face of his sentience of impending death likewise causes him to reflect on the foundations of his isolation. At this point in the series, the audience is painfully aware of these foundations: Morse has never been able to find a comfortable place in society because he defies constructions of class. His blue-collar background makes him an outsider at Oxford; his intellect and education make him a pariah in the police force. He is the common man, empowered through education, that Anthony championed, but that was never granted acknowledgment in the social order.

Although Taylor's appeal to Anthony is an obvious homage to Morse, its application to the Irish context creates a more resounding effect than the original. Only a year after publication of *The Guards*, *The Wire* satirized the idea of detectives requesting intervention from Anthony when faced with conflicts between their consciences and the criminal justice system. Like Taylor, Detective Michael Santangelo has an abhorrence for snitching. Advised that he has a choice between reporting to his commanding officer about the unprofessional habits of his colleague Jimmy McNulty or clearing a cold case, Santangelo determines that solving the case, while seemingly impossible, is the only solution. In desperation, he falls prey to the prank of his jeering sergeant, who sends him to a local psychic to ask for help. Seeing the psychic's religious artifacts, Santangelo draws her attention to his name, a derivation of Saint Angelus, who was a contemporary of Anthony. While he shared Anthony's passion for education and preference for forgiveness over punishment—he famously prayed for the pardon of his murderer from his deathbed—Angelus is known more for his unquestioning devotion and his skills at conversion than for a clear-eyed and objective assessment of the nature of law, ethics, and church practices. When the psychic informs him that it is Saint Anthony, and not Angelus, who has a message for him, Santangelo quickly abandons his loyalty to his namesake and embraces the proposed alliance with Anthony instead: "Ain't he the guy you call when you lose something?" Though he has doubts about the psychic's reliability—the statuette of Anthony she offers him bears no resemblance to the Franciscan—he nevertheless follows the prescribed, albeit ridiculous, ritual of burying and exhuming the statuette as a gesture of supplication. As tongue-in-cheek as the story line is, it concludes with the surprise resolution of a different cold case, and Santangelo is thus rescued from any punishment or concession of his values: a seeming miracle, for which he unhesitatingly credits Anthony.[13] For Santangelo, it makes little difference that the efforts of McNulty and his partner are the direct cause of his reprieve; as in the cases of Taylor and Morse, Santangelo's prayer to Anthony is, in some sense, a metaphoric appeal for living people to deliver justice consistently and in a way that averts the compromising of ethics.

In its treatment of Anthony, *The Wire* posits the saint as inextricably linked with Ireland and with Irish detectives in particular. Santangelo is initially dismayed when the psychic introduces the idea of his connection to Anthony by asking if he is Irish. Confoundedly, he replies that his ancestors are from Italy—the country in which Anthony spent most of his life and with which his miracles and sainthood are associated—but his protest is dismissed. The correlation of Anthony with Jack Taylor and Ireland is crucial to the dark social commentary of the series at this juncture; though Santangelo's conundrum about snitching and his sense of discord between law and ethics are here embodied specifically in the question of whether to inform on McNulty, the story thread is also a thinly veiled iteration of the series' running theme about the corruption, power struggles, and institutionalized bias of the police force. McNulty has become the target of his superiors through his dogged insistence that the case of a murderous drug ring be investigated thoroughly. This creates an unusual amount of work for a unit that is more concerned with clearance rates and the appearance of progress than actual justice; it also leads to a money trail with the potential to incriminate high-ranking members of the police force and government officials. The nod to Taylor is both an acknowledgment of the way in which Irish noir has furthered discussion about the nature of justice and the reliability of the legal justice system in crime fiction and a suggestion that such a discussion is applicable outside of an Irish context. By the time *The Wire* itself receives a similar nod on *Justified*, considerations of the conflicts between ethics and legal standards are so deeply linked to Ireland that they continue to be discussed in terms of patron saints, despite the Pentecostal context of the series. Though he is a born-again Evangelical Christian whose religion rejects the

Catholic understanding of sainthood, Boyd Crowder nonetheless tries to educate the protagonist, Raylan Givens, about the patronage of saints such as Jude. More poignantly, in a scene echoing *The Wire*, he recommends that Givens limit his detective work and thus implicitly reject the balance of religion, ethics, and law represented by Anthony. Instead, he advises a more traditional Christian approach—that of Anthony's mentor and check—wherein faith is superior to acquired knowledge or legal justice: "In the words of Saint Francis, 'it is only by forgiving that we ourselves are forgiven.'"[14] Like many of his detective counterparts, however, Givens is unable to embrace religion uncompromisingly; anticipating the same quote by Francis, Jack Taylor replies that it is "bollocks,"[15] so it is not surprising that Givens's frowning response is far less enthusiastic than Santangelo's and highlights the inappropriateness of the suggested saint: "He the one with the birds?"[16]

In the second novel of the Jack Taylor series, Bruen plays with the association of Irish noir and recognizable tropes in American crime fiction through a British suspect who inexplicably characterizes detective fiction as an Irish construct: "A private eye, twenty a day and expenses? I love it; only in Ireland. I've seen the movies."[17] The irony here is obvious: apart from attributing the development of American hard-boiled standards to Irish authors, the suspect seemingly overlooks the fact that, while crime fiction—of the amateur and procedural varieties in particular—has enjoyed enormous popularity in Britain, and while there have long been echoes of the mystery genre in the Irish literary canon, forays into crime writing by Irish authors have been relatively sparse and have not received substantial and serious attention until the twenty-first century.[18] This delay is likely owing to a number of factors, including the widespread suspicion of police and informants underscored by Bruen and others. In *Irish Crime Fiction*, Brian Cliff makes the compelling case that an inundation of so-called Troubles trash novels—reductive crime narratives about the conflict in Northern Ireland, written largely by non-Irish authors—also contributed to a devaluation of the genre.[19] Perhaps most notably, the persistence of Revivalist approaches to

Irish literary studies has inevitably had the effect of prioritizing liter-ature that reflects on the Irish condition and contributes to discourse about postcolonial Irish identity.

If a sluggish embrace of crime fiction in Ireland is understand-able because of a convergence of cultural and social conditions, the recent boom in the subgenre requires more speculation. Currently, authors both north and south of the border are producing work at a staggering rate, to great critical acclaim. In "Murderous Mayhem: Ken Bruen and the New Ireland," Paula Murphy argues that the newfound respect for the genre is partially attributable to tribunal inquiries into politicians, which have led to "a significant change in attitude from juvenile admiration for those who trick the state to a more mature demand for social responsibility"[20] and thereby made legal justice—and thus crime fiction—more palatable to an Irish audience. These tribunals, however, have not been universally popular and continue to be regarded with suspicion as potential vehicles of further corruption. It has also been suggested that they obfuscate the lines of investigative duties, thereby creating an excuse for the Guards to shirk responsibilities. Bruen's numerous references to the tribunals highlight this public mistrust, even implying that the Irish blame them for "conflicting information" and miscarriages of justice.[21] Bruen's unease with encumbering Jack Taylor with a staple noir title, such as "detective" or "investigator"—an unease echoed by several subsequent Irish crime writers—also suggests that the recent popularity of the genre in Ireland is not predicated on a newfound confidence in the law. On the contrary, Taylor's protests that he is not a detective might be viewed as a cautiously ironic and self-reflective authorial commentary: an indication that Bruen understands that the success of a traditional detective novel is as unlikely in Ireland as the success of a private eye and a self-conscious distancing from this formula.

In "Religious Belief in Recent Detective Fiction," Bill Phillips remarks that "Taylor's refusal to accept the title of detective, or private eye, contributes to Bruen's general policy of interrogating and subverting the traditional hard-boiled detective model."[22] This formula of interrogation and subversion is perhaps a more convincing explanation for the recent surge in crime fiction from Ireland, and it is reflected in Irish noir in part through reassessments of the nature of justice and attempts to redefine the role of the detective within the legal justice system. For Taylor, such a reassessment is complicated and not particularly fulfilling. It involves abandoning the structured systems of justice that formerly provided him with a sense of self and belonging to search in isolation for a purer, unchartered course through a sequence of trials and errors. As a former police officer, he regrets his dismissal from the Guards, clinging to his regulation all-weather coat as a connection to a time when he could clearly define himself in relation to a particular preoutlined philosophy,[23] but he is extremely aware of corruption in the legal system and the failure of legal procedures to inevitably produce justice. His yearning is not for the Guard system itself, but for the naïveté that enabled him to feel that the end of colonialism in Ireland meant that he would be participating in a new, trustworthy type of police force, "a tangible power for the betterment of the nation,"[24] through which, "in [his] uniform with the buttons gleaming, [his] cap at a firm angle, the baton to hand, [he] thought [he] could make a difference."[25] While Taylor insists that his nostalgia for religion and the police are both merely force of habit, he enters the barracks only when compelled but frequents churches of his own free will, remarking on the sense of comfort they provide. The training committee's ostensible philosophy for guards, which painfully lodges itself in his dreams, describes the role of the police almost exclusively through religious metaphors, suggesting that they should *have the wisdom of Soloman, the courage of David, the strength of Samson, the patience of Job . . . the kindness of the good Samaritan . . . the faith of Daniel . . . the tolerance of the carpenter of Nazareth.*[26] This is consistent with Taylor's outlook in general, which articulates justice and decency in terms of religious, rather than legal, ethics. He regularly uses the concepts of love, purity, and holiness to describe the best aspects of the world, while consistently describing those individuals who would seek to cause harm or chaos—notwithstanding psychological ailments or childhood trauma—as evil. Upon encountering the most heartless predator of his career, Taylor is largely convinced—and strives to convince his audience—that the man is the devil incarnate.

But Taylor is nearly as disillusioned with the promises of the church as he is with those of the legal system. He refers to himself frequently as a recovering Catholic, is often outwardly hostile toward the perceived authority of priests, and returns repeatedly to the subjects of the church's pedophilia scandals, cover-ups, and financial greed.[27] Nevertheless, his faith in the existence and power of God is unwavering.[28] In this sense, Taylor's seeming preference for what he perceives as a corrupt church over a corrupt legal system is an understandable by-product of his independence and distaste for authority; it is more clearly possible to have a personal relationship with God that exists outside of the standards of the church than it is to have a personal relationship with the law that exists outside of the standards of law enforcement. Moreover, it is possible to negotiate one's relationship with religion—to create a subjective hierarchy of religious codes and thus to forge one's own rule book of justice and morality—while the law allows for little such flexibility. Taylor is able, for example, to at least partially excuse himself for violence and even murder in the pursuit of a greater good: an approach that is irreconcilable with the law. His ability to draw a distinction between faith and its flawed human manifestations might thus be perceived as reflective of his ultimate quest to find a place for himself within the context of the legal system: a place that, ideally, would allow him to further the cause of justice according to the dictates of his own conscience. At the same time, he is acutely aware that the guidelines he finds so distasteful in both the legal and the religious approaches to justice are society's only protection against subjective vigilantism, and he frequently finds himself in the position of investigating vigilantes whose distorted perceptions, personal wounds or fetishes, or misinterpretations of science or literature lead them into perpetuating injustice even as they seek to rectify it. Taylor's frustration and self-loathing principally stem from the cognizance that the only thing that allows him to distinguish himself from these targets is the fact that he believes in his own principles and not in theirs. In this regard, his awareness of the limitations of structural justice is tempered by a correlated understanding of the impossibility of a conception of justice that is universal to all members of a society. Unlike Morse, he knows precisely what miracle he wants, but he is unable to envision what that miracle would look like in a society with as many perspectives as people. It is, for him, an unsatisfying conclusion, and he is frequently forced to remind himself that there is much to be said for honesty, even when it is less alluring than illusive hope, certainty, or complacency.

Taylor's bleak view of the possibility of finding a successful route to justice leads him into frequent bouts of depression, emotional self-laceration, and thoughts of suicide, but as often as he protests that he is devoid of faith or hope, he invariably pulls himself back from the precipice because of a sense of obligation to at least attempt to advance the cause of justice. At such moments, he returns to Anthony's altar, shunning priests and entreating the saint directly to protect his deceased loved ones and to assist him in protecting the living. Here, his imagining of Anthony as an embodiment of elusive, unqualified justice helps him to outline some of the attributes of justice that, for him, are nonnegotiable. Unlike the church, which extorts donations from an impoverished public, requiring payment for Mass cards, candles, and the prayers they represent, Anthony stands aloof from appearances and consumerism.[29] To Taylor, he seems to offer solace regardless of social or financial status and the possibility of forgiveness for mistakes made in the quest for righteousness: mistakes that Taylor finds difficult to entirely forgive in himself. Although he never manages to devise a clear course of action or a personal standard of behavior that he finds acceptable, Taylor comes to define his role as "finder" as, at base, a provider of the same comfort he has been tendered by Anthony: a "gatekeeper" to prevent others' complete loss of hope and suicide.[30]

Aside from Taylor's symbolic association of Anthony with a pure form of justice that he finds difficult to define in principle, let alone enact in practice, Anthony's emphasis on the importance of literacy and reading in the promotion of empathy, empowerment, and comfort becomes a defining theme in the novels. Taylor's greatest passion is for all forms of literature; his longest-sustained relationship is with his bookseller, and through his many changes of residence, books are the only furnishings for which he seems to feel any attachment. Through Taylor's remarks about his reading habits and his numerous, specific references to authors and their works, Bruen creates a dialogue with other authors that allows him to remark not only on the relationship between literature and humanity but also on his feelings about developments in crime fiction. He offers nods of respect and encouragement to Irish crime writers that succeed him, including Declan Burke, Brian McGilloway, Gerard Brennan, and Adrian McKinty. Similarly, he responds with mutual admiration to the screenwriters who have referenced his work, alluding repeatedly to *The Wire* and framing Raylan Givens from *Justified* as the detective Taylor most envies because of Givens's ability to enact his personal interpretation of justice without being subject to qualms of conscience or serious trouble with the law. Late in the series, Bruen brings his authorial commentary to the forefront by introducing himself as a character that Taylor encounters in a pub: a lost and guarded individual who Taylor explains has "done some hard time in a South American jail. So rumor said. He certainly had the lost eyes to give it credence. I'd heard too he had a minor rap going as a crime writer." Bruen's decision to interject himself in the story line is, in part, a desire to respond to criticism of his work: his character refers dismissively to a review that "tore [his] book to shreds," implying that his difficult life experiences have made him at once uniquely capable of writing relatable fiction and immune to pain from disparagement. Refusing to condescend to more detail himself, he lets Taylor's bookseller complete his thoughts: "The critics crap him off because they say. . . . He uses too many cultural references, pop music, crime writers in his books. . . . [B]ollix to them. Because for me, it grounds the story in stuff I know, that I can relate to."[31]

Later, Taylor returns to this theme of unwarranted disrespect for Bruen's brand of postmodern, humanized, intertextual crime writing, lamenting that "every literary hack was taking time out from the *serious vocation of literature and slumming in [the crime fiction] genre*" and referring to such behavior as opportunistic.[32] For Bruen, this "slumming" is clearly an attempt to appropriate a form made acceptable to the Irish as a result of developments by himself and others, without appreciating the significance of these developments. Bruen's allusion here is to John Banville, the Booker Prize–winning Irish novelist who, at the Theakston Old Peculier Crime Writing Festival, claimed to be "slumming it" when writing crime fiction[33] and, in an interview for the *Paris Review*, asserted that the procedural novels he wrote under the pseudonym of Benjamin Black were "bloody easy" to write compared to dramatic fiction, by virtue of the "consciously crafted" nature of detective fiction and its "clichéd" elements of character: "Most of the thrillers that I pick up, after three pages I throw them at the wall because the wise-guy tone grates on my nerves. Every hero in crime fiction knows everything about everything. Nothing surprises or baffles him. What I like about Quirke is that he's rather stupid, like the rest of us. He misses the point of things, he stumbles over clues, misreads people. He's far too dim to be a Philip Marlowe. But this is what I treasure in him— his human frailty."[34] Banville's assessment raised eyebrows in the crime writing community, particularly in Ireland, in that it seemed to overlook some decades of progress in the genre, depicting fictional detectives other than his own as cozy amateur caricatures or hardboiled men-of-the-streets whose ethical failings do not interfere with their ability to maintain "emotional distance" from their cases and unfailingly restore order to chaotic situations.[35] Bruen's singling out of Banville for censure is hardly surprising, as Banville's assessment reflects at best an unfamiliarity with and at worst a willful dismissal of the aspects of crime fiction that Bruen has embraced and built upon in the structuring of Irish noir.

Bruen's consideration of the imperfection of justice relies heavily on postmodern crime fiction narratives about the imperfection of people: an imperfection to which detectives, including Taylor, are not immune. Despite Banville's appraisal, sophisticated plots that acknowledge the complexities of crime and ethics—narratives that DCI Banks describes as "no good, no evil, just a bunch of men and women getting in a mess"—are hardly unusual. The detective, more often than not, is a fallible person within the drama, wondering "how . . . you clear it up when you're part of the mess."[36] British crime writer Jay Stringer emphasizes that the contemporary fictional detective "needs to have something wrong with them, either mentally, physically, or socially. They are the world around them, and they wouldn't be trying to fix the world if there wasn't something about themselves that also needed fixing,"[37] while Shaun Evans, who plays Inspector Morse in *Endeavour*, suggests that "you often find that in . . . crime dramas, the central character . . . is quite a dark, tortured person and finds some kind of release in solving crime and bringing justice."[38] Certainly, even early hard-boiled detectives like Sam Spade and Philip Marlowe, to whom Banville refers extensively, sought to work through questions of personal disequilibrium and selfhood through their cases, though they did so in a manner that was largely tangential and un-self-reflective.[39] What is suggested in these assessments is something more human, fallible, and relatable: a detective driven to solve crimes not only to restore social order, but also to generate a surrogate order as balm for his own psychological wounds: "The question of the literal truth or universal validity of the story is an irrelevance. Its crux is that it represents the possibility of overcoming trauma through the process of representation itself."[40]

In a brief but insightful overview of historical trends in crime fiction, author Mark Billingham reflects on imperfections and idiosyncrasies of character that date to Arthur Conan Doyle's creation of Sherlock Holmes, suggesting that the "cosy" novels produced during the interwar period might be viewed as a kind of aberration in the development of increasingly worldly, sensitive, and even damaged detectives. Within this timeline, Billingham also notes the significance of work by P. D. James, Ruth Rendell, and Colin Dexter, whose investigators were "cultured rather than privileged,"[41] thereby challenging both character tropes—the aristocrat dabbling in crime; the violent, streetwise private eye; the cog in the police machine—and stereotypes about class. Of the three detectives in question—Adam Dagliesh, Reginald Wexford, and Endeavour Morse—I would argue that the third, in particular, foreshadows Irish crime fiction through his subjective approach to crime, his personal shortcomings, and the author's persistent interrogation of social prescriptions that impact our understanding of identity. When Dexter launched the Inspector Morse series in 1975, he introduced a detective whose personal struggles were tangible and relatable and whose role within the system of law and order was equivocal at best. A man in constant search of his place in society, Morse is too intellectually driven to feel at home in his blue-collar family, too emotionally fragile and disenfranchised by his outsider status to complete his course at Oxford, too enamored of chaos to choose a mate wisely and thus create his own family structure, and too skeptical of authority and regulations to rise through police ranks in a timely fashion. Far from being a symbol of order, he reflects the turmoil and inconsistencies of the human psyche in its attempts to understand and relate to the world. Moreover, his vanity and prejudices are more than foibles: frequently, they cause him to make mistakes—sometimes, even fatal mistakes. He is driven to solve crimes by intensely personal motives, namely, a desire to find a place for himself in the world, to understand people so that he might find a way to relate to them, and to impose some kind of meaning and worth on his painful and chaotic life. In *The Remorseful Day* (1999), he solves the case that he has decided will be his last before retirement—and promptly dies. The resolution of cases has become so complete a surrogate for the social and emotional milestones he hoped to attain in his personal life that without it there is seemingly no way for him to live at all.

The Dexter-era detective may seem, psychologically, only a natural development from his predecessors, but that development is crucial in terms of his ability to transcend social and political context. There is thus some irony in Banville failing to acknowledge the distinction, as it may be argued that, along with interrogations of the nature of justice, it is precisely this distinction that led to a shift in perception of the genre's possibilities and allowed it to flourish in Ireland among his predecessors in the form, such as Bruen. Just as Jack

Taylor has to reformulate private eyes as "finders," crime fiction had to be reformulated from plot-driven procedural to existential metaphor. While deliberately referencing standards of the genre so as to contextualize its differences, in Irish crime fiction, solutions to cases often become substitutes for unforthcoming solutions to problems in the detectives' own lives. The search for a murderer or a missing person reflects the detective's desire to define his own identity: his ethics, his place in society, and the challenges he must overcome in order to be happy. Simultaneously, it is a means of avoiding this more subjective quest and the emotional difficulties involved in addressing personal shortcomings. Taylor's request to Anthony for help with a case, his confession that he actually longs to ask for help finding himself, and his ultimate refusal to do so set a clear paradigm for the Irish detective. The detective's individual identity, relationship to justice, and role in society are at once conflated, interdependent, and at conflict.

The detective's conundrum is reflective of a larger tension at play in Irish crime fiction. By rejecting the puzzle-game formula in favor of a more metaphorical approach, Irish noir writers both interrogate standards of the genre that might be unpalatable to an Irish audience and contextualize the genre in terms of long-standing national literary traditions. The quest for self-identity is an understandably common theme in the literature of a region that historically defined itself in contrast to a colonialist other and was forced to renegotiate this definition when globalization and modernization blurred the distinctions between Irish and British subjectivity and increased secularization obfuscated ideological distinctions between Catholics and Protestants.[42] For W. B. Yeats, delineating Irish identity meant turning inward to collective memory and traditions of language, religion, and orality that were suppressed under British occupation. For postmodern writers, identity becomes more complex as a result of perceived conflicts between nationalism and the establishment of a modern, tolerant, liberal society.[43] Additionally, Revivalist pressure to subjugate other aspects of identity to cultural heritage might be viewed as ultimately stifling or antithetical to self-knowledge. The

nature of Irishness is also called into question because of the imposi-
tion of idyllic American conceptions of Irish tradition: conceptions
that Ireland has increasingly been pressured to replicate to bolster a
tourist industry that is pertinent to its economy.

This opacity of cultural identity, coupled with the waning power
of the Catholic Church, has made room for increased speculation
about personal identity and the ways in which it has been encumbered by cultural and religious expectations of public persona. Brian
Friel's *The Enemy Within* (1975), in its emphasis on the emotional
life of Saint Columba and his efforts to reconcile his private self
with public perception and obligations, might be viewed as a model
for the Jack Taylor series as clearly as the work of any hard-boiled
author; just as "Columba's exile from Ireland on Iona can . . . be
interpreted as a metaphor for his exile from a sense of self,"[44] Taylor's exile from the Guards and partial dissociation from the church
leave him floundering for a sense of personal identity—and, in turn,
an understanding of what justice means to him personally—outside
of structured public norms. Likewise, Irish crime fiction attempts
to negotiate literary and individual identity both within and without the prescriptions of genre and cultural heritage, simultaneously
emphasizing the instability and the freedom that arise from crossing
the bounds of these prescriptions. In so doing, it examines ways of
approaching identity in an era when traditional social markers seem
increasingly inadequate and reductive.

The Irish detective is an idiosyncratic character, conforming neither to obsolete, stereotypical crime fiction devices nor to sentimen-
talized notions of Irishness engendered by the American imagination
and popular culture representations. Just as Taylor attempts to reconcile and evaluate standards of religious and legal justice, assessing
and ranking their value in a search for absolutes to incorporate in the
basis of his own individual system, Irish noir makes use of heritage
and genre in the establishment of a new approach: one that considers what it means to be both an individual and the product of social
systems, both acculturated and globalized, both affected by the
past and assuming a role in progress, both aware of imperfections

of the self and the world and desirous of having a positive impact. Above all, it challenges the trope of the detective as an individual who "knows everything about everything,"[45] destined for his role because of exceptional qualities of perception, deduction, and intellect. Rather, it suggests that, inasmuch as the postmodern condition creates new possibilities for subjectivity, awareness, and empathy as well as uncertainty, isolation, and reactionary intransigence, the contemplative individual is of necessity a sort of detective, appraising the behavior and ideologies of himself and others, negotiating his identity, his shortcomings, and his relationships—and, ideally, examining what it means to be a force for justice.

Until recently, scholarship on Irish crime fiction was limited, but this situation is rapidly changing. Apart from journal articles by scholars of both Irish studies and crime fiction, Brian Cliff's survey *Irish Crime Fiction* (2018), and three recent anthologies, Declan Burke's *Down These Green Streets: Irish Crime Writing in the 21st Century* (2011), Elizabeth Mannion's *The Contemporary Irish Detective Novel* (2016), and *Guilt Rules All: Irish Mystery, Detective, and Crime Fiction* (2020), edited by Mannion and Cliff, have contributed substantially to discourse on this subgenre. Such foundational texts have established a context and framework for more specific examinations.[46] I have not, in this study, set out to create a broad survey of Irish crime fiction, but rather to specifically consider the way that Irish crime writers redefine the notions of justice, faith, and identity—sometimes in multiple and heterogenous ways—in response to changes in the economic, cultural, and political climates of Ireland and Northern Ireland. Because the use of religious symbolism is a distinctive quality of Irish crime fiction, and because it is often employed in particular to emphasize the malleability of these terms and to denote efforts to reframe them in ways that conform to the individual detective's (sometimes equally variable) priorities and understanding of the world, the text is divided with respect to this convention. Sections reflect the representative qualities of Catholic saints who appear as reference points in the primary texts, both directly and indirectly.

Part 1, "Finders of Lost Things: Saint Anthony, Identity, and the Limits of Structural Justice," considers efforts by Irish authors to establish multiperspective (and, especially, multicultural) discourse in their approaches to crime fiction. In particular, it examines works by John Connolly, Ken Bruen, Alex Barclay, and Tana French that negotiate boundaries between America and Ireland, tradition and modernity, vigilantism and the law, and religion and secularism to consider the complexities of dissecting personal and cultural identity, redefining faith, and exploring various approaches to justice in a postlapsarian, globalist society.

Part 2, "Michael Tramples Satan: Northern Ireland's Troubled Police," looks at Adrian McKinty's Sean Duffy series, Brian Mc-Gilloway's Lucy Black series, and Claire McGowan's Paula Maguire series, each of which features a Catholic police officer in Northern Ireland as its protagonist. In the Black and Maguire series, these characters are also women operating in a male-dominated profession. The officers' status as outsiders—both on the force and in their broader social environments—serves to reflect on the unique problem of identity in Northern Ireland caused by sectarianism and postcolonial disagreements over national and cultural identification. These characters exhibit more apprehension than their counterparts from the Republic about the dismantling of social, legal, and political structures, channeling the Troubles[47] as a warning about the dangerous subjectivity of vigilantism. The emphasis is on scrutiny of existing structures with an eye toward making them more just, transparent, and inclusive. The early release clause of the Good Friday Agreement[48]—which offered pardons to former paramilitary members in order to secure a cease-fire—is used as an example of the sometimes complex and difficult "price of peace": that is, the suspension of immediate, explicit, and satisfying justice to ultimately secure a more fair, safe, and benevolent society.

Part 3, "Saint Christopher: Redemption and Narrative," examines works that push the prospect of redefining justice, faith, and identity to its logical extreme, suggesting that the malleability of these terms casts serious doubt on the value of words as signifiers and the reductiveness of our categorizations of human nature and interactions. I discuss novels by Gerard Brennan, Stuart Neville, and Steve Cavanagh with special attention to their protagonists, who defy classification in terms of their relationship to both the law and the pursuit of justice in a more comprehensive sense. Through these paradoxical characters, the authors interrogate and reformulate the classic redemption narrative, proposing at once that truth might be a more tenable goal than justice, and that the obscuring of truth through hypocrisy, pretense, corruption, or self-deception is, in some ways, more dangerous than criminality. Finally, I look to Eoin McNamee's Blue trilogy, focusing on the author's use of true crime research to explore the subjectivity of narrative, and his ultimate conclusion that the elusiveness of truth is both a product and a cause of subjectivity. For McNamee, however, subjective narration is frustrating, problematic, and potentially risky—but also imperative. It is a means through which people make sense of things they are unable to understand or accept, including violence and murder, certainly, but also discrepancies between the way they have constructed their personal identities, their own idiosyncrasies or ethical failings, and the way they are perceived by others.

I chose to conclude this study with McNamee because the metatextuality of the Blue trilogy—which is highly self-referential, offering straightforward glimpses into the author's research process and consciousness of the inevitable subjectivity of his own accounts of history—offers a pertinent reminder of the cognitive and emotional significance of narrative, particularly crime narrative, not only for characters and readers, but for writers as well. Using a genre whose prescriptions have been largely devised by British and American authors, and hailing from a region in which considerations of cultural identity have tended to dominate literary tradition, Irish crime writers have nevertheless adroitly managed to carve out their own individual narratives, weaving firsthand perspectives of history, politics, violence, and changes in economic and social climate together with singular interpersonal experiences to reflect on the nature—or *natures*—of justice, faith, and identity. It would not be overstating matters to suggest that, in so doing, they have reclaimed their stories from a number of powerful influences (Revivalism, genre snobbery, cultural literary standards, colonialism, nationalism, and American idealism, to name a few) and made an assertion about the value of their perspective—and, indeed, of any firsthand perspective—to broader discourse about justice. Out of respect for this achievement, this text is guided as much by interviews and conversations with the authors as by previous scholarship and my own analyses of the texts.

PART ONE

Finders of Lost Things

Saint Anthony, Identity, and the Limits of Structural Justice

The powers of Saint Anthony of Padua, the patron saint of lost things and missing persons, are interpreted as both literal and metaphorical. Anthony is invoked for help recovering missing objects but also for assistance in finding love and providing guidance for the physically, emotionally, or spiritually lost. This tradition of Anthony as a *finder* makes him an obvious point of alignment for detectives as they search concretely for people and evidence and, abstractly, for truth and justice. The symbolism is especially poignant as a means of characterizing detectives whose cases parallel attempts to navigate their way through complex considerations of personal identity—to find themselves and to locate their belief systems, as it were.

As a champion of the disenfranchised and downtrodden, the Anthony of tradition might be viewed as an early model for the hard-boiled detective. Legends about Anthony emphasize a perception of justice that is at times dissonant with both the legal justice system and, more surprisingly, the hierarchy of the Catholic Church. He notably speaks out against the tradition of imprisoning debtors, arguing that poverty should not be considered a crime; as the first teacher of the

Franciscan order, he also emphasizes the importance of education and sometimes uses his own research and logic to challenge authority within the church. In this sense, he is an apposite reference point for contemporary considerations of justice in crime fiction, since he acknowledges the ways in which systems designed to support justice can become critically flawed through corruption, greed, and power, and believes that addressing and attempting to rectify these flaws is a crucial aspect of his vocation.

Anthony's appearance in the final novel of Colin Dexter's Inspector Morse series strikes a bitter chord about the legal justice system. Despite his frequent disputes with authority, Morse is a fairly standard fictional detective in terms of his dedication to pursuing justice through legal means and his outright rejection of religious and spiritual considerations. Throughout the series, we are led to believe that his education and critical thinking skills are what put him at odds with his superiors; in *The Remorseful Day*, however, his trouble—the most serious in his career—stems from a steadfast adherence to morality and personal ethics that are contrary to the rule of the law. For the first time, he seems to ponder whether religion has something to offer in its emphasis on kindness and humanity above all else, and, more particularly, whether its logical shortcomings, as he perceives them, are actually less problematic than the law's failure to prioritize compassion.

With his intertextual reference to Morse's conundrum, Ken Bruen applies the metaphor of Anthony to post–Celtic Tiger Ireland: a country in which, from Jack Taylor's perspective, both religious and legal systems have proved gravely disappointing, but still retain some value. Bruen's incorporation of Anthony has two distinct but related effects: first, it reinforces a standard set by John Connolly in the Charlie Parker series, which rejects crime fiction's outright dismissal of religious faith, spirituality, and the supernatural. Unlike Connolly, Bruen specifically frames this discussion through Catholic symbolism, acknowledging that the historical influence of the church in Ireland has inevitably affected discourse about justice and ethics, despite rising secularism.

Second, Bruen's use of Anthony builds on Dexter's implicit suggestion that a basis for clearer paths to justice and empathy might be formed by examining multiple models of thought to assess their benefits and shortcomings. The four detectives discussed in this section—Ken Bruen's Jack Taylor, John Connolly's Charlie Parker, Alex Barclay's Joe Lucchesi, and Tana French's Rob Ryan—struggle with a number of seeming dichotomies in their attempts to come to terms with their understandings of themselves, their societies, criminal behavior, and systems of justice. All of these detectives have tenuous relationships with the police: Taylor and Parker are disgraced ex-police officers, Lucchesi is on extended leave after a questionable application of deadly force, and Ryan spends much of the narrative fearful of being fired for his unprofessional behavior. To various degrees, each of them considers, encourages, or participates in vigilantism (or rule breaking, in Ryan's case) as an alternative to the shortcomings of the criminal justice system, but none of them is willing to entirely cut his associations with the force.

Each of these four detectives also ruminates on the notion of faith in the broadest sense of the word, questioning whether it is possible to embrace religion but reject religious institutions, whether one can trust in the potential of the criminal justice system despite its imperfections, or whether other types of faith— in oneself, in other people, or in individual priorities or beliefs—can help to ease the personal instability that arises from a loss of faith in the prescribed rules and ethics of institutions. These attempts to come to terms with what they believe, where they can place their trust, and how they can best serve justice are one aspect of the characters' larger efforts to understand their identities as individuals. The outsider detective trope is used to emphasize the characters' ambivalent relationships to tradition, modernity, cultural stereo- types, and globalization, which create discord in their perceptions of themselves and their roles in society.

In this sense, all of the texts address issues that are specifically relevant to post–Celtic Tiger Ireland, but it would be reductive to suggest that they are in any way insular or limited to this context. Rather, each of the texts sets up a sort of dialogue among cultures and ideas, adopting and offering different perspectives. The Charlie Parker series is set in the United States, while the Jack Taylor series embraces the effects of immigration even as it expresses wari- ness of American cultural influence in Ireland. Joe Lucchesi is an American displaced in Ireland, and Rob Ryan is an Irishman who spent his formative years in England. The straddling of cultures by the detectives is a tangible reflection of the authors' pro- cess in applying an Irish perspective to a traditionally British and American form.

Ultimately, the emphasis in each of these texts is on process and progress, rather than on obvious choices or tidy solutions. Economic disparity and evi- dence of malfeasance—resulting in the need for tribu- nals of inquiry—have made the government appear less reliable, abuse scandals have cast doubt on the ethics of the church, and globalization has shaken the Revivalist view of identity in Ireland, emphasizing that paths to justice, self-knowledge, and equity are neither clear nor straightforward. Rather, they require constant reexamination and reforging. The varied settings of the novels emphasize that these lessons are universally applicable: innocence and ignorance are dangerous but easy; experience and transparency lead us down a rabbit hole of frustration, confusion, and contradiction. By the thirteenth novel in Bruen's series, *The Ghosts of Galway* (2017), Jack Taylor finds himself symbolically metamorphosed into Saint Anthony—an event he has claimed as a goal throughout the series—when he assists a priest, Father Malachy, by locating an ancient text that has gone missing from the Vatican archives. Rather than being pleased about his freedom from institutional regulations and his liberty of thought, Taylor finally admits how much he wishes to be readmitted to the Guards—his "heart [lurches]" and he "[feels] dizzy with hope" when he thinks it is a possibility—and is furious when Malachy conflates him with the freethinking Anthony:

> I asked,
>   "How did he [Malachy] find it [the book]?"
>   "Oh, he gave all the credit to Anthony."
>   "Who?"
>   "Saint Anthony. The go-to guy for lost things."
>   I was truly shocked. The treacherous bastard. . . .
>   I now knew what the expression meant.
>   *It stuck in my craw.*
>   Did it fucking ever.[1]

1

The System, Changed

Ken Bruen's Jack Taylor, John Connolly's
Every Dead Thing, Alex Barclay's Darkhouse,
and Tana French's In the Woods

> We do not believe in evil anymore, only evil acts that can be
> explained away by the science of the mind. There is no evil
> and to believe in it is to fall prey to superstition, like check-
> ing beneath the bed at night or being afraid of the dark. But
> there are those for whom we have no easy answers, who do evil
> because that is their nature, because they are evil.
> —John Connolly, *Every Dead Thing*

While humanization of the detective and profound interrogations of
the nature of justice can be easily tied to the work of late-twentieth-
century British crime writers, there is little question that Irish noir
also owes much to the American hard-boiled tradition. Many Irish
authors claim Dashiell Hammett, Raymond Chandler, James M.
Cain, and John MacDonald as their earliest influences: writers whose
work suggested that cases were not always resolved tidily and that
the detective, notwithstanding a clear sense of morality and honor
that makes him "the best man in his world and a good enough man
for any world,"[1] is nevertheless subject to human flaws.

Maureen T. Reddy suggests that Irish crime writers symbolically
express anxiety about modernization and a tendency toward chau-
vinistic, heteronormative, and xenophobic attitudes by adopting the
standards and tropes of early American hard-boiled fiction. Reddy
argues that "recent Irish crime writers have been deeply interested

in working through the problem of redefining Irishness. . . . but the hardboiled form that has profoundly influenced so many contemporary crime writers works against a progressive or liberatory conception of Irishness." There is some irony in Reddy's assessment, in that several Irish crime writers point to the pressures of addressing national identity in Irish literary tradition as a reason for breaking from that tradition to embrace a historically American form. Writing under the pseudonym of Ingrid Black, Eilis O'Hanlon and Ian McConnel lament that Revivalist writers such as W. B. Yeats and Lady Gregory fostered a situation in which "Irish writers who followed were expected, to varying degrees, to partake in the same mission. . . . The English had misrepresented and abused the native Irish for centuries. The writer's job was to reclaim and remake that identity." For O'Hanlon and McConnel, crime fiction is the literary equivalent of emigration: a way to "[forget] where they came from . . . ignore the past and reinvent oneself anew." Doing so, they argue, is vital to self-expression in that "freeing oneself of the burden of speaking for Ireland is, for an Irish writer, the start of being able to speak for oneself." Similarly, John Connolly asserts that the relative youth of Ireland as a nation means that it is "compelled to engage in a period of questioning its identity" and that "any writing that is not actively contributing to this discussion may be disregarded entirely." Like O'Hanlon and McConnel, Connolly views genre literature as a means of escaping this prescribed cultural responsibility, adding that the American hard-boiled tradition is particularly appealing in its *breach* from cultural and institutional norms. The attraction of Hammett and Chandler is not in the nostalgia they evoke for the past, but in their attempts to define justice once traditional approaches have been deemed untrustworthy and a society is forced to acknowledge that "the poor and the vulnerable [have] no recourse to the law."[2]

One of the cornerstones of Reddy's argument is a critique of John Banville's traditionalist approach in his Benjamin Black novels and his decision to write them as period pieces:

Black adopts, entirely uncritically, the whole of hardboiled ideology, structure, and tropes; his embrace of a bygone tradition also explains why the novels are set in the 1950s instead of in a more contemporary period. The Quirke series is suffused with beliefs and attitudes, particularly regarding women, that would seem anachronistic in the twenty-first century. . . . Black's Quirke is the voice of white, male, heterosexual, settled Irish experience in a period in which those terms equated with Irishness itself. Although those terms no longer suffice to describe Irishness, the Quirke series labors to reinstate only slightly revised versions of them.[3]

Reddy posits Banville's 1950s-era setting as an extreme manifestation of a discomfort with modernization and globalization that permeates Irish crime fiction. While acknowledging the misgivings of other authors toward Banville resulting from his dismissive remarks about crime fiction, Reddy does not here consider that these misgivings imply a rejection of Banville's notion of the hard-boiled as a formula with limited possibilities that has remained essentially unchanged since its inception.

Of his construction of the Charlie Parker series, Connolly says that "the absence of any recognisable Irish models" led him to look to American and British crime writers for inspiration, but he is quick to point out that he views his use of the form as a means of opening a dialogue about it, and not as an unquestioning adoption of its standards: "For me, the choice was either to import genre conventions from the UK or the US to an Irish context, which I felt was neither appropriate nor, indeed, interesting; or to apply a European, outsider's perspective to those conventions, to try 'to change the system from within,' to borrow a line from Leonard Cohen."[4] The Irish approach to crime fiction might thus be viewed as an attempt to launch a conversation among cultures and conventions.[5] Rather than unconditionally accepting the standards of American hard-boiled fiction, it might be more accurate to say that Irish crime writers make use of the form in part to challenge some of its presumptions. They expose the shortcomings of institutional justice but also acknowledge its benefits; they maintain that an outsider status enhances a detective's objectivity but insinuate that it can likewise result in stereotyping, isolation, or a loss of ethics; they promote secular reason and deduction but warn that attempts to understand the world in terms of logic alone are inadequate. Ultimately, authors such as Ken Bruen, John Connolly, Alex Barclay, and Tana French reject dichotomous constructions—rationalism versus faith, community versus free thought, tradition versus modernization—as simplifications that discourage open-minded assessments, shroud inconvenient truths, and impede the course of justice.[6]

Certainly, some discomfort with modernization is obvious in Bruen's Jack Taylor series. Taylor seeks out pubs, restaurants, and inns that have retained an unpretentious authenticity: places with dark wood and lighting, the habitual drinkers he affectionately refers to as "sentries," and simple food and drink, rather than elegant cocktails designed to appeal to tourists and a new generation raised on American television. His frustration with teenagers who affect American dialects, mannerisms, and speech patterns and with people who fail to display modest decorum is palpable, and as Andrew Kincaid notes, he frequently makes use of the Irish language as "an act against letting older social, more egalitarian forms disappear" in order to "[appeal] to the reader's desire for simplicity and honesty."[7] At times, he wistfully recalls the days when he could walk down a street in Galway and recognize every face he encountered.

Yet Taylor more frequently recalls those same days with rage, grimacing at the former power of the church, its many abuses of that power, and the code of silence and conformity that helped to cover up these abuses: "evil [flourishing] and [spreading] because decent people don't want to make a fuss."[8] *The Magdalen Martyrs* (2003) is a glaring critique of the Magdalene laundries'[9] cruelty toward women who failed to adhere to strict societal standards, while *The Killing of the Tinkers* (2002) studies the historical disenfranchisement of Romani Travellers in Ireland. In the latter novel, and throughout the series, Taylor repeatedly expresses his opinion that, if anything, in terms of social equality and accepting outsiders, postmodern Ireland has not come far enough.

Taylor's antipathy for Ireland's past is concretized in his volatile relationship with his mother. He feels indebted to her and has moments of nostalgia for childhood, but these moments are always followed by an acknowledgment that the childhood he longs for is a fantasy of comfort and stability, rather than the painful upbringing marked by shame and emotional cruelty that he actually had. He frames his mother as a tormenter without empathy, who, like the old Ireland, is more concerned with maintaining the appearance of piety than with fostering honest human communication or addressing and redressing miscarriages of justice. In his mother's feigning of religiosity, there is no room for individuality or forgiveness of human frailty, least of all his own. At their strongest, Taylor's impressions of his mother manifest themselves as a conviction that she revels in his failures because they give her something to feel self-righteous about, in much the same way that the failures of the Magdalene women gave the church and members of traditional Irish society occasion to celebrate their own supposed goodness and adherence to church doctrine. Taylor concludes that the pseudoreligious, homogenous culture of his youth is responsible for victimization of the vulnerable. While recounting the true news story of a woman who died in a Galway hospital after she was refused the abortion that could have saved her life, Taylor fumes at the residual adherence to religious tradition over common sense, thundering, "whoever else is involved" in such decisions, "it sure as shootin isn't Jesus."[10] When a client suggests that the people responsible for serial killings of Travellers are likely masquerading as respectable churchgoers, Taylor is nonplussed: "I thought of my mother, didn't argue."[11] Taylor's nostalgia for a nonexistent past, then, does not reflect a fear of modernization; rather, it provides a base point for Bruen's critique of the false, rural, idyllic narrative of Ireland's past engendered by Revivalism.[12]

While Taylor seeks out traditional spaces to evade gentrification and tourism, his reactions to changes brought about by globalization take on a decidedly different tone: "A little along that road is what the locals now term Little Africa. A whole area of shops, apartments, businesses run by Nigerians, Ugandans, Zambesians, people from every part of the massive continent. To me, a white Irish Catholic, it was a staggering change, little black kids playing in the streets, drum beats echoing from open windows, and the women were beautiful. I saw dazzling shawls, scarves, dresses of every variety. And friendly . . . if you smiled at them, they responded with true warmth." Taylor's visit to Little Africa is marred by anti-immigrant graffiti—which he calls "a shame of epic proportion"—but redeemed by the kind greeting of an elderly Black man: a marked contrast to his usual interactions with native Irish who approach him only because they want something. As he proceeds through a gay neighborhood that would make his "father . . . turn in his grave," he unqualifiedly asserts that he is "delighted" by the new district. For Taylor, the integration of unfamiliar lifestyles and perspectives offers more than the prospect of exposure to the beauty of other cultures; it is also a means by which the Irish might extricate themselves from the limited points of view that have resulted in centuries of sectarian violence: "Keep the city moving, keep it mixed, blended, and just maybe we'll stop killing our own selves over hundreds of years of so-called religious difference."[13] In *The Emerald Lie* (2016), Taylor befriends a former British soldier who, he implies, worked against the Catholics in Northern Ireland but whom he grows to trust implicitly because of their personal commonalities: "We had reached our own separate peace . . . whatever flags we flew under."[14] His closest ally on several cases is a lesbian guard whom he comes to regard in a familial manner, investing himself deeply in her well-being even when her strict, legal approach to justice is at odds with his more independent inclinations. Together, they foster a relationship so complex and unusual, even in postmodern fiction, that the creators of the television series based on Bruen's novels transformed it to a heterosexual love affair.

Taylor's regret is thus not for the old, monocultural Ireland, but for Ireland's loss of faith in institutions; he believes that faith once fostered an adherence to morality, albeit engendered by fear of ostracism and punishment. He laments that the void created by the lack of confidence in the church has left the country scrambling for a replacement, acknowledging that "religion, however heavy its hand, had for centuries provided a ballast against despair";[15] moreover, he fears that cults, consumerism, and obstinate bigotry seem poised to fill that void, as if the country has, while ridding itself of the benefits of the church, nevertheless determined to stubbornly advance its injurious aspects. For this state of affairs, he blames the country's institutions themselves, suggesting that the self-interest that prevents them from promoting public welfare—both economic and personal—has driven people to search elsewhere for fulfillment, while providing them with an ominous model of how power and success can be obtained. As a result, belief and decency are as corroded as the post–Celtic Tiger economy;[16] having lost faith in the government, the clergy, and the banks, "the only item people trust is money—greed is the new spirituality."[17] Taylor's framing of morality and ethics in ecclesiastical terms is in part attributable to habit, but, more pertinently, the unfulfilled promises of the church, such as understanding, acceptance, forgiveness, and compassion, strike him as things devoutly to be wished for—much like the unfulfilled promise of his childhood.

Taylor's longing for rituals of the past, then, is a longing for what he once believed Ireland to be, rather than what he now knows it was. "With all the recent scandals" in the church, he argues, "it was less a place of refuge than the belly of the beast." This reality is, for him, represented in modernizations such as electric prayer candles that remove the sheen of ritual in favor of convenience, highlighting the commercial aspect that was always a hidden part of the church: "Time was, I took my candle business to the Augustine till they went techno. Yeah, automated buttons to light your wick. That doesn't do it for me, I need the whole ritual of the taper, the smell of the wax, to see the candle take flame. It comforts me, makes me feel like some items are not for sale."[18] While he has no qualms insulting members of the clergy, Taylor cannot abide disrespect for the symbols of religiosity: in *Sanctuary* (2008), he is tormented by a serial killer who blows out a prayer candle for each life she takes,[19] and in *Headstone* (2011), he is infuriated by the theft of a religious necklace given to him by a decent nun.[20] It is noteworthy that, while agnostics and people of different religions are generally presented as trustworthy and capable of good judgment, individuals who infringe on these symbols are always lacking in conscience. Kincaid recognizes a parallel attachment to symbols in the form of Taylor's Guard coat, through which "he is reminded of his loss, but also of his promise. He gave up an income, a community, and power, but gained independence, pride, and resourcefulness. . . . Taylor's former Garda coat, number 1834, serves as a security blanket, a marker of identity, self-reliance, and hope for stability."[21] It also serves as a symbol of the possibility of a type of faith that transcends the limits or shortcomings of a single institution. For Taylor, reassurance lies in people who still believe[22] in something positive. It doesn't much matter what shape that belief system takes, so long as it provides an ethical code.

A portion of this attachment to ritual is also more personal: Taylor worries that his own lack of faith in institutions has left him without a strict moral system and that this lack of direction has, at times, caused him to behave unethically. He misses the structure of the police force but not the "bullshit"[23] in the force's pretenses to justice and equal treatment; when asked if he regrets the punch to the pedophile government official that cost him his job, he replies that his sole regret is that he struck the official only once.[24] He levels similar accusations at the church, contending that, in his experience, religion does not promote justice either.[25] While he credits his dismissal from the force for initiating his emotional pain and dissociation from the comforts of community, he is abundantly aware that these problems predate that dismissal, as indicated by the struggle with alcohol and drugs that triggered his discharge. Intuitively, he understands that the isolation he feels stems from knowledge and understanding, which force one to confront the evils of the world but also are necessary in combating those evils; there is "no greater curse" than "[seeing] . . . clearly,"[26] he suggests, quoting Håkan Nesser on the inherent chaos of goodness and the tidiness of evil.[27] Moreover, he surmises, there is an intrinsic loneliness in pursuing a subjective morality as opposed to a codified one, since the versatility of the human race makes it nearly impossible for two people to develop the same set of ethics when left to their own devices.[28] As a result, freedom from institutionalized thinking—and the consequential need to forge individual systems of ethics and understandings of identity outside of it—has, while potentially liberating people from corrosive prejudices, made it more difficult for them to find common ground and form supportive connections. Such a conclusion, it should be noted, is distinctly at odds with the established norms of early American hard-boiled fiction, in which detectives facilely develop personal codes when forced to work outside of the legal system, and the presumption that these codes are superior to legal or religious standards is rarely called into question.

While John Connolly's Charlie Parker is an American detective, his character has much in common with the Galwegian Taylor; in the first novel of the series, *Every Dead Thing* (1999), he is introduced as an ex-cop whose alcoholism has served as a catalyst to his excommunication from structured morality. While Taylor is dismissed from the Guards as a result of his addiction, Parker's drinking and his routine of spending extended hours in bars provide motive and means to the Traveling Man, a serial killer who brutally slaughters Parker's wife and child, resulting in guilt, grief, and an obsession with finding the culprit that make it impossible for him to function in his career. Parker has no illusions about whether his problems predate his exclusion from the force; on the contrary, he blames the stress of the job for driving him to alcoholism. Like Taylor, while the lost impression of belonging pains him—the reader can feel him wincing when a mob boss scrambles for a way to address him in the absence of a title—he has little trust in the police, prefers to involve them in cases only when necessary, and clarifies that it is the naive sense of belief in the force that he had upon joining, rather than the reality of the force, that evokes his nostalgia.[29]

Also like Taylor, Parker seeks redemption by helping others, suggesting that it is the only means through which he can resist the temptation of suicide. He admits that his drive for justice has more to do with himself than the victims, indicating that he needs to save them more than they need his saving, and he has enough self-awareness to realize that this dependency on fulfilling a heroic role sometimes makes him wish for harm to come to others so that he might intervene. In the most literal sense, then, Parker pursues other cases because he is unable to solve the case that most concerns him or, notwithstanding his abstinence from alcohol, to resolve the emotional crisis that facilitated that case to begin with. He is profoundly aware that any resolution in surrogate cases will not lead to relief and fears that even finding the Traveling Man will be unsatisfactory because it will neither prevent him from blaming himself nor allow him to understand what causes people to kill without any clear benefit. Closure, he suggests, does not imply a solution or explanation, and attempts to understand the murderous psyche through logic are often futile. Aside from his conviction that the police blame him for the death of his wife and child, it is this sense of futility that leads Parker to feel more comfortable with criminals than with members of law enforcement: "They had no illusions about the world in which they lived, no philosophical constructions that allowed them to be at once a part of, and apart from, that world. . . . Now they [the delusions] had also been taken away from me, like scales falling from my eyes, leaving me to reestablish myself, to find a new place in the world."[30]

Parker's approach to developing a personal code in the quest for justice outside of the police force is similar to Taylor's in its concurrent convictions that legal approaches are insufficient and that straying from these codes can result in dangerously subjective vigilantism. He feels guilty for his first murder of a criminal, arguing that it is a "vicious justice" that enables a person to feel he has the right to pass judgment on and take the life of another, regardless of that other person's actions. This assessment is deeply linked to his understanding of his personal motivations and his subsequent fears about his nature and identity. He recognizes that, notwithstanding his surface arguments in favor of the killing, he actually did it to appease something in himself, giving him a commonality with the very suspects he hunts down. He argues that evil becomes contagious when those who seek to rectify it lose faith in the system. Despite his self-loathing, over the course of the novel, his exposure to cruelty and the impotence of police tactics increasingly anesthetizes him to the implications of street justice and cooperating with criminals for the sake of expediency; eventually, it is insinuated that he is better at tracking killers because he is a killer himself and therefore understands something of their nature. Nevertheless, he is unable to completely convince himself of the righteousness of vigilante justice; he yearns for the possibility "to reestablish [his] place in the world" and seeks an antidote to his immersion in criminal culture by reflecting on the better aspects of humanity and human relationships: "I wanted to touch, however briefly, something positive, to try to awaken something good within myself."[31]

Parker's status as an outsider is perfectly in keeping with the standards of early American hard-boiled fiction, but it also challenges these standards in that it is largely informed by Connolly's Irish perspective. Although he is an American, Parker is distinctly alienated from any specific region of America; even when he is in Manhattan, where he has spent most of his life, he claims that he feels like a visitor because he has traveled and lived in other places. In this sense, he is able to view the cultural, social, and legal norms of various areas objectively. Spatial relations in the novel also have a feel that is distinctly not American: characters in New York, New Orleans, and a small town in Virginia have multiple connections with each other in the various regions, downplaying the vastness of the United States in favor of an approach more fitting of a smaller country. This traversing of space inevitably challenges the hard-boiled trope of a particular city as a character with a distinct and familiar relationship to the protagonist; Parker describes the landscapes of Maine, New York City, and the South with equal clarity. Of all of the novel's locations, the atmosphere of New Orleans comes through as the most distinct, but it is the exotic nature of the city and its residents for Parker, and not his previous experiences with it, that most directly influence his observations. For Parker, New Orleans is a mysterious place mired in heat, wetlands, predatory animals, history, music, and cultish magic:

in short, an appropriate place to suspend logic and to examine the world and human nature from a metaphysical perspective. Connolly seems to suggest that, unlike location, the consideration of humanity and criminality is universally relatable; not surprisingly, then, the killer who torments Parker in New Orleans seems equally idiosyncratic for a character with American roots, quoting from ancient theology and, more remarkably, from James Joyce.[32]

Parker's lack of a definitive affiliation with a specific city makes him somewhat immune to melancholic considerations of the past or antipathy for change; like Taylor, his biggest regret is for what he views as a collapse of human ethics in favor of isolation and greed. He is attracted by places that have retained their traditional flavor despite modernization, but his frustration at developments is directed at gentrification rather than globalization. More pertinently, as an outsider, he is able to look past physical changes and assert that, despite these changes, the character of New Orleans has remained fundamentally the same. The struggle to depict social modifications as something not necessarily to be feared might be another reason behind Connolly's decision to set portions of the novel in the American South, a place where the history of the culture and the architecture is decidedly shorter than that of Ireland and where that history is, in any case, not consistently desirable. Connolly emphasizes this through repeated references to the slave trade, plantations, mistreatment of Black people by the police, and the way in which historical disenfranchisement in the region has led to a spike in criminal activity. There is also the hint that, considering the history of legal justice in the South, the Irish citizenry's uncomfortable relationship with the law is not an isolated phenomenon: in New Orleans, as in Ireland, offering information to the police or anyone affiliated with them is socially unacceptable. In a show of solidarity with Black Americans, Parker refuses, almost as adamantly as Taylor, to refer to himself as a detective or an investigator.[33]

Parker's sense of communion with the Black community is not at all subtle. His name is a reference to the notable jazz musician, a fact emphasized by the nickname "Bird"—which he shares with the original Charlie Parker—and his insistence that, though he obtained the name without design on the part of his parents, in much the same way one might inherit race, he fully embraces its implications. Upon hearing young men playing music in a New Orleans neighborhood, he is gratified by his familiarity with the tune, proudly proclaiming himself an "honorary homeboy." More important, he instinctively trusts in the decency, honesty, and competence of the Black characters in the novel, although he is generally suspicious of the other characters. Despite the lack of clear logic and evidence in her tale, he wholeheartedly believes the clairvoyant Tante Marie when she describes the knowledge she has obtained about his wife's killer through psychic means. He also dedicates time to researching similar supernatural leads provided by Tante Marie's son and feels relief at encountering a Black cop in Virginia, whom he posits as more intelligent than the rest of the force based on his look, before any words are exchanged between them.[34]

If the novel is in any way to be taken as continuing the Irish literary quest to define national identity, it might be through nuanced suggestions that Black America could provide a role model for the Irish as a community that has managed to evade the temptation of self-isolation in its progress toward recovery from subjugation. To make this point, Connolly delineates two possible by-products of suffering and disenfranchisement: on the one hand, an increased sense of community and empathy; on the other, the conviction that prosperity is most easily obtained through mimicry of one's former oppressors. This latter possibility is in line with Taylor's conception of a postmodern Ireland where the greed of institutions has led to a similar greed among citizens; now liberated from exploitation by the British and the church, Taylor suggests, rather than working communally, the Irish have turned to exploiting each other. For Parker, such a response is embodied by Joe Bones, a man of mixed race who suffered in childhood as a result of racial discrimination and violent bigotry. Rather than seeking to rectify such injustices as an adult, Bones uses his ability to pass as white to align himself with the white community and to exploit impoverished Black people in advancing his power as a drug lord. So thoroughly determined is Bones to repudiate the Black community that he trains his dog to attack and dismember Black people who trespass on his land.[35]

Like all of the most detestable characters in the book, Bones is devoid of any belief system and consumed by hatred and a drive for self-advancement. By contrast, the most thoroughly benevolent characters are invariably religious; that Parker has equal admiration for memories of his wife in a Catholic church, Tante Marie's associations with voodoo, and her son's well-worn cross pendant suggests a lack of emphasis on a particular religious code in favor of the concept of faith in general. Parker's meeting with Tante Marie reflects a markedly different attitude than what is usually seen in American crime fiction. A scene not dissimilar in structure to Santangelo's meeting with the psychic on *The Wire* is, in this case, approached without a touch of irony; though Tante Marie is visually impaired, Parker is convinced that she is "not blind, not in any way that [matters],"[36] and thoroughly believes that her relationship with the supernatural facilitates her ability to form connections with other people, including himself. In its most literal iterations, Tante Marie's talent allows her to visualize the cause of Parker's suffering and send him a telepathic warning about the return of his wife's killer, but more broadly, it enables her to sympathize with the pain of other people and makes her desirous of assisting them.

Connolly acknowledges that "the roots of the detective novel lie in rationalism, in the belief that the basis of truth is intellectual and deductive," and outlines the way this is exemplified in early crime fiction, before explaining his own resistance to this approach: "Perhaps it's because I come from a Catholic tradition . . . but I've never really believed that rationalism is the sole—or even the most appropriate—means of gauging human behavior, or of understanding the world we inhabit. At the very least, people are a lot odder than rationalism allows, and make decisions based on a great many criteria, of which what might be the most rational or sensible thing to do in any given situation is often pretty far down the list." Accordingly, Parker frequently asserts his experience through an understanding of the futility of trying to impose any sense of meaning or order on the chaotic implications of murder. For Parker, there are two classes of criminals: the ones who cause harm for logical reasons and the ones who do so just to create chaos, for reasons that are incomprehensible to the rest of us, or perhaps for no reason at all. The first category is represented in the novel through his own criminal friends—including a paid assassin—and through a mob boss whose code of honor forces him to adhere to specific rules. Parker expresses a kind of respect for these criminals; even when he doesn't agree with their actions, his ability to understand them and predict their behavior is comforting to him. The second class of criminal is something else altogether, represented to varying degrees by the Traveling Man; by immigrant gangs who reject the codes of business and honor established by the Italian mob; by the mob boss's cruel and tumultuous son, who horrifies even his own murderous father; by a criminal who tortured Parker when he was a child; by Joe Bones, who enjoys inflicting pain on people with whom he should empathize;[37] and, particularly, by Adelaide Modine, a serial rapist and murderer of children. Parker consistently describes these killers as creatures to whom no sense of logic can apply; in cases involving them, he suggests, detectives looking for motives will be sorely disappointed.

But Connolly also takes it one step further, depicting these chaotic killers as something other than human. After describing Parker's story as a quest for redemption in the introduction to *Every Dead Thing*, he also gives examples of other characters, Morphy and Rachel, whose brushes with unethical behavior—as perpetrator and victim, respectively—heighten their dedication to seeking justice for others, thus establishing a norm of human behavior and reaction. The second class of murderers, however, responds to such experiences in a completely contrary manner, in that they are inspired by injustice to inflict cruelty on others. Rather than seeking to embrace humanity, they desire to eradicate it, with all of its associated consciousness, compassion, and subjectivity. This extreme misanthropy is most clearly seen in the Traveling Man, who, unsatisfied with mere murder, compulsively removes his victims' faces.

Parker and the other characters in the novel do not hesitate to describe these murderers as evil, with all of the supernatural implications of that word. The mob boss's unfeeling gunman seems, to Parker, an embodiment of the harm the boss wishes to do, while the Traveling Man claims that he was brought into being by Parker's own hatred. If such things can manifest as the result of unethical impulses in otherwise decent people, Parker surmises, then perhaps a person who is evil by nature can be driven by this evil to metamorphose into a demon. Adelaide Modine is presented as a sort of beast, unable to grasp concepts of justice and righteousness; she is described to Parker by the cop in Virginia as "a thing out of Hell." Perhaps our biggest clue to the nature of these murderers is in the Traveling Man's suggestion, before he is exposed as the culprit, that the killer of Parker's family is inherently different from criminals "who had crossed some line, but . . . were so pathetic that they were still recognizably human." This killer, he argues, is not motivated by any comprehensible force, but "[sees] the world as just one big altar on which to sacrifice humanity, someone who [believes] he [has] to make an example of us all."[38]

In "A 'Honeycomb World': John Connolly's Charlie Parker Series," Brian Cliff cautions against presuming "that his [Connolly's] real materials or his real concerns, if you just look closely enough— and past the numerous American influences—are Irish," but notes that the series' rejection of the crime fiction standard "that the world is ultimately or essentially knowable" in favor of "the idea that something fundamentally unknowable is at the heart of the series and of Parker's life . . . suggests both supernatural fiction and Irish culture have influenced this very particular detective."[39] Connolly's unflinchingly religious approach to crime fiction is representative of his aim to create a dialogue in which, as an outsider to America, he challenges presuppositions in the American hard-boiled, such as the idea that logic and deduction can adequately confront and quash injustice and the conviction that spirituality is insignificant or even detrimental to that process. Fittingly, the Traveling Man teases Parker with illusions of religiosity, playing to the standard suspicion of such views in hard-boiled novels, but ultimately reveals himself as an atheist, dedicated to undermining faith. Parker, contrarily, is aided by his own faith in the pursuance of justice: "I believed in the devil and pain," he says firmly, insisting that to understand evil as a thing in itself, without seeking to qualify or search for reason in it, enables one to recognize it and, in destroying what parts of it one can, contribute to eradicating its spread.[40] A lack of community and closeness in the postmodern world, he suggests, leads to an inability to comprehend others and the basic tenets of humanity; because we view everyone as foreign, we can no longer distinguish the people we actually need to be afraid of. In this sense, Connolly's approach is not dissimilar from Bruen's in its implication that, despite its benefits, the dismantling of trust in institutions and the rise of subjective morality has led to a situation that is unfavorable to human connection and understanding and, moreover, unfavorable to a cooperative sense of confronting injustice.

Not surprisingly, then, Parker lists as his chief goals the ability to establish human connections and understanding—things that he asserts are also unfathomable in a purely logical context—and the ability to thereby recognize the aberrant evil of killers, before they are able to inflict harm. He equates these abilities with innocence of the sort that both he and Taylor had before they were forced to confront the inadequacies of their institutionalized belief systems, suggesting that only children can see the bogeyman,[41] and that that might not be because he doesn't exist, but rather because skeptical adults often fail to identify him.[42]

Ultimately, and perhaps because the American context necessitates a stauncher perspective, Parker is far more resolute in his defense of spirituality than Taylor. There is even some indication that it is only because of religion that he is able to pursue justice at all, as he is incapable of making any real progress on his case, or, indeed, toward healing himself, until a Christian organization assists him in giving up alcohol. Still, it would be difficult to read the novel as an unquestioning vindication of religious structural justice; like Taylor, Parker never fully rejects the idea that vigilantism and the willful abandonment of structural norms are sometimes necessary to combat evil. He does, however, experience more guilt about this outlook than Taylor and is more attuned to its potential consequences; for Parker, these consequences are reflected not merely in their physical effects but also potentially in something more significant: that is, enabling the further spread of evil. Both Taylor and Parker come face-to-face with supernatural, evil characters that seek to prevent them from redemption and the furtherance of justice, but regardless of his failure to adhere to the tenets of the church, Taylor's devil views him as a nemesis—a force in opposition to evil—while both the Traveling Man and the dark angels that Parker encounters later in the series regard him as essentially one of their own because of his moral failings. That Parker is less dedicated to firmly critiquing a religious approach to justice than Taylor might explain why he is less committed to finding an alternative; nevertheless, such an alternative is subtly offered when another character suggests that Parker considers himself "the patron saint of dead children":[43] in the Catholic faith, this comment might be construed as a reference to Saint Felicitas, Saint Nicholas—or Saint Anthony of Padua.

Like *Every Dead Thing*, Alex Barclay's *Darkhouse* (2005) can be read as a dialogue between Irish and American experiences in the construction of detective fiction. Alternating between events involving the disappearance and murder of Katie, a young woman in a small village in Ireland, and flashbacks that describe the abusive childhood of her abductor, Duke Rawlins, in Texas, *Darkhouse*'s omniscient narration offers insight into the perceptions of several characters—police and amateurs, Irish people and Americans, and rural and urban dwellers—offering a variety of different perspectives on the pursuance of justice. Primarily, though, the novel follows an American detective, Joe Lucchesi, in his attempts to solve the case.

Following the horrific murder of a mother and child and Lucchesi's subsequent killing of Donnie, the unarmed perpetrator, Lucchesi is on leave from the New York Police Department while he contemplates whether to remain in a job that has led to stress, trauma, and self-laceration. An attempt at a relaxing break in Ireland becomes frustrating for him; he is essentially aimless, halfheartedly assisting his wife, Anna, as she refurbishes a lighthouse for a magazine spread and trying to communicate with his increasingly secretive son, Shaun. Lucchesi is unfamiliar with the landscape of Ireland, its culture, or its legal justice system, making him an outsider in terms of both his surroundings and his career. In a technique resembling Connolly's, Barclay describes Lucchesi's situation in America as similarly alienating; his mother is dead, and his relationship with his father is distant. Rather than providing him with a sense of community, his role on the force has led to further isolation, as his exposure to the worst of human nature and violence makes him mistrustful and guarded, even toward his own wife and son. Like Parker, Lucchesi had an unstable upbringing, involving multiple moves to various cities, rendering him as much an outsider in any region of America as he is in Ireland.

Lucchesi is thus depicted as capable of reflecting on both the Irish and American societies and their prejudices objectively, a fact that is underscored through amusing examples of each culture's ignorance and stereotypes about the other: Americans' belief that Ireland is "all sentimental ballads" and their presumption that Irish names should be pronounced with American phonetics; the red, white, and blue gaudiness of an American-themed burger joint in Ireland; an Irish taxi driver's shock at being criticized for calling Black men "boys" in America because the appellation doesn't have the same connotations in Ireland; and the same driver's insistence that Ireland needs a politician like Rudy Giuliani, whom he associates with order without comprehending the discriminatory implications of certain of his zero-tolerance policies. At its worst, this cultural ignorance morphs into outright prejudice, with Irish characters referring to Americans as dysfunctional, as "wacko" or "weirdo," and as "arrogant Yanks" who "think [they] can save the world." When Shaun's girlfriend, Katie, goes missing, his classmate insists that Shaun must be responsible owing to the violence of American culture and, in particular, the school shootings that have been on the news: "We should be lucky he didn't come in here in a trench coat and blow us all to shit."[44]

Barclay suggests that, if they can step beyond such preconceptions, America and Ireland might learn something from each other and create a cooperative discourse that enables both countries to better address the sources and facilitators of criminal behavior and thus to more effectively pursue justice. Ireland, and particularly rural Ireland, is described as overly naive in the face of modernization; there are no locks on the doors in this small Irish town, and its residents and police force are unprepared to prevent, address, or react to Katie's disappearance and murder in any meaningful way. Though Lucchesi initially admires the innocence of Irish girls, thankful that Shaun is no longer in a position to date "predatory" Americans,[45] he later discovers that the sheltered lives of young Irish people have served only to make dangerous situations seem alluring and exciting to them. This amalgamation of innocence and curiosity turns deadly for more than one character in the novel; on his arrival in Ireland, Duke is able to exploit a bored and disenchanted young waitress, luring her to assist him with his crimes and ultimately murdering her. Likewise, Katie's vulnerability is the result of a conflict between her desire for unfamiliar experiences and her mother's concurrent ignorance about the postmodern world and determination to enforce strict rules to protect her daughter. Katie becomes accessible to Duke because she feels compelled to lie to her mother when she meets Shaun for sex; after arguing with Shaun, she is obliged to walk home, because she cannot reveal where she has been. Any chance of discovering Katie alive is also obliterated by this compulsory deception; the investigation into her disappearance begins in obscurity because the police are searching for her along the wrong route.

The distance between people that allows evil to flourish in the works of Connolly is here encapsulated in the tension between innocence and experience or unpalatable truth. Apart from her inability to communicate honestly with her mother, Katie's argument with Shaun, a result of their incongruent understandings of and experiences with sexuality, causes her to walk the streets alone on the night of her abduction, regardless of his protests. Throughout the novel, such intractable naïveté is posited as an enabler of crime in Ireland;

in particular, drug abuse and delinquency flourish among teens because their parents cannot believe that such things can affect their own families. In an ironic twist at the end of the novel, the classmate who initially believes that Shaun's experienced American upbringing makes him potentially dangerous is led, through his own gullibility, into facilitating Duke's escape from arrest.

The relative experience of Americans is not, however, framed as a superior alternative to rural Irish naïveté. On the contrary, America is infected by a culture of violence and vigilantism that, left unchecked, inevitably spreads and infiltrates other countries. Ultimately, it is revealed that Katie's death and other tragic events are the result of Lucchesi's maverick decision to kill Danny, which has lured Duke to Ireland in order to seek revenge on Lucchesi and his family. While more aware of danger than the Irish, Americans are similarly blind to the problems that plague their society and cause these dangers; in particular, American justice attempts to address crime without examining its underlying causes, especially in terms of prejudice and disenfranchisement. In the flashbacks to Duke's childhood, we learn that his mother, once revered for her charm and beauty, was compelled to turn to prostitution when she was deemed too old to be worthy of anything else. Addicted to drugs, numb, and devoid of compassion, she easily forced the same fate on her very young son in order to pay the bills and feed her habit. Barclay spares the reader none of the horror of these experiences; extreme sexual violence and resultant injuries are described in detail, evoking a sense of sympathy for Duke and suggesting that he might not have become a murderer were it not for the economic disparity of the United States and the lack of reliable resources for its most vulnerable citizens.[46]

Barclay's inclusion of Duke's background does not refute the existence of evil; it implies that there might be a solution to evil in recognizing and addressing the factors that give rise to it, but it also suggests that there is a darkness in certain people that renders them more susceptible than others. Duke's foray into cruelty begins with mimicry; he is inconsolable when his mother kills his dog, but is inspired to slaughter the dog she brings him as a replacement. Just the same, his escalating violence surpasses anything he has witnessed or experienced; he lures Danny into his schemes and progresses to rape and murder, dehumanizing his victims by hunting them and mutilating their bodies, much as Connolly's Traveling Man does by removing his victims' faces. He becomes immune to human notions of compassion, guilt, and responsibility, shamelessly allowing his uncle, who protected him in childhood, to go to jail for him and suggesting that his crimes are no longer a response to the abuses he has suffered: "Surviving is bullshit," he tells Danny unflinchingly. "I've done all my surviving. It's time to go out and just get." Like the Traveling Man, he seems to have transformed into a demon, motivated by the sheer pleasure of destruction rather than by personal gain or revenge. His pupils dilate in excitement when he assaults women, offering "windows to the soul . . . and the soul [is] black."[47]

Such lovers of chaos exist in Ireland as well, where they have the benefit of operating in a society that recognizes them even less, obstinately adhering to the notion that crime and violence are things that occur elsewhere. Duke's Irish counterpart is a young police officer named Richie Bates; while Duke has been forced into a marginalized situation in order to commit his crimes, Richie operates in plain sight with the assurance that his community is blind to his nature. Exploiting the religiosity of the townspeople, he couches his lack of empathy as a quest for redemption; his coldness and abuses of power are easily accepted as the ill-informed by-products of an adherence to structural justice designed to compensate for his inability, as a child, to rescue a drowning friend.[48] When he is exposed as Duke's coconspirator in the murder of Katie, we learn that Richie actually enjoyed this childhood experience and that watching his friend die made him desirous of witnessing and abetting the deaths of other people. That we are not offered evidence that Richie has ever been victimized himself, examples of any crimes he has committed as an adult, or any explanation for his involvement with Duke underscores the idea that the evil in Ireland is a result of American influence, but this origin is of little consequence: it is in Ireland now, and to ignore it is to enable it.

Although Barclay clearly suggests that evil must be recognized in order to be resisted, she concurs with Bruen and Connolly in her assessment that people who are exposed to evil are in danger of being infected by it. Owing to his time on the force, Lucchesi has developed a bleak outlook on the world and repeatedly injures the people closest to him with his negativity. In direct contrast to the Irish parents in the novel, he imagines danger everywhere and is suspicious of everyone, including his own son. A portion of this pessimism stems from his culturally induced failure to consider the causes of criminal behavior. Unaware of Duke's background, he fears that the actions of Duke and others like him are incomprehensible and therefore cannot be effectively combated. He is also acutely aware that this lack of comprehension has, at times, hardened his own heart and made him an unwilling cause of the deaths of innocents, most notably through his act of vigilante revenge against Donnie. Accordingly, when he tells Duke that his pretenses to nobility in seeking vengeance for Donnie are fallacious, Duke reminds him that that they are similar characters, both driven to vigilante justice in search of retribution.[49]

Lucchesi's desperation to understand what triggers people to harm others without benefit to themselves differs from Parker's in that his adherence to rationalism, a standard of American detectives, prevents him from accepting that some things simply cannot be explained. Just as innocence and curiosity make for a dangerous mixture among the Irish, Lucchesi's sustained contact with evil becomes treacherous in conjunction with his lack of a positive belief system. The implications of this void are put into relief by Frank Deegan, an older rural Irish officer, whose unwavering religious faith allows him to pursue justice without becoming tainted. Frank is depicted as an ideal middle ground between innocence and experience. His faith is in no way hypocritical or blinding; he is simultaneously optimistic, empathetic, and rational.[50] His faith extends to the possibilities of the police force under proper management; he is extremely aware of the failures that have led to public mistrust and is determined to behave in a manner that will reestablish confidence. He believes that imperfect institutions can be improved and views such improvement as essential in that the potential for trust and belief inspires communion and healing. For Frank, these effects are illustrated in the consolation Katie's friends find in their elders' prayer rituals, even though they are less certain than their parents that prayer is effective. The dissonance between the outlooks of Frank and Lucchesi is highlighted when Katie's mutilated body is discovered. Frank insists that the shocking state of the corpse is all the more reason to believe in the soul, while Lucchesi's attempts to picture Katie as an angel are overwhelmed by gruesome memories of "all the evil [he has] ever seen." Lucchesi mourns his loss of innocence, wishing to be anything other than "a person who [has] lost forever the chance to view the world as good."[51]

Lucchesi's lack of faith extends to the criminal justice system. Once outside of the force, his mistrust in its effectiveness becomes even clearer; unconvinced that the police are capable of solving Katie's case, he takes on the role of amateur detective. When it becomes clear that his wife has also been targeted by Duke, he reflects on the irony that, after years of telling people that the police can help them in their hour of need, he prefers not to notify them. In this instance, his unwillingness to involve the police stems from a fear that their involvement could actually be dangerous, considering that the mother and child who were killed by Donnie might have been spared if the police presence hadn't been detected. Later, however, he returns to the same conviction that led him to vigilantism—namely, that even when criminal justice is effective, it doesn't always go far enough. He concludes that he would prefer to catch Duke himself and presumably kill him than to allow the police to arrest him.[52]

The novel itself takes an ambivalent stance toward the police and Lucchesi's skepticism of them. On the one hand, Lucchesi is correct in assuming that he can solve Katie's case more effectively than the police; on the other, were it not for his initial act of vigilantism, there would not be a case to solve. Though this vigilantism brings Duke to Ireland, his murderous behavior results in part from the brutal rapes he suffered as a child; by the end of the novel, we discover that his most vicious assailant was a police chief. There is also some suggestion that dedication to legal order and procedure has dehumanizing effects not dissimilar to the ones brought about by crime; tellingly, Richie, the officer most invested in these rules, turns out to be actively working against justice, rather than pursuing it. Moreover, the adherence to legal codes alienates the public from the police, making them feel victimized rather than protected by them. The townspeople detest Richie because of his codified behavior, which emphasizes the importance of minor parking and rubbish violations over common sense and compassion, and prefer to turn to Lucchesi with information and requests for assistance. Though he agrees to help, Lucchesi notes that, despite the conclusions they may have drawn from detective novels and television series, the police don't actually call in private investigators to assist with their cases.[53] In this exposure of the unrealistic nature of classic detective fiction, Barclay offers a reminder that, while the idea of an amateur or private detective with special skills and a passion for justice is appealing, the fact is that most people have to rely solely on the police in such matters, so it is imperative that the police stop estranging and disappointing them.

The police force's potential for redemption is embodied by Frank, who encourages Richie to be less stringent in his application of the rules in order to promote public trust. Clearly, the problem is not with the legal justice system itself, but with the unquestioning adherence to norms and structure in general. The Irish citizenry also has difficulties transcending these norms; notwithstanding their initial reliance on Lucchesi, when Katie's body is discovered, they instinctively blame the American outsiders for their tragedy. Although he knows it defies common sense, even the open-minded Frank assigns culpability to the Lucchesis. Barclay's point seems to be that blaming the unfamiliar is less painful than confronting and addressing true sources of danger but that such an approach allows crime to spread unchecked. Shaun's classmate is able to help Duke escape because the Irish will say "nothing to no one" to incriminate one of their own, while Richie relies on the probability that the locals will believe him over Lucchesi, because the latter is a stranger.[54] Ultimately, Richie

is exposed because of the testimony of a young man who, too intellectually impaired to be blinded by cultural considerations, is not
unlike the children Parker describes as able to recognize the bogeyman because they have not yet been socialized not to.

Tensions between cultural standards and between legal and
hard-boiled approaches to justice become conflated in the novel, as
the Irish characters attribute Lucchesi's maverick investigation to his
nationality. The police, in particular, are inclined to this interpretation, suggesting that Lucchesi's mistrust in their competence stems
from his incomprehension of Irish society. While they warn Lucchesi
not to stereotype them as lazy because of their culturally appropriate, measured approach, they concurrently insinuate that it is his
autonomous American attitude that leads him to believe he can solve
the case on his own, referring to him alternately as "Dirty Harry,"
"Magnum," and "the great American detective." When Lucchesi
reminds them that he is an experienced police officer, they emphasize
the issue of ethnicity, asserting that he is "an amateur over here."[55]

Of course, it is precisely Lucchesi's objectivity as an outsider that
makes him more efficient than the police at solving the case; while
his outsider status is complicated by cultural connotations, it is also
a holdover from the American hard-boiled tradition, in which private
investigators are more effective because they are unconstrained by
the alliances and biases associated with the criminal justice system.
The disdain for outsiders is also not culturally specific; American
police officers in the novel are just as inclined as the Irish police to be
suspicious of interlopers. Although Lucchesi is more successful working independently, his revulsion at becoming one of the amateurs
that he has always derided ultimately leads him to return to the force.

Lucchesi is unable to liberate himself from the temptation of prescribed norms, but *Darkhouse* offers little nostalgia for the past or
for tradition. Instead, it optimistically envisions the possibility of a
better future, in which the shortcomings of institutions are recti-
fied and globalization leads to increased empathy. Lucchesi notes
that Shaun's exposure to a variety of people and cultures makes him
more compassionate than he was as a teenager,[56] and it certainly

seems to be the case. Prior to Katie's disappearance, Shaun is more dedicated to improving communication between himself and Katie than Lucchesi is with Anna, just as Lucchesi's imperfect relationship is nevertheless an improvement on that of his parents. While it ends disastrously, Shaun and Katie's relationship also suggests that millennials are more inclined than previous generations to establish relationships with people who are different from themselves, to their mutual benefit.

In contrast to *Darkhouse*'s international contexts and hopeful implications about postmodern society and its potential for informed global discourse, Tana French's *In the Woods* (2007) concentrates unrelentingly on the city of Dublin as a case study, framing the modernization of Ireland as at best suspicious and at worst a mirage. The focus on a specific city conjures American hard-boiled associations with crime, corruption, and disaffection while adding a suggestive element of confinement and suffocation for the narrator, Detective Rob Ryan, who, after a lifetime of masking his personal history and working-class Irish roots, is finally compelled to confront both. The case of Katy Devlin, a young girl found murdered on an archaeological site, brings Ryan back to the housing estate where he grew up and the woods that border it, which are the location of a severe childhood trauma. At twelve years old, Ryan ran away from home with his two best friends and was later discovered in the woods by a search party, blood-soaked, terrified, and so plagued by amnesia that he was unable to assist the police in their quest for his missing friends, who were never subsequently located. Like many postmodern detectives, Ryan both avoids addressing his own wounds and remains connected to them through the surrogate of other cases, but the parallels between his experience and the murder of Katy, in terms of location and the victims' ages, indicate the possibility of a connection and force him to interrogate his own memories, under the presumption that they might be the key to finding Katy's killer.

In "Voicing the Unspeakable: Tana French's Dublin Murder Squad," Shirley Peterson argues that French's "peripatetic upbringing in Ireland, Italy, Malawi, and the United States . . . situates her well as both a subjective and an objective observer of the Celtic Tiger years."[57] Indeed, as French is the only American-born author discussed in this chapter and spent her formative years outside of Ireland, it is tempting to view her work as a response to Connolly's call for a dialogue between cultures about crime fiction, in which French suggests that, before they can be viewed through a global lens, social issues must be addressed by looking inward and formulating honest historical and cultural assessments. While this notion follows Barclay's line of reasoning about recognizing and addressing the problems of one's own society, it differs in its implication that global contexts are a distraction. Somewhat ironically, French is uniquely positioned to make such an argument, given her familiarity with Ireland and her extensive exposure to other societies. Her narrative enforces this dual and at times contradictory perspective; her attention to detail underscores an intimate knowledge of Dublin, while frequent allusions to American television, literature, and politics seem designed to emphasize the objectivity of her perspective.

Mimosa Summers Stephenson suggests that French's background influences the manner in which she constructs her characters, who also exist "both within and without the society." This point is true in a very practical sense, in that the role of French's detectives in the criminal justice system is fundamentally American. In the author's note to *In the Woods*, French remarks that the murder squad within which her detectives operate does not actually exist in Ireland as homicide units in America do, but that "the story seemed to require one";[58] furthermore, unlike the majority of police officers in Ireland, French's detectives carry guns, adding an element of protection—and dissociation—from their society. The within/without dichotomy is equally relevant in the metaphorical sense to which Summers Stephenson alludes; Ryan has in common with French both the subjective experience of an Irish native and the distanced perspective imposed on him through memory loss and his exile to a British boarding school,[59] a move made by his parents to protect him from the publicity of his friends' disappearance. Ryan condones his parents' decision to change his name from Adam to his middle name following the incident; alienation from his roots has become a comfortable habit and a source of pride. He deliberately dresses in an elegant manner to disguise his class and is frequently mistaken as British because of the accent he picked up at boarding school. While he implies that this perception is out of his control, it is suspicious that his speech is more affected by a few years abroad than by his childhood and adulthood in Ireland. He feebly protests that "being taken for English infuriates me to an irrational degree," but also makes it clear that he associates his accent with the affected class situation and grandeur for which he strives: "I sort of enjoyed the absurd idea of me as James Bond." Indeed, Ryan seeks to exaggerate his own sense of otherness. He refuses to keep up with the current events of his own country, arguing that proximity leads to a lack of clarity: "I don't watch Irish news; it always morphs into a migraine blur of identical sociopath-eyed politicians mouthing meaningless white noise. . . . I stick to foreign news, where distance gives enough simplification for the comforting illusion that there is some difference between the various players."[60] His preference for an objective role in resolving other people's cases over the subjective role required to address his own mysterious past thus includes an additional symbolic commentary about the inclination of Irish society to ignore its complex and painful history in favor of narratives of present and future success and prosperity.

In contrast to hard-boiled tradition, Ryan's semifaux outsider status is not delineated as in any way positive or beneficial to his investigative skills. On the contrary, his refusal to confront his subjective reality, like the evasion of truth in *Darkhouse*, has the effect of muddling his capacity for exacting justice. If "Celtic Tiger Dublin" is "a virtual crime scene in which victims of its inconvenient past refuse to stay buried until justice is served,"[61] Ryan himself is also a representative crime scene, and his judgment and motivations are highly distorted by the impact of the past he declines to address. One can assume this state of affairs has existed throughout his career; he is in complete denial about the influence of his past experiences on his desire to become a detective and uncritical of the white-knight complex that has obviously developed from his survivor's guilt and need to counter feelings of impotence associated with his inability to rescue his childhood friends. In the Devlin case, this complex makes him susceptible to the manipulations of the person who plotted the murder, Katy's seemingly vulnerable and girlish sister Rosalind, whom his partner, by contrast, recognizes as a calculating psychopath. Ryan's unconscious desire for self-healing also compels him to involve himself compulsively in the case, hiding the conflict of interest from his superiors and thus undermining the legal merit of accumulated evidence. Finally, his distraction causes him to make a disastrous error, as he misreads Rosalind's birth date and erroneously concludes that she is not a minor, leading to a confession that is inadmissible in court and to Rosalind's evasion of prosecution for her crimes. Ultimately, as Peterson notes, "Ryan's inability to confront the 'buried truth' of his own past steadily erodes his judgment until he actually destroys the Devlin case."[62]

The novel uses the promise and withdrawal of truth as a device through its structure as a discomforting, anticlimactic confession. Ryan introduces himself as mendacious but quickly dismisses this characteristic as a requirement of detection. As he describes his developing relationship with Cassie, his partner, confidante, and eventual lover, his linguistic style morphs from formality and coldness to confidentiality; he acknowledges the reader, addressing us as "you" and offering us information that he claims even Cassie has not been privy to. As he becomes increasingly open about his feelings, he encourages the reader to trust in his honesty, even when his actions and reactions seem misguided, and to feel hopeful about the eventual resolution of both of the novel's central cases. This hopefulness comes to an abrupt conclusion when, on the verge of reclaiming his memory and beginning a romantic relationship with Cassie, Ryan suddenly retreats, reminding us that he warned us of his dishonesty, denying any foreknowledge that his relationship with Cassie was more than an average friendship, and simultaneously displacing blame onto Cassie by suggesting that she is lying about her feelings for him and onto the reader by insisting that we were, like him, fooled by Rosalind.[63] In this way, French artfully exposes the reader firsthand to the effects of denial: like Cassie, we are lured, misled, rejected, and gaslit.

The cycle of Ryan's openness corresponds to his cycle of willingness to admit a need to address his past. Initially, he insists on the sagacity of his decision to avoid discussing it, arguing that it will cause people to inaccurately assume that it affects him, even as he describes meticulously reading articles about it in secret and then flushing them down the toilet. He claims that he has no real desire to revisit his own case, blaming the reestablishment of his proximity to it on fate, though he could easily be released from the Devlin case by admitting to his conflict of interest. He seems not to comprehend why seeing the body of the young child in the location of his own former trauma has an emotional impact, dismissing his reaction as a normal facet of the job: "Every detective has a certain kind of case that he or she finds almost unbearable, against which the usual shield of practiced professional detachment turns brittle and untrustworthy." Briefly, he admits that his attempts at dissociation have been unfruitful and that, "in ways too dark and crucial to be called metaphorical, [he] never left that wood," but he quickly withdraws this assertion, exploiting and ridiculing fictional detective tropes to insist that he is not "some kind of tragic figure with a haunted past, smiling sadly at the world from behind a bittersweet veil of cigarette smoke and memories" who requires "a therapist and redemption and a more communicative relationship with [his] supportive but frustrated wife."[64]

Although he increasingly admits to being desperate to remain on Katy's case, Ryan is unable to connect that desperation to his past until Rosalind offers him an excuse that caters to both his desire to be a hero and his need to deny his personal investment, by suggesting that his experience makes him uniquely capable of obtaining justice for her sister. For the first time, he makes a conscious effort to retrieve his lost memories, a process he finds as "beautiful and dangerous as a bright spinning blade." He even comes to understand the extent to which his past has influenced his decision to become a detective, admitting that "this was the real thing for which all the other times and all the other cases had been nothing but practice." He determines to spend the night in the woods in an effort to unlock his subconscious, perfectly comfortable with the prospect of reporting anything he remembers to his chief, thus concurrently solving the only case of real import for him and revealing his true identity, which will likely bring an end to his career. Ultimately, however, this confrontation proves to be more than he can handle; he recoils from both the case and the communion he has developed with Cassie, recognizing too late that what feels like relief is actually "not a deliverance but a vast missed chance, an irrevocable and devastating loss."[65]

Ryan's failure to reconcile with his past is frequently presented as a kind of physical exile. He associates his pain with the displacement of boarding school rather than with the events leading up to it, comes nearly to tears hearing Cassie's contention that "Adam" can never return home, and finally begins to think of his slowly returning memories as path markers that, as in a folktale, he relies on to find his way home.[66] For Peterson, Ryan's alienation is a reflection of the Irish situation in an unrecognizably modern society, while for Rachel Shaffer, his quest to regain his identity and a sense of home represents the struggles of the Irish to come to terms with the changes brought about by the Celtic Tiger.[67] Ryan's ambivalence about modernity seems to support both of these views. He expresses disdain for traditional Irishness, critiquing prejudices he attributes to "deep stubborn veins of nostalgia for the 1950s"—a remarkable contrast to Benjamin Black's first Quirke novel, published less than three months prior to *In the Woods*. Ryan also ridicules residual hatred of the British in Irish society, which he feels disguises an inferiority complex; Irish adherence to folklore and superstitions; and even social conventions like the necessity of accepting food when one is not hungry to avoid offending a host.[68] In this sense, he promotes "the kind of backward concept of Irishness that proponents of Celtic Tiger culture place in opposition to Celtic Tiger progressive influences":[69] a concept of Irishness that, above all, is posited as responsible for all of the country's social wounds. Ryan attacks sectarian allegiances and the inability to move beyond the colonial mindset as causes of crime in the country and impediments to justice, in that they prohibit citizens from cooperating with the police for fear of being labeled as informers. At times, like Jack Taylor, he insinuates that Ireland has not modernized enough, pointing to the inconvenience of streets that were built for carriages rather than cars as a sign of the country's inability to embrace the implications and requirements of the postmodern world.[70]

Nevertheless, Ryan concurrently shares Taylor's sense of comfort in the remnants of Ireland's past. He reminds himself that his own experience is a rarity and that grave crimes like the abduction of children are still much less common in Ireland than elsewhere. He gravitates to old architecture, such as a bar that remains unchanged while the street has modernized around it and the preserved exterior of Dublin Castle, which he contrasts favorably with its refurbished interior. Despite his generally antipathetic response to superstition, he remarks on the appeal of a country that retains mysterious, unmonitored corners where even skeptics might imagine that hidden creatures lurk and suggests that contemporary approaches to the unknown, which encourage blindness to mortality through immersive consumerism, are in no way superior. Moreover, he is shocked by the apparent worldliness and understanding of sexuality among the young friends of Katy whom he interviews, contrasting these traits with the way he remembers his own more innocent childhood.[71]

In the vein of Jack Taylor, Charlie Parker, and Joe Lucchesi, however, Ryan's nostalgia is not for the past, but for the naïveté that shielded him from an understanding of the dangers of the world and the corruption of systems designed to protect society from those dangers. He muses that "it seems ingenuous to say that the 1980s were a more innocent time, given all that we now know about industrial schools and revered priests and fathers in rocky, lonely corners of the country. But then these were only unthinkable rumors happening somewhere else, people held on to their innocence with a simple and passionate tenacity, and it was perhaps no less real for being chosen and for carrying its own culpability."[72] Additionally, like

Taylor specifically, Ryan yearns for a past that he feels he was prom-
ised and of which he has been deprived, namely, a stable upbringing
in a familiar place with the communion of his two best friends.[73]
Since the denial of truth under old systems was responsible for misleading Ryan, Peterson views his disorientation as representative of
the plights of people who suffered under those systems and whose
struggles have been ignored for the sake of convenience, while Moira
Casey adds that it might also shed light on the false promises of new
prosperity, which has done little to assist the economic situations of
the working class.[74]

Unable to reconcile his discomfort with modernity and distaste
for tradition, Ryan attempts to satisfy his yearning for stability
through his role as a police officer. He is unique among the Irish
detectives in his intransigent faith in the legal system; although the
day-to-day hostility, competitiveness, and drudgery of his career fail
to live up to his fantasy of the murder squad, he continues to envision
his role as a detective as epically heroic and beautiful. His attachment to the force stems largely from a need to belong; he argues
that the drawbacks of the job merely reinforce his sense of community and allow him to forget about his own problems, "surrender
everything else . . . and become nothing but one part of a perfectly
calibrated, vital machine."[75] Even following his dismissal from the
murder squad, he finds himself unable to stray from the security of
the force.

Despite his idealized impression of the police, Ryan's views about
belief and faith in general are somewhat more contradictory. In contrast to Parker's response to Tante Marie, Ryan dismisses people who
claim to have psychic knowledge of Katy's case as "whackjobs," and,
despite his self-presentation as a heroic force of justice, he is particularly disturbed at the possibility of others having faith in him. With
Rosalind, he attributes this discomfort to an advanced understanding of the limits of justice, while he insinuates that his roommate and
ex-lover, Heather, uses her disappointed trust in him as a weapon in
her construction of martyrdom, much like Taylor's mother. When
Cassie expounds on the cruciality of belief systems, echoing other

Irish detectives in her contention that eroded faith in the church and government has led people to embrace materialism, corporeality, and self-gain as religion in mimicry of corrupt politicians, Ryan is entirely dismissive. His assertion that an archaeologist who is passionate about preserving the heritage site on which Katy's body was found is "batty" is met with a rebuke from Cassie: "That's his faith. . . . [I]t's a concrete part of his whole life, every day, whether it pays off or not. . . . That's not batty, that's *healthy*."[76]

Yet some of Ryan's derision appears to stem from envy of the belief systems of people such as the archaeologist and his compatriots in the fight for preservation. Both Morse and Taylor also express such jealousy, but for Ryan, it evokes spite and compulsive mockery; rather than expressing admiration for those who genuinely adhere to religion, he jeeringly envisions the candles he would light to saints were he religious. He couches his frustration for his loss of innocence as mature understanding, expressing no sympathy for people who become aware of corruption and disappointment late in life. This hostility also stems, in part, from an inability to forgive himself for the ignorance of his youth, but his conviction that he is immune to naïveté blinds him to the fact that experience is an ongoing process. When he arrests Damien, who was tricked by Rosalind into murdering her sister, the parallels between the two men are obvious: they share the boyish fantasy of knighthood, which makes them vulnerable to Rosalind's manipulations, and Ryan's inability to sympathize with Damien is a clear displacement of his own sense of blame. In this instance, Ryan's enviousness of Damien's innocence seems particularly misguided and lacking in self-awareness, as does his confession that he fears his experience made him too flawed to become a victim along with his childhood friends.[77] Clearly, it is Cassie, who recognizes Rosalind for what she is, that is too experienced to be susceptible.

An underlying factor in Ryan's naïveté is his conviction that all things can be explained logically. He rationalizes evil as a mirage of psychology, sympathizing with a rapist, Jonathan, who offers disenfranchisement and lack of economic opportunities in pre–Celtic

Tiger Ireland as excuses for his crime. French's use of the supernatural seems sometimes to support this point of view; Jonathan,
Damien, and Ryan share the perception of a large animal, perhaps
the black dog of folkloric tradition, as they are committing crimes
or facing their uncomfortable pasts, but it appears to be an unconscious effort to externalize the danger that lies in themselves, their
memories, and their capacity to commit harm. On the other hand, it
is Cassie's ability to delineate Rosalind as evil, rather than searching
for a meaning behind her actions, that makes her more successful
than Ryan in terms of bringing the case to a resolution. Ryan eventually comes to understand this fact, realizing that what he had hoped
was "a hideous misunderstanding. . . . a girl made vicious by trauma
and grief" was actually "something as simple and deadly as razor
wire." Once exposed for what she is, Rosalind appears hideous and
animalistic to him; like Adeline Modine in *Every Dead Thing*, she
is depicted as a beast disguised as a human being. Still, the experience serves only to drive Ryan back to the safety of what he can
understand and confront painlessly; he concludes by using his failure
to recognize Rosalind's nature as an excuse for retreating from his
memories, arguing that he no longer deserves them.[78]

In a certain light, French's novel might be viewed as more insis-
tent on the retention of cultural tradition in Ireland than is typical
in Irish crime fiction. That her narrator rejects this tradition with
little hesitation only serves to reinforce this standpoint; despite the
fact that his trust in the postmodern criminal justice system allows
him to largely avoid sullying himself with vigilantism, Ryan's refusal
to honestly address the past and the conflicting forces in his changing society makes him distinctly unsympathetic. At the same time,
French herself seems little inclined to invest in these cultural traditions; indeed, her attribution of perceived evil to psychological
aberrance—ultimately, even Rosalind's behavior is explained as psy-
chopathy—might be one factor in the popularity of her novels in
America.

In "'Down These Mean Streets': The City and Critique in Contemporary Irish Noir," Kincaid argues that Irish crime writers

embrace the tropes of American noir in their novels because of parallels between social and economic changes in America during the twenties and thirties and the transformation of Ireland during the Celtic Tiger and its aftermath: "The origins and ideology of noir . . . make a direct link to their reappearance in Ireland at this juncture. . . . Its literary origins in Hammett and Chandler lie in the Great Depression, in the extremes of wealth and poverty. The detective helps to expose the connection between corruption and glamor. . . . Philip Marlowe and Sam Spade are men of honor in a false age. . . . [W]hat the detective uncovers is large-scale unfairness, the result of an unbridled, unchecked economy, and his mission is not only to bring a criminal to justice but in some small measure to right this larger wrong."[79] Certainly, Irish noir is in part a reaction to stimuli similar to the ones that instigated the American hard-boiled: modernization, economic disparities, the development of urban centers, a spike in crime, immigration, and a heightened awareness of institutional corruption.[80] That Irish noir is less inclined to entirely reject the potential of institutions than its American counterpart seems remarkable in that oppressive colonization is a significantly more recent phenomenon in Ireland; however, the delineation of self in terms of freedom from federally imposed religious oppression is also more recent. Early American settlers fled England in order to escape religious persecution, but Americans have, at least nominally, lived under the presumption of a separation of church and state since the eighteenth century, while Irish Catholics did not enjoy equal rights with their Protestant counterparts and the freedom to worship according to their beliefs until the twentieth. In this light, it is not entirely surprising that Irish crime writers have more difficulty abandoning a faith that, until recently, was viewed as the alternative to forces of oppression.

It follows, then, that Irish noir is more invested in a type of truth that defies logic. Religion, notwithstanding its shortcomings, promotes communion and ethics and offers people a reason to show compassion to each other. The ability to clearly define right and wrong—or good and evil—prevents a society from being overwhelmed by muddled attempts to impose logic and motivation on chaotic or inexplicable behavior. On the other hand, the Catholic concept of redemption has an ironic twist in Irish noir, since it is frequently associated with the need to atone for abuses of the church and the code of silence and willful ignorance that enabled them. None of the authors considered in this chapter posits modernity as inferior to the past; rather, they share the conviction that, in order to progress effectively, the past must be considered and addressed in a manner that is neither sentimental nor dismissive. For Bruen, doing so means acknowledging the historical abuses of women and minorities to avoid making the same mistakes under a postmodern system; for French, it implies understanding the roots of economic disparities in an effort to address their effects. In the work of Connolly and Barclay, we are invited to consider that the need to heal the wounds of the past might not be limited to Ireland and that the relative rapidity of change in Ireland might allow for a clarity of vision that enables its writers to remind America of the problems that, in its own eagerness to reject the past, it has also failed to rectify.

PART TWO

Michael Tramples Satan

Northern Ireland's Troubled Police

In the book of Revelation, Saint Michael the Archangel leads God's armies to victory by conquering Satan's forces in the war in heaven; a warrior saint, he is considered the patron of police officers and the military. As with Saint Anthony of Padua, Michael's powers are interpreted as symbolic as well as literal: he is called upon for assistance by individuals facing internal struggles between compassionate and malevolent impulses. In this way, Michael serves as a reminder of the multifaceted nature of personal identity, emphasizing that people comprise a number of sometimes contradictory character traits. Likewise, the tradition of Michael suggests that imperfections—in people, institutions, or a society—are not cause to abandon hope; with enough force and effort, good can overcome evil, even if they coexist in the same entity.

Adrian McKinty's recurrent references to Michael in the Sean Duffy series form a complex web of symbolism that is both unique to the series' Northern Irish setting and studiously applicable outside of it. Viewed as a response to Ken Bruen's use of Saint Anthony, McKinty's incorporation of Michael suggests that positing vigilantism as a viable alternative to legal justice is at best misleading and at worst extremely dangerous. Set during the Troubles in Belfast and Carrickfergus, the Duffy series goes to great lengths to demonstrate that institutional corruption, however widespread or insidious, is less difficult to address and less potentially destructive to a society than exploitative vigilantism. Building on the same metaphor, the series steadfastly contends that people do not need to be perfect or unconflicted to participate in repairing broken systems and improving their communities' approaches to justice. On the contrary, such work, while often frustrating, overwhelming, or even seemingly Sisyphean, offers a means through which one might come to terms with one's values and priorities and thus better understand one's identity.

This latter theme is especially poignant in the North, where the question of identity has long been subject to conflicting narratives and ideologies. The emphasis on self-delineation in opposition to an *other*—Irish or British, Catholic or Protestant, nationalist or loyalist—was, according to McKinty and other authors, exploited by paramilitaries for power and financial gain at the expense of the security and well-being of the general populace. The three series examined in this section—Adrian McKinty's Duffy series, Brian McGilloway's Lucy Black series, and Claire McGowan's Paula Maguire series—acknowledge the effects of cultural immersion in dichotomous perceptions of identity while emphasizing personal values and ethics over such prescriptions. Each of the series features a Catholic detective working for or in conjunction with the traditionally Protestant police force of Northern Ireland, underscoring the urgency of breaking free from limiting notions of the self in order to create a more just and equitable society.

All three of the series stress the potential of the legal justice system; even McKinty's series, set during the eighties, when the Royal Ulster Constabulary (RUC) was notoriously partisan and subject to British intervention, envisions officers whose moral compasses enable them to surmount such challenges to remain impartial in the service of justice. The McGilloway and McGowan series use contemporary settings to reflect on progress made by the Good Friday Agreement and the establishment of the Police Service of Northern Ireland (PSNI), designed to be more neutral and balanced in terms of community representation than the RUC. Although both of these series acknowledge shortcomings of the PSNI, they also praise its new mission of inclusion and community outreach and express hope for continued improvement. While none of the three authors in this section argues for an abandonment of religious principles, then, the faith of the detectives is largely reserved for the promise of the police and the law. The implication is that, as evidenced by the new standards, the legal system can be influenced and improved by all members of a community—and can help all members of a community to find shared priorities and universally beneficial goals and solutions—while identification that prioritizes religious affiliation has historically proved divisive.

Like the detectives in the previous section, Duffy, Black, and Maguire are all "outsiders": Duffy not only works in a largely Protestant police force but also chooses to live in a Protestant neighborhood; Black and Maguire are not only Catholics but also women in a male-dominated field. While these distinctions cause substantial angst, they also lead to increased empathy, unlikely connections, and learning experiences that enable the detectives to address their personal demons, thus distinguishing them from Jack Taylor, Charlie Parker, Joe Lucchesi, and Rob Ryan. The lonely, despondent Duffy finds love with a Protestant woman and hope in the prospect of a family; Black's workplace experiences with sexism allow her to resolve her conflicted relationship with her mother; unexpected assistance from a Protestant officer helps Maguire to solve the mystery of her mother's disappearance, which has haunted her since childhood. The success of these detectives is reliant on their ability to transcend prescriptions of identity in order to better understand others but also on their capacity for accepting that viable paths to justice are of necessity complicated and imperfect. References to the early release clause of the Good Friday Agreement emphasize that long-term benefits must sometimes take precedence over immediate satisfaction; while all of the detectives are tempted by the immediacy and extremism of vigilante justice, they ultimately view it as shortsighted and self-defeating. This is not to suggest that the texts diminish the trauma involved in not obtaining sufficient justice for personal injuries; rather, they contend that such sacrifices are the unfortunate but necessary "price of peace."

2

"A Middle Finger to the Darkness"

Adrian McKinty's Sean Duffy

> *Yeah, I know what you're thinking: gun battle, rain, Ireland.*
> *But you don't know. You have no idea. You weren't there.*
> *For you, the eighties are: Thatcher triumphant, the Argies*
> *bashed, North Sea oil, the unions broke, the Reagan-Thatcher*
> *two-step. For you, but not for us. For us, it's helicopters, low*
> *clouds, soldiers, curling umbilicals of ash over the great, grey,*
> *dying city . . .*
> —Adrian McKinty, *Rain Dogs*

Gun Street Girl (2015), the fourth novel in Adrian McKinty's Sean Duffy series, opens with a typically eventful night in the life of Detective Inspector Duffy, a Catholic peeler in the Criminal Investigations branch of the Carrickfergus Royal Ulster Constabulary. In a joint operation among the RUC, the Irish Gardaí, the Federal Bureau of Investigation (FBI), MI5, and Interpol, Duffy waits on a beach to intercept an American ship carrying guns and ammunition for the Irish Republican Army (IRA). He is disaffected: mistrustful that so much competing bureaucracy will be able to carry off the operation smoothly, numbed to the point of boredom by the incessant violence of the Troubles, unconvinced that his own efforts or those of his colleagues are remotely useful in combating it, and wary of the looming risks to his life in the form of stray bullets, bombs, threats by Protestant paramilitary groups, and the IRA's bounty on Catholic police officers, whom they view as traitors to their cause.

While the other officers prepare for the arrival of the ship, Duffy remains silent and checks his two most trustworthy safeguards: his revolver and a small print of a painting by Guido Reni, *Michael Tramples Satan*: "I discreetly make the sign of the cross and, in a whisper, ask for the continuing protection of St Michael, the Archangel, the patron saint of policemen. I am not sure I believe in the existence of St Michael the Archangel, the patron saint of peelers, but I am a member of the RUC, which is the police force with the highest mortality rate in the Western world, so every little bit of talismanic assistance helps."[1] This print surfaces five more times in the series: once when Duffy seeks redemption after a mission he is in charge of ends in chaos and violence, despite his best intentions;[2] once when a suspect pulls a gun on him and he finds courage by grasping the print, ultimately contending that he survives as a consequence of Michael's protection;[3] once when he has been kidnapped by an IRA cell and fears that Michael will not be able to save him from summary execution;[4] again when he credits Michael for his getaway;[5] and finally when he considers a pilgrimage to Lough Derg with his father. By this last instance, Duffy's good fortune in escaping numerous life-threatening situations has increased his faith in Michael, though he indicates that this faith should not be confused with an unquestioning conviction in either the Catholic religion or the existence of God: "I didn't know if I believed in God . . . but I believed in St. Michael the patron saint of policemen."[6] For Duffy, Michael—the point of convergence between spiritual and legal order—is less a marker of religious or political identity than a symbol of hope that an antidote to the chaos in which he is engulfed will arise from the ashes of one or both of these crumbling systems.

Indeed, for a character whose identity is so entangled with his religious background, Duffy is surprisingly unaffected by faith per se. His Catholicism is the chief factor in establishing his role as an outsider; he has alienated himself from the Catholic community by joining the RUC and enforcing British law, and he lives in a Protestant neighborhood because it is substantially less dangerous for police officers. At the same time, he worries that his neighbors could turn on him as a result of sectarian considerations and is perpetually subject to the suspicions and derisive comments of other government employees;

by the sixth novel, he is easily framed by a corrupt superior as an IRA mole. Aside from these unwarranted suspicions, Duffy describes his immersion in the Protestant world as a kind of culture shock wherein the rejection of ornamentation, mysticism, symbolism, and high emotion—attributes habitually linked to Catholicism—makes it difficult for him to forge the personal bonds he yearns for. As a Catholic, he argues, he requires a level of communication, warmth, and confidentiality—not to mention an understanding and appreciation of art, music, and literature—that his dour, Bible-centric Protestant neighbors and colleagues are unable or unwilling to provide. His loneliness is emphasized through his disappointment when the people around him express distaste for his choices in music or fail to understand his literary references, and even his closest and most reliable friend, Detective Sergeant McCrabben, is described by Duffy as an emotionless "Vulcan,"[7] uncomfortable with any discussions of a deep and personal nature. In this sense, religion in the series is more a designation of background and custom than of a system of beliefs; Duffy does not regularly attend church or give any indication that his personal morality is particularly affected by religion, and the only signs of his religiosity are infrequent prayers in times of distress or for the souls of the dead.

McKinty explains Duffy's ambivalence as a realistic reflection of the time and location: Duffy is not a "postmodern character who's an atheist"; he is "more naff and dull" in that he clings to his religion as a mark of his identity, even as he berates himself for his superstition in the face of the ugly, unromantic aspects of human behavior he witnesses every day. In *The Cold Cold Ground* (2012), he breaks his usual boycott of the depressing news because "someone tried to assassinate the Pope and Duffy was really, really upset about it. He's devastated, and while all this shit's going on in his life, he's constantly checking the news: is the Pope ok?"[8] At the same time, he distances himself from the philosophy of his religion, attending confession only once in the series and habitually breaking the rules of his faith, even assisting his girlfriend when she contemplates having an abortion.

Duffy's reluctance to embrace Catholicism is not, as in the novels of Ken Bruen, a reaction to church scandals involving abuse and pedophilia; he mentions these scandals only once over the span of the series, and the situation of the novels in the 1980s predates the most extensive inquiries of clerics in Ireland. Rather, his conflicted response stems from frustration at the emphasis placed on religion in Northern Ireland and the decades-long sectarian violence that has ensued from this emphasis. His decision to become an RUC detective is a rejection of the classifications underscoring this acrimony; he expresses ongoing sympathy for the cause of historically oppressed Catholics and dismay at working for the colonialist government that oppressed them, but explains that he joined the RUC—as opposed to the IRA, which was his original intent—because the need to put an end to the chaos and divisiveness was paramount. Ultimately, his ability to overcome his expectations and discomfort in his Protestant surroundings allows him to form powerful intersectarian bonds: he develops a mutually protective and literally life-preserving relationship with Bobby Cameron, a paramilitary leader; finally achieves the relatively stable and mutually supportive family unit he has long desired with a Protestant woman and their daughter; and comes to fully appreciate the value of McCrabben's loyalty and reliability, despite his seemingly cold exterior.

Through Duffy's immersion in "otherness," then, McKinty underlies the superficiality of perceived secular divides, offering an alternative outlook on the forces perpetuating the Troubles in Northern Ireland. Paramilitary groups on both sides, he suggests, have good reason for wanting the Troubles to continue in order to maintain power and the ability to conduct illicit business without interference by the overworked and mistrusted police. Because Duffy is not especially attached to Catholicism, it is tempting to view his communion with Saint Michael as an intertextual reflection on Bruen's use of Saint Anthony. McKinty implies that bucking traditional structural systems is all very good and well in the Republic or elsewhere, but in the North, powerful and self-serving criminal enterprises have usurped the power of the police in a way that is anything but neutral or beneficial to the public. Since the paramilitaries have become the new order, Duffy's decision to become a policeman and his symbolic attachment to Michael as his patron saint are, paradoxically, rebellious acts against the corrupt establishment, much like the choice of Jack Taylor and others to become private investigators outside of the more powerful police forces of their societies.

As a Catholic, Duffy obviously has qualms about working for the RUC, remarking on his embarrassment at being linked to the insensitive and ineffective British policies that have led to the Bloody Sunday massacre in Derry[9] and the deaths of the IRA hunger strikers.[10] He asserts that these policies have perpetuated the violence by inadvertently evoking sympathy and support for the IRA, while the Special Branch simultaneously empowers Protestant paramilitary groups through collusion. When he is arrested by the Special Branch as a suspected mole, rather than asserting his neutrality, Duffy cannot refrain from an accusatory outburst about the way he and other Catholics have been treated: "One day there's going to be a reckoning for all the civilians, all the Catholic civilians, you've let die in Loyalist attacks, to protect your agents."[11] Additionally, Duffy paints the IRA as a force of extreme intellect in comparison with its Protestant counterparts, periodically describing its organizational and technical skills with something bordering on admiration. Unlike his colleagues, and contrary to procedure, he also maintains contacts with IRA affiliates. *In the Morning I'll Be Gone* (2014) has Duffy seek assistance from republicans in the search for his childhood friend Dermot McCann, now a high-ranking member of the IRA and a recent escapee of the Maze prison; in exchange for information about Dermot, Duffy agrees to privately investigate the murder of Dermot's former sister-in-law so that the family can exact revenge on her killer. In *Police at the Station and They Don't Look Friendly* (2017), Duffy relies on information from a friend who is highly placed in the Derry IRA to protect him from a Dublin cell that has condemned him to death. McKinty explains these irregularities as a means of countering reductive interpretations of the Troubles:

> If you grew up in the seventies and eighties, almost all of the fic-
> tion and films dealing with Northern Ireland . . . were extremely
> un-nuanced. . . . As you turn the microscope, you'll find that it's
> much more complicated: there's good IRA men, bad IRA men,
> sometimes the bad IRA men can occasionally be good. There's a
> bit in *Police at the Station and They Don't Look Friendly* where
> he [Duffy] goes out to be executed by an IRA hit squad and what
> I wanted to do with that story is . . . to show that all these people
> were individuals with their own agendas and own ideas and not
> just faceless villains out to kill our hero.[12]

Despite his sporadic doubts about his occupation and discomfiting sense that he is "one of the oppressors, not the oppressed,"[13] Duffy
exemplifies this nuance in his persistent conviction that both sides
of the paramilitary battle are essentially the same and that, while
neither is entirely evil, neither wholly and earnestly has the rights or
security of citizens at heart. He insinuates that the sectarian struggle
is an elaborate ruse in which, despite appearing to be "sworn enemies
who . . . [try] to kill each other at every opportunity," the IRA and
Protestant paramilitary groups actually work together "to facilitate
the distribution and the collection of protection money."[14] This practice includes forcing small shopkeepers already struggling under a
failing economy to pay exorbitantly in order to avoid being violently
targeted, under the pretext of collecting donations for causes such as
the hunger strikers or Ulster Defence Association (UDA) prisoners.[15]
By reinforcing divisive attitudes and asserting that they can enforce
justice more effectively than the police, the paramilitaries are also
able to maintain a monopoly on the country's drug trade, hypocriti-
cally passing the murder of independent competitors off as vigilante
crime fighting as they divide cities "between themselves for the dealing of hash, heroin, and speed, and the two newest (and most lucra-
tive) drugs in Ireland: ecstasy and crack cocaine."[16] Clearly, both
sides also participate in the killing of innocent civilians in order to

assert their power and advance their respective causes, leading Duffy to feel that he has most in common with people who have "contempt for all sides in Northern Ireland's pointless religious wars" and for whom "nationalism [is] a perverse hangover from the nineteenth century."[17]

While he admits to British culpability for the situation in Northern Ireland, then, Duffy assigns the mass of the blame to paramilitary greed and to outdated philosophies and prejudices that render its citizens vulnerable; after all, he argues, even England has long since progressed from its own religious wars[18] and is poised to extricate itself from Northern Ireland's as well.[19] For McKinty, the people of 1980s Northern Ireland are more ideologically stunted than their English counterparts because the Anglo-Irish Treaty of 1921, which enabled the division of the North from the Irish Free State, has left them mired in questions and frustrations about their identity: "I remember thinking when I was a kid how complicated it was to be from Northern Ireland because you're not Irish, you're not British. Northern Ireland is a completely invented identity; it means nothing. It was invented in 1921. There is no Northern Ireland; it's completely fake. And I remember thinking how easy it would be to be Scottish or English or American or whatever."[20] Unlike much of the rest of the world, which seems prepared to soften borders and work collectively, the North during the Troubles is engaged in a struggle between polarized ideals in an attempt to define national identity. As a result, its citizens are willing to turn a blind eye to the criminal activities of organizations they perceive as advancing their causes, despite the deeply personal and profoundly detrimental effects these groups and the clash among them have on their lives.

As a city effectively ruled by criminals under the guise of vigilantism, Belfast is portrayed by McKinty as a kind of dystopia, where riots, bombings, dismantled industry, unemployment, emigration, substance abuse, and depression are the norm. Duffy's painful perceptions are of a "gap-toothed city sinking into the mud. . . . Belfast as Gormenghast, Belfast as Fallen World, Belfast as Cursed Earth."[21] He drives the point home by depicting events that would seem catastrophic in other societies—explosions, violent insurrections, petrol bombs hurled at police, attacks on RUC stations—as not particularly contextually serious, and by the fifth novel, he describes these daily threats to the safety of himself and others with sardonic ennui: "A day of riding in Land Rovers. Of shields and formations and Molotovs. . . . Milk bottles filled with piss or petrol tumbling through the air. Seen it all before. Too bored even to describe it."[22]

Duffy's increasing desensitization to violence is a reflection of McKinty's own experiences with personal and societal numbness during the Troubles. When discussing one of the many bombings of the Europa Hotel in Belfast, he emphasizes the delight that he and other unemployed people with glazier experience felt at the prospect of earning enough to support themselves during a period of extreme economic hardship, in spite of the violent circumstances that had created such an opportunity: "They planted a bomb . . . outside the Crown Bar, and they blew a thirty-foot crater, and the hotel was destroyed . . . so we came up here and picked up all the broken glass from those windows and put them into a truck, and I think I got like 150 quid plus 50 quid bonus for clearing up the bomb damage. . . . And I'm sure every glazier in Belfast, when they heard this bomb went off, they went, 'Ah, happy days!'"[23] In the Duffy series, McKinty offers poignant reminders of the danger of such anesthetization to violence and of the fallacy of reducing human fatalities to numbers, as Duffy frequently does in downplaying their seriousness: *In the Morning I'll Be Gone*, for example, details one of many unexceptional attacks on a police station, which is said to have resulted in "only two fatalities";[24] however, one of these fatalities is Matty McBride, whose progress from youthful, apathetic, bumbling forensics officer to one of Duffy's most profound and trusted allies has been carefully detailed for the reader over the course of three novels, encouraging investment in the character and his future development. While depictions of the Troubles, particularly outside of Ireland, often stress the ideological clash and deemphasize the resultant casualties, McKinty shifts the focus to a humanization of these casualties, reminding us that they are people with families and potential, whose deaths have as much of an impact on their personal circles as any other murder.

That McKinty is compelled to make an argument for the importance of individual human life makes the Duffy series a kind of foil for traditional detective novels—in which one particular case is perceived as all-important and is given the full resources of the detective and the law—exposing their lack of realism for societies that have become habituated to violence and an absence of justice and thereby immunized to the personal implications of tragedy. At the same time, McKinty asserts that murder and injustice are personal and unconscionable and that we should not be blinded to this by the milieu in which they occur. While the titles of all of the novels are references to songs by Tom Waits, the most poignant in this context is *I Hear the Sirens in the Street* (2013), a line from "A Sweet Little Bullet from a Pretty Blue Gun," which criticizes the devaluation of human life that results from acclimatization to violence. McKinty reminds us that deaths that would be "big news" in other societies ought not to be overlooked simply because "Ulster in 1981 had other things on its mind."[25]

The central question in the series thus becomes how to reemphasize the importance of the individual over ideology, as represented by Duffy's attempts to thoroughly investigate individual murders in the context of a civil war.[26] Obviously, this task proves difficult. The RUC's resources are spread thin as it contends with persistent riots[27] and has difficulty maintaining personnel because of the extraordinary dangers and stress of the job. Even in cases involving the deaths of their own members, the paramilitaries refuse to cooperate, fearing that police investigations will undermine their semblance of strength and distract attention from their respective causes.[28] Citizens are also unhelpful, both because they are afraid of paramilitary revenge for providing witness statements and because these same paramilitaries have convinced them that the RUC is working against their interests and that informers are therefore worse than drug dealers and murderers.[29] Consequently, interrogations and requests for information invariably lead to the same refrain: the first rule of the North,

Duffy regretfully contends, is "whatever you say, say nothing."[30] The chaos of the Troubles provides convenient cover for nonsectarian murders as well; because of the lack of available evidence or avenues of inquiry, these murders are frequently attributed to the IRA and are left unpursued, since the police are all too aware of the futility of trying to build a case. Even if they manage to determine who the perpetrator is, successful prosecutions are rare owing to the lack of witnesses and public cooperation; as a result, "the vast majority of murders in Northern Ireland are never solved. The clearance rate is under fifteen percent when there's a terrorist dimension." For Duffy, this state of affairs means that, despite his tireless efforts, his cases inevitably conclude with "no closure and no justice."[31]

Understandably, Duffy ruefully contrasts his job with that of police in other countries and film and television detectives. Traveling to relatively peaceful Italy, he is staggered by "what normality [looks] like" in other societies,[32] and he repeatedly emphasizes that the stress of working for the RUC results in the highest suicide rate among police in Western Europe.[33] So common was this phenomenon, McKinty asserts, that the RUC developed an unspoken code for dealing with it without undermining the deceased officer's life-insurance benefits:

> another thing they don't tell you about . . . is the number of police officers who would die by "accidental discharge of a firearm," which basically means they killed themselves, but it would never be reported as a suicide, because that would invalidate the life insurance policies. And so you'd see these weird statistics: nineteen police officers died by accidental discharge. So how many accidents are these guys having? What was going on here? And then you'd look at the statistics a little bit and go, oh, right. I get it. You're an alcoholic; your wife's left you; you're fed up with the patrol and you can't take any more; the stress is killing you, and you just think . . . I'll give my children a better life. Blow your brains out because you know that the investigating officers will come and just go, "Well, clearly this is an accident," and your kids will get the life insurance and maybe move to England.[34]

In Duffy's collaborations with the law in other countries, the discrepancies between this life-on-the-brink and the role of officers outside of Northern Ireland are particularly evident: police in Norfolk have enough time on their hands to provide a team of officers and grief counselors for a death notification,[35] a Scottish officer is astonished that the RUC detectives carry guns,[36] and, notwithstanding its reputation owing to Colin Dexter's Inspector Morse series, the Oxford police force's inexperience with murder and crisis has the effect of muddling one of Duffy's investigations. His description of the renowned headquarters in Oxford is steeped in both bitterness and undisguised envy: "No one wearing body armor, no one wearing side arms, no stench of fear. This was what policing was like over the water. This was policing in civilization. These guys didn't know how lucky they had it. Burglaries, stolen bicycles, the odd rape, a murder every five or ten years—the real Morse World."[37] During a rare moment of idleness in *Rain Dogs* (2015), Duffy again remarks that "this must be what it's like to be a copper over the water";[38] when his tranquility is disrupted by the discovery of a bomb under his car, he returns to work after a few days, noting that "if this was any other police force in the world, you'd be in counseling for months after something like that. But RUC men and women were made of sterner stuff. Here, this was par for the course."[39]

McKinty does not, however, leave room for emotional detachment or exoticism. Along with the shocking death of McBride, he was originally determined to kill off Duffy himself, under morosely degrading circumstances, in order to unnerve his readers by making the reality of the Troubles feel personal to them:

> I tried to kill him at the end of book three, the Brighton bombing one. . . . Duffy hates Thatcher, obviously. . . . I thought it would be the perfect ending to the series: he dies saving Thatcher and . . . because he's this crazy Paddy and nobody knows what he's doing there, MI5 disavow him. They actually think he's involved, and so he dies, saving Thatcher, utterly dishonored, shamed, and his body is, like Mozart, thrown into a pauper's grave, and he's got no

honor, no life, no nothing. . . . [T]he only one who will know is the reader and the reader will be so, "No, wait! He saved her! How can you be so cruel? Don't you understand?"

While his editor talked him out of creating such an irreversible ending for his best-selling character after only three novels, McKinty tried again in the fourth book: "There was this real-life incident where they took all the top Special Branch guys and MI5 guys, and they put them in this helicopter. . . . And I thought . . . Duffy will be in the helicopter . . . and I'll make it so beautiful: he's just found love, maybe, and a way out, and a new career. . . . [H]e's just on the verge of transcendence and then, boom, he's killed in this accident."[40]

Although his efforts to kill Duffy were thwarted for a second time, McKinty manages to invest his international audience through a slow, consistent, and deliberate assurance that, wherever they live, they are not immune to the possibility of a convergence of circumstances that might create their own version of the Troubles. Northern Ireland, and Belfast in particular, is unique in its desperate and chaotic situation, but it was not always this way. Before it was a city bent on destroying itself and its citizens,[41] it was a place renowned for its noble patriots, its preservation of literacy and education, and its production of some of the world's most influential and eloquent literature. *In the Morning I'll Be Gone* describes the Belfast of the past as a city of architectural beauty and economic prosperity, brought down by the 1921 partition from the Free State, blitzes during the Second World War, and, finally, the bombings, burnings, and riots of the Troubles.[42] Not satisfied with suggesting that such a downfall could happen anywhere, Duffy repeatedly asserts that it *will* happen *everywhere*: "Belfast is the prototype of a new way of living. In 1801 it was a muddy village, by 1901 it was one of the great cities of the Empire, and now Belfast is the shape of things to come. Everywhere is going to look like this soon enough after the oil goes and the food goes and the law and order goes."[43]

This emphasis on the importance of "law and order" distinguishes the Duffy series from much of the crime fiction of the

Republic. Following two early exceptions, Duffy's periodic recourse to vigilantism is generally either minor and inconsequential or a matter of omission rather than commission: he lifts confiscated drugs but uses them sparingly, picks locks when he deems it necessary, and sometimes disobeys his superiors' orders, particularly when they involve closing a case prematurely. In one instance, he decides not to save a murderer who is bleeding to death;[44] in another, he refuses to extricate Strong, the former mole, from a dangerous meeting with the IRA in his new role as a Special Branch informant, musing that justice will be done for the deaths caused by Strong if the IRA discovers that he is wearing a wire.[45] The situation with Strong, however, reflects a conscious effort by Duffy to overcome the human temptation of "natural justice":[46] this late protest that Strong deserves to die follows an episode in which Duffy himself might have easily and justifiably killed him but chose the more difficult path of arrest.[47]

Duffy's rejection of vigilantism is portrayed as a growth curve in the series, culminating in this resistance of his instinct to kill Strong. In the first novel, he describes his youthful interest in joining the IRA following the Bloody Sunday massacre in Derry, in which Catholic protesters were shot by British soldiers during a march for civil rights, and the subsequent bombing of his college pub, which led him to embrace a structural approach to justice instead. This bombing was attributed, in succession, to the Ulster Volunteer Force (UVF),[48] the UDA, and the IRA, but seeing its effects firsthand led Duffy to realize that the attribution and associated ideology were unimportant compared with the destruction and loss of life:

I didn't care about any of that.

The alphabet soup didn't interest me.

I wasn't badly hurt. A burst eardrum, abrasions, cuts from fragmenting glass.

Nah, I was ok, but inside the bar was carnage.

A slaughterhouse.

I was the first person through the wreck of the front door.

And that was the moment—

> That was the moment when I knew that I wanted to be some small part of ending this madness. It was either get out or do something. I chose the latter.[49]

Nevertheless, Duffy commits one of his two major acts of vigilantism—the only one that involves taking a life—at the end of this novel. When he discovers that the murders he has been investigating were committed by a spy for the British government who has infiltrated the IRA and cannot be prosecuted without exposing and damaging operations, Duffy follows the spy to Italy, where he murders him in his home. Although there is no doubt of the man's guilt and Duffy's actions are a response to suggestions from MI5, by the second novel, Duffy confesses that the psychological impact of acting as the man's judge, jury, and executioner has been overwhelmingly negative and that even the gratification of justice has been tainted by feelings of guilt: "Revenge is the foolish stepbrother of justice. I understood that. I had lived with that thought for eight months. *Ever since that night on the shores of Lake Como.* What I had done then was a crime, and it was also a sin."[50]

Still, at this early point in the series, Duffy wavers on the subject of vigilantism. In the third novel, he burns a brothel owned by a pimp who has, through drugs, manipulation, and violence, coerced Dermot's sister into working as a prostitute. In this instance, Duffy ensures that no one is in the building; because there are no casualties involved, his reflections on his actions are not only untroubled, but actually suggest a satisfaction and a sense of closure that he has found evasive in his police work: "For once, I slept the sleep of the just."[51] Much of this irresolution stems from a conflict between Duffy's desire to pursue justice and help to reestablish peace and his acknowledgment that he must work for a government he considers dishonorable in order to do so. Encountering Dermot, Duffy contemplates which of them is more immoral: the IRA man who kills innocents with bombs or himself. He seems equally conflicted about whether he is more to blame for being a government employee or for his own vigilantism: "Could you work for Mrs. Thatcher's government and still be a good man? Could you shoot a man in cold blood and expect to avoid the fires of hell?"[52] Later, when Duffy discovers that, although they dismissed his prediction that the IRA would bomb Thatcher's hotel and refused to evacuate citizens for fear of bad publicity, MI5 took the precaution of moving the prime minister, he wonders whether, in fact, the IRA has the right idea in using violence against such a government.[53]

Nonetheless, all of this scrutiny ultimately leads to a reaffirmation of Duffy's belief in structural justice. Unlike Jack Taylor, whose doubts about vigilantism stem from the fear that ignorance or bigotry might lead independent justice seekers to actually subvert the cause of justice, Duffy's concern is with the confusion of justice and revenge and the weight the decision to take the law into one's own hands by injuring another can have on the human psyche. When he feels compelled, by his pact with Dermot's mother-in-law, to give her the name of her daughter's murderer, he does so grudgingly, along with a plea for her to reconsider what he knows will be her response: "Revenge is a mug's game. . . . The person getting revenge injures himself far worse by the act of vengeance than he was ever suffering before. He ends up living miserably. I've seen this first hand. A few years ago I revenged myself on a man who did terrible wrongs and it has brought me no satisfaction and considerable regret."[54] Ironically, of course, Duffy contributes to another murder by not withholding the name, but there is no consequential "sleep of the just." Rather, he becomes increasingly committed to his role as a police officer, even in matters of law with which he disagrees. While he sympathizes intensely with Irish women who are forced to travel to England due to Northern Ireland's antiabortion laws, upon accompanying his girlfriend at the end of the fifth novel, his lack of religious qualms does not prevent him from berating himself, since his actions run contrary to his oath as an officer: "*Aren't you supposed to be a policeman? Aren't you supposed to enforce the law? Abortion is illegal on the island of Ireland. . . . Assisting someone in the procurement of an abortion is a criminal offense under the catch-all clause of the Offenses Against the Persons Act (1861).*"[55]

For Duffy, then, the police and the laws they enforce may be imperfect, but they represent an order, a relative neutrality, and an acknowledgment of the humanity of citizens and of the importance of protecting them, all of which are lacking in the paramilitaries' approaches to controlling Northern Ireland. He reconciles himself with the discomfiting aspects of his job by asserting that he is "doing bad . . . for the greater good"[56] and describes the RUC's valuation of human life in stark contrast with that of the paramilitaries. In *Cold Cold Ground*, for example, Duffy pursues a killer who initially appears to be a serial murderer of gay men. Although one of the victims is a high-ranking member of the IRA, the Catholic organization impedes the investigation in order to avoid any public association with homosexuality. This reaction is as much a matter of practicality as of bigotry; the hunger strikes following the withdrawal of political status for IRA prisoners, the election to Parliament of Bobby Sands (one of the hunger strikers), and Margaret Thatcher's refusal to negotiate with the prisoners have led to increased global attention and sympathy for the IRA, and the organization is loath to allow any scandal to detract from that support. The Protestant paramilitaries are equally resistant to serving justice in the situation. They suggest that they are less invested in traditional Christian sexual mores than the IRA, but argue that Belfast society as a whole will likely perceive that the killer has done it a favor; they also admit that, had the victim been a member of a Protestant organization, they would have been forced by the higher-ups to murder him themselves.[57] While witness testimony is always scarce, Duffy attributes the complete absence of leads in this case to prejudice and citizens' fear of being labeled as homosexuals themselves for assisting: "The gay angle was probably hurting us. No one wanted to leave a tip about a homosexual murder. . . . [T]his was Northern Ireland in 1981 which was slightly less conservative than, say, Salem in 1692."[58]

Over the course of this case, we also get some foreshadowing of the manner in which Duffy ultimately resolves his qualms about working for the government, as he begins to draw clear contrasts between the motivations of government officials and of the police and clear designations between laws created by the government and the manner in which they are interpreted by the RUC. Politicians in this novel have more in common with the paramilitaries than with the RUC in that they are more invested in using the killings to advance their bigoted ideologies than they are concerned for the loss of life. A Democratic Unionist Party Belfast City councilor, for example, responds to news of the murders with the assertion that gay men are "an 'abomination under God deserving of the very worst torments of hell.'"[59] Only the police feel an obligation to seek justice for the victims, and they do so regardless of the fact that homosexual acts are against the law in Northern Ireland. Duffy and McCrabben deal sympathetically with the partner of the IRA victim, urging him to trust them and assuring him that, as RUC officers, they genuinely want to find the killer, unlike the paramilitaries, who wish to cover up the crimes for their own convenience.[60] When asked by the media if their efforts in the investigation will be affected by the illegality of homosexuality, Duffy's colleague McCallister replies without hesitation, in a manner that underscores an understanding of the difference in severity of various crimes and emphasizes the importance of life above all other considerations: "Keeping pigeons without a license is illegal as well, but we can't have people going round shooting pigeon-keepers, can we? It is the job of the RUC to enforce the law in Northern Ireland, not paramilitary groups, not vigilantes, not 'concerned citizens,' it's our responsibility and ours alone."[61]

This refrain of "our responsibility and ours alone" becomes a running theme in the series. In *I Hear the Sirens in the Street*, Duffy blocks a gang of racist paramilitary members in his neighborhood from attacking a vulnerable Black mother with the admonition that "you're not the law, my lads, I'm the fucking law. . . . I'm the law, my brave boys, and you'll have to go through me."[62] That Duffy has been asked to intercede in this situation by Bobby Cameron, the leader of the local paramilitaries, indicates that the wisest members of these groups also understand the importance of legal order at crucial moments. Although RUC officers are officially agents of the government, there is thus some acknowledgment of their superior impartiality in instances such as this one. For Duffy, this impartiality, coupled with a genuine interest in solving crime and protecting the public, renders the police significantly more respectable and reliable than the people they work for. Success "from a political or diplomatic standpoint," he concludes, is not the same as successful police work;[63] subsequently, despite his devotion to police regulations, he does not hesitate to periodically defy the government that, he believes, sometimes prioritizes politics over citizens. His guilt over the murder he committed in the first novel, which was done with the blessing of MI5 but ran contrary to police procedure, encourages him, at times, to even posit the police and the government as opposing forces. In *Rain Dogs*, he responds very differently to an MI5 suggestion, refusing to drop his investigation into a dignitary who is considering opening a plant in Belfast and arguing that the pursuit of justice and the prevention of crime should outweigh any economic or political considerations: "I am fucking persistent . . . and I'm going to bring the bastard down for it. The UK government might not like it, the Irish government might not like it, but if I can make a case, the RUC will support me, and the police down south will support me, too. Cops everywhere love nicking villains."[64] As it turns out, Duffy is not mistaken: both his superiors in the RUC and the Irish Gardaí support him in his pursuit of the killer, despite the opinions of their respective governments.[65]

The Duffy series thus makes use of the procedural trope of well-meaning and persistent officers who resist constraints imposed by their superiors in order to attain justice for the common man, but it also subverts this trope by suggesting that the police *in general* are a benevolent force and that the constraints are largely imposed by the government for which they work, rather than by higher-ups on the force. While the government concerns itself with, at best, the larger picture of economic development in Northern Ireland and, at worst, its own image in the international media, the RUC focuses on catching culprits and obtaining justice for individuals, without regard for self-interest or praise. In *Gun Street Girl*, Lawson, the third member of Duffy and McCrabben's small team, summarizes their devotion and lack of concern with accolades: "I'm not interested in promotion. I just want to do good for the community."[66] Conceding to governmental concerns about security and publicity, Duffy frequently accepts a total lack of recognition for his competent deduction and self-sacrifice, even when he is responsible for saving the life of Prime Minister Thatcher. When the Special Branch and the Ulster Defence Regiment take credit for one of their operations, he and McCrabben are unconcerned, asserting that the desire for headlines is useless vanity.[67] In *Police at the Station and They Don't Look Friendly*, Duffy gives up the opportunity for praise—and even endangers his career—by taking independent measures to save the life of a wounded IRA member who tried to kill him, rather than going through formal channels that might be too slow to rescue her: "Who wants to be a hero? And hero at the expense of some wee lassie's life?"[68] Although he technically breaches procedure in this last incident, Duffy insists that it is just another example of the prioritizing of human life—even when it runs contrary to government standards—that is fundamental to RUC officers: "Crabbie [McCrabben] was a policeman who would never manufacture evidence or take fruit from the jurisprudential poison tree or knowingly break the law. Crabbie had doomed-Edwardian-expeditions-to-the-Pole concepts of rectitude and discipline. But . . . he would have done exactly the same thing. He would have saved the girl too."[69] After all, Duffy suggests, those individuals who become detectives do so out of a commitment to truth and justice, and at times, bypassing a sluggish chain of command and a government with different priorities is necessary in the pursuit of both of these ideals.[70]

In this sense, Duffy resolves his qualms with working for "the oppressors" by endowing the RUC as an entity with a personal morality normally reserved for mavericks in procedural fiction. While he describes some of his colleagues as less ethical than others, the only officer without a real interest in justice turns out to be an IRA mole, who is brought to bay by Duffy and his team. In the series' most extreme example of the benevolence of the RUC and the perilousness of straying from its values, the departure of Duffy's once-trusted colleague McIlroy to join the public sector actually turns him into a murderer; even before Duffy realizes that McIlroy is the culprit, he determines that McIlroy's newfound interest in money, rather than justice, has made him vulgar[71] and concludes that, like the chaotic paramilitary leaders, now that McIlroy is no longer part of the system, "he [isn't] my senior anymore. He [isn't] anybody's senior anymore. He [is] nothing."[72]

The suggestion that a policeman's morality and identity are diminished upon leaving the force echoes the Jack Taylor series and other crime fiction of the Republic, but while most of these works search for a middle ground between vigilantism and imperfect structural justice, the chaotic backdrop of the Duffy series significantly heightens the protagonist's desire for and tendencies toward structural order. Apart from an overall adherence to police procedure, Duffy's yearning for regulations, reliability, and control manifests itself in an attachment to ritual and repetition that borders on the compulsive. He wears the same clothing almost consistently throughout the series: black jeans, Doc Martens, and a Che Guevara T-shirt, detailing them to the reader at regular intervals. He also makes note of checking for mercury tilt shift bombs each time he enters his car. While this consistency ultimately preserves his life when he discovers a bomb, he argues that the ritual itself is as important as the safety it promotes: "In a situation like this what saves you is the routine. There is something about process and procedure that distances you from the reality. We were professionals with a job to do. That's also why you're supposed to look under your car every morning—it isn't just the possibility of finding a bomb, it's the heightened sense of awareness that that routine is supposed to give you for the rest of the day."[73]

It is, of course, slightly ironic that Duffy's championing of individual human lives and rights leads him to erase some of his own individuality in favor of following preordained structure and procedure. This point is noted with disdain by the women with whom he attempts personal relationships: Laura, his first serious girlfriend in the series, remarks that she cannot connect with him because being in the RUC has "institutionalized" him, prevented him from tending to his own physical and emotional well-being, and stripped him of his vigor and personality,[74] while Annie, a woman with whom he has long desired to have an affair, tells him that the job has changed him and overwhelmed every other aspect of his life, making him simply "a cog in the machine."[75] While he argues vehemently against this critique, his thoughts following the encounter suggest that he is not only aware of his self-erasure but is actually glad of it: "I ran the bath and as the room filled with steam my reflection blurred and faded and finally disappeared completely, which was the way I wanted it to be."[76] Only in the sixth novel does Duffy seriously question whether his need to cling to ritual and repetition to survive the Troubles might be as destructive as the Troubles themselves; after reiterating twice in quick succession that Belfast is the unfortunate prototype for all cities in the future, he berates himself for talking in circles and remarks that here is strong evidence that he should leave the country, while there is something left of himself to salvage.[77]

Duffy's decision, at the end of this novel, to work part-time in Carrickfergus and to reside part-time in Scotland with his girlfriend and child represents the possibility of an alternative approach to his role in "ending this madness": one in which his ability to function within the chaos of his surroundings stems from the respite of self-care rather than that of ultimately inconsequential rituals. This approach is the culmination of a slow progress: in the second novel, he rejects McIlroy's suggestion to transfer to the Met, insisting that he must "stay and be part of the solution."[78] In the third novel, his suspension from the RUC makes him suicidal,[79] and though he tries to persuade himself to leave the country, he ultimately agrees to assist MI5 on a case instead, on the condition that they reinstate him to his former position on the force. His discomfort with this situation and his fear that, as a police officer, he can never truly escape being a pawn in the British government's plans makes him contemplate a spontaneous departure from Northern Ireland once the case is resolved; however, he cannot persuade himself that he is "free of honor and obligation" and instead returns home to "what [is] evidently going to be a long, long war."[80] In the fifth novel, after the discovery of the bomb under his car, Duffy is encouraged to take paid leave to recover from the stress of the incident, but he continues to pursue police inquiries instead;[81] at the beginning of the sixth novel, following months without a case, he is thrilled to be presented with a murder. Despite his newfound contentment with his family and his conviction that the case will not likely be solved for the usual reasons, Duffy contends that the possibility of investigating it is fundamental to his sense of identity and well-being: "A man's nothing without a purpose."[82]

Throughout the series, Duffy exhibits envy of people who can "cut through the guilt and the loyalties and the emotions" and leave Northern Ireland in pursuit of their own happiness.[83] His own inability to do so even temporarily and his constant immersion in the Troubles steadily erode his faith in the potential for justice and his capacity to contribute to it. The third through sixth novels are replete with evidence of an advancing sense of hopelessness. In *Gun Street Girl*, Duffy considers the possibilities that the pursuit of justice is quixotic[84] and that, despite hard work and good intentions, a single person can do little to rectify social wrongs.[85] This revelation brings him to an existential crisis, in which he questions whether the principle for which he has forsaken self-knowledge, independence, and the ability to be involved in a functional relationship actually exists: "I didn't know what the hell I was doing with my life anymore. . . . [W]hen I joined the police I thought I could help keep back the anarchy, but . . . every day the chaos was worse. . . . Sara wanted to know about the real Sean Duffy, but there is no real Sean Duffy. There was once, but there's not now. There's just a tired, broken, compromised wreck of a man."[86] By the end of the novel, he seems resigned to the limitations on accessing and exposing the truth in the face of a government and society that are perpetually trying to cover it up, adding that, to save oneself hassle and frustration, perhaps *"whatever you say, say nothing"* is the best course of action after all.[87] However, this concession is partially illusory, and Duffy rallies in *Rain Dogs* to counter people who express similar sentiments; he tells a superior officer that "the arc of the universe is long . . . but it bends toward justice," brushing off the officer's insistence that this maxim does not apply to Northern Ireland,[88] and resolutely refutes a government official's conviction that he is too cynical to believe that justice can be attained.[89]

In *Police at the Station and They Don't Look Friendly,* Duffy struggles more seriously with the evasiveness of justice; his kidnapping by the IRA cell leads him to consider that he has been working pointlessly against the inevitable future of the country and that his pride in believing otherwise will now be his downfall: "The future belongs to the men behind me with the guns. They're welcome to it. Over these last fifteen years I've done my best to fight entropy and carve out a little local order in a sea of chaos. I have failed. And now I'm going to pay the price of that failure."[90] Throughout this novel, his attempts to recover himself with thoughts of how some degree of order can be reinstated are fruitless; at one point, he interrupts his own hopes about the possible success of a case with pure dismissal.[91] Later, he asserts that he and his colleagues have achieved nothing at all in Northern Ireland, despite their hard work and devotion, and again considers leaving the country;[92] this train of thought is reinforced when he is accused of being a mole, giving him the sense that he has not even succeeded in combating prejudice among some of the people he works with.[93] For the first time, Duffy's faith in the RUC begins to waver, and he concedes that they play their own corrupt role in the Troubles by turning a blind eye to the paramilitaries' protection rackets and drug running.[94] Again, however, when he sees this cynicism reflected in others, he rebels against it, delivering a powerful sermon about personal responsibility to Strong, who claims that his illicit work for the IRA is excusable, given the hopelessness of bringing order to the chaos:

> Civilizations rise and fall and rise and fall, and eventually the sun goes out and the earth dies, and then all the suns go out and all the civilizations die, and eventually entropy maximizes, the second

law of thermodynamics wins, and there's nothing in the universe, no light, no atoms, nothing . . . But just because the world's ending, doesn't mean you give up. It was the great heretic Martin Luther who said "If the Apocalypse was coming tomorrow, today I would plant a tree." Wise words. And that's how we win: by sticking up a middle finger to the darkness closing in.[95]

If there is a moral to the Duffy series, it is that justice is not always attainable—certainly not in the very absolute and orderly way in which it is traditionally depicted in detective novels, and perhaps not at all in the span of a human lifetime—but its elusiveness does not absolve us of the obligation to pursue it. For Duffy, contradictory senses of powerlessness in the face of chaos and conviction that justice may yet "win" are embodied in the small print of Saint Michael that he carries with him for protection. McKinty explains that, on the one hand, he wanted to depict Duffy's slow loss of faith "as he becomes more cynical and he sees that no one's helping anybody; there's no God; there's no justice; the only justice has to be done by people like him, reluctantly forced into that situation." On the other hand, surviving the bomb at the Brighton hotel and multiple other life-threatening situations has made him consider that perhaps "the finger of God is reaching down from the sky and is saving him for better things." That Duffy carries the print of Michael in the pocket above his heart, McKinty adds, is extremely significant; after machine guns were supplied to the IRA by Americans, RUC officers were forced to add an extra element to their riot gear. Because multiple bullets fired at the chest by sharpshooters had the capacity to eventually puncture the Kevlar of bulletproof vests, officers began to wear an additional metal strip above their hearts to deflect bullets. Duffy's print of Michael is thus situated in the same place as this metal strip, representing a compromise between cynical rationalism and belief—both in the power of goodness and in his own role as a manifestation of Saint Michael, the patron saint of policemen, the "warrior who fights evil."[96]

A similar resolution of contradictory sentiments is also evident in the conclusion of *Police at the Station*. Duffy's decision to move to Scotland and work part-time in Northern Ireland seems inconsistent with the attitude expressed in his earnest lecture to Strong about personal accountability. However, Duffy's move does not equate to retirement: it merely suggests that he no longer feels that the responsibility for ending the Troubles can be—or should be—"[his] . . . and [his] alone." It also denotes a newfound, mature comprehension of the importance of self-care in renewing his resources, staving off despondency, and thereby becoming more effective at his job. In this sense, Duffy manages to strike a balance between investment in crime solving and investment in self that is antithetical to postmodern detective character tropes. McKinty notes that "he [Duffy] is saying 'just because entropy's happening all around us, just because there's chaos doesn't mean we can't try,' but he's also saying 'but I want my little parcel of happiness, and I've got this little chance of happiness, and maybe I can be selfish here.'"[97]

The conclusion of *Police at the Station* represents a balance of contradictions for McKinty as well. Over the course of the six novels, he only once strays from the first-person narrative of Duffy. Chapter 23 of *Rain Dogs* begins with a passage, highly emphasized through its use of italics, told from a different narrative perspective—presumably that of McKinty: "*I wish we could spin the clock back to the beginning of the day. Freeze Duffy there, as he drives to Carrick Castle. Let him avoid the melodrama. Let him lose the girl and get the girl and go to Liverpool and grow up and become a man. Let his story be the parsing of the human condition. But, alas, we can't do that, because we're dealing with truth here. Ugly, vulgar, violent, clumsy truth.*"[98] McKinty's explanation for the divergence of this passage suggests that Duffy's struggles echo his own authorial ones. Like Duffy, McKinty expresses a sense of conflict between his obligation to truth and justice and the lure of peace and happiness; also like Duffy, he articulates a mild envy of members of his profession who are unencumbered by the heavy, violent, frightening reality of the Troubles, contrasting his own work with the novels of Nick Hornby and Martin Amis:

> That's what I was trying to go for in that scene. Wouldn't it be great if we could just tell this guy's story, about his philosophical evolution, his maturation as a man. Because he's very much a man-boy at the beginning, and throughout the series, he matures and becomes a man who . . . thinks about other people. Wouldn't it be great if we could do all that without him having to shoot anyone? But we can't. He's going to have to shoot someone, and someone's going to have to shoot him, because that's the shit that happened, all the time, every day. So, yeah . . . that was my little authorial plea: I would love to tell it in another way, but I'm interested in telling it more or less the way it was.[99]

Because Duffy is unable to concentrate exclusively on himself and his personal development, McKinty seems to suggest, it would be unrealistic for Duffy's author to do so; however, the Duffy series underscores the importance of personal identity precisely by highlighting what occurs when that identity is confused, repressed, or obfuscated. While Tana French's Rob Ryan has some agency in refusing to face the trauma of his past and subjugating his private self to institutionalized teamwork, Duffy is limited in his ability to explore his subjectivity by the chaos in which he has come of age. In this sense, he is a reflection of the sui generis circumstances of an entire generation in Northern Ireland: a situation exacerbated by the efforts of outside forces to willfully disregard or control the narrative of Northern Irish identity. For McKinty, then, a crucial step toward reclaiming the individual narrative is reclaiming the narrative of an entire society.

McKinty's dedication to telling the story—of Duffy, of the Troubles, and of the generation that was shaped by them—is thus primarily rooted in a desire to edify. The passage in which he interjects an authorial voice directly follows a frustrated diatribe, also in italics, about the misunderstanding and misrepresentation of the Troubles outside of Northern Ireland (quoted at the beginning of this chapter).

In its references to Margaret Thatcher, Ronald Reagan, and the Falklands War, this segment designates two distinct imagined audiences for the series: the British, so enmeshed in their own political issues that they failed to take adequate responsibility for the situation they helped to create in Northern Ireland, and the Americans, whose sense of entitlement to the management of other countries and dedication to the reductive David-and-Goliath narrative of virtuous Catholic freedom fighters battling an oppressive, bigoted, tyrannical government led them to significantly worsen the damage of the Troubles, in terms of destruction of architecture and property and, more significantly, human casualties. In a review for the *Irish Times*, Brian Cliff notes that the "sense of Northern Ireland as subject to larger forces: MI5 and MI6, transnational corporations, American interests, and the downward spiral of the British Empire" is a running theme in the series, adding that "such forces bat Northern Ireland around at will, in the service of their own external priorities."[100]

Cliff's use of the phrase "bat . . . around" here is particularly apt, summoning the dehumanized image of an animal toying with its prey and conjuring the darker implications of Northern Irish exploitation in McKinty's work. Certainly, these "larger forces" use the North in their own service—politically, economically, and sentimentally—but more poignantly, they do so without acknowledgment of the consequences on the people who actually live there. Throughout the series, Duffy juxtaposes the local news with British media reports, which largely ignore the ongoing violence on the ground in Northern Ireland. *I Hear the Sirens in the Street* takes place during the Falklands War, which Duffy paints as an insignificant scuffle meant to reinforce the mirage of British power. He has difficulty containing his outrage upon learning that forces in the North will be relocated to the Falklands, thinning their already inadequate numbers. Moreover, the incessant media updates about the Falklands contrast markedly with the sparse coverage of the Troubles: "Some wars, it seemed, were more important than others."[101] In *Police at the Station*, Duffy reflects on all of the historical events he has described in the novels, with particular attention to the Milltown Cemetery attack, in which three unarmed mourners at an IRA funeral were killed by Michael Stone, a member of the UDA, and the subsequent corporals killings, when two off-duty officers, wrongfully suspected of conspiring with Stone, were beaten and shot to death by the IRA. The chilling irony of these two events is that they remind the reader that the Troubles took place in a postmodern society, with the technological capability to broadcast footage of these incidents on live television, but seemingly without the drive or capacity to have stopped them from occurring in the first place. For the British, more consumed with a future of economic, technological, and social progress than with rectifying problems caused by past colonization, these tragedies are quickly forgotten, but for the people of Northern Ireland, the "progress" that enabled them to view the events firsthand serves only to compound the damaging effects of their situation: "The Troubles simmered in the background, an entire generation scarred by the brutal murders of the two corporals and the three IRA funeral mourners on live TV. Throw in the 'punishment' shootings and the fire bombings and the attacks on cops and soldiers. . . . Most of that stuff wouldn't make page one of the Irish papers and wouldn't get mentioned at all in the British ones."[102]

By contrast, American society in the Duffy series is overly interested in the Troubles, a phenomenon implicitly linked to its sentimentalization of Irishness and of the Irish Catholic struggle. Irish Americans, generations removed from their emigrated ancestors, have little real understanding of Irish culture, politics, or society. Their perception of the culture about which they are so passionate actually derives from reductive and romanticized film, television, and literary accounts contrived by their fellow Americans. When he travels to the United States in *I Hear the Sirens in the Street*, Duffy is appalled by the carnivalesque interpretation of his society and its problems: "I found an Irish pub called Molly Malone's. It was an embarrassing explosion of kitsch and sentimental Oirishness. Comedic leprechauns jostled for space with photographs of the dead hunger strikers and framed newspaper headlines celebrating infamous bombings. There was a collection tin for the IRA on the bar and posters that said things like 'Death to the RUC,' and 'Death to the Brits.' No Mick with any self-respect would ever drink in a place like this, which is why it was packed to the rafters."[103] Not without reason, Duffy anticipates overt, fawning attention from members of this community, but he discovers that his Northern accent is unrecognizable to them; when he hazards conversation, he is invariably perceived of as Australian.[104] Apart from underscoring American ignorance about Ireland, this misconception is also symbolic. Americans have a particular idea of what it means to be Irish: a stereotype that excludes the people of the North in whose war they feel entitled to be involved. While Duffy finds humor in their mawkishness and lack of education—in *Gun Street Girl*, American gunrunners kissing Irish soil downwind from a major sewage plant in Derry seem particularly clownish—he also emphasizes that, for Northern Ireland, this ignorance is lethal: "These young American men . . . have come across the sea to bring us death in the form of mortars and machine guns."[105]

If the British are hypocritical for professing a desire for peace in Northern Ireland while they continue to fuel the fire of the Troubles, Americans are equally so in their willingness to overlook casualties in the society they claim to revere in order to preserve their black-and-white vision "of peace-loving Irish patriots starving themselves to drive out the evil British imperialists."[106] Duffy sardonically contrasts scenes from American films in which the IRA subjects captured policemen to philosophical dissertations on the evil of imperialism with the actual torture and murder inflicted under such circumstances.[107] Apart from high-velocity weapons that both intensify police reactions and result in the death of more civilians, the Americans send politicians, such as Joe Kennedy, to endorse the cause of Sinn Féin and, by extension, the IRA.[108] For Duffy, these men and the Irish American diaspora as a whole are "rich, interfering, good hearted but essentially kind of stupid,"[109] unable to process that their actions merely postpone the commencement of a peace process in a region from which the British are already preparing to withdraw. In this way, they unintentionally worsen the situation for Catholics and Protestants equally, a fact emphasized by the attempted murder of Duffy by a group of Irish Americans when he visits Boston. Because he does not easily fit their dichotomous stereotypes, Duffy is attacked as a police officer and oppressor of Catholics, despite the fact that he is a Catholic himself, invested in a safer and more just future for other members of his religion.

Moreover, although the British and the Americans appear to be on opposite sides of the war in Northern Ireland, much like the Protestant and Catholic paramilitaries, they actually work together for their mutual benefit and at the disservice of the North. Visiting Americans get away with violence and murder, excused by their own society as freedom fighters and by the British owing to the money they bring into the region. *Gun Street Girl* is a particularly cynical take on this arrangement, opening with the aftermath of the assault of a prostitute by an American actor, who threatens the police who attempt to hold him accountable, simultaneously arguing that his wealth gives him power over them and conflating their accusations against him with their oppression of Irish Catholics.[110] The central case of this novel, which involves the murders of a couple and the disappearance and apparent suicide of their son, is complicated because a prime suspect, John Connolly, is an American residing in the guest house of the US consul. The Special Branch is hesitant to pursue the lead for fear of upsetting the American government,[111] but Duffy forges ahead, only to discover that, as an American, Connolly is "holy. Precious. Untouchable."[112] Having arrested Connolly for using a fake Irish passport, Duffy is chastened and forced to release him, regardless of the damage it will do to the investigation: "The lesson here: stay away from Americans in Ireland. This was their backyard, this was their playground."[113]

As it turns out, Connolly is not directly responsible for the deaths, but the lure of his government's money most certainly is. As an operative in the Iran-Contra affair, Connolly persuaded the son of the murdered couple and a warehouse supervisor to assist the American government in smuggling missiles, and the supervisor ridded himself of his partner and his family to increase his share of the recompense. More deaths occur during a botched American attempt to obtain these missiles, but this event is erased from history through the joint efforts of the British and American governments, and the Special Branch ultimately drops the investigation into the missiles altogether.[114] In McKinty's reimagining of Iran-Contra, the role of the British government is more substantial than the public has been led to believe, blurring the distinctions between governmental and paramilitary behavior and making Thatcher's refusal to negotiate with IRA prisoners on moral grounds seem hypocritical: "The plan had been to buy missiles that were to be given to 'moderate' elements of the Iranian government in exchange for their help in securing the release of American and British hostages in Lebanon. Reagan and Thatcher had been doing deals with terrorists while declaring that they would never ever do deals with terrorists."[115] Additionally, the use of falsified Irish passports by Oliver North and his men when traveling to Iran is reinterpreted and conflated with Irish America's sense of ownership of the old country: Connolly chooses Northern Ireland as a base for his operation because, he says, "My mother's family is Irish. . . . And there's always been excellent relations between this country and Ireland. We felt that the Irish would be amenable to our interests. Ireland is a place where Americans can do business."[116]

Despite Duffy's escalating mistrust in the transparency and good will of governments, the nuanced assessments of the novels never incline toward anarchism, vigilantism, or nihilism. On the contrary, apart from the British and the Americans, there is a third implied audience for the Duffy series, to whom McKinty directs the weight of his pleas for critical thought, humanitarianism, and a reimagining of justice. This wider audience includes anyone who, not having come of age in the midst of a civil war and seen the repercussions first-hand, might still be inclined to weight ideologies above individuals, allow anger to devolve into intolerance or bigotry, or imagine that violence is ever the best response to inequity. The novels are replete with comparative reactions to British colonization; the King David Hotel bombing might have driven the British out of Palestine, McKinty suggests, but Gandhi's passive resistance was no less effective in gaining Indian independence.[117] Gandhi is a favorite reference point for Duffy, who uses his example as armor against the temptation of believing, as many of his fellow citizens do, that change can be effected only by violence.[118]

Like many of his contemporaries in Irish crime writing, McKinty's work reflects a broader conversation about the manner in which different societies can learn from each other's experiences to evolve better strategies toward attaining justice. Northern Ireland might have spared itself considerable casualties by following India's pacifistic approach, but the lessons of the Troubles also make its citizens uniquely capable of teaching other societies about nuance, identity, nationality, tragedy, violence, and tolerance:

> I think living in that zone where it's confusing and you don't know who you are or where you're from . . . you always have to interrogate yourself. Scott Fitzgerald had this idea: the mark of a civilized man is to keep two contradictory ideas in his head. And that's sort of like being from Ulster: keeping at least two or three contradictory ideas in your head. Are you Irish? Are you British? Is there a place called Ulster? You come from this place that doesn't really exist. And then you think to yourself: but *nowhere* really exists. England doesn't exist. Scotland doesn't exist. They're all fake, and it's all lies. . . . [I]t's confusing, but it's also just an interesting journey that you have to do and to think about. And, also, it gives you compassion for people in stateless worlds, people who are just confused about everything. You could be confused about your gender identity . . . your race, your ethnicity, your language. I just want to say to them it may be confusing and awful now, but that's actually a really interesting place to be.[119]

3

Borders

Brian McGilloway's Lucy Black

> Nothing cements a community like a common enemy.
> —Brian McGilloway, *Bad Blood*

Bad Blood (2017),[1] the fourth novel in Brian McGilloway's Lucy Black series, advances Adrian McKinty's suggestions about the lessons of tolerance, acceptance, and empathy that might be learned from the Troubles. The narrative offers a striking departure from the first three books, shifting the focus from the inner workings of the heroine to tackle the worlds of politics and social justice. Following Lucy's investigations during the week prior to the historic Brexit vote in the United Kingdom, *Bad Blood* explores the economic hardship and xenophobia that contributed to Britain's decision to withdraw from the European Union. In so doing, it hearkens to McKinty's Sean Duffy series, drawing parallels between the Troubles and the increasing normalization of hard right-wing values in the West.

Borders are a recurrent theme in McGilloway's work: his Inspector Devlin series, for example, features cross-force police investigations on the border between County Tyrone in the North and County Donegal in the South. For some time, McGilloway notes, his interest in the physical border between the two countries "waned as the object itself appeared to vanish from sight":[2] owing to the withdrawal of military checkpoints in accordance with the Good Friday Agreement, the border has been open and effectively invisible since 2005. For McGilloway, though, physical borders are only one manifestation of the boundaries people establish in a counterproductive

103

effort to define their identity: freed from the specter of the Irish border, the first three Lucy Black novels examine the metaphorical borders Lucy creates between herself and other people—particularly her mother—as she grapples with her conception of herself and her ethics and responsibilities as a professional woman.

That McGilloway would return to a focus on borders in the context of politics and nationalism in *Bad Blood* is hardly surprising: the British vote to leave the European Union in 2016 inevitably raised the possibility that customs checks—and a hard border—would be reinstated between Northern Ireland and the Republic. Many argued that such a border would, in effect, undermine the intent and progress of the Good Friday Agreement. Ultimately, a hard border on the island was avoided, and a trade border was instead established in the Irish Sea; however, in an article written prior to this decision, McGilloway suggests that, regardless of the physical resolution to the border question, Brexit and associated discussions about the border run the risk of reopening wounds that have barely begun to heal: "So long as we couldn't see it [the border], we could pretend it wasn't there. We were free to choose our own national allegiances, whether Irish, British or Northern Irish. . . . If ever something would help reinforce feelings of social division and the tribal mentality of both religion and politics in Ireland, surely a Border crossing would do it. . . . And for all the talk of technology and frictionless boundaries after Brexit, we should be in no doubt that, whatever of the physical structure, the psychological Border is already hardening. Tribalism and sectarianism are not far below the surface here."[3] In *Bad Blood*, we see the very real threat of reversion to a world not unlike that of Sean Duffy, where such tribalist attitudes obfuscate personal questions of identity; the "community" that is brought together in the quote that opens this chapter is one that defines itself in opposition to an other—or, in this context, many others—as opposed to one that emphasizes individual development.

The Black series is set in Derry during the UK recession, some fifteen years after the Good Friday Agreement. Lucy is a Catholic detective sergeant who has returned to her small hometown to serve in the Police Service of Northern Ireland (PSNI), a force designed to be more neutral, equitable, and subject to community oversight than the Royal Ulster Constabulary (RUC). However, McGilloway suggests that changes in policy are easier effected than changes in attitude. In *Little Girl Lost* (2011), Lucy considers the transformation of the city since the Troubles: "It still shocked her how much it had changed since she had left. Then it had seemed on the verge of destroying itself; two banks of the river, two names, two tribes. . . . Now, though, the place seemed to have found its feet. . . . [O]ne by one bridges literal and metaphorical were traversing the river, drawing the two sides closer."[4] Nevertheless, the tenuousness of this peace is equally emphasized through statues along the river representing men from the two communities reaching out to each other, which have been dressed by citizens in opposing tribal colors.[5] The sense is very much that, though technically over, the Troubles still bubble under the surface of this society; their vestiges remain in the structure of its architecture, particularly in the high, airless windows of the police station where Lucy works, designed to protect its occupants from bombings.[6]

There are other vestiges as well. Working-class neighborhoods are still largely segregated, designated by curbs painted in the colors of the Union Jack or the Irish tricolor.[7] Mistrust of the police remains palpable in these neighborhoods, where Lucy and her colleagues are encumbered in their investigations by menacing teenagers who threaten them or pelt them with rocks, and where witnesses are wary of talking to them for fear of being targeted as informants. Certainly, the peace process and the transition from the RUC to the Police Service of Northern Ireland has had some major benefits: violence has substantially declined, Lucy is not especially targeted as a Catholic officer, and she can rely on cooperation from at least *some* members of the community, albeit often behind closed doors and out of sight of their neighbors. Still, maintaining the new and delicate cease-fire comes with its own set of complications. Obtaining CCTV footage, in particular, is a slow and cumbersome process for the PSNI, since the footage must first be reviewed and processed by the City Center Initiative to avoid public outcry about police surveillance.[8]

During the Troubles, crimes frequently went unprosecuted as a result of obfuscation from the paramilitaries and a lack of assistance from the community. In contemporary Derry, the police must compromise in their reactions and arrests in order to preserve stable community relations. Certainly, this restraint is extremely valuable in terms of limiting police abuse, but it also inhibits the PSNI's ability to contain riots and vigilantism which, while less frequent, are still common occurrences. In *Someone You Know* (originally published as *Hurt* in 2013), police and firefighters are unable to rescue a man mistakenly accused by his neighbors of murdering a young girl; after setting the man's house on fire with him inside of it, the neighbors form a riotous barrier that the police fear to breach because "any heavy-handed attempt by the PSNI to break through the line of youths would be immediately politicized and could undo years of painstakingly developed cooperation between the residents in the area and the community policing teams."[9] Nor do these limits on police displays of force always prevent the government from exercising control in an equally corrupt and more surreptitious fashion. In the same novel, Lucy unearths a cover-up from the early years of the peace process. Knowing they would be dependent on the cooperation of community leaders, the PSNI and the Special Branch wrongfully convicted a leader who refused to collaborate for the murder of a young girl, replacing him with the father of the actual killer, who was more sympathetic to the peace process.[10]

Just as Sean Duffy frames his work for an oppressive British government during the Troubles as "doing bad . . . for the greater good,"[11] Lucy's mother, Assistant Chief Constable (ACC) Wilson, insists that "doing deals with bad people to try to do some good. On all sides"[12] is an integral part of modern policing in Northern Ireland. While Lucy is unconvinced that the cover-up was warranted, she concedes that lack of community cooperation leads to more widespread injustice.[13] Her own mission to determine the whereabouts of Alan Cunningham, a man who killed a young girl with whom she formed an attachment in *Little Girl Lost*, has been significantly impeded by the protection of Cunningham's republican ties. As in the Duffy series, even nonsectarian crimes are difficult to resolve owing to sectarian considerations and residual hostility toward the police; Lucy contends that "none of those who knew Cunningham necessarily agreed with what he had done, nevertheless they had not been prepared to help the police to find him."[14] Although she criticizes the flouting of legal justice by the individuals involved in the cover-up, Lucy undermines the system in turn. In exchange for assurance that Cunningham will lose his protected status, she offers classified information to an IRA convict about his daughter's killer, knowing that her actions will result in vigilante violence.

McGilloway's Northern Ireland is thus a region that, while no longer exhibiting the most obvious manifestations of civil war, nevertheless contends with both enduring social norms created by the Troubles and a new generation that, not having witnessed the deleterious effects of ideological extremism firsthand, is not immune to its appeal. Ex-paramilitary members are regarded as heroes in their communities;[15] working-class areas are still controlled by people who formerly participated in sectarian violence;[16] the drug trade is still operated by sectarian groups that violently target dealers who refuse to pay protection money;[17] the police still struggle with inadequate equipment and manpower because their resources are deployed to contain riots.[18] In *Bad Blood*, each of two men struggling for control over their community portrays the other's violent attacks as accidents, indicating a higher valuation of ostensible enemies' right to conduct business without police interference than of structural justice, even when such an outlook is against their interests.

Moreover, the peace process has served not to eradicate anger and guilt caused by the Troubles, but rather to internalize it, leaving people with no direct outlet for their frustrations and causing some to turn to nonsectarian crime or even suicide.[19] McGilloway describes the process as a "salve" that has "not proved as purgative as people had perhaps supposed" because "many of the old animosities remained, just below the surface." Forebodingly, he warns that "in the wrong hands, or with the wrong words, any one of the issues was enough to bring people out to the streets, not to protest about the specific issue necessarily, but more to vent their frustrations at enforced compromises."[20] Northern Irish society is depicted as an unexploded bomb, ready to detonate with the slightest of changes to its delicate ecosystem. While each new protest, riot, or contention over a loyalist parade leads the media to presume that long-dead sentiments have suddenly and unexpectedly returned, Lucy contends that these sentiments have never disappeared, but that people have merely been persuaded to repress them in the name of progress: "The issues had always been there, just below the surface. Like love, the first flush of peace was idyllic, such a contrast to what had gone before, that you were prepared to overlook the flaws; indeed were blind to them. The real test was always going to be the long haul: the ability to face the imperfections and still decide that it was worth sticking with, that the good outweighed the bad."[21]

Lucy's understanding of the ongoing anxieties from the Troubles stems from personal experience. While her own involvement in the new policing system is relatively unaffected by bigotry owing to her religion, both of her parents were Catholic officers in the former RUC. Like Duffy, her family "hadn't been welcome in the Catholic areas because her father was a cop; nor welcome in the Protestant areas because they were Catholics."[22] Ultimately, they were burned out of their house and forced to move, an event that caused enduring trauma for Lucy, particularly because her parents' divorce and a subsequent alienation from her mother followed soon after. Upon returning to Derry to care for her father, who, "in some personal act of defiance" moved back to the same neighborhood from which they were driven,[23] Lucy confesses that, as a consequence of how unwelcome she was made to feel there as a child, she is not at all sure that it is her home and is not entirely convinced that it has changed substantially. Fleming, her PSNI supervisor, asks her to keep an open mind, asserting that "places can't change. . . . Only the people who live in them. You might be surprised."[24] Indeed, though Lucy's adult life initially seems to be mirroring her childhood when she returns home to discover the words "Lucy Black. PSNI Scum" spray-painted on her gable wall,[25] she is astonished to discover a very different and more supportive response from members of her community. A neighbor arrives to repair her wall, to inform her that the community does not support the way she has been targeted, and to invite her for a cup of tea. "With those words," we learn, "he [confers] on her a sense of belonging she [has] not felt since she was a child."[26] Despite McGilloway's persistent commentary on the corruption and resentment that have not been entirely eliminated by the peace process, then, the first three novels in the Black series underscore a change in attitude in Northern Irish society: a willingness to transcend sectarian mentality, to extend empathy to people as individuals, and to trust in the potential of the new police force and the new direction of the country.

Of the shift in the series' tone from cautious optimism about signs of progress to frustration, alarm, and exhortation in *Bad Blood*, McGilloway offers that the tribalist discourse surrounding the Brexit vote is disturbingly familiar and has the potential to do serious damage in a region that has not had the time to fully address and recover from its past:

> I suppose the point was that during the violence here, people were encouraged into tribalism. It suited politicians and some clergymen to encourage certain perceptions of "the other" as a way to ensure blind faith from their followers. The end of the violence here and the almost Damascian change of heart about their one time enemies some of our leaders exhibited when they got a taste of power simply highlighted the fact that, for 30 years, they'd been playing their followers, selling a message that suited them to achieve their own personal aims. But when you start a fire like that, it's hard to control it again. The other problem here, I think, was that the end of violence was presented as bringing financial improvement for all. In fact, while some areas did see increased investment, that wasn't across the board and those who lived in areas of social deprivation began to feel left behind. Rather than seeing this as a class issue, old enmities meant that tribal splits were ripe to be exploited again; except in more recent days, that was aimed against immigrants who became the new "other." I'm disgusted

by anyone who blatantly uses tribalism (or the vilification of "the other") as a recruitment agent. *Bad Blood* is born of that.[27]

Thus, the kindness of Lucy's neighbors is contrasted dramatically at the beginning of *Bad Blood*, when the house of an immigrant Roma family, the Lupeis, is targeted with racist graffiti. In this case, Lucy notes, the community does not offer help removing the graffiti, and the Lupeis are left feeling isolated and threatened.[28] The implication seems to be that, though some lessons about tolerance and inclusion have been learned through the peace process, applying these lessons outside of the context of Protestant-Catholic sectarianism is a different matter entirely. Other examples of bigotry run concurrently with the vandalism: a pro-Brexit, anti-immigrant leaflet is distributed in the Lupeis's neighborhood; a pastor named Nixon preaches vehemently against homosexuality; Mr. Lupei is severely beaten on his way home from work; and two gay men are murdered. The assessment of Jackie Moss, a former paramilitary leader, echoes McKinty's contention that the Troubles did not arise from a set of circumstances peculiar to Northern Ireland; rather, they were the inevitable result of the human tendency to blame people unlike ourselves for our problems and the exploitation of this weakness by individuals and groups seeking power: "Nothing cements a community like a common enemy," he notes. "The crowd that are doing this are trying to get a foothold, get some community cachet. The Provos did it targeting drug dealers and joyriders. This crew are targeting immigrants. It's not a new concept."[29]

Fittingly, the anti-immigrant group behind much of the violence in *Bad Blood* mimics the tactics through which the paramilitaries attained community support and subservience during the Troubles. Stephen Welland, the leader of this group, makes use of his community's frustration with the compromises of the peace process and the economic crash, providing people with an outlet for their anger by positing immigrants as threats to the economy and lifestyle of Northern Ireland. He uses this sentiment to disempower the police, much as the paramilitaries effected a mistrust of the RUC by emphasizing the danger of sectarian otherness,[30] suggesting that the people of the North have been failed by the PSNI and the government and must therefore rely on vigilante justice.[31]

Welland's efforts, and the hard-right values popularized during the Brexit debate, energize former players from the Troubles era. Nixon, the homophobic pastor, makes use of the current environment to stoke fear and broaden his audience, just as he did thirty years earlier.[32] Moss competes with Dougan, another local criminal, to form an alliance with Welland to control the local drug trade.[33] Anti-immigrant sentiment provides convenient cover for such trade; just as the loyalist paramilitaries and Provos secretly worked together to attack independent dealers during the eighties, people with opposing ideologies now collude to drive out Roma dealers who threaten their monopoly.[34] The old guard believe that they are effectively using Welland and his followers to regain their previous foothold; though he disagrees in principle with the bigoted sentiments stoked by Welland, Moss coddles the younger man, arguing that "there's always a need for new blood once the bad blood's been let." Lucy perceives the older men as naive, unable to recognize that it is they who are being used by Welland.[35] Far from the bad blood being let, Welland is a sign that it has evolved into something even more insidious and potentially more dangerous.

McGilloway utilizes this narrative as a vehicle for strong social commentary. The end of the novel sees the passage of Brexit and Lucy's pensiveness about the message it sends to the many immigrant families like the Lupeis. Her housemate ventures that "it's like the world's changed in some way. . . . But I don't know how," highlighting that the echoes of the Troubles are familiar, but the sense of progress reversed is not. The exposure of dishonest claims that Brexit will enable enhanced funding for the National Health Service is conflated with the scars of spray paint on the Lupeis's house,[36] underscoring that the public has been duped into believing it will benefit from borders, both physical and metaphorical. At the same time, in another implicit comparison to the Troubles, McGilloway takes a swing at the exploitation of religion to control the population and to promote bigotry. Nixon frames himself as a victim, arguing that gay-rights protesters are threatening his entitlement to his religious beliefs and freedom of speech. Lucy describes him as a hypocrite, suggesting that instigating harm against others is contrary to the Christian point of view he claims to be defending.[37] Fleming, likewise, argues that Nixon is "legitimising personal opinion using the language of prayer"[38] and that "spreading the word is one thing. Spreading hate is something else entirely."[39] Ultimately, Nixon's own son, Ian, agrees to assist Lucy's investigation into the murders of the young gay men, asserting that what he has learned from Nixon in theory is far different from what his father does in practice: "He always taught me to do what was right. . . . It's just that his idea of right seems wrong."[40] There is a glimmer of hope in Ian's courage and in the Lupeis's neighbors finally offering assistance, along with regrets that they did not do so earlier;[41] if people look to their own consciences and resist the temptation to be led by fear and pack mentality, McGilloway suggests, perhaps this difficult time, like the Troubles, shall also pass.

Unlike many of his contemporaries in Irish crime fiction, McGilloway rarely makes use of intertextual references in the Black series; exceptions in *Bad Blood* therefore seem significant and extremely deliberate. Ian's slow progress toward coming to terms with his own homosexuality and his father's hypocrisy, along with his resolution to follow his own moral code despite the potential consequences, coincides with him watching reruns of *Inspector Morse*.[42] This detail is likely an allusion to the frequent considerations of homophobia—and, indeed, its intersection with religion—in Colin Dexter's novels and the three television series based on them.[43] A reference to Adrian McKinty's Sean Duffy series also appears at the end of the novel when, finally beginning to empathize with her mother and recognize the lessons she might learn from her, Lucy becomes interested in the elder woman's reading habits: "There was a bookcase with an assortment of paperbacks, mostly crime, which were well read. . . . She lifted one of the titles, vaguely recognised it as the name of a Tom Waits album she'd once bought." Entering the room, Lucy's mother assures her that it is a worthwhile read.[44]

This conclusive nod to McKinty acknowledges the clear influence of the Duffy series on *Bad Blood*; likewise, it underscores the motive behind the novel's departure from the largely character-based drama of previous books in the series to include a wider consideration of social justice and politics. While McKinty foreshadows the way that social atmosphere, economic problems, and the insidious work of opportunists might lead to a recurrence of the conditions of the Troubles at any time in any society, McGilloway's use of a contemporary setting allows him to highlight twenty-first-century circumstances to confirm that such foreshadowing is more than just speculation.

Although the shift in tone of *Bad Blood* is substantial enough to warrant McGilloway's implicit explanation, the novel's subject matter is, in many ways, a different iteration of themes that persist throughout the series; Lucy's struggles with misogyny, relationships, and her identity as a professional woman are part and parcel of McGilloway's broader concern with borders. McGilloway has repeatedly emphasized that, for him and for his characters, borders are not only physical but also symbolic: "The borderlands," he notes, "are the grey area that most of us inhabit, the distance between what we'd like to do and how we'd like to be, and what we actually do and who we actually are."[45] Borders can represent the artificial divisions we create when we define ourselves in terms of our differences from other people, or, as Carol Baraniuk concludes, they can be "a meeting place between neighbors."[46] Most poignantly, McGilloway suggests that national and political borders are very much entwined with individual borders, each influencing the other. For this reason, just as reinstatement of a physical border risks reviving tribalist sentiment, the ability of individual characters—Lucy's neighbors, the Lupeis's neighbors, or Lucy herself—to transcend such sentiment offers a hope that distinguishes the Northern Ireland of the Black series from the dystopian society of the Duffy novels.

Lucy Black's story is, from its inception, one about borders and reconciliation. The rejection of her family by both Protestants and Catholics during the Troubles and their violent exile from her childhood home are only one component of her isolation; as a woman in a male-dominated profession, estranged from her mother and charged with the care of her father as he struggles with Alzheimer's, Lucy's status as an outsider is also gender specific. The exposition of the first novel, *Little Girl Lost*, outlines Lucy's religion, her father's illness, and the challenge of balancing her career and her duties as a caretaker. This challenge also contributes to an alienation from her own concept of self that verges on the pathological and impedes her from forming relationships with other people, whom she regards either with fear and suspicion or as the objects of her personal responsibility. Her slow progress toward self-care, recognizing her own limits, and understanding the disparate struggles that form the perspectives of others is, in this sense, a microreflection of the peace process under way in the society in which she lives.

This is not to suggest that the Black narratives are mere allegories for the Troubles and their aftermath; rather, they highlight the fact that the human tendencies and conditions at work in everyday personal lives and interactions also form the basis of our broader political and societal spheres. In this sense, they are a reminder that, while the Troubles are unique to Northern Ireland, they are also a reflection of interpersonal and identity issues that exist globally, on both small and large scales.

Just as the Duffy series underscores the manner in which persistent violence and sectarian ideologies inhibited the subjective development of a generation in Northern Ireland, *Little Girl Lost* is, to a certain extent, an examination of the social pressures placed on girls and young women that deny them the healthy potential of growth and self-knowledge. Because she was not offered nurturing and guidance by her mother, who left her in her father's custody after the divorce, Lucy views herself as orphan-like and doubles down on her own feelings of responsibility for taking care of others, in order to distinguish herself from her mother. As a result, she muses, she has "little time to herself, despite being frequently alone."[47] She allocates no time for pleasure or companionship, and even this sacrifice is challenged by men who wish to pursue romantic relationships with her.

Lucy's prioritizing of others above her own physical and psychological health is a running theme in the novel. Rather than sleeping, she spends most of her nights in the hospital with her father or female victims; when an accident at work causes her to be hospitalized herself, she checks out prematurely to assist Mary, a young girl involved in her case. After conflicting responsibilities prevent her from rescuing Mary at the end of the novel, Lucy is haunted by the failure and hangs Mary's photo in her office at work as a form of self-laceration.

Through the tales of several young girls whose circumstances mirror Lucy's, McGilloway emphasizes that his protagonist's situation is not unique. In *Little Girl Lost*, Lucy encounters four such girls: Kate, the abducted daughter of a wealthy property owner; Alice, a child initially mistaken for Kate when she is discovered in the woods, who refuses to speak and thus cannot readily be identified; Mary, whose absence from school leads her principal to think she might be the girl found in the woods; and, finally, Janet, a former informant of Lucy's father, whom Lucy seeks out when her father's disease makes him believe she is Janet. That these characters appear interchangeable to others is telling; each has been compelled to forgo her identity to compensate for the failures or weaknesses of others. Kate's kidnapping and motherless childhood are a direct result of her father's insurance fraud, which involved bombing one of his properties while her mother was inside, and his subsequent debt to the men who assisted him, including Alice's father. Alice, in turn, must release Kate from her imprisonment, at great risk to herself. Mary, whose mother suffers from unhealthy addictions to both drugs and her abusive boyfriend, Alan Cunningham, takes charge of the care of her mother and baby brother, ultimately sacrificing her own life to protect her brother when Cunningham sets their house on fire.[48] Targeted as an informant by paramilitaries during the Troubles, Janet's investment in justice and assisting Lucy's father has ruined her life. Neither the police nor her parents intervened as she was tarred and feathered,[49] and this tragedy, along with sexual exploitation by Lucy's father, has left her broken and homeless. Fleming ventures that the carelessness with which these girls have been treated and the necessity of subjugating their own needs to those of other people has left them voiceless: "It's no wonder the child [Alice] doesn't want to speak. Maybe she knows that no one would listen anyway."[50]

This theme continues through the second and third novels of the series. *Someone You Know* focuses on an investigation into the murder of a young woman named Karen, who was driven to self-harm by the responsibility of caring for her alcoholic mother[51] and who, while being abused by a pedophile ring, took it upon herself to look after the other victims.[52] Sarah, a second abuse victim, is also neglected by her drug-addicted mother, is required to perform adult responsibilities in the household, and ultimately concedes to being raped by older men in order to protect her mother, since the abusers have threatened to spike her mother's stash with poison if Sarah does not comply.[53] In *The Forgotten Ones* (2015), Lucy encounters Lisa, a teenage orphan in charge of her younger sister, whose loneliness has driven her into a relationship with a disreputable young man. She also meets Grace, who was disowned by her mother to please her second husband and has been reduced to homelessness and prostitution. Lucy relates deeply to all of these "little girls lost"; she frequently outlines the similarities between her own situation and theirs—particularly in terms of ineffective parenting—and feels more comfortable spending Christmas at a homeless shelter than with her own mother. At the end of *Forgotten Ones*, she rejects her boyfriend Robbie's invitation to move in with him, determining to take on Grace as a housemate instead.

Apart from her empathy for Grace and other lost girls, Lucy's decision reflects progress in terms of placing her own well-being above her sense of responsibility for others: Robbie has been injured in a car bomb intended for Lucy, and she struggles with the sense that her feelings for him have more to do with guilt than with love. However, her decision also underscores her guardedness with men in general, which is particularly evident in her work environment, where her first priority at new postings is "making it clear that she [is] not looking for an office fling."[54] Each time she interacts with a male colleague, her attempts to interpret his behavior—and whether it constitutes condescension or danger to her—are described at length. At times, the attention to detail and analysis seem to verge on paranoia: she notes how close men stand to her, the manner in which they look at her, and for how long; she mulls over the tone of their words and even imagines them laughing at her behind her back. What is most striking about these insights into Lucy's perceptions is the way in which they serve as reminders of the particular difficulties faced by woman working in male-dominated fields. For Lucy and her female colleagues, the dangers of the job extend beyond the potential of community violence to the very real possibilities of harassment and bias from their coworkers. That so many of Lucy's male colleagues inadvertently raise her suspicions, even when they mean no harm, highlights their lack of awareness and sympathy for the challenges female officers are forced to contend with. In *Little Girl Lost*, when Lucy is summoned to the office of lecherous Chief Superintendent Travers, the men on her team "[feign] anxiety, believing that Lucy would have to explain her lateness at the briefing," while Tara, the other woman officer, assesses the situation differently, telling Lucy to ensure that Travers does not lock the door.[55]

McGilloway's criticism of men's failure to recognize women's reality is, he says, deeply personal: "I'd love to say that I'm contributing to a wider debate, but to be honest, I'm probably just writing my own concerns, as I always have. I started the Lucy books with the birth of my own daughter Lucy. The books reflect my concerns about father/daughter relationships. Failing as a father, letting down your child and damaging that relationship is at the heart of the book because those things lie at the heart of most fathers' deepest fears, I suspect."[56] Fittingly, Lucy's struggles with trust largely stem from her deeply complicated relationship with her father. The series opens with Lucy committed to the difficult task of caring for her father as his Alzheimer's progresses. His confusion causes him to obsess over his former police files and to wander and endanger himself, which is obviously trying for her. But a greater source of emotional discomfort is his inability to consistently recognize her, and she struggles with jealousy when he mistakes her for her mother or Janet.

The father-daughter relationship is framed as the most intimate and crucial in Lucy's life; while her childhood memories of her mother involve little apart from the pain of abandonment, she fondly recalls her father doting on her, raising her onto his shoulders to take in surroundings, and protecting her when their house was attacked with petrol bombs. Her vigilance for his welfare and insistence on caring for him at home, rather than committing him to a medical facility, is portrayed as an understandable if challenging recompense for his kindness and affection.

Despite McGilloway's hesitance to claim that he is "contributing to a wider debate," a turning point in the narrative of Lucy and her father, when she discovers that he molested Janet when she was a teenager, offers a disturbing reminder that men who exploit women may appear, to the people closest to them, to be above such behavior. Lucy struggles to reconcile her positive memories of her father with the fact that, while he was raising her, he was exploiting a vulnerable young woman close to her own age. The knowledge of her father's history colors her interactions with him and her sympathy for his frailty; as he seeks assistance and comfort from her, "against her wishes, she [imagines] him forcing himself on a fourteen-year-old girl, [imagines] the hand now flailing in the air looking for hers, tugging at the young girl's clothes."[57] Similarly, the new information heightens her mistrust in other men; in *Bad Blood*, she considers that the reason she was unable to commit to Robbie was not that she was unsure of her feelings for him but that his decency made him seem suspicious to her: "He was a good man, just like her father had been. And she couldn't help but remember how that had turned out."[58]

The other lost girls in the series have similarly problematic relationships with their fathers. In *Little Girl Lost*, Alice's deliverance of Kate from her father's basement mirrors Lucy's discovery of Janet as she is about to die from sepsis on the streets. In both cases, the fathers, while criminal and abusive to other girls, are willing to risk their lives to protect their own daughters: Alice's father submits to torture to avoid telling the other kidnappers that Alice is in the house and has released Kate, while Lucy's father takes the blame when Lucy is forced to shoot a rogue and murderous police official. Kate's father, though culpable for her kidnapping and her mother's death, goes to great lengths to rescue his child. In *Someone You Know*, Karen's father, Eoghan Harkin, is an imprisoned IRA man, who mistakenly believes that his daughter has been killed because of his paramilitary connections. He is willing to assist Lucy by withdrawing republican protection for Alan Cunningham in exchange for information about his daughter's murder. Harkin's fear that his own imperfections have adversely affected his child encapsulates the concerns McGilloway asserts are at the heart of his novels: in the works of Sophocles, Harkin says, "the daughters die because of who the father was."[59]

None of the lost girls in the series actually dies because of the actions of their fathers, but all are immeasurably affected by them; by the fourth novel, Lucy's rage at the violence and betrayal of men, embodied in her father, is given full expression when she is attacked by Lloyd, a corrupt police officer who, Lucy has discovered, is in collusion with drug dealers. As Lloyd beats and attempts to sexually assault Lucy, she manages to get the better of him, cursing and striking him repeatedly with a lampstand, even after he has clearly been subdued. She has to be reminded to stop by Huey, another female officer, who nevertheless approves of Lucy's excessive force, asserting that Lloyd "got everything he deserved."[60] Likewise, the woman doctor who attends to Lucy after the attack congratulates her for injuring Lloyd so severely, and Lucy's mother condones her daughter's actions, adding that she does not care whether Lloyd survives the beating.[61] Lucy herself swiftly overcomes any misgivings about her behavior, obstinately refusing to take time off of work because she does not wish to give Lloyd any power over her feelings or choices.[62]

In a rare moment of lucidity, as he apologizes to his daughter at the end of *Little Girl Lost*, Lucy's father asks her to remember that "things get lost and things get found."[63] Rather than further isolating her, Lucy's loss of her naive faith in her father serves to remove some of the barriers that have prevented her from forming a bond with her mother, now Assistant Chief Constable Wilson. At the beginning of the series, Lucy denies that her mother has had any influence on her life, suggesting that "[she became] a police officer in spite of her mother, not because of her,"[64] and hiding her relationship with the assistant chief constable from even her closest colleagues, with the excuse that she does not want them to inaccurately assume that she receives unfair advantages at work. In reality, Lucy distances herself from her mother because she equates her mother's prioritizing of career over family, of reason over emotion, with an unnatural coldness: "Her mother had never done what was expected of her, had seemed determined to ignore proprieties. In so doing she had broken the glass ceiling. And it was not all that she had broken."[65] To a degree, Lucy's ability to earnestly explore her own identity is initially limited by a tendency to define herself in opposition to these characteristics; her subjectivity is less a positive stance than a negative insistence on establishing herself as a different kind of woman than the "other" that Wilson represents.

In "Nancy Drew, *Dragon Tattoo*: Female Detective Fiction and the Ethics of Care," Caroline Reitz considers that "a global feminist ethics perspective invites us to think about what feminism can bring to conceptions of justice beyond a personal code of justice that is only as just as the individual actor. In conceiving of detective work as care, female detective fiction recovers a sense of tending to needs that is at the centre of care ethics." The female detective, Reitz suggests, effectively balances familial and work obligations, in addition to compensating for the flaws of the criminal justice system by "performing care not only for individual clients, but, arguably, for a society whose official justice system structurally prevents it from being fair to all its members in all circumstances." In this sense, Lucy very much conforms to a classic feminist model, internalizing responsibility for the needs of victims that structural justice is unable to meet. However, Reitz also reflects on the problematics of care ethics in female detective fiction: not only do the female detective's actions "let the 'system' off the hook," rather than challenging its inadequacies to devise strategies for improvement, but they also contribute to stereotyping that runs contrary to feminist principles, positing women as a collective rather than as individuals and prescribing specific, acceptable—and ultimately clichéd—characteristics, such as maternal instincts and a predisposition to nurturing.[66]

McGilloway addresses this paradox through Lucy's developing perspective of ACC Wilson. Because Wilson's behavior does not conform to Lucy's limited notions of feminine empathy, care, and solidarity, Lucy initially regards her as heartless and unnatural. She is dismissive of her mother's tempered displays of concern for her health and safety, insinuating that they are inconsistent with Wilson's failure to seek custody during her parents' divorce, and must therefore be attributable to a desire for control, rather than genuine interest. Instinctively, though, Lucy seems to understand that her stubbornness prevents her from acknowledging the full picture. In *Little Girl Lost*, her jealousy of Kate's promising reunion with her father is immediately followed by Wilson's arrival and support;[67] likewise, when Lucy's father strikes her in a moment of confusion, Lucy "[cries] for her mother"[68] and drives to Wilson's house for comfort and advice. Nevertheless, she remains suspicious of her mother's warmth and efforts to improve their relationship: "It disconcerted her; at least they'd both known where they stood when she [Wilson] was simply Lucy's superior officer. Now, Lucy couldn't help but wonder for whose benefit was this attempted reconnection most intended: her own or her mother's."[69] Not until the end of the third novel does Lucy allow herself to smile at her mother's familiarity and attentions;[70] by the end of the fourth, she begins, for the first time, to visit Wilson without ulterior motives, simply for the sake of getting to know her better.[71] In keeping with *Bad Blood*'s theme about tolerating differences and overcoming the tendency to place the blame for personal and social problems on people unlike oneself, Wilson tells Lucy that she wants to eradicate the "bad blood between" them.[72] Unlike the perfidious alliance between Moss and Welland, this reconciliation is presented as earnest progress: Lucy lets go of the preconceptions she has long held about Wilson and remarks that the future is "uncertain but rich with promise."[73]

Furthering the novel's contention that otherness is a fallacious construct, Lucy increasingly realizes that, despite their different lifestyles and social strategies, she and her mother have much in common. In *Someone You Know*, as the stress of her job begins to affect her looks, she sees her mother reflected back at her in the mirror and quickly averts her eyes;[74] later, she fears that the similarities between them might run deeper than physical appearance.[75] In the same novel, a man whose daughter's murder was among Wilson's early cases comments that Lucy reminds him of Wilson,[76] though he is oblivious to the familial connection. Lucy's father also mistakes her for her mother,[77] and Wilson asserts that Lucy is more like her than she wishes to concede.[78] Fleming, too, remarks on the likenesses between the two women, drawing on his recollections of a young Wilson to compare their looks and behavior as Lucy stifles her compulsion to challenge him.[79] Upon deducing that the two women are related, Lucy's colleague Tara argues explosively that Lucy's unwillingness to share this information about herself, while intended to prevent her coworkers from presuming she is like her mother, is actually solid proof of their resemblance: like Wilson, Tara argues, Lucy masks her emotions, withholds personal information to keep potential friends at a distance, and prioritizes her career above bonding with others.[80]

Indeed, Lucy frequently shifts the subject to work-related issues to avoid confronting tricky personal situations; her job is her central topic of conversation with Robbie, and she relies on her work relationship with Wilson to create diversions in lengthy discussions about her father. She gradually comes to realize that she and Wilson share this technique of using police work to impose a surrogate order on the difficult and disappointing aspects of their personal lives. Lucy's ethic of care is, to her mother, a kind of mask designed to excuse self-protective and callous behavior; by immersing herself in the needs of victims, Lucy is able to avoid giving anything of herself to the people closest to her. Likewise, Wilson contends that Lucy's self-imposed ethics are a means of justifying her safe isolation through self-righteousness and a spurious sense of being misunderstood; in *Someone You Know*, she challenges her daughter's self-perception with surprising acuity: "But no one feels as deeply as you do, isn't that right? . . . Because that's what we should do. Invest everything in our work. Care so deeply that we forget about everything around us."[81] Finally, Lucy's ethics allow her to envision the world in black-and-white, without considering the consequences of her actions. Lucy stalks the family who adopted Mary's brother, ostensibly to ensure that he is well cared for; she dismisses the effect her transgressions might have on Robbie, who used his connections as a social worker to obtain the address for her.[82] Similarly, Lucy attempts to cover Fleming's slide into alcoholism out of misguided loyalty and does not take into account that, in so doing, she may be preventing him from obtaining the assistance he needs to tackle his addiction.[83]

Although she resents Wilson for abandoning her as a child, then, Lucy's own conduct emulates that of her mother, who single-mindedly devoted herself to her work to avoid dealing with her husband's offenses, at Lucy's expense: "I had worked hard to get as far as I had got," she explains. "It wasn't fair for me to give that up because of what he had done. And I couldn't have done it with a child."[84] Like Lucy, Wilson justifies her choices as necessary sacrifices for the greater good; however, rather than accepting the imperfections of the justice system and embracing an ethic of care like her daughter, Wilson's approach is to change the system from within: specifically, by paving the way for enhanced gender equality in the police force.

For McGilloway, Lucy's gradual realization that she and Wilson share the same priorities and struggles, despite their disparate solutions, is the central premise of the series: "Lucy is like her mum—the books are very much about her learning her perceptions have been wrong and having to accept that her mother did what she had to do to survive and succeed as a woman. In doing so, she made the way for Lucy and Tara that bit easier."[85] At the conclusion of *Bad Blood*, Lucy conquers her tendency to view Wilson as the root cause of her problems, finally humanizing her and regarding her from a place of empathy. She comes to understand that her parents' divorce had a major emotional impact on them, instead of viewing herself as the sole casualty of the situation.[86] At the same time, she registers that

Wilson's success is plagued by the loneliness that accompanies it, noting that men, including her father, are intimidated by Wilson's authority.[87] Although she dismisses her mother's warning against behavior that will leave her similarly isolated, the plaintive admonishment brings her to a sudden awareness of Wilson's frailty: "Lucy was surprised, and a little saddened, by how thin her mother felt in her arms, how sharply her bones protruded through her skin, just as her father's had."[88]

Lucy's newfound cognizance of the difficulties Wilson has faced helps her to attain a greater understanding of other women in general. In the first three novels, she unconsciously places women into one of two categories: the ones who are unfeeling and unapproachable like her mother and the little girls lost whom she relates to, but whom she also feels compelled to protect, creating imbalanced and one-sided relationships. In *Bad Blood*, Lucy begins to view women outside of the subjective lens of her own experiences. In so doing, she learns that her disillusionment and fears—particularly the ones that stem from the abusive, controlling, or inconsiderate behavior of the men she encounters—are not unique to herself. As Lucy comes to terms with the fact that institutional sexism affects all women, her focus shifts from the ways in which other women are different from her to the challenges she shares with them and the potential value of their perspectives and support. For the first time, she actively seeks Wilson's advice, asking her whether gender discrimination and harassment are best confronted through direct action or by playing along, in order to attain the power and position to effect change at an institutional level.[89] After she is attacked by Lloyd, Lucy allows Wilson, Huey, and the female doctor to comfort her, accepting their support as a sign of solidarity.[90] She also determines to emulate this solidarity, backing Tara in a harassment case against a fellow officer, although she knows it will create tension for her at work and possibly damage her potential for advancement. For Lucy, supporting Tara is "the right thing to do," but in a gentle reminder that there are different yet equally acceptable paths to the same end, her mother confirms that "it's *a* right thing to do at the very least."[91]

Lucy's reconciliation with her mother provides another glimmer of hope in the retrograde society of *Bad Blood*; through this story line, McGilloway demonstrates that even the most deep-seated notions of otherness can be surmounted and even the most powerfully defended borders can be bridged. The suggestion is clearly that a society is nothing if not a collective of individuals and that social biases, conflicts, and fears can thus be addressed in the same ways as personal ones: through humanization, respect for different perspectives, and an emphasis on commonalities. Ironically, then, the darkest novel of the Black series concludes on a more optimistic note than its predecessors: through the progressive courage and empathy of Lucy, Wilson, Ian, and the Lupeis' neighbors, we are encouraged, despite appearances, to envision a future in which "there's no bad blood."[92]

4

Bridges
Claire McGowan's Paula Maguire

> It's a common belief in the rest of the UK that "the Troubles"
> in Ireland are long over. It's true to an extent that people now
> feel safe to walk the streets. We have a regional government
> who spend at least some time on issues like healthcare and
> schooling. There have been only—only—three police officers
> killed since "peace."
> —Claire McGowan, The Silent Dead

It would be difficult to miss the correspondences between Brian Mc-
Gilloway's Black novels and their close contemporary, Claire Mc-
Gowan's Paula Maguire series. According to McGowan, the Maguire
series is "not a deliberate nod" to McGilloway—she had already
begun writing the first novel when *Little Girl Lost* was published—
but, she notes, "definitely there are parallels."[1] In particular, *The
Lost* (2013) resembles *Little Girl Lost* in both its title and its central
mystery: the search for the missing daughter of a shady businessman.
The themes of the novels are also analogous, conflating physical disappearances with the devaluation of women and girls that allows
them "to be lost in plain sight."[2] Moreover, although she is a forensic
psychologist rather than a police officer, Paula's situation is remarkably similar to that of Lucy Black: having left her small hometown
in Northern Ireland because of personal traumas suffered during the
Troubles, Paula returns to Ballyterrin during the recession to work
with the Missing Persons Response Unit (MPRU) and the local police force. Like Lucy, Paula is the daughter of a Catholic RUC officer
who was forced into retirement, who continues to obsessively peruse

his old notebooks and case files, and who worries that his daughter's devotion to her work will cause her to end up alone.

Like the Black novels, the Maguire series also touches on circumstances particular to women in male-dominated professions. Since Paula's mother, Margaret, is herself a missing person, who disappeared from their house when Paula was thirteen, the maternal role of Assistant Chief Constable Wilson in Lucy's life is here assumed by a supervisor, Detective Chief Inspector Helen Corry. Like Lucy's mother, Corry is compelled to adopt a mask of coldness and rigidity in order to gain rank as a woman and change the force from within: "I like to put the fear of God in the young fellas," she tells Paula, "but it's the only way to get their respect, you see, if you happen to have a pair of breasts. . . . [W]e need more women up there. Sexual assault, domestic abuse—sometimes people just want to see another female face, you know."[3] Corry speaks from personal experience: she was driven to join the Police Service of Northern Ireland (PSNI) and "be the change [she wanted] to see in the world" after a boyfriend abused her and the all-male police force with whom she filed a report failed to take her complaint seriously, focusing instead on what she might have done to provoke the abuse. Corry's view of men and their ability to understand and support women is especially bleak; she regrets both her failed marriage and her decision to become a mother, advising Paula that men "think they're so liberated, just because they change a nappy now and again, but when it comes down to it, it's you that has to sacrifice your body, your career, everything. So put it off as long as you can."[4] Just as Wilson's career is jeopardized by her husband's criminal behavior, Corry's hard work, heightened awareness, and caution are not enough to shield her from bearing responsibility for the treachery of men. In *The Silent Dead* (2015), her involvement with a forensic scientist gives him access to her cell phone, enabling him to leak information and compromise an investigation; as a result, she finds herself demoted to the rank of sergeant.

In *Irish Crime Fiction*, Brian Cliff writes that a focus on contemporary women's issues in the Maguire series "[minimizes] the presumptive centrality of Troubles themes without erasing those themes from the landscape or from her [McGowan's] characters' lives."[5] I would take this a step further to suggest that, just as McGilloway's Lucy Black series uses its narratives about Brexit, gender discrimination, and female bonding to consider the topics of otherness and empathy more broadly, McGowan approaches both the history of the Troubles and issues of women's health, safety, and equality in terms of larger questions about identity and reconciliation with the past, particularly in the absence of justice or closure.

Through Paula, McGowan reflects on the multifaceted nature of subjectivity: Paula's identity as an individual, as a woman, as an investigator, and as a person who came of age during a time of civil war in Northern Ireland are inextricably entwined, and each of these aspects of her history and subjectivity informs (and, at times, conflicts with) the others. Her approach to solving cases, for example, benefits equally from her ability to relate to the outlooks and needs of other women and her personal understanding of the experiences of families of missing persons. By contrast, her exposure to life in small-town and large urban environments, and her acute recognition of both the advancements and the shortcomings of the peace process, result in ambivalence about other characters' ideological stances on community and globalism, legal justice and vigilantism, and progress and resolution. Perhaps without design, Paula's contradictory impulses suggest a kind of antidote to tribalism, implying that categorizations of identity are reductive and disingenuous, because people by nature and experience comprise multiple and sometimes seemingly incongruous subjectivities.

Crucially, Paula's multidimensional identity also allows McGowan to examine the ideological stances of other characters as various shades of gray while avoiding a sanctimonious illusion of objectivity, since Paula's ambivalence about various issues central to the series stems from subjective experience. Her internal struggles—in particular, the conflict between her desire to move forward with her life and her need to address unresolved issues in her past—mirror the situation of Irish women, who must strive for future advancement in terms of civil rights, bodily autonomy, and equality in the workplace, while also contending with a past riddled with institutional sexism and inequitable social and political norms. Likewise, Paula's struggles reflect on the circumstances of people who suffered from paramilitary violence during the Troubles, but have been urged to leave the past behind them and embrace the potential of the peace process. McGowan's implicit questions about how we define identity and whether people are emotionally capable of moving forward without closure—even when their logic dictates that it is in their best interest—are, ironically, made more universal by their specific applicability to Paula's life. In a sense, the challenges faced by women and the complications of the Northern Irish peace process are presented both as unique problems and as manifestations of conflicts that are common to the human condition. As Paula contends with her personal issues through logic, empathy, and insight from a variety of perspectives, we also get some sense of how similar issues might be addressed on a broader scale.[6]

Despite the surface similarities in theme, plot structure, and supporting characters, then, Paula is a very different detective than Lucy Black. She is never dogmatic or inflexible, as Lucy is at the beginning of the Black series; rather, Paula is thoughtful and self-aware. She seeks out and digests the advice and professional assistance of Corry and others, ruminates extensively, and ultimately comes to her own conclusions. Although she keeps secrets about her past from others because she does not want to appear vulnerable,[7] she is not herself in denial, and she explores various avenues as means of better comprehending her childhood and loss. While Lucy has difficulty explaining why she chose to become a police officer,[8] Paula is extremely aware that she is driven to finding missing persons by her family history—and equally aware that, as long as Margaret is still missing, locating others will never be enough to satisfy her.[9]

Paula is also more sophisticated than Lucy in terms of her understanding of gender identity and relations. Although her neighbors in Ballyterrin expect her to assume a caretaker role with her father, PJ, whose mobility is inhibited because of a broken leg, she recognizes and accepts PJ's desire for independence, the pleasure he gets from

maintaining a protective parental role, and her own lack of nurturing tendencies. Paula's relationship with PJ is largely one of equals,
who care for each other deeply and hold each other's intellect, professionalism, and disparate experiences in high esteem; she describes
her interactions with him as "typical father-daughter [chats] about
tea, the IRA, and dead bodies."[10] Her rapport with Aidan, her former boyfriend and editor of Ballyterrin's only newspaper, is similarly
balanced and collaborative. Despite their troubled past—their relationship ended when Aidan was unfaithful and Paula left Northern
Ireland, determined to cut him out of her life—Paula and Aidan's
shared history and connections forge a mutual respect. Since his journalist father, John O'Hara, was murdered in front of him by the Irish
Republican Army (IRA), Aidan is uniquely capable of understanding
Paula's ongoing distress from the disappearance of Margaret. The relationship between Aidan's mother, Pat, and PJ—which begins as mutual support over the loss of their spouses and progresses to romance
and, finally, marriage—also brings the two closer together. Regardless of their personal differences, Paula and Aidan rely on each other
for assistance in researching cases, and in a mark of professional acknowledgment, Aidan insists on referring to Paula by her last name.

Additionally, Paula possesses a great amount of agency in her
romantic interactions with men. At the beginning of *The Lost*, we
learn that, like Lucy, she has little time for dating as a result of her
dedication to her career. Following a chapter break, however, it
becomes clear that this state of affairs does not cause her to deny her
sexual appetite; on the contrary, she is perfectly comfortable having
sex with an attractive younger man and hustling him out the door so
that she can return to her paperwork.[11] McGowan emphasizes that
"there's . . . a female gaze" at work in her novels, adding that "Paula
often notices how attractive different men are."[12] She further subverts stereotypes through Paula's reactions to her new male supervisor, Guy Brooking. Initially, we are told that Paula considers Guy's
attentions dangerous; she explains away his invitations for drinks as
normal collegial interaction but adds that "the more he [acts] this
way, the more nervous she [gets]."[13] In a bait and switch, it becomes

clear that the danger Paula senses in the situation is not the potential of harassment by Guy but her own attraction for him and the possible complexities of a relationship with a colleague. Ultimately, she pursues him sexually while he hesitates and finally concedes; following the encounter, she is offended by his concern that he has abused his position of authority and his assertion that he will understand if she files a complaint against him.[14] For Paula, Guy's learned sensitivity about gender relations in the workforce falls short of the mark, delineating women as victims regardless of the circumstance and undermining their strength of will and sexual independence.

Though Paula has moments of regret about her failure to conform to female stereotypes, they are always fleeting: she feels guilty for not being a caretaker to her father but reminds herself that this would be impossible given the nature of their relationship and the stress of her job;[15] she becomes jealous when Aidan praises the cooking of her friend Saoirse but ridicules herself for imagining that her time would have been better spent on acquiring domestic skills than on tracking missing persons;[16] she contrasts herself with Guy's estranged wife, suggesting that "she was still his wife. . . . And Paula was . . . nobody."[17] In each of these instances, Paula's transitory insecurities stem more from respect for the differences of other women than actual self-doubt: she admires the caretaking capabilities of Pat, the domesticity of Saoirse, and the monogamous commitment of Guy's wife. Likewise, she trusts and empathizes with female colleagues, even when their approaches and priorities are dissimilar to hers. Her sympathy for other women also extends to the missing persons involved in her cases: she shares Lucy Black's affinity for lost young girls, but Paula's ability to view these girls as active agents, rather than hapless victims, is crucial to her success in locating them. She persistently reminds her colleagues that most girls who disappear do so by choice rather than as a result of abduction and that the key to finding them thus generally lies in understanding what they are trying to escape from or what they are running toward.

Of her goal in writing the series, McGowan notes that she "really wanted to write something where the missing and vulnerable girls and women have often disappeared of their own accord, or where something else is going on beyond the typical narrative of being preyed on."[18] Far from being the objects of desire or quarry of many crime fiction novels, then, women in the Maguire series are often the instigators of action, both personally and politically. When she finds herself pregnant following sexual encounters with both Guy and Aidan, Paula takes for granted that the decision about whether to have the child is entirely her own and does not even tell either of the men about her pregnancy. Likewise, she declines a genetic test, determining that it is her right to choose which man she wants to have a paternal role in her daughter's life. While the men possess interchangeable and relatively insignificant positions, the pregnancy increases Paula's sense of urgency in locating Margaret, whose role as a grandmother she views as vital. As she learns more about Margaret's disappearance, her understanding of her mother's own agency increases. In the first two novels, it is largely assumed that Margaret was targeted by the IRA because she was married to a Catholic RUC officer, and Paula even muses about "PJ and John O'Hara's shared pursuit of what they called justice, while their wives stayed at home and worried about phone calls, balaclavas, shots ringing out."[19] Later, she discovers that her mother was likely involved in the Troubles in her own right, feeding information about IRA operations to the British out of a determination to assist in ending the violence: "She was like her husband, believed in the black and white of it, the right and the wrong, even though here they were living in the kingdom of grey."[20]

In the "kingdom of grey," McGowan suggests, it would also be reductive to assume that women are more consistent than men in using their agency as a benevolent force; female characters might be justice seekers, perpetrators of heinous crimes, or, in some cases, a combination of both. *The Dead Ground* (2014) features violent female ideological extremists, *The Lost* and *Blood Tide* (2017) involve women who are overlooked for their crimes because men are deemed more likely suspects, and both *Silent Dead* and *A Savage Hunger* (2016) examine young girls who are determined to exact brutal revenge on the people who have wronged them. These latter two characters, in particular, highlight the series' themes about the way in which the past influences the present, the negative consequences of unresolved injuries, and the capacity of such injuries to deteriorate personal ethics.[21]

Since her ability to recognize her own strengths and weaknesses and to appreciate the diverse paths taken by women makes Paula—like other female characters in the series—largely immune to the sort of womanhood-as-identity-crisis that plagues Lucy Black, McGowan is able to focus more decisively on the questions of identity that arise from being a citizen of Northern Ireland who has lived through the Troubles. Like McKinty, McGowan is concerned with what it means to have come of age in a place that was essentially occupied by two tribes, each claiming that the region rightfully belonged to a different country. Because she emigrated to England as a young woman, Paula's situation is especially complicated in that her personality and outlook are impacted by her experiences with both Northern Ireland and England, as well as with both intimate small-town and impersonal city life. McGowan notes that "definitely [Paula is] torn between staying in Ireland, which has so many painful memories, or going back to her safe, anonymous life in London. It's something I have experienced myself, when I left home at 18 to go to university in England."[22] That McGowan refers to the North as "Ireland" is particularly telling in its implications of occupied space; the choice, for Paula, seems to be between embracing her own culture, which has been threatened both by imperialism and by the paramilitaries that rebelled against it, and returning to a more neutral urban existence in another country.

Although McGowan notes that she was not being consciously metaphorical in this context, Paula's love triangle with Aidan and Guy clearly reflects her sense of these two conflicting identities and the life paths that they constitute. Her challenging past with Aidan is among her first considerations when she arrives back in Ballyterrin, particularly because his betrayal was one of the catalysts for her initial departure from the town; following her encounter with London-raised Guy, she begins to associate that city with him uniquely, although she lived there for many years herself. Each of the men appeals to her on different levels: her interactions with Aidan are highly passionate and grounded in a near-familial history, while she admires Guy's coolness, objectivity, and professionalism. As a crisis point is reached in the cases of both Margaret and Aidan's father, Guy returns to London and offers her a job in his unit there, conflating her choice between the two men with a parallel choice between addressing the wounds of the past and pursuing a future in anonymity.

Although each of the men is a seeker of justice—Guy through police work and Aidan through journalism—their different approaches also reflect contrasting tendencies in Paula's personality. She relates to Aidan because they share a historical and sociocultural background and thus an emotional investment in local missing-persons inquiries; likewise, she empathizes with Guy's status as an outsider, since her time outside of Northern Ireland has given her enough distance to view certain cultural norms and assumptions from an outsider's perspective. The most critical difference between the two men, however, lies in their incongruent opinions about how justice can best be attained. Both men understand the limits of the law's capabilities in obtaining justice, particularly for victims of the Troubles, but Guy, who has not been directly affected by the North's civil war, *"really believes in it, a fair trial and acquittal and innocent until proven guilty,"*[23] while Aidan, largely owing to his own subjective pain and desire for revenge, insists that he has his "own brand of justice—telling people the truth, and letting them decide,"[24] even if that means inciting mob violence.

While Paula criticizes Aidan for his techniques, telling him he is obstructing justice in the long term, he reminds her that her own approach "isn't always the exact definition of the law."[25] Indeed, Paula frequently disobeys her superiors' orders, uses Aidan's connections and ability to obtain information outside of the restrictions of legal standards and has to be reined in by her colleagues for pursuing inquiries in a haphazard manner based on emotion and intuition, without regard for how her actions may affect the outcome of the cases at trial. Just the same, she rails against vigilantism, arguing that "people can't just dispense justice however they see fit. We have laws,"[26] and finally determines, at least in theory, that it is important to support the neutrality of the justice system and "trust that it [is] right, even if so often the outcome [is] very, very wrong."[27]

As with Sean Duffy, much of Paula's regard for legal justice stems from a notion that it is the only viable option to the paramilitary violence of her childhood. Her most persistent argument against vigilantism is that contemporary Northern Irish society has advanced from a focus on tribalism and revenge to one of compromise and humanitarianism: "We're not like them. They killed without remorse or regret, but there has to be some end to it. . . . To the killing. Or else there'll be no one left alive."[28] Though she appears to be unaware of it, Paula has obviously come to her own compromise between conflicting instincts by dogmatically refusing to forget the past but also embracing the progress of the present. Her role in the MPRU enables her to utilize the country's new emphasis on cross-border and non-sectarian cooperation in order to provide answers for people who, like herself, have been as much wounded by the obfuscation of truth during the period of civil war as by the loss of their loved ones. In this sense, she is perhaps the most obvious "finder" in Irish crime fiction, as she literally searches for missing persons while figuratively searching to expose the truth, both about events that occurred during the Troubles and about her current society's reluctance to address them. In so doing, she negotiates a middle ground between closing the door on the Troubles and their ongoing effects and presuming that these effects cannot be managed through diplomacy, understanding, and the albeit imperfect justice of the legal system.

Like the Prehen of the Lucy Black novels, the fictional town of Ballyterrin on the Irish border is a place where the peace process has enabled significant change, but where underlying tensions, fears, and tribalism remain. The local population clings to tradition and ritual, homosexuality and abortion are stigmatized, citizens are still reluctant to assist the police, and the British press continues to trivialize or ignore crimes in Northern Ireland. Americans, with their influential cash flow, still cause trouble through meddling—though now in the form of missionaries touting religious extremism rather than support for the IRA—and the immediate dangers of the Troubles have been replaced by postmodern threats to personal security such as drugs, sexual exploitation, and abduction. Rioting, while less frequent than during the time of civil war, is still common enough to be largely taken in stride and dismissed as a seasonal occurrence: "There was something that stirred in the blood in Northern Ireland when summer hit—a brief heat that could take you by surprise, and equally be followed by days of stinging rain. It made people restless, reminding them they were sharing a small, wet island with another tribe. . . . Every summer a restless wind began to blow and people seemed to decide en masse—it was time for a riot."[29]

In their first conversation, Paula encourages Guy to remember that the Troubles are over, and he replies that "the past seems quite . . . present round here."[30] As an Englishman newly arrived in Ballyterrin, Guy is not subject to Northern Ireland's most crucial cultural norm: relegating the past to the past and pretending that sectarian loyalties, animosity, and paramilitary extremists have been entirely nullified by the peace process. Paula's unit is a reflection of this attitude, comprising equal numbers of Catholics and Protestants and of men and women in order to create a specific impression of unified progress. The MPRU is designedly set apart from the PSNI, who are "based in a nice modern building but still behind their high security fence. New name, but everything else the same."[31] Pulsing under the new way of life is the constant reminder that peace in Northern Ireland has been attempted and has failed in the past: "You grew up holding your breath while shaky ceasefires lasted a year, eighteen months, then exploded into shootings and bombs . . . you hardly dared hope 1998 could be the end."[32] For Paula, Guy's outsider's perspective is unnerving in its exposure of her own underlying fears about the tenuousness of peace in her country; she notes that "the word IRA always sounded different in the mouths of English people. Round here they were the Provos or the Ra, familiar names to cover up the fear and pain they'd caused. Reducing them to a joke, like so many painful things in Ireland,"[33] but she later concludes that the demotion of sectarianism to "a gentle joke. . . . It was all easy, too easy."[34]

The Maguire series tackles this notion of peace as "too easy" in particular by confronting the complexities of the Good Friday Agreement, which stipulated early release for paramilitary members sentenced for crimes before April 10, 1998, whose organizations agreed to maintain a complete cease-fire. A hotly debated aspect of the agreement, this clause was designed to ensure the cooperation of the paramilitaries and to underscore a distinction between the violence of the Troubles and the new progressive direction of Northern Irish society. In practice, of course, it meant that people in contemporary Northern Ireland were forced to cohabitate with former paramilitary members who may have injured or killed their friends and relatives and to accept that these people had evaded punishment for their actions. It also meant that any attempts to enact vengeance to compensate for the government's failure to deliver justice would not be similarly exempt from legal consequences. Finally, in some cases, it meant that the people who had spent years terrorizing a region were now allowed to direct the same region in a political capacity.[35] In *Silent Dead*, the mayor who officiates at a memorial service for victims of a bomb that was set after the peace accord is himself a pardoned paramilitary member; Paula considers the hypocrisy of this, questioning "how it made him feel, knowing he'd caused equal loss to other families. If he even felt at all."[36] Nevertheless, she notes that any expression of discomfort about the mayor's past would reflect "a very old-fashioned attitude nowadays. You were just supposed to put it behind you."[37]

McGowan's point is not to undermine the importance of the Good Friday Agreement but rather to highlight its challenges and to question the adoption of a stance of denial as the best possible response to them. The veneer that there are no lingering resentments from the Troubles is one of dehumanization; while Catholics and Protestants work together to keep sectarian violence at bay, it is only natural that "it was always there between you, when you spoke to someone from the other side. How many of ours have you killed? And us yours?"[38] Even Paula, who is educated and aware enough to understand and despise the concept of tribalism and the way it has been used to control the population of Northern Ireland, is not immune to its effects: "She was aware of it, the nasty nugget in the core of herself, the same raw ore of sectarianism she loathed in others. . . . It was in everyone, however much you liked your Protestant neighbors and colleagues, however tolerant you liked to think yourself in this post-conflict society. . . . When it came down to it, down to bombs and shootings and blood running in the road, you had to pick a side."[39] By ignoring the persistence of such feelings, the government of Northern Ireland—and its society by extension—simultaneously prohibits citizens from working through their grief and turns a blind eye to the latent forces that may lead to a resurgence of violence. In *Blood Tide*, a third potential outcome of denial is examined, when it seems likely that Aidan will be convicted for a crime effected by former republican paramilitaries because the investigating officer "[does] not want the scrutiny of the world on the town— after all, if the IRA [has] disbanded, how could their members still be executing old grudges?"[40]

For McGowan, as for McKinty, healing from the Troubles involves an honest recognition of the frailties of human nature and a refocus on compassion over doctrine. Ideologues in the series are described as devoid of natural empathy: an extremist missionary's eyes have "nothing in them, no humanity";[41] dogmatic antiabortionists think of a woman's body as "nothing but a husk."[42] These characters have much in common with the paramilitary members of the Troubles, who "learned to believe it was all justified, gunning men down in front of their children, blowing up kids who got in the way. All part of their tinpot war."[43] While the peace process has served to moderate the behavior of these men and women, it would be misguided to believe that it has altered their principles or rendered them less dangerous: "Most of these men are dead inside . . . so sure of their cause they literally don't care about who gets killed on the way."[44] In this sense, "evil" in the series is not a religious construct, but a pathology stemming from absolutism—and a pathology that is both understandable and contagious. *Silent Dead* follows the MPRU's investigation into the disappearance of five republican dissidents who are widely believed to have placed a bomb in a neighboring village after the Good Friday Agreement, killing and injuring several innocent bystanders. Paula notes that there is nothing singular about these bombers: they are "ordinary people. That [is] the worst bit."[45] A central tension in the series stems from the fact that pretending that Northern Ireland has entirely progressed from the Troubles—and that "ordinary people" are not also susceptible to the lure of vigilantism when the government has not provided them with justice—is a type of ideological extremism in itself.

McGowan brings this point home not only through Paula's confession about her own difficulties overcoming tribalism—a struggle to which many other detectives in Northern Irish crime fiction seem largely immune—but also through the way in which the past informs, and ultimately becomes, present to her in a personal manner. Because Margaret has never been located, either dead or alive, Paula is unable to find closure; she considers the many ways in which families have been denied such closure, acknowledging that "it [is] a fucked-up world" in which the discovery of the corpse of a friend or family member, rather than the revelation and punishment of the murderer, is the best one can hope for: "a fucked-up Northern Irish world."[46] Paula's ongoing pain from the events of the Troubles and her inability to quietly accept her mother's disappearance underscore the human condition that is at odds with the ideology behind the peace accord. On the surface, she accepts the rationale of the country putting the crimes of the Troubles era behind it, even if she finds the process difficult to digest: "Her mother's case, like so many others, would be swept under the carpet of reconciliation and peace and it's-not-really-worth-the-bother, if it meant people not dying in the street again."[47] Internally, however, she recognizes that accepting a lack of closure and justice is one thing on paper and quite another in a personal context, as emphasized in her perusal of the paperwork on

Margaret's disappearance: "It was only an envelope. Dun-coloured, slim, dog-eared. It was exactly the same as all the others they handled at the unit every day. Except those were just names. This was blood and bone and the wrenching loss that woke you deep in the bowels of the night, grasping for something you couldn't name. This was her mother's file."[48]

Paula is not the only character to feel the effects of the Troubles in the present. *Dead Ground* begins with a flashback of PJ's experiences as an RUC officer, confronting gruesome scenes from which he will never fully recover. Paula notes that it was common for members of the RUC to live through "the Troubles and their onslaught of bombs, bullets, and fire, only to keel over from delayed stress and fear."[49] This was the case for PJ's colleague Mick Quinn, father to Paula's own coworker Fiacra, who continues to be affected by the loss. PJ, on the other hand, was decommissioned during the transition from the RUC to the PSNI, like many other Catholic policemen, because of residual sectarian prejudice. He is forced to resign himself to this decision; meanwhile, his former Protestant colleague Bob Hamilton, who was promoted in his stead, must turn a blind eye to "the terrorists he'd spent his life hunting now running the town."[50] Aidan is also required to contend with an absence of justice when Sean Conlon, one of the men responsible for but never convicted of his father's murder, is released from prison, where he has been serving a sentence for an unrelated crime. Nor is Aidan "the only one in Northern Ireland who had to share the streets with the person who'd smashed their life to pieces . . . what they sometimes called *the price of peace*";[51] in *A Savage Hunger*, it is revealed that political maneuvers made during the Troubles continue to have an effect on former paramilitaries as well. Conlon is also guilty of murdering an IRA compatriot in order to prolong the hunger strikes and protract both the Troubles and international sympathy for the republican cause, and friends and family members of the murdered man are as angered and frustrated by his freedom as Aidan. Through all of these examples, the Maguire series circles an essential question: "*If you ever ask yourself the price of peace, then this is it—to go out in your home town and see the man who murdered your child filling his car with petrol, whistling a Republican tune, free and alive and getting off scot-free. Ask yourself—is that a price you'd be willing to live with?"*[52]

Ultimately, as implied through Paula's arguments for structural justice over vigilantism, McGowan answers this question in the affirmative. While she rallies against the cultural silencing of victims, she constructs a notion of justice that is deeply complicated and includes an acknowledgment that, at times, a more just society can be achieved only by pardoning the sins of the past. Despite Guy's assertion that the past is present in Northern Ireland, the situation of the books is founded on an understanding that it is not: the MPRU is a cooperative unit designed to trace missing persons, while the Troubles and the British efforts to contend with them were marked by an inability to devote police resources to missing and murdered girls and women: "Everything fracturing into deep fissures. No surprise if people fell through them."[53] In *The Lost*, Paula considers that because the RUC and the Irish Guards were so overstretched during the civil war and did not communicate with each other effectively, both forces were significantly more likely to attribute disappearances to emigration or elopement, without looking into them seriously.[54] Likewise, she notes that police on both sides of the border may have been less willing to assist in cases involving citizens of the minority religion in their area.[55] In *A Savage Hunger*, Paula and her colleagues manage to solve a Troubles-era missing-persons case and arrest the murderer of the missing girl, who has evaded justice for decades because "the RUC were too busy to bother with some girl going missing."[56] The end of paramilitary reign in Northern Ireland has not only concluded an era of eye-for-an-eye tactics that prolonged violence between tribes, but has also enabled the police to better investigate nonsectarian crimes and effect justice for average citizens.

While the series does not ignore the ways in which the law and criminal justice could be improved in Northern Ireland—bigotry against Romani Travellers and the illegality of abortion are recurring themes—it largely posits the police as a benevolent, interpretive force, particularly as personified in its female officers. In *A Savage Hunger*, Paula and Corry discuss a case from the nineties, in which a young girl who had been raped was forcibly prevented from procuring an abortion: "Doing this job, you have to know you're on the right side. . . . Because if we don't have that, we have nothing. And when it's the state doing stuff like that—it makes it harder."[57] Despite what she perceives as unjust applications of a law that restrict women's rights, Paula also considers that the PSNI and MPRU are sometimes the only champions of women and girls in need of help; while her unit searches for Alice, a teenager who disappeared from her internship at a church along with a holy relic, the townspeople seem more concerned about locating the relic than the girl, Alice's parents are convinced that their daughter is staging an elaborate hoax, and her friends seem determined to deliberately obstruct the investigation: "They were the only people who seemed worried about Alice. Not even her own parents. Not even her closest friends." Paula notes that, whether Alice has been abducted or is missing of her own accord, the concern and objectivity embodied by the police might be imperative in locating her: "If I went missing . . . I think I'd at least want to know someone was looking for me."[58]

Although Paula and her colleagues come from disparate religious and cultural backgrounds, they are thus united in championing neutrality and structural order, despite the fact that many of them have just cause to desire vengeance for events from their pasts. Aside from the experiences of Paula and Fiacra, Guy has lost his young son to a gang hit in London, while Gerard, another member of the MPRU, is the nephew of a man who was wrongfully imprisoned for twenty years because of evidence planted by the RUC. When Paula expresses astonishment at Gerard's decision to join the police despite the mistreatment of his uncle, he responds with an emphasis on the bigger picture behind their mission, the need to be a force for justice untainted by personal or sectarian considerations: "I'm no Provo. Uncle Pauric, maybe he didn't do the bombing, but he did other stuff. He wasn't a good man, and I've no time for the IRA. They ruined more people's lives than the police ever did. . . . We have to try to be rational. We have to do it right, you know? We have to be the impartial ones."[59] This sentiment is echoed by Guy in *Silent Dead*, when he instructs the unit to remain neutral as they search for the abducted republican dissidents who are likely responsible for a civilian bombing: "They were acquitted in court, and even if they had been convicted they're entitled to the same justice as anyone else. That is in fact the meaning of 'inalienable rights.' . . . We're going to do the same for the Mayday Five as we would for anyone else. That's the reason we have laws—it's not up to us to decide on who gets justice, with all our own history and pain."[60] In the same novel, Corry likewise asserts her determination to adhere to the law, despite her sympathy for the victims of the bombing and their families: "I don't do allowances. . . . There's been far too much of that in this country. I do the law and nothing but."[61]

Certainly, the adherence to structural justice would seem to place Paula and her colleagues at odds with the residual tribalist sentiment of a portion of the population, but Paula views this tension as a type of accomplishment: "The PSNI was not seen, as the RUC had been, as the tool of the Protestant majority. Rather it disgruntled everyone equally, as should probably be the case."[62] It is also suggested that, although they have been conditioned to the contrary, even former paramilitary members secretly yearn for peace, authority, and neutrality. In *The Lost*, as the MPRU homes in on an ex-IRA man as a suspect in the disappearance of his daughter, he initially contends that he wishes the police would let things slide as they had in the past; however, when Paula reminds him that their loved ones had died as a result of such negligence, he confesses that he had hoped that the peace process would enable his daughter to be the first in their family to grow up in a conflict-free society, rather than "hiding under her bed from the men at the door with guns."[63] Through a flashback in *A Savage Hunger*, we learn that even the hardened Sean Conlon felt the same yearning for structural order on the fateful evening when he was instructed by higher-ups in the IRA to murder one of their ranks: "You'd been brought up to hate the RUC. If someone robbed your car or your house you'd ask the Provos to sort it out. Not the peelers, never the peelers in a million years, it would be betraying your kin and country. So how come now . . . all you wanted was to pull over to one of the cops and tell them everything? *Please, arrest me. Don't make me do this.*"[64]

Silent Dead's plot about the vigilante kidnapping of bombers who slipped through the cracks of the legal system is a particularly poignant commentary about the shortcomings of vigilantism and the need for objective structural justice, however flawed. The ringleader of the vigilantes, thirteen-year-old Kira, is determined to seek revenge for the death of her mother in the explosion by giving the bombers "the proper trial the government failed to provide."[65] Early in the planning process, she is too young and overwhelmed by fury to think critically about her actions, arguing that her personal investment makes her better equipped than the legal system to contend with the bombers: "The judge and jury people, they don't really know, they get to go home to their own families and forget." She refuses to listen to people with more experience, who have lived through the Troubles and thus understand the way in which subjectivity—and subjective retribution—prolong violence and damage vigilantes as much as the individuals upon whom they exact vengeance. John, whose son was also killed in the bombing, advises her that the bombers "took so much. Don't let them take your heart too,"[66] while Flaherty, one of the bombers, explains that Kira's grief is the result of his own attempt to obtain justice not provided by the government, since his father was killed by British soldiers who were not held to account for their conduct. When she witnesses the violent consequences of her actions, Kira is filled with regret. Childishly, she attempts to retract her efforts, while Flaherty tells her: "You can't take things back, girl. . . . That's what I kept trying to tell you. Do you feel you've got justice now . . . ?"[67]

Kira's response to the loss of her mother underscores the complexities of restraint for Paula and others like her who lost loved ones in the Troubles and offers a reminder of what might unfold if that restraint is not maintained.[68] Her coming-of-age progress from vengeance to understanding, forgiveness, and remorse also reflects the maturing of Northern Irish society and, in particular, the realization that being a victim "doesn't make everything allowable. . . . Grief . . . it's not an absolution."[69] The book concludes with Kira, newly released from a home for young offenders, determined to let her mother lie in peace and to work on building relationships for the future, particularly with her father, rather than letting anger about the past consume her.

In an author's note to *Silent Dead*, McGowan remarks on "the losses which are still being endured every day" in Northern Ireland, praises "the unbelievable strength of the victims and bereaved" for their difficult role in embracing a complicated peace process, and offers the caution that "the worst days are behind us now. May we never go back."[70] Fittingly, the final novel of the series, *The Killing House* (2018), sees Paula finally coming to terms with the seeming contradictions that have plagued her—peace versus justice, past versus present, London versus Ballyterrin, Guy versus Aidan—in order to arrive at new compromises that allow her to move forward. This progress is effected, in part, through a breakdown of apparent dichotomies. In particular, Paula realizes that it is possible to avoid being hampered by regret for her past without abandoning those aspects of it that are most meaningful to her. As the novel concludes, we see her living in London but retaining strong ties to Ballyterrin: a balance she has been unable to attain until this point. She has also come to a clearer understanding of the intricacies of human nature, as characters she has perceived of as enemies to her happiness and her quest to uncover the truth about Margaret are revealed to have been working in the best interests of her and her family all along. Most poignantly, she learns to accept that the knowledge and transparency she has always viewed as crucial to recovery from trauma are, in themselves, imperfect things, beneficial to some people but potentially devastating to others. While she continues to research her mother's disappearance, she finally admits that she has been "pretty good at lying to herself,"[71] acknowledging for the first time that, in some ways, she prefers the ignorance that allows her to retain hope that Margaret is still alive to the closure she would receive if her body were discovered.

Accordingly, as she follows her mother's trail to its ultimate conclusion, she withholds the delicate information she uncovers from PJ
and Pat, allowing them their own route to recovery: an acceptance of
unanswered questions, and a willingness to put the ghosts of the past
behind them. McGowan's conclusion to the series offers a nuanced
assessment of the confrontation of pain in the post-Troubles era, suggesting that knowledge may very well equate with power, but only if
it can be obtained without "destroying the fragile peace."[72]

PART THREE

Saint Christopher

Redemption and Narrative

Although he is the patron saint of travelers, Saint Christopher is also commonly associated with redemption.[1] In Catholic tradition, Christopher aspired to serve the most powerful ruler in the world. Disappointed by his employment with a reputedly mighty king (who feared the strength of the devil) and by his encounter with the devil himself (who cowered at the thought of Jesus Christ), Christopher struggled to find a means of serving Christ that suited his talents, which did not include traditional methods of worship, such as prayer and fasting. Advised to make use of his naturally strapping frame to help travelers cross a treacherous river, Christopher eventually assisted a child, who became increasingly heavy as they traversed the water. The child, of course, was Jesus Christ; in the final stages of his transformation from evil to good, Christopher had been made to carry the weight of the world.

Christopher's path to redemption includes two curious elements: first, it is implied that he is drawn to God out of a love of power rather than religious faith, adherence to a particular system of ethics, or a conviction that his actions can in any way contribute to righteousness or justice. Christopher's lack of idealism gives him something in common with fatalistic noir heroes, particularly the characters of certain Irish crime novels, who, as Fintan O'Toole describes, operate in "an Ireland with no faith in authority and no belief that the bad guys will be vanquished by naming their names."[2] Second, Christopher resists the common, expected routes to grace (prayer and fasting), accepting his own limitations and emphasizing his individual strengths. As a symbol in Steve Cavanagh's *The Defense* (2015), Christopher underscores the unorthodox methods of the protagonist, Eddie Flynn, in his efforts to save his daughter from the Russian mob and to obtain justice for the victim of a vicious attack. Part con man, part lawyer, Flynn's redemption comes from embracing both sides of his personality, abandoning his heretofore self-defeating efforts to fit into a conventional role in his relationship with the law.

In this sense, redemption in *The Defense* is closely associated with honesty about one's identity, motives, and abilities. While Flynn becomes a force of justice after coming to terms with who he is and channeling his distinctive strengths and experiences, Tommy Bridge in Gerard Brennan's *Disorder* (2018) and Gerry Fegan in Stuart Neville's *The Ghosts of Belfast* (originally published as *The Twelve* in 2009), two other characters with dualistic personalities and complicated relationships to justice, are less successful. Bridge attempts to quash his morals to attain vengeance for his daughter, but his subversion of the law and exploitation of his power as a police officer escalate to acts he is literally unable to live with. By contrast, Fegan's decision to rectify past wrongs ironically provides a justification for continuing to act on his deadly criminal impulses.

Just as the tragic inability of Tana French's Rob Ryan to face the truth of his past might be viewed as an authorial commentary on Ireland's need to honestly address its history (discussed in part 1), the self-deception of Bridge and Fegan can be read as a warning about post-Troubles complacency in Northern Ireland. Brennan and Neville stress that the underlying social factors that triggered the Troubles still exist, even if they are apparently dormant at present, and that many of the key players from the war still retain positions of power—albeit legal ones. The "price of peace" analyzed by the authors in part 2, particularly Claire McGowan, is here seen as potentially explosive if it is left undiscussed as a result of politesse, social conventions, or a desire to sweep a painful and embarrassing past under the rug as Northern Irish politics and society embrace progress toward a more peaceful and equitable future. True redemption, these authors seem to suggest, includes carrying the heavy burden of the past, acknowledging the pain of those individuals who have suffered from it, and taking steps to ensure that it endures in the collective memory, as a measure against calamitous history repeating itself.

Eoin McNamee's Blue trilogy does precisely this, looking to a series of related crimes and trials in pre-Troubles Northern Irish history to examine the ways in which politics, power, and bias can and have impeded justice. Like Cavanagh, Brennan, and Neville, McNamee also reflects on the lies people tell themselves about their identities and roles in society. For McNamee, truth is a slippery construct, blanketed in layers of human perspective, self-deception, and the influence of fiction tropes on the collective psyche, even when deliberate obfuscation is not in play. In the Blue Trilogy, narratives perpetuate narratives, as people construct their own interpretations and stories to make sense of facts that are hidden or concepts, behaviors, and actions that they are unable to understand or accept. If justice, faith, and identity are confusing or ineffable; if these three concepts can be reframed, reoriented, or even redefined based on perspective; if peace is tenuous and truth is elusive, then the cohesive narratives we create for and about ourselves and our societies might be the only things keeping us grounded. Individually, these stories can be reductive and damaging as well; collectively, however, the multiple perspectives and narratives of a society might provide us with the closest approximation of truth we are likely to attain.

5

A Disordered World

Gerard Brennan's Disorder,
Stuart Neville's The Ghosts of Belfast,
and Steve Cavanagh's The Defense

> I had occupied two different worlds—the world of the hustler
> and the world of the lawyer. . . . [I]n reality, they weren't so
> very different at all.
> —Steve Cavanagh, *The Defense*

The Maguire series frames the early release clause of the Good Friday
Agreement as a deeply complicated and extremely expensive "price of
peace," but crucially, it also highlights the progress of Northern Irish
society following the peace accord and envisions the legal pardons
of paramilitary members as a temporary suspension of justice for
the sake of better serving its cause in the future. Even the notion of
former terrorists in powerful political positions is treated in terms of
its emotional effects on their victims, rather than as a potential danger in the present. From a different and less optimistic perspective,
however, the fluid transition from paramilitary to political power
might suggest that the boundaries between criminality and the law
are somewhat murky. Unsurprisingly, then, a number of Northern
Irish crime writers tackle the question of whether the appearance of
law and order is merely a palatable masking of ongoing corruption.
In Gerard Brennan's *Disorder*, Detective Inspector Tommy Bridge
is a bent cop contending with a corporation that fans the flames
of sectarianism for profit, even as he pursues a personal vendetta

that ultimately involves the murder of innocents. Stuart Neville's *The Ghosts of Belfast* follows Gerry Fegan, a former killer for the Irish Republican Army (IRA) who seeks vengeance for his own victims by murdering the other people involved in their deaths. In so doing, he threatens the peace process and the establishment of a new government by exposing the violent pasts of current politicians. In *The Defense*, Steve Cavanagh uses lessons learned from the Troubles and the transition to peace to reflect on the American justice system, positing that the goals and strategies of lawyers have much in common with those of the criminals they prosecute or defend. Each of these novels aligns its readers with a protagonist who is equal parts self-serving lawbreaker and justice seeker, blurring the distinctions between them and their adversaries and suggesting that morality, justice, and the law are really just matters of perspective.

Both *Disorder* and *Ghosts of Belfast* portray contemporary Belfast as, in essence, two vastly different cities. On the one hand, the old ways seem to be fading: the civil war is officially over, and the streets in the city center and surrounding Queen's University are safe and inhabited by students and young professionals with no personal memory of Northern Ireland's dark history. On the other, the conditions that gave rise to violent tribalism—most notably, the lack of opportunities for the working class in terms of both economics and social mobility—remain unchanged. Anger and frustration make a large portion of the population vulnerable to the same sort of exploitation exercised by the paramilitaries during the Troubles for personal gain, but now the exploitative forces also masquerade under the guise of legitimate commerce or politics.

Disorder begins by contrasting the perspectives of young men from different social classes in the wake of a loyalist protest. For working-class Clark Wallace and his cousin Vic, the peace process has changed very little, and the protest is very clearly "a warm-up to a riot,"[1] not least because they are determined to ensure that violence occurs. While Vic mindlessly follows his cousin's lead in pursuit of a thrill and a purpose, Clark is more calculating; for him, violence is a game of profit: an assertion of his dominance that allows him to collect protection money from local businesses just like paramilitaries during the Troubles. He leads the crowd at the protest in chanting: "P-S-N. I-R-A,"[2] implying that the inclusion of more Catholics in the police force inclines it to support the republican cause. Later, he furthers his narrative about the oppression of Protestants by claiming that the riot he assisted in instigating himself was actually just a peaceful protest, unfairly misrepresented by Catholics in the media: "That's just propaganda. Fucking Taig journalists, know what I mean?"[3] Bit by bit throughout the novel, however, Clark's stance of bigotry and mistrust of the police are revealed for what they are: not true ideologies, but a means of prolonging a chaotic environment through which he can maintain power and status.

Meanwhile, Jimmy McAuley, a student from an upper-middle-class family, decides to go to the protest out of curiosity and to potentially embark on a career in journalism. Jimmy is so far removed from the violent underbelly of the city and the ongoing threat of tribalism that it never occurs to him that the protest could become dangerous; when his friend Steve tells him to be careful, Jimmy replies that "it's Belfast not Bosnia."[4] Before his fateful decision to attend the protest, Jimmy's biggest problem is feeling entrapped by the amount of time he spends on social media; at the protest, however, he is shocked when his filming of the event becomes an excuse for the trouble-seeking Vic to attack him, smashing a bottle across his face. Ironically, this dose of reality turns social media into a genuine threat to Jimmy's life and to the community: while he is being treated by paramedics, Jimmy is interviewed by Grace Doran, a reporter. His anger, fear, and shock at being attacked cause him to rant against the Protestant rioters in extremely bigoted and classist terms: "I am so sick of these subhuman imbeciles hogging the limelight and making our country look like some sort of red-neck, backwater, inbred dung-heap. They're a genetically inferior version of Irish Catholics. Completely out of step with reality. Throwing their toys out of the pram over flags and marches? I mean, who even cares about any of that stuff these days? Let it go, morons!"[5] While Jimmy later confesses that his speech was prompted by stress and does not reflect his true feelings, the damage has already been done: the video goes viral on the internet, inspiring the former generation of republican paramilitaries and evoking the wrath of loyalists like Clark, who tracks Jimmy with the intent of injuring or killing him. Of the message behind this story line, Brennan suggests that tribalist violence has always had more to do with inflammatory speech that stirs up natural human aggression than with belief systems, adding that the rise of social media has offered a much broader platform for this type of discourse:

> What I'm trying to get across with Jimmy and his viral video is that we need to be careful with the role of social media in terms of justice. While writing the book I could see how Facebook and posts to other popular platforms fed anger within Northern Irish communities, while the PSNI attempted to contain and follow the trend of appealing for peace by using the same wit or 'banter' as our so-called community leaders. In this context, community leaders are basically retired paramilitaries trying to find their own place in a small and complex society. . . . And in a wider context, you can see this tribalism in, say, an animal rights group on Facebook. Vegans look down on vegetarians, who look down on pet-owners who eat meat . . . In the end, the animals are pretty much forgotten by the time each tribe is done picking at the others' ribs.[6]

It is particularly poignant that, in assuming that tribalist hostilities are the result of defunct ideologies and are therefore irrelevant in modern society, Jimmy falls victim to their influence himself; however, he is not the only character to underestimate the potential of violence by misinterpreting its roots. Grace assumes that she is safe as a journalist covering the protest because the loyalists are simply looking for attention: "Without the cameras and the possibility of the whole world seeing it, what the fuck do *you* think *they* think is the point of all this stupidity?"[7] She appears to be as surprised as Jimmy when she is attacked by the rioters and, despite suffering a broken tailbone, largely diminishes the importance of the event, refusing to cover its aftermath because "people are bored of this shite already."[8] Even the fact that Jimmy's video has gone viral does not faze her; she assumes that it will be forgotten once its shock value has worn thin. The police, too, do not take the violence particularly seriously; they chat nonchalantly, attribute the situation to recreational rioting and the heat,[9] and even make jokes as they unleash water cannons on the protesters.

Each of these perspectives stems from an inability to fully acknowledge that the Troubles were the result of a confluence of issues, all of which are still in existence. Certain media personalities aid Clark and other ostensible sectarians in stoking resentment for the sake of ratings and profit. While the Police Service of Northern Ireland (PSNI) aims to be more modern, neutral, and just than the Royal Ulster Constabulary (RUC), the legal system is biased in favor of entitled young people like Jimmy, whose status as a student gives him "the potential to become an upstanding member of the community."[10] Jimmy and his friends are not immune to criminal behavior: Jimmy readily admits that he is high at the protest, and his best friend, Steve, is a drug dealer and a hacker, whose privilege allows him to frame his crimes as a noble pursuit: "I prefer the term hactivist. Hackers are gremlins. What I do . . . it's something else. It's about justice."[11] The PSNI is largely unconcerned by the actions of Jimmy and Steve; by contrast, the working-class rioters, who are also convinced they are breaking the law for the sake of justice and who have not had the same opportunities for advancement as the students, are met with "so-called non-lethal force" in the form of water cannons that take away their "breath, sight and dignity,"[12] reinforcing their personal narrative of victimhood.[13]

The only character who is seemingly capable of understanding both versions of Belfast is Detective Inspector Tommy Bridge. The child of a Catholic mother and an RUC officer, a member of the PSNI and an associate of local thugs and hitmen, Bridge operates both in the modern vision of Northern Ireland and in the remnants of the past that continue to haunt it. When he is introduced in the novel, his role in the police force is deliberately withheld, and he is described in terms that suggest something different about his relationship to the justice system: specifically, Bridge has "a fist-sized anarchy symbol, tattooed between his shoulder blades"[14] and a "twitching jawline," and he spends his leisure time clenching and unclenching a Glock 17.[15] For Brennan, Bridge is at once adept at seeing the ongoing injustice of his society—he attempts to educate Jimmy about the lower classes in order to encourage his empathy—and, because of his lack of faith in the new police system, a contributor to this injustice: "Tommy Bridge is named after his purpose, as was Spade in *The Maltese Falcon*. He's a bridge between my perception of the gap between the RUC's short-comings and what the PSNI should be. He also bridges the religious and class divides that Belfast is infamous for. Within the class divides lie varying levels of criminality, and so everybody is a person of inter-est to him. Basically, Bridge is trying to be a bit of everything, and in that attempt he overstretches himself. He has a place in every part of the community and yet he belongs nowhere."[16]

During and immediately after the riot, Bridge's roles as police officer, vigilante, and criminal converge. He contributes to control-ling the rioters, but like Clark and the media, he also exploits their anger to his own ends: in order to rescue Grace from a man who is attacking her, he shouts to the crowd that the man is a rapist and a pedophile, knowing that they will descend on him as a result.[17] More strikingly, when Bridge comes across Vic being beaten by local thugs, we discover that he is not there to save him, but has actually hired the thugs to get Vic away from the crowd so that he can kill him. Far from being the face of neutrality the PSNI purports to embrace, Bridge's primary obsession is a personal vendetta: the avenging of his daughter's suicide after she was lured into drug abuse and used for sex by Clark and Vic. Bridge's behavior serves as a reminder that the cycle of violence and retribution during the Troubles, though triggered by sectarianism, could as easily arise through any sense of perceived injustice. Though his family background allows him to straddle the religious divide, Bridge is not immune to the tendency to seek justice and revenge outside of the law.

Rather than serving to rein Bridge in, the new expectations of the PSNI offer him accessibility and cover for his crimes. As much as they claim to be oppressed and endangered by the police, lawbreakers like

Clark and Vic actually naively rely on the PSNI's duty to be neutral and to protect all citizens. Although Bridge has been suspended for attacking Vic in the past, Vic assumes that Bridge's readmission to the force implies a reinstatement of this sense of duty. He is not on guard as the inspector approaches him; rather, he smirks at his assaulters and tells them he is about to be rescued: "You're fucked now. . . . He's a cop, so he is." As he begins to recognize Bridge's intentions, Vic continues to insist that it is impossible for Bridge to hurt him because he is a police officer,[18] a delusion that he maintains until his murder at the inspector's hands. Upon realizing that his cousin is missing, Clark also anticipates help from Bridge; despite his role in the death of Bridge's daughter, Clark insists that Bridge is bound by the oath of his office to assist him in locating Vic, and he is startled when the detective informs him that, rather than helping him, he plans to ensure that Vic's case is not pursued.[19] During this exchange, it becomes clear that Clark intuitively understands what Bridge himself cannot: Bridge's attempts to simultaneously enforce the law and to break it for personal reasons are ultimately self-defeating; had Bridge been "thinking like a peeler should," Clark insists, "all that shite with your daughter might have worked out better. . . . You'd have found a reason to put me *and* Vic away back then if you'd done it the right way. . . . But instead you got suspended for beating up my wee cousin. Was it worth it?"[20]

Bridge's murder of Vic, while brutal, might be viewed as a type of justice: in addition to being partially responsible for the death of Bridge's daughter, Vic is prone to violent behavior. His unprovoked assault on Jimmy, for example, leaves the student badly wounded and scarred for life, and it seems certain that he would have injured many other innocents if his life had not been cut short. However, Brennan does not allow his readers to easily align with Bridge as a flawed yet well-meaning vigilante in the style of Bruen's Jack Taylor. On the contrary, Bridge's hypocrisy renders him decidedly unsympathetic: he asserts that Jimmy does not deserve his protection since his video has inspired sectarian divisiveness,[21] yet he promotes sectarian violence himself, deceiving Clark into believing that Jimmy's father is a republican dissident, and that the family is thus a danger to Clark and his companions, in order to detract attention from his own culpability in Vic's death.[22] As his plan to punish Clark progresses, we see the lengths to which Bridge is willing to go in order to exact revenge: he threatens the children of one of his coconspirators in order to ensure the man's silence and kills Clark's lover with a pipe bomb in an attempt to frame his nemesis for her murder.

In contrast to Bridge, his partner, Detective Sergeant "Dev" Devenney, is a stringent proponent of the idealistic values of the peace process and the PSNI. For Brennan, the relationship between the two detectives "is an inversion of the classic femme fatale dynamic";[23] rather than being a corrosive or dangerous influence, Dev repeatedly tries to pull Bridge back from the precipice of criminality. While she insists that, despite the fact that she is technically Bridge's junior, his corruption makes her "the real superior officer,"[24] she clings to the notion that he can repent and adhere to the law and neutrality. Their discussion about Bridge's resentment of Clark echoes McGowan's reflections on the dilemma created by the early release clause of the Good Friday Agreement: Bridge insists that it is impossible for him not to be consumed by his history, while Dev contends that personal wounds can be worked through, albeit with some difficulty, for the sake of a greater good.[25] Dev's devotion to her own principles of forgiveness is evident in her treatment of Bridge; even after she realizes that he is guilty of murder, she maintains that he is still redeemable and worthy of pardon: "There's a part of you left in there, isn't there? A little bit that wants the real Bridge back. And I'll be here with you to welcome him home."[26] According to Brennan, Dev is an embodiment of the potential of the new PSNI and the threat that this potential will be "corrupted by the influences of the 'old school' of Northern Irish policing." Although "she's bigger and stronger than Bridge, in a physical sense, and can even drink him under the table . . . as a woman she'll never be accepted by her colleagues as a real peeler."[27] For this reason, while Dev is clearly more reliable and devoted to her work than Bridge, she is forced to operate within a system that has promoted her male partner more quickly than her.

This injustice makes her susceptible to Bridge's influence; she finds herself breaking police rules in minor ways and insinuates at the end of the novel that she will decline her forthcoming promotion because she fears that the combination of power and the effects that Bridge has had on her put her at risk of corruption.[28]

While Dev's self-awareness offers a glimmer of hope for progress in the police force, Bridge and his ilk of bent police officers are not the only holdovers from the Troubles that threaten to return Northern Irish society to its previous state of discord. Joe Soap, an American businessman, has discovered a means of profiting from the riots in Belfast. Much like the Irish Americans whose meddling prolonged the Troubles, Soap is entirely ignorant of the culture and politics of the North. His goal, however, is financial rather than sentimental or ideological: he intends to set up a private security force to intervene in the riots, which he claims will enable the PSNI to improve their reputation, since they will not be responsible for the use of force in such situations. Soap clearly misconstrues the goals of the peace process, viewing it through the lens of commerce. To him, the transition from the RUC to the PSNI is simply a "rebranding exercise,"[29] rather than a legal measure designed to enforce neutrality and the protection of civilians. His vision for his company includes the worst characteristics of the RUC, including sectarianism: while the RUC mainly comprised Protestant officers and has been widely criticized for its bias against Catholic citizens, Soap's company largely employs former republican paramilitaries, with the excuse that "ex-IRA men are much more professional than their Loyalist counterparts." Also like the RUC, Soap's security agents are almost exclusively male.[30] Any suggestion that Soap's approach is an earnest, if misguided, attempt to assist the PSNI and to quell the residual violence in Northern Ireland begins to unravel as he spouts about the inadequacy and class bias of the police: "Unless you're royalty or some sort of politician . . . well, you just don't get the special kind of treatment that those who are more equal than others are afforded."[31] In addition to discrediting the police, Soap has much in common with former paramilitary leaders: he suggests that he wishes to "tap into" the anger of Northern Irish youth[32] and attempts to persuade people that the government does nothing to assist its citizens and must therefore be overthrown.[33] Finally, it is revealed that Soap is actually planning and instigating riots through social media, even offering payoffs to the rioters in order to increase demand for his product.

Through Soap, Brennan offers an implicit warning to the contemporary American populace from the point of view of someone who has seen the damages that can be done to a society through tribalism, prioritization of wealth, and a mistrust of structural justice that extends beyond a quest to repair the system to an outright attempt to dismantle it. From a certain perspective, Soap serves as a clear embodiment of recent political figures in America: he equates money with class and disparages low-income workers even as he pretends to be on their side; he asserts that people who have no experience with or education about politics are the best equipped to make political decisions;[34] he views politics as a corporate enterprise and is prepared to "[move] on to the next gig"[35] if his enterprise fails, with no concern for its effects on the people of Belfast. Brennan acknowledges a frustration with America's failure to learn from the historical mistakes of other countries: "I channelled my anger at certain contemporary American characteristics through him [Soap]; the crumbling American Dream, the rise of alt-right politics, the suggestion that money will speed up the time it takes to heal a broken and divided nation." While he remarks that Soap is "less of a threat to the community than Clark Wallace because there's a tendency in Belfast for some natives to smirk at America," he also indicates that the association of America with wealth and prosperity makes the country—and its priorities and errors in judgment—extremely globally influential: "In this version of Belfast, people look at American tourists, diplomats and entrepreneurs with hungry dollar-sign eyes. They represent the potential for money."[36]

Ultimately, Brennan's treatment of the possibility of progress is inconclusive: on the one hand, by the end of the novel, Soap has been exposed as a fraud; both vestiges of Belfast's violent and vengeful past, Bridge and Clark, are safely in their graves; and Dev, Grace, and Jimmy come together to commiserate and support each other in their visions of a more just and transparent future for the police and the media. On the other hand, it is clear that the lessons of the Troubles have not been absorbed by everyone: both Soap and his personal assistant seem to take for granted that there is no danger that the mass disorder of the Troubles can recur outside of that specific situation of sectarian resentment; for them, social disunity is a thing to be trifled with, which allows for little optimism that Americans will be safely steered from the growing tide of tribalism in their country before large-scale violence ensues. Closer to home, PSNI officers on riot duty turn on each other, first owing to sectarian concerns and then because of conflicting ideals between the old guard who were members of the RUC and younger officers who are committed to the modernity of the PSNI. Brennan suggests that, optimism and expectations of police neutrality aside, "we're all human first, prone to mindless mob mentality when the lizard brain kicks in";[37] no matter the point of contention or the players involved, society frequently reverts to "us against them. Same old story."[38]

Like *Disorder*, Stuart Neville's *Ghosts of Belfast* approaches the optimism of the peace process with several grains of salt. Its protagonist, Gerry Fegan, is a former executioner for the IRA who has been freed from prison as a result of the early release clause of the Good Friday Agreement and whose past has come back to haunt him—literally. Fegan is followed, tormented, and prevented from sleeping by the spirits of the twelve people he has murdered; while there is some suggestion that Fegan has a history of mental illness resulting in hallucinations, Neville underscores the palpability of Fegan's remorse by refusing to concede that the spirits are entirely figments of his imagination: in particular, children, whose idealism is not yet tainted, are able to see the twelve as well.[39] Neville's take on the suspension of legal justice during the peace process is unique in that it suggests that the perpetrators of crimes during the Troubles have, in some sense, been as injured by their pardons as have their victims and their families, because they have been denied the possibility of serving adequate time to atone for their wrongdoings.

Because he was incarcerated, Fegan was isolated from the concessions, compromises, and social and political transitions that constituted the peace process. Whether this distance allows for more lucidity on his part or an inability to recognize progress—or a combination of both—is deliberately left unclear. Essentially, he is released to discover that the same people who were responsible for criminal acts during the Troubles have now attained legitimate power in the political sphere; while he is encouraged to embrace the new order, he is unable to forget the past, largely owing to an awareness of the self-serving nature of his former compatriots in the IRA and a conviction that, regardless of the way they present themselves, their motivations and tendencies toward criminal behavior have not changed. Fegan has adequate evidence to support such a conviction, since he is the recipient of a regular salary for a government job that does not actually exist: the salary is a payoff for his silence about events of the past and an assurance that he will be available if needed to threaten or torture people who undermine the success of "the party"—an unsubtle reference to Sinn Féin—or the personal prosperity of its leaders and their friends. Fegan's reluctance to play the role that is expected of him as recompense for the party's support and loyalty is initially attributed to emotional shortcomings; he is thought to be an unstable alcoholic and is informed that, as "a Republican hero," he must put on a brave face for the sake of the next generation: "The young fellas need a role model, someone they can respect." Like Tommy Bridge, Fegan is able to pursue a personal vendetta because of presumptions about how someone in his situation ought to behave. In reality, he is extremely aware that "there's no respecting what [he has] done,"[40] and he is therefore determined to punish his former friends in order to satisfy the demands of the vengeful spirits of his victims.

Fegan's haunting, like the threat of the contagion of old-school police methodologies in *Disorder*, reflects a profound fear that the progress in Northern Ireland is partially illusory and extremely fragile. Fegan is astonished by the appearance of prosperous normality on the Lisburn Road, now replete with boutiques and coffee shops, inhabited by well-off young professionals and Queen's University students, who Fegan muses were probably not "even born when they scraped the body parts off the streets with shovels."[41] Fegan is slightly envious of these young people, acknowledging that they are able to enjoy a sense of security and potential that was denied to him, but finally determines that he is glad that they will "never comprehend the awful, constant fear that had smothered this place for more than thirty years."[42] Just the same, he wonders if their trust that the civil war is finally over is misplaced: *"Over for who?"* As the citizens of Northern Ireland head to the polls to elect their first real government at Stormont, Fegan's old compatriots stuff the ballot boxes with multiple votes each to tip the election in favor of their preferred candidate, Paul McGinty, whom even the party would have liked to pass over as "tainted by the old ways, no matter how hard he tried to play the politician."[43] Nor are illicit votes the only thing that allows former paramilitaries to maintain power in the region, as the Northern Irish electorate is entirely willing to "vote for criminals in full knowledge of their nature"[44] along sectarian lines. Any real hope for "a future here" is, evidently, challenged by the fact that "men like McGinty are still running things."[45] While the party leadership earnestly wishes to dissociate itself from the old guard, if only for the sake of appearance, it is reliant on men like McGinty to curry the favor of those individuals who prefer the violent solutions of the past and to be available for help lest those solutions return as a dominating force: "The old ways [are] dead and gone, but still their ghosts might come to haunt the political process. The politicos might be smarter, but smart never stopped a bullet."[46] Problematically, of course, the concession of allowing McGinty and his friends to remain in power gives them an avenue through which they might, eventually, find a way to fully regain the influence and control they had during the Troubles.[47]

As Fegan stalks the people he feels are responsible for the murders he committed, we get a clearer understanding of the danger of allowing these men a say in the government, either directly through politics or via connections with politicians. Michael McKenna, an associate of McGinty, is a man whose true face is far from the one presented on television: a "face that burned with white-hot pleasure as McKenna set about [a] boy with a claw hammer, [a] face that was dotted with red when he handed Fegan the .22 pistol to finish it."[48] Fegan views McKenna as inhuman and irredeemable: a man with no heart, who gets pleasure from the suffering of others, though he is an expert at disguising it. Even in death, McKenna continues his deception of the public; his modest casket masks the wealth he has accumulated through his position so that he might be remembered as a man of the people. McGinty and McKenna have several similar hypocrites on their payroll, who enable them to evade justice for criminal activities: Father Coulter, a priest who is paid to feed them information and to look the other way as they commit egregious sins; Patsy Toner, who frames himself as a human rights lawyer while growing rich from defending members of the party in court; and a corrupt police officer. They also continue to employ men like Vincie Caffola, a professional torturer, and to work cooperatively with Bull O'Kane, a former IRA strongman who adheres to the old ways, laundering money and obtaining land from his neighbors through threats and physical force. While he is not on Fegan's kill list, O'Kane serves as a reminder that there are fundamental similarities between the old guard and the new: both claim to be working for the benefit of the country while their only real interests are in obtaining power and lining their own pockets, and each serves to reinforce the influence of the other: "McGinty and O'Kane were two sides of the same coin. O'Kane still commanded the loyalty of the old foot soldiers . . . and McGinty and the party leadership relied on them for their power on the street. At the same time, the party's political influence had allowed the Bull to operate his fuel-laundering plants in relative peace for the last ten years. Each needed the other."[49]

Like Joe Soap, McGinty promotes violence in order to sell his importance as a force that can contain it, both to the party and to the community. His foot soldiers encourage young people to start riots to create photo ops of him arriving and dispelling the chaos, giving Fegan flashbacks of the days when "journalists gave kids five-pound notes to throw stones and bottles at the Brits, hoping to set off another battle for the cameras."[50] Although he quickly deduces that his men are being picked off by Fegan, McGinty's initial response is to exploit these murders and the media attention they receive to garner more power for the party in the new government and to reinforce his position within it. By blaming the police for the attacks on his men, McGinty is able to leverage his ostensible outrage to threaten a withdrawal of party support for the PSNI, putting the British government on the defensive and making himself indispensable: "As long as I've got the press lapping this stuff up, the Brits are on the back foot. I stir up enough shit, they'll give us anything we ask for. They know we can bring Stormont down if we want to, and they'll bend over backwards to stop it. They'll be eating out of my hand, and the party won't dare pass me over. . . . [T]he media's a better weapon than Semtex ever was."[51] McGinty concludes that Fegan's first two murders were actually a kind of favor to him: McKenna, who was involved in illegal smuggling and prostitution rings, and Caffola, a dissident who believed that the republicans should refuse to participate in the government or support the police, were both threats to his public image. The people of Northern Ireland are no longer willing to tolerate the old ways, he argues, and because of 9/11, the Americans who once gladly supplied the IRA with weapons and money now view violence in a different light: "Used to be we could sell them the romance of it, call ourselves freedom fighters, and they loved it. The money just rolled in, all those Irish-Americans digging in their pockets for the old country. They don't buy it any more."[52] When Fegan murders the corrupt PSNI officer in McGinty's lawyer's car, McGinty likewise views the event only in terms of its potential effects on his political clout: in this case, however, he fears that his association with the scandal will result in him losing his position in the party and in the unionists attaining the type of leverage he had hoped to gain himself by pinning the murders on the police.[53]

The British government is not ignorant of McGinty's history and tactics—on the contrary, they have had an operative, Davy Campbell, working in his circles for nearly two decades. Because of his proximity to and understanding of the situation, Campbell is no fan of the allowances offered to McGinty and his ilk; to a certain extent, he views these allowances as an indication that the tribalism and systems of power and manipulation from the Troubles era are still firmly in place: "The city's invisible borders remained the same as when Campbell first walked its streets holding a rifle eighteen years ago. The same lowlifes still fed off the misery they created, deepening the divisions wherever they could. The same hatreds still bubbled under the surface. But the city had grown fat, learning to mask its scars when necessary and show them when advantageous."[54] While he is thus sympathetic to what he perceives as an attempt by Fegan to cull the party of former paramilitaries, Campbell is ultimately compelled by both pragmatic and personal concerns to try to put an end to Fegan's crusade. His handlers prioritize the successful creation of a new government at Stormont to the degree that they are willing to concede to McGinty's false accusations against the police for the sake of expediency,[55] and they refuse to allow Fegan to complicate matters by killing McGinty or exposing his corruption because they know that "for every politician like McGinty there [are] ten thugs who would gladly take his place and guide the party away from weapons like newspapers and television cameras, and back to AK47s and mortar bombs."[56] Far from being a force of untainted structural justice, the British government is willing to turn a blind eye to crime and to sacrifice innocents in its own self-interest; even when Campbell is ordered by McGinty to kidnap a woman and her young child and deliver them to him and his men, Campbell's handlers order him to play along rather than risk blowing his cover or arresting McGinty, remarking that the lives of these people are less important than the work and money that have gone into building Stormont.[57]

In this sense, the appearance of all sides working together for peace is shadowed by the insinuation that they are also working together to disguise the corrupt and violent remnants of the past that continue to have an effect on Northern Irish society, thus preserving and enabling them.[58] But Neville does not suggest an easy answer in transparency and the pursuit of justice or redemption. On the contrary, Fegan's attempts to atone for injustice inevitably give rise to more injustice, a fact with which he is forced to reconcile when he encounters Caffola's mourning children at his funeral: "Some insane part of him wanted to beg their forgiveness. Caffola might have been a mindless thug, but he had been a father to these boys."[59] Moreover, Fegan's efforts threaten more than the struggles for power at Stormont: they create a real danger of a return to more violent times. Caffola's death escalates rioting in the city beyond McGinty's power to control it, while the refusal of certain leaders to attend McKenna's funeral highlights and exacerbates ideological rifts in the party. In the event that McGinty is publicly tainted or murdered, the party's choice of replacement has the potential to anger McGinty's followers, creating chaos among the politicians, weakening trust in legal avenues, and increasing support for the old-school methods of men like O'Kane. In the "precarious balance between the old ways and the new," Fegan's vigilantism is ultimately tipping the balance toward the old;[60] even as he tries to make up for the crimes of the past, he is ironically increasing the likelihood that more such crimes will be committed.[61] The pursuit of truth and justice, Neville seems to imply, doesn't always equate with the furtherance of peace.

Fegan's quest to avenge the murders of his victims is problematic in other ways as well. Even as he bristles at the notion that people remember the sins of others but not their own, contending that his own sins are inescapable,[62] his presumption that other people are more responsible than him for the crimes he has committed is clearly a displacement of guilt. This dissociation is most evident in that, despite his expressions of regret at killing certain of the people on his list—particularly Father Coulter, who, hypocrisy notwithstanding, has never actually killed anyone or ordered anyone killed—he is persuaded that there is no other option, because the twelve will accept nothing but eye-for-an-eye justice. When he discovers that the last person on their hit list is himself, however, he begs for mercy and receives it. If the twelve are to be taken as manifestations of Fegan's unease with the past, this clemency is a clear indication that he believes himself worthier of forgiveness than others involved in criminal activities during the Troubles.[63]

This belief is not entirely indefensible. Fegan makes the compelling argument that, as a person with few ambitions and little passion for the republican cause, he would not have become a murderer without the manipulative intervention of McKenna, who drafted him into the IRA, and McGinty, who brainwashed him into becoming a soldier. He describes himself in childhood, completely devoid of tribalist mentality and bewildered when a neighbor told him that her parents had forbidden her from being friends with him because he was *"the other sort."*[64] In an impassioned speech, he berates McGinty for depriving him of this innocent outlook and exploiting his youthful naïveté by persuading him that Protestants were an enemy bent on destroying the future of Catholics in the country. Fegan contends that McGinty never actually believed in the republican cause and that his only real aim, both as a paramilitary leader and as a politician, has been to stir up discord in the pursuance of power: "You used people like me. You told us we didn't have a future. You said we had to fight for it. You put the guns in our hands and sent us off to do your killing for you."[65] Fegan perceives himself as fundamentally different from his former compatriots because his crimes were inspired neither by tribalist hatred nor by a desire for advancement; for him, killing was merely work in service of the Catholic community: "Just a job to be done, with no care or feeling behind it."[66] He remembers in detail the celebrations of his fellow prisoners after the Chinook helicopter crash that resulted in the deaths of MI5, British army, and Special Branch agents and his own sense of dissociation with the event.[67] Essentially, he envisions himself as a kind of worker bee who acted under the guidance of more powerful and intelligent forces; thus, as much as he protests that the blood on his hands makes him undeserving, he allows himself some hope for a future in which he is forgiven and at peace.

When he meets Marie, McKenna's niece who has been exiled by the party because of her former marriage to an RUC officer, Fegan is introduced to a perspective on disagreement that is utterly at odds with the way he has been programmed. Although she has been treated with disrespect by her family and the friends of her uncle, Marie refuses to respond in kind because she believes that animosity and revenge ultimately harm the people who harbor such feelings more than their objects.[68] Marie becomes almost sacred to Fegan; in her company, he is finally able to feel real emotions and to experience beauty and laughter. There are, however, several glitches in this redemptive story line. First, Fegan's insight into the character of men like McGinty casts doubt on his protestations of innocence; he claims, for example, that the twelve made him aware that a particular hit on a butcher's shop, which McGinty framed as a statistical attack on a Protestant paramilitary meeting, was actually a deliberate assault on civilians in furtherance of McGinty's political ambitions. Unless we are to believe that the twelve are *only* actual spirits, which seems unlikely,[69] this deduction represents an acknowledgment that Fegan knew exactly what he was participating in, but simply chose to conceal it from himself. Such an interpretation is supported by his confession that "sometimes he [wonders] if, deep inside, [he has] always known the true desires of men like Michael McKenna and Paul McGinty."[70] Moreover, although he asserts that McGinty caused him to act by fueling his outrage, Fegan also admits that he is unsure "if he . . . ever believed in any of it." Certainly, he witnessed attacks on the civil rights of Catholics as a youth, but he confesses that his participation in the IRA "was more than that. Fegan had been a solitary boy, quick with his fists but slow with words. When McKenna befriended him thirty years ago, it seemed to be a path to a bigger world. A world where he mattered."[71] The distinctions between Fegan's motivations and those of McGinty thus begin to blur; Fegan's ambition to "matter" might not include a public spotlight, but it nevertheless suggests that his actions were more self-serving than he generally admits. Fegan's attempts to rectify what he has done also ironically reflect an unwillingness to change; although he has developed a conscious awareness of the damages caused by violence, he seeks his redemption through the same means that caused him to feel guilty in the first place, with as little sense of conscience or regret. When he kills Caffola, for example, he "[closes] his eyes and [searches] his heart, looking for some sense of what [he has] just done," only to discover "nothing but the cold hollowness of his wishes."[72] Nor is there much evidence that following Marie's path of nonviolence and forgiveness would serve Fegan any better: despite her efforts to avoid a confrontation with the party, Marie becomes a target and is tracked down and kidnapped by McGinty's men. Her attitude, as idealistic as it seems, appears to have no place in the society in which they live.

Perhaps the biggest problem with Fegan's methodology, however, is evidenced in the character of Davy Campbell. Campbell has obtained a place on Fegan's kill list by falsely implicating two men to disguise a crime he committed: when one of McGinty's associates discovered that he was a British spy, Campbell killed him and claimed that the associate had been working with two Protestant paramilitary members to undermine McGinty. Having accepted this account, McGinty sent Caffola and Fegan to torture and murder the two loyalists—an outcome Campbell would have known was inevitable. Clearly, Campbell did what he thought was necessary in furtherance of his job, making his actions in the case of the two loyalists very similar to Fegan's. In fact, the parallels between Fegan and Campbell are difficult to miss: like Fegan in his former iteration as an IRA hit man, Campbell acts in blind service to his handlers, committing atrocities without feeling.

Although we are privy to internal and external dialogue that suggests that Campbell would prefer to avoid harming people if possible, his lack of passion for his work and his understanding of himself as a laborer for a larger system make him more dangerous than some of the criminals whose circle he has infiltrated. During a small-time robbery of a post office, dissident republicans are content to steal a trivial amount of cash and cartons of cigarettes; Campbell, however, proceeds to brutally beat the elderly postal worker. When McGinty compels Campbell to kidnap Marie and her daughter, Coyle, the violent thug who has been sent with him, exhibits more compassion than Campbell, flatly refusing to participate in any action that might result in the death of a child. However, Campbell most assuredly has a conscience. During the exchange with Coyle, he comes to the conclusion that the viciousness with which he treats others is actually a redirection of his own self-loathing: "He didn't hate her [Marie], he didn't even know her. But hate was in his heart. Who for? When the answer came, as hard and sure as any single thing he'd ever known, he could hold her gaze no longer."[73]

Fegan evidently recognizes the likenesses between Campbell and himself; when he first confronts and tries to kill Campbell, he insists that his vengeance is just because Campbell's victims "weren't killers. Not like you and me."[74] Campbell is also the only of Fegan's targets whom Fegan assumes has been haunted by the ghosts of regret in the same manner as himself: "When you close your eyes at night," he asks him, "do they scream?"[75] Fegan appears to have identified Campbell's buried conscience and anticipated its resurgence: just before his death, Campbell does indeed have an encounter with his dead victims that is not dissimilar to Fegan's own experiences with the twelve: "Those men with the shaven heads and tattoos . . . were dead years ago, broken into pieces in a cold concrete room. What did they want with him now? Their faces blazed in ecstasy. . . . The other faces, the bodies, the limbs, all dead and rotting, swarmed on him."[76] Unable to bear these embodiments of his guilt, Campbell actually begs Fegan to kill him. Campbell's narrative complicates the story line, as it examines the possibility that other players in the Troubles—perhaps many other players—were used and manipulated for political gain in much the same way as Fegan. For Campbell, however, there is no mercy; in fact, when Fegan finally gets to him, Campbell has already been shot and is likely to die, but Fegan is determined to shoot him again, not only accepting more blood on his hands, but actually welcoming it unnecessarily.

The murder of Campbell is something more than hypocritical; it is, paradoxically, symbolic of Fegan's rejection of the end of the violent era in which he came of age—an era that he claims to regret and despise and for which he believes he is atoning through his vengeance on former compatriots. For both Fegan and Campbell, however, the peace process is also a process toward personal irrelevance. Fegan notes that, while he was in prison, the world outside was altered irrevocably. The Celtic Tiger made the Republic a rich nation, with little desire to reclaim its poorer northern provinces; in the North, former paramilitary leaders found an easier path to power and wealth through politics: "The cause he once killed for was long gone, swallowed up by the avarice of men like McGinty."[77] He describes in detail the sleepless nights he and his fellow inmates experienced after receiving their release letters; the prospect of freedom, he suggests, was overshadowed by an unbearable question: "If there's peace, if it's really over, then what use are we?"[78] Fegan frequently returns to this query, asserting that, since they were robbed of any chance at constructing alternative identities or futures and were consigned to work as killers for a cause that no longer exists—and, indeed, perhaps never did—men like him no longer have a place in Northern Irish society, nor do they have the skills or resources to relocate and thrive elsewhere. Campbell feels similarly about his own situation, particularly after his handlers begin to urge him toward retirement. He recognizes that his talents are virtually useless in peacetime and that the sacrifices he has made for his job have left him without family, friends, or a more permanent career to fall back on. For Campbell, the prospect of retirement is "like walking off a cliff. A long drop into nothing," and he struggles to make sense of the fact that his efforts for the British government have secured a future for Northern Ireland while destroying his own prospects.[79]

There is, however, a fundamental difference between Fegan and Campbell, made obvious through their disparate reactions to the ghostly embodiments of their victims. Campbell's confrontation with these figures occurs in the last moments of his life and is described as a Dantean experience of retributory torment. Fegan, on the other hand, finds comfort in the presence of the twelve, even though they cause him anxiety and prevent him from sleeping. At the apex of his relationship with Marie, as they drive into the countryside together, it occurs to him that he yearns for the spirits in this moment of relative tranquility;[80] later that night, he seeks them out in the darkness, hoping for "some assurance they would protect him from the horrors that waited in his mind."[81] For Fegan, the twelve provide a justification for the suspension of his current reality; as long as he pursues their agenda, he is able to extend his sense of utility and postpone the inevitable necessity of beginning a new course in life. He is also able to resume his career as a killer—which, though ethically complex, contains an element of comfortable familiarity—and to continue to absolve himself of his crimes by shifting the blame to others. The twelve have, in effect, filled the void in his life created by the paramilitary leaders' progress toward nonviolence. In this sense, while both Campbell and Fegan followed destructive paths during the Troubles to establish a sense of self-importance, Fegan's resolve to do the bidding of the twelve, particularly as it pertains to Campbell, demonstrates that, unlike his outlook on his former compatriots, his motivation remains unchanged.

A comparable interrogation of the classic redemption story can be found in Steve Cavanagh's legal thriller *The Defense*. Like the other two novels discussed in this chapter, *The Defense* is concerned with questioning the established dichotomy between criminality and the law and with contrasting the appearance of structural order with the seedy undercurrents beneath it. Of his decision to set the novel in New York City, Cavanagh remarks that, like many of his contemporaries, he grew up reading American crime fiction, but he adds that his "heroes in the genre are Lee Child, Michael Connelly and John Connolly," who are British, Irish American, and Irish, respectively, suggesting particular interests in heterogenous approaches to the genre and in the diverse perspectives on American culture reflected therein. Like Connolly, Cavanagh also contends that an objective point of view can be useful in considerations of justice: "Like Lee and John, I don't hail from the US and perhaps I can give an outsider's view on some of the issues."[82] Much of this "outsider's" perspective involves applying lessons from the Troubles and their aftermath to a consideration of the American legal system. Indeed, as Brian McGilloway notes, while the book is set in America rather than Northern Ireland, "Cavanagh's concern with the law and justice and the frequent distance between the two is very much born of a lifetime living here."[83] Like the Belfast of Brennan and Neville, Cavanagh's New York is "a city of dualities. You have Wall Street and the richest people in the country, then you have abject poverty in other areas."[84] It is, likewise, a city where the side of the law from which one operates is not in the least reflective of one's role in the pursuit or obstruction of justice.

The central character of *The Defense*, Eddie Flynn, embodies this fine line between criminality and the law. Once a con artist, Flynn was encouraged by a sympathetic judge to pursue a more legitimate career as an attorney, only to be eventually driven into a hiatus by the disastrous consequences of a case. At the beginning of the novel, Flynn is forced out of retirement when Olek Volchek, the head of the Russian mob, demands that Flynn defend him at a murder trial. It is theoretically impossible to win the case owing to the profusion of evidence against Volchek, particularly the testimony of Little Benny, a triggerman who claims that Volchek ordered the hit. The goal, then, is for Flynn to use his familiarity with the court's security guards to smuggle a bomb into the courtroom to kill Little Benny and, quite possibly, a number of innocent bystanders. In the best-case scenario, Flynn will be blamed for the bombing and sent to jail, while Volchek will have an opportunity to evade justice; however, Flynn's own experience with crime and deception leads him to believe that Volchek will never risk leaving him alive because of the possibility, however unlikely, that the police might find his version of events credible. Nevertheless, Flynn has little choice but to follow Volchek's orders, as Volchek's men have kidnapped Flynn's ten-year-old daughter and have threatened to kill her if he does not go along with their plans.

Flynn's predicament is complicated significantly by the difficulty of distinguishing between people who might be relied upon to secure the safety of his daughter and bring Volchek to justice and those individuals whose motives are self-serving and corrupt. Initially, he imagines that his biggest obstacle will be making contact with a police officer or government agent without raising Volchek's suspicions and persuading that person to trust his account and assist him. In itself, doing so would be no easy task, since the story sounds far-fetched and the bomb strapped inside his jacket is highly incriminating. However,

Flynn quickly learns that a job within the justice system also does not equate with a desire to serve it; Volchek has both a security guard at the courthouse and Tom Levine, a member of the FBI, on his payroll, making government officials as potentially untrustworthy as the deadliest of mafia thugs: "If the mob could buy a federal agent," he concludes, "they could buy a hundred New York cops."[85] Ultimately, he determines, he cannot put his daughter's life at risk by relying on the honesty of the police.[86]

Like *Disorder* and *Ghosts of Belfast*, *The Defense* thus explores the fallacy of expectations as defined by anticipated loyalties and relationships to the law. Tommy Bridge gets away with criminal behavior because both cops and criminals presume that PSNI officers will prioritize the safety and well-being of citizens; Gerry Fegan succeeds in murdering several of his former compatriots because they do not suspect that he will act in the service of justice or against his own financial interests. In *The Defense*, Eddie Flynn's ability to evaluate people outside of their anticipated roles gives him an advantage over other characters in the novel. As he predicts, when he finally manages to establish the integrity of Kennedy, an FBI official, he receives no help from that quarter: Kennedy is unable to process Flynn's story because it requires him to accept that Levine is in league with the Russian mob, which he deems impossible for a fellow agent. Kennedy actually dismisses proof of Levine's corruption, contending that it must be a misinterpretation of his colleague's former undercover work. Such naïveté is not only evident among ethical members of law enforcement: Volchek, too, is being double-crossed by members of his own gang. Flynn uncovers evidence that Arturas, Volchek's right-hand man, has been meeting with drug suppliers behind his boss's back and that the murder committed by Little Benny was actually the result of an attempt to secure and destroy photographic proof of these meetings. The bomb scenario is merely a smoke screen; once Little Benny is produced in the courtroom, Arturas intends to kill Volchek, help Benny to escape, and take over as head of the Russian mob. Such a possibility of betrayal has never occurred to Volchek, who works under the presumption that all members of his crime family are devoted to him and to the established power structure of the mob; when confronted with incontrovertible proof of Arturas's treachery, he is confounded and reluctant to accept the truth: "It seemed as though this was too much for him to take in. He had built his life around the loyalty of his men. Indeed, his very existence depended on utter obedience, honor, and allegiance. . . . Now those lifelong foundations were crumbling away."[87]

Because he is the only character who has operated in two distinctly different social spheres and is thus capable of assessing people based on individual characteristics rather than stereotyped expectations, Flynn is able to regain control of the situation. First, he calculates that his two most important potential allies are Harry Ford, the judge who helped him to become a lawyer, and Jimmy Fellini, the head of the Italian Mafia. While this seems an unlikely pairing, the two men share an adherence to their own self-assigned codes of ethics. Ford, Flynn realizes, will do whatever it takes to ensure that killers do not evade justice, and his willingness to mentor Flynn despite his past as a con artist is evidence that he is not averse to breaking rules for the sake of the greater good. Fellini, like Volchek, prioritizes an old-school system of loyalty, and his childhood friendship with Flynn ensures that he will put his life on the line to protect Flynn's daughter. With allegiances secured both within and without the legal system, Flynn wagers that Volchek, who also strictly values and observes codified personal standards of conduct, is his best chance at striking a bargain for his daughter's life within the Russian mob. He carefully lays out Arturas's plans, exploiting Volchek's disgust at the prospect of disloyalty and offering his assistance in exchange for Volchek's assurance that Flynn's daughter will not be harmed.

At the same time, Flynn relies on Volchek's tendency to consign people to predictable, one-dimensional roles in order to run a counterattack on Volchek and his perfidious underlings. Flynn's advantage is evident early in the novel, when the mob men laugh at his seemingly ridiculous threats of revenge: "They knew me as Eddie Flynn, the lawyer; they didn't know the old Eddie Flynn: the hustler, the backstreet fighter, the con artist."[88] In fact, the arts of dissimulation and criminality are an intrinsic part of Flynn's nature; he styles these talents as both hereditary traits and familial traditions. Flynn teaches his daughter how to hone her skills at sleight-of-hand techniques, just as his father, an Irish emigrant, taught him "the grift" and the best way to respond effectively if he ever got caught.[89]

Cavanagh's explanation of Flynn's initial plunge into a life of fraud offers a critical perspective on how illegal or immoral activity is defined by a society and the manner in which custom obstructs clear evaluation of such definitions. This perspective is pointedly informed by Cavanagh's background: as a citizen of a country with universal health care, he is positioned to offer an outsider's assessment of the flaws of the American medical system. Flynn's cons are almost exclusively directed at purveyors of insurance; after a health-care company refused to pay for the medical treatment that would have saved his father's life, he dedicated himself to a full-on assault on health and liability insurance companies through fraudulent claims.

Although illegal, Flynn's scams are framed not merely as victimless crimes, but as a means of redressing the harms inflicted on Americans by a system that exploits them. The licit dealings of insurance companies, which collect monthly premiums in exchange for a promise of care that is not always forthcoming, pose an ethical conundrum; by contrast, Flynn's ability to find the weaknesses in these companies' structures and to use them to his own advantage is depicted as a form of art. He describes creating a fake law firm by scouring obituaries for recently deceased lawyers, approaching their widows under the guise of former clients of their husbands, offering the widows cash and gifts, and requesting their husbands' practicing licenses as mementos. He then stages auto accidents by hiring drivers to stop suddenly at traffic lights, causing the cars behind them to collide with them; laws mandating the maintenance of safe stopping distances ensure that Flynn's drivers will be legally recognized as victims in the accidents. Subsequently, he uses the practicing licenses he has acquired to impersonate the deceased lawyers and represent the drivers in their claims against insurance companies. As a final coup de grâce, he sets up a fraudulent medical practice with the sole purpose of creating letters, supposedly written by medical practitioners, advising his fake accident victims not to settle out of court because their cases are worth a fortune—letters that he "accidentally" encloses with the insurance claims.[90] Flynn, his employees, and the lawyers' widows all profit from the scheme; the drivers accused of causing the accidents do not pay out of pocket; and the disadvantage is only to the insurance companies. It is, in effect, a classic David-and-Goliath tale of outwitting and undermining a powerful and abusive enemy.

Flynn's cons are not merely presented as justified and somewhat heroic, either: from the first lines of the novel—"I'd grown sloppy. That's what happens when you go straight"[91]—it is implied that his efforts to leave his criminal past behind him in order to pursue a legitimate career have left him vulnerable. This is true both in a literal sense—because Flynn is not constantly on guard, he becomes easy prey for Volchek's gang as they initially approach and kidnap him—and also in a figurative one. By attempting to work within the confines of a legal structure, Flynn betrays his own nature and becomes mired in hypocrisy. He concludes that he never actually left the world of hustling behind, but merely learned to apply his expertise in a socially acceptable setting. The shared characteristics of lawyers and con artists are outlined at length in the novel; the goal of a lawyer, Flynn argues, is not to present the facts objectively but to convey a distorted impression of truth to the jury that best serves the needs of the prosecution or a client: "The skills and techniques that I'd developed and used as a successful con artist—distraction, misdirection, persuasion, suggestion, the load, the switch, the drop—I'd used these methods just as much on the street all those years ago as I had for the past nine years in the courtroom. I hadn't really changed. I'd just changed the con."[92]

Cavanagh suggests that this overlap of technique in the law and con artistry is not always a bad thing, offering a rendition of a popular anecdote about Clarence Darrow, the lawyer noted for defending John Scopes in the "Scopes Monkey Trial," by way of example. Darrow is regarded as something of an American intellectual and civil rights hero; apart from his defense of Scopes's decision to teach the theory of evolution in his classroom contrary to state law, he also used his position to argue vehemently against the death penalty and for the right of minorities to use self-defense when targeted for their race. In the anecdote, Darrow inserts a hat pin into the cigar he lights at the beginning of each trial in order to keep the ashes from falling; eventually, the jury becomes so fascinated with the length of the ashes that their attention is entirely distracted from the arguments of Darrow's opponent.[93] While this story is likely apocryphal, it is one of many such tales of Darrow's use of manipulation to win his cases; in some of these stories, it is even suggested that he bribed witnesses or jury members. From a postmodern perspective, Darrow's alleged undermining of the legal system he purported to support might be perceived more as a form of justified civil disobedience than as unprincipled illegal activity. When the law is unreasonable or inequitable, Cavanagh implies, subversion becomes an acceptable and even laudable tool in the pursuit of justice.

Ford's perception of similarities between Darrow's legal strategies and Flynn's carefully planned assaults on insurance companies are the basis of his conviction that Flynn can give up his life of crime and apply his talents to a career in the law. For Flynn, however, a major complication arises in that the obligations of this career actually constrain him from following his personal sense of ethics. If exacting revenge on exploitative institutions is a type of justice from Flynn's perspective, skewing evidence to enable clients to evade legal repercussions for their actions most certainly is not. Flynn remarks that he initially sought to avoid responsibility for this discomfiting aspect of his job by cloaking himself in feigned ignorance: "I never represented anyone I knew to be guilty because I never asked any of my clients if they were guilty. I never asked because there was always the terrible possibility that they might just tell you the truth. The truth has no place in a courtroom. The only thing that matters is what the prosecution can prove."[94]

Just as Fegan's abrupt awakening from his willful blindness about paramilitary procedure results in a murderous crusade in *Ghosts of*

Belfast, Flynn's self-loathing, stemming from his role in exonerating dangerous criminals, drives him to vigilante violence. Flynn recounts how his ability to find recourse in denial came to an end after he successfully defended a client, Ted Berkley, charged with the assault of a young woman, Hannah Tublowski, despite his gut feeling that Berkley was indeed culpable of the crime. Berkley later kidnapped, raped, and tortured Tublowski, leaving her permanently disfigured and disabled and thrusting Flynn into a cycle of guilt and alcoholism. "I would not make the same mistake again," he notes, adding that violent predators "had to be stopped or they would go on destroying lives." In this instance, Flynn did indeed stop the predator, with a compromise between vigilantism and the law: he called the police but made use of the time it took them to arrive to beat Berkley within an inch of his life.[95]

Cavanagh describes *The Defense* as a tale of redemption, noting that recurrent references to a Saint Christopher medal worn by Flynn are deliberately symbolic: "Saint Christopher is the patron saint of travellers and is often depicted carrying the child Christ across a river. Eddie is starting out on a long road to redemption in that first book, plus he is trying to save his child. Saint Christopher seemed to fit with the predicament he had in that book."[96] The twist to this redemption story, of course, is that Flynn's deliverance involves distancing himself from a strict adherence to legal standards in order to pursue a more complex notion of justice that includes both vigilantism and the employment of criminal alliances. In this sense, Saint Christopher serves much the same purpose for Flynn as Saint Anthony does for Bruen's Jack Taylor: he becomes an embodiment of Flynn's efforts to establish a comfortable ethical compromise between the law and alternate understandings of justice. The medal itself was a gift from Flynn's father—notably, the only property the senior Flynn carried with him when he emigrated from Ireland—reflecting the utility of Flynn's education in con artistry and subtly reinforcing the idea that an outsider's perspective is invaluable in assessing the shortcomings of a society's structural conventions.

As Flynn smuggles the bomb into the courthouse, security officers attribute the reaction of the metal detector to the Saint Christopher, depriving Flynn of the police intervention he might initially have hoped for and forcing him to resolve the crisis using his own hybrid—and ultimately more effective—methods. The weight of the medal reminds him of his father's priorities and steels him to do whatever is necessary, legal or not, to secure the safety of his daughter: "I knew what he [my father] would do. He would fight—he would do whatever it took to protect his family. This wasn't about revenge. It was about survival."[97] As he takes cautious steps to bring the multifarious aspects of his plan together—assisting one mob boss in averting a takeover by mutinous underlings, enlisting the help of another to locate and secure his daughter, sending a judge out for supplies for his sleights-of-hand, and attempting to persuade an FBI agent to serve as backup—Flynn is fortified by "the cold touch of his [father's] medal against [his] skin."[98]

When he first determines to take matters into his own hands with Volchek and his men instead of entrusting his circumstances to criminal justice officials, Flynn takes an emblematic leap. Escaping through the window of the court office where he is being held by the Russian mob, he scales the side of the building to seek out Ford. In order to do so, he must, with great difficulty, physically cross over the statue of Lady Justice on the outside of the courthouse. Flynn describes the statue in great detail, with particular attention to the sword and scales she wields, "balancing mercy with retribution just as she balances her hands." Even in the midst of such a precarious situation, Flynn takes a moment to reflect on the hypocrisy of this figure as a symbol of structural justice: "She is blindfolded to symbolize her indifference, her blindness, to race, color, or creed. *Yeah, right*."[99] The dismissal is not unlike Brennan's critique of the police system in Northern Ireland, where the severity of punishment is inversely proportional to the wealth and social status of an offender. Contextually, however, it proposes a different response to the shortcomings of legal justice: while Brennan largely rejects vigilantism, instead expressing hope for increased transparency and equity in police procedure, Cavanagh envisions boundaries between the law, vigilante justice, and criminality as decidedly less distinct. If Flynn's physical ability to traverse the statue allows him to secure assistance for himself and his daughter, his symbolic ability to cross over from one side—or form—of justice to another is imperative to the success of his plan, and to saving his daughter's life.

The Defense concludes with Flynn fully embracing who he is by nature: both a lawyer and a con artist. His "redemption" affords him the strength to visit Hannah Tublowski's house for the first time since she was attacked by Berkley. Flynn gives Tublowski close to a million dollars, which he managed to fleece from Volchek during the course of the trial, thus offering her a type of compensation and justice she has failed to receive from the courts. He describes his former adherence to legal standards and success in his profession as an abandonment of personal ethics, a temporary shortcoming he has now managed to put behind him: "I knew what I had done; I knew that I would never make that mistake again; I knew that there were bad people in this world and that as long as I played my part in the justice game and I remembered who I really was, those people wouldn't get a second chance to harm anyone else."[100]

Ultimately, then, Cavanagh's novel ends on a more positive note than either *Disorder* or *Ghosts of Belfast*, largely because it avoids scrutinizing the potential ramifications of subversion and vigilantism. Instead, Flynn's narrative suggests that paths to justice are fluid and that the capacity to balance contradictory positions with respect to the law is not necessarily a bad thing. For Cavanagh, the principal threat to justice is not criminality, but hypocrisy. Flynn's rejection of pretense to acknowledge his natural disposition places him in sharp contrast with Tommy Bridge, whose guilt about his own corruption and resistance to both forging a different path and facing repercussions for his past actions drive him to suicide. Flynn's evolution is also markedly different from that of Gerry Fegan, who shifts his sense of culpability onto others. When forced to confront the truth about the paramilitary crusade with which he was involved, Fegan launches a different crusade, reinventing his motivation as a need for retribution. In this way, he excuses himself for continuing to act on his violent impulses while hiding behind an—albeit untenable—mask of righteousness. In their attempts to rectify one injustice, Bridge and Fegan both become responsible for many more, largely because their dissimulation—their characterization of their purposes as paramount to all other considerations and of their methods as the only possible courses of action—leaves little room for critical thought, honest self-reflection, or growth. In this sense, these characters are almost impossible to differentiate from their hypocritical and loutish enemies. Flynn, on the other hand, is more distinguishable from the villainous characters in *The Defense*, overlapping with them only in terms of technique. This distinction is a result of his capacity for introspection, which allows him to recognize his mistakes and to change procedure multiple times in the quest for self-worth, moral tenacity, and a comfortable path to justice. While Cavanagh displaces the discussion to an American context, then, a perspective on the peace process in Northern Ireland might be inferred: one that suggests that the most problematic aspect of the process is not the early release clause of the Good Friday Agreement itself, but a lack of social acknowledgment and transparent discourse about the crimes of the past—both of which are essential to healing, progress, and, most important, an assurance that the bloody legacy of the Troubles is not, through denial, permitted to repeat itself.

6

The Stories We Tell

Eoin McNamee's Blue Trilogy

> "That's what people do. Tell stories when something like this
> happens." Their stories all they had to set against the dark.
> —Eoin McNamee, *Orchid Blue*

Clearly, an urgent need for honesty and transparency—whether in government, religious or social structures, understanding of self, or interpersonal relations—is a recurrent theme in Irish crime fiction, both north and south of the border. The increasing popularity of Irish true-crime stories might be viewed as an attempt to come to terms with the past, to interrogate comfortable narratives, and to confront some of the legal shortcomings and inequitable social standards that have led to both systemic injustice and, indeed, civil war. In theory, true crime appears better situated to address such issues than crime fiction, since it relies on historical evidence, rather than tropes, to piece together narratives about criminality, its roots, and responses of the legal justice system. In the Blue trilogy, however, Eoin McNamee confronts this assumption about true-crime stories, suggesting that what we perceive as historical evidence is in fact distorted by memory, perspective, and, most important, the way that perspective is colored by expectations established by fiction. *The Blue Tango* (2001), *Orchid Blue* (2010), and *Blue Is the Night* (2014) tackle three infamous and interrelated murder cases from the Newry and Belfast regions in Northern Ireland, scrutinizing the effects of class, social expectations, and political corruption on the process and outcome of these cases. At the same time, the blending of fact and fictionalized accounts of the major players in these cases underscores the limitations of historical research alone in reconstructing the past. McNamee's central thesis seems to be that, while examining history can help to promote discourse about the problematics of standardized justice, it also serves to reinforce the notion that transparency and honesty in such discourse are ultimately elusive constructs.

Blue Tango covers the 1952 murder of Patricia Curran, daughter of Northern Ireland High Court judge Lance Curran, for which a technician from the Royal Armed Forces, Iain Hay Gordon, was convicted. Deemed psychologically unsound, Gordon was spared the death penalty, committed to Holywell mental hospital, and released seven years later. Gordon maintained his innocence, asserting that his confession, the only substantial evidence against him, "was dictated by [Detective Chief Superintendent John] Capstick" and edited to sound like Gordon's own language; Capstick, Gordon claimed, made "changes like 'went' for 'proceeded' because it sounded less legalistic."[1] In 2000 the confession was deemed to have been coerced by Capstick and was declared inadmissible; Gordon's conviction was overturned. In his introduction to the novel, McNamee contends that, notwithstanding the assignation of blame to Capstick, the outcome of Gordon's original trial exposes a more systemic corruption and disregard for human life and dignity, in which both law enforcement officers and the community were willing participants: "It is a fake confession, a fiction couched in the mocking language of death; the death penalty was not to be abolished for another four years and the trial was to be carried out in the full knowledge of this. . . . Few of the words in the confession were ever spoken by Iain Hay Gordon but the true profanity of the text is that many of the participants in his trial were aware of this."[2]

The second novel of the trilogy, *Orchid Blue*, examines the 1961 trial and conviction of Robert McGladdery for the murder of Pearl Gamble. McGladdery was the last person to be executed in Northern Ireland, and while he was never legally exonerated like Gordon, McNamee strongly insinuates that he was also innocent, outlining parallels between the two cases, which both relied heavily on circumstantial evidence. Another link between the two trials is the involvement of Lance Curran, who was allowed to preside over the McGladdery case despite a clear conflict of interest: Gamble, like Curran's daughter, was nineteen when she was murdered; both young women were stabbed repeatedly, and neither was sexually assaulted. Curran's determination to work on the McGladdery case could easily be construed as a displaced effort to obtain justice for Patricia, since the man convicted of her murder was not hanged for the crime; ultimately, however, McNamee frames this scenario as the least onerous of many potential interpretations.

Each of these first two novels carefully delineates similarities between the victims and the accused, suggesting that they are casualties of corruption and social prejudices on a near-equal scale. In *Blue Tango*, both Patricia and Gordon are described as misfits because of their failure to conform to conventional gender roles. Patricia evokes the long-standing ire of her mother, Doris, by accepting a job as a truck driver—a move that Doris equates with a willful abandonment of femininity and grace: "There was something about her daughter at the wheel of a truck. The heavy, leather-covered steering wheel. The burnished chrome, smells of aftershave, diesel, cigarettes. Men with tattoos. Men wearing gold jewellery. A sense of grizzled maleness to the whole business, men's unpredictable and deathsome elations."[3] Patricia has a reputation for promiscuity, particularly with married men, placing her at odds with the chaste ideal of a young woman of her social status. Moreover, she frequents clubs with gay men, considers a dalliance with a lesbian model, and is forthright in her conviction that her brother, Desmond, is a closeted gay man. Gordon, for his part, also seems conflicted about his gender identity and sexuality: he is described as sensitive and effeminate, and his closest confidants are gay. The actual Gordon appears to have had bisexual tendencies; despite having relationships with women, he also experimented sexually with at least one young man, Wesley Courtenay.[4] Ultimately, Gordon's fear that these experiences might be exposed, in a society where homosexuality was viewed as both a mark of perversion and a criminal activity, seems to have been the impetus behind his concession to Capstick's forged confession.

Likewise, in *Orchid Blue*, Gamble and McGladdery are both fantasists whose understanding of the world is largely shaped by literary tropes. They share a drive for excitement, relevance, and accomplishment, imagining themselves as heroic characters from the fiction they obsessively absorb, despite the limitations imposed by their working-class backgrounds. Because of a distinctive combination of attractiveness, self-assurance, and naïveté, they are magnets for people of questionable ethics. Gamble's friend Ronnie Whitcroft is portrayed as jealous, selfish, and thoughtless about Gamble's safety, abandoning Gamble on the night of the murder for a liaison with her boyfriend. Similarly, Will Copeland is a young man with an obsessive and exploitative outlook on women, which McGladdery finds distasteful. We are told that Copeland once manipulated McGladdery into participating in an attempted burglary and disappeared when the police arrived, leaving McGladdery to face the consequences alone. During his trial, the historical McGladdery suggested that Copeland may have been responsible for Gamble's murder; although this suggestion is widely regarded as a desperate attempt to evade justice,[5] McNamee's incorporation of the burglary narrative frames it as a distinct possibility.

While the first two novels in the series focus on questionable convictions, *Blue Is the Night* looks at the unjust dismissal of charges in the 1949 case of Robert Taylor (also called "Robert the Painter"), a young Protestant man who was tried for the murder of a Catholic woman named Mary McGowan. The central narrative is a flashback of sorts, occurring before the murder of Patricia Curran that begins the trilogy; at this time, Lance Curran is still an attorney general with hopes of a judgeship and a career in politics. The actual Taylor case occurred at an especially politically charged time in the Duncairn Gardens district of Belfast, an area that comprised both Catholics and Protestants, where the unionist member of Parliament habitually resorted to tribalist propaganda in order to appeal to the sentiment of working-class Protestants and maintain his party's hold over the district. The election of February 1949 was particularly contentious, with politicians engaging in fearmongering tactics and using imagery associated with William of Orange in order to counter growing support in favor of a united Ireland: "During the election, the Prime Minister, Sir Basil Brooke, rousingly called on all loyalists to deal the new Anti-Partition movement a crushing blow: 'I ask you to cross the Boyne . . . with me as your leader, and to fight the same cause as King William fought for in days gone by.'"[6] Under other circumstances, the weight of evidence against Taylor would have been damning, but McNamee paints a vivid picture of a society in which justice must be sacrificed in order to maintain the peace; the execution of a Protestant for the murder of a Catholic would serve to further incite rioting in the region, so the trial is thrown and Taylor is exonerated. In this particular story line, Curran comes off as the sole seeker of truth in a corrupt and compliant system, refusing to capitulate to sectarian considerations and pursuing Taylor with the full force of the law. However, the novel also jumps forward in time to explore irregularities in the investigation of Patricia Curran's murder and back to consider Doris Curran's unconventional upbringing in the Broadmoor psychiatric institution, where her father worked as a superintendent. Cumulatively, these scenes insinuate that Doris—or someone else in the Curran family—may have killed Patricia and that the judge may have orchestrated a cover-up, suggesting that his devotion to justice does not apply to circumstances where it might become a liability to either his professional reputation or his family.

The central irony of the Blue trilogy is that, in order to correct inadequate or misguided narratives of these trials in public discourse, McNamee must piece together alternate, more comprehensive narratives, which are nonetheless subject to their own limitations. The novels frequently recall the same events and rehash the same pieces of evidence multiple times in order to incorporate various perspectives and interpretations, to demonstrate how these perspectives and interpretations evolve over time, and to reflect on the malleability of perception and the limited reliability of personal accounts. Taken together, however, the disparate points of view of the characters become pieces of a larger puzzle, which, while imperfect, offers a more complete and unbiased picture than any single perspective could provide.

The basic premise of the trilogy concerns the human compulsion to construct stories in order to make sense of complex or frightening situations. "They have to tell the whole thing because they're terrified," explains Eddie McCrink, a detective brought in from London to assist on the McGladdery case. Inevitably, people are "searching for the formula of words that would protect them. The telling. The incantation of story."[7] In the Newry murders, this incantation involves framing the crimes as aberrations: situations that generally happen in larger cities that have somehow managed to temporarily infect the local habitat. It also involves a personal distancing from those individuals directly affected by the murders: a searching for shortcomings in the victims that have made them more vulnerable than the rest of the populace and a reconceptualization of the accused as monstrous, inhuman, and deserving of whatever punishment they receive—even death—regardless of how their convictions are obtained.

McNamee views these embellishments of truth as similar in nature to fairy tales:[8] unimaginable horrors reconstructed as lessons in morality, incorporating stereotyped characters that provide convenient alternatives to the complex realities of human nature and relations. He observes that the trial photo of Iain Hay Gordon that most captured the public's imagination portrays Gordon in a defiant light, looking uncharacteristically cocky and intelligent, and remarks that photos of Robert McGladdery and Pearl Gamble offered less satisfaction: "In the photographs, McGladdery looked boyish and open. People were aggrieved about this. They thought that this should have belonged to a subtle monster. . . . Equally the public felt let down by the images that appeared of the murdered girl. Pearl Gamble's laughing face. . . . There was nothing ominous in it."[9] *Orchid Blue* envisions a public desperate to compensate for these perceived shortcomings, creating a persona for McGladdery as a crime fiction villain[10] or a folk demon, inventing wild tales about his violent sexual deviance and an imaginary dungeon in his house.[11] Ultimately, a single piece of evidence in the McGladdery case—a copy of Mickey Spillane's *The Long Wait*, punctured by a tool similar to the one that was used to kill Gamble—does more than provide circumstantial evidence of premeditation. By offering a fictional surrogate for the real McGladdery, the novel and its cover image allow the public to become more comfortable with his impending execution: "It appears that Robert's story, in the mind of the jury and of the public, had merged with that of the hunted couple on the cover, the faithless girl and the struggling man in a fix of their own making."[12]

McNamee concurrently uses and interrogates this struggle to reframe crime and corruption as manifestations of evil, emphasizing Patricia Curran's perception of a demonic presence in her family's house,[13] the view of jurors in the McGladdery case that "something beyond evil had slipped its bounds" to sport McGladdery's clothing and murder Gamble,[14] and the sensation of Harry Ferguson, Judge Curran's fixer, upon watching his client play cards: "In his childhood Ferguson had listened to stories of men who played games of chance with the devil, with their immortal soul for stake, and those stories came back to him. . . . He had an impression of the Judge locked in debate with an unseen adversary."[15] Indeed, McNamee sometimes makes comparable associations in his own narrative voice, describing an assault on Patricia and her friend prior to Patricia's murder as an act not committed by humans but by "a somber and occult will made manifest" in a forest "fecund with historic evil."[16] Similarly, he portrays the elusive Will Copeland as "a traveller in some infernal region"[17] and provides no counterpoint to Doris Curran's belief that "there were those without souls in whom the light of mercy did not shine."[18]

In this way, McNamee makes it clear that he understands the appeal of "storybook evil":[19] the temptation to attribute violence and criminality to diabolic forces, outside of the realm of human control. Just the same, he points out that the allure of stereotyped villains and victims and of clear and tidy plotlines is dangerous in that it can easily be exploited. Juries look to confident witnesses "to take control" and "to help them find a way through these shifting and allusive tales" in hopes of "the threads of the story being pulled together again, structure reasserting itself."[20] In the Taylor case, Curran exposes the possibility of false testimony by attacking the hollowness of language and syntax in the absence of proof;[21] in the McGladdery case, however, he spins his own web of deceit by insisting that he can be more impartial than other judges, who would feel bound by their loyalty to him to ensure that McGladdery hangs to compensate for Gordon's escape from execution.[22]

Moreover, the influence of fictional tropes prevents people from recognizing the threats that surround them. If murder victims are consigned to their fates by immoral behavior or Calvinist predestination, it follows that neither personal accountability nor improvements to the criminal justice system are necessary. However, if the photos of Gamble and the other victims do not exhibit the foreboding desired by the public, it is likely because, like everyone else, they did not anticipate that they were at risk. In an important way, then, both the victims and the accused in the Gordon and McGladdery cases become ensnared in perils as a result of preconceived notions about the way their stories should proceed and conclude—notions largely derived from fiction. They share the same ideas about clear plotlines and the inevitability that justice will prevail as the rest of the populace, but in their own narratives, they are the heroines or heroes who will invariably be saved or exonerated.

For this reason, Gordon and McGladdery are both driven to implicate themselves through a desire to feel significant, shortsightedly constructing important roles for themselves in the only remarkable circumstances they are likely to encounter in their lifetimes. Gordon puts himself on the radar of the cops, who are searching for a scapegoat, by contacting Patricia Curran's brother in an attempt to play up his inconsequential relationship with the family. Likewise, McGladdery is flattered that he has become a prime suspect and behaves suspiciously and arrogantly in order to maintain the interest of the police. Both men seem oblivious to the consequences they might face, trusting that the cases will conclude with the easy and absolute justice of traditional crime fiction. We are told that "Gordon was thinking of detectives he had seen in films. Blunt men in raincoats with a capacity for gruff individualism," and that he "had no conception of real policemen with their ability to elevate moral ambiguity to a guiding principle."[23] Similarly, McGladdery enters the witness box at his trial with misguided expectations: "It was a moment he'd read about a hundred times in crime novels. The innocent man faces down his accusers."[24] McGladdery is bewildered when he encounters resistance to his testimony, and he starts to understand that others have constructed a different narrative in which he is the bad guy, destined for retribution. So powerful is this second narrative that McGladdery himself is seduced by it, and the actual details of the night of the murder start to slip away from him: "Part of him wanted to admire the story that was emerging from the cross-examination, the jury being guided towards the old tales, the fireside tellings of the innocent and the guilty."[25]

McGladdery's perspective is one of several that shifts according to circumstances. His mother is willing to embrace his guilt as long as the community feels sorry for her, painting her as the long-suffering mother of a psychopath. Once the narrative turns against her, with speculation about the role of her son's upbringing in his violent behavior, she begins to empathize with him and to feel that he has been unjustly persecuted. Initially speculating that her son was adversely affected by time spent in London, a city that she associates with crime and depravity, she reframes this hypothesis to imagine that he would have been safer if he had stayed in London, rather than returning to a corrupt and unjust "town of decay."[26] But the most substantial modification of perception in the trilogy is seen in Detective Chief Superintendent Capstick, a purveyor of falsehoods in *Blue Tango*, who later comes to regret the outcome of the Gordon case and dedicates himself to genuinely investigating Patricia Curran's death. When Harry Ferguson approaches Capstick with suspicions that Gordon may have been scapegoated to protect the Curran family, he notes a remarkable change in the detective: "The outcome of the [original] investigation had been predetermined, Capstick's brief to redirect suspicion away from the Curran family. This was a different man. This was the archetypal detective, lone and hampered."[27]

There is, of course, some irony in Ferguson's assessment. Since Capstick was summoned to replace the politically uncooperative Inspector McConnell in the original Gordon investigation, it is unsurprising that, in turn, he and Ferguson find themselves restrained in their research by powerful governmental forces. Thus, the role of the "archetypal detective" becomes particularly crucial in the trilogy, precisely because it is a role that is impossible to fulfill. The absence of an effectual investigator, capable of advancing the cause of justice, creates a chasm between the actions and expectations of the public and the way in which the trials actually proceed. In *Orchid Blue*, McCrink obsessively bemoans his inability to obtain the evidence he requires to solve the McGladdery case, reflecting that every witness he interrogates is "at the centre of their own tale, subject to encroaching fictions . . . skulking, untrustworthy."[28] Moreover, he believes that the townspeople and the local police officers are actively withholding information from him, both because he is an outsider whom they feel is encroaching on their "interior dialogue"[29] and because they have preconceived notions about the way the case should play out—notions that would be unlikely to withstand a thorough and objective examination of the facts. As he attempts to make sense of the disparate tellings and gaps in the story of the night of Gamble's murder, "knowing he wasn't getting the full truth. Knowing that wasn't the way the town worked. The story had to be pieced together, dredged out of the alluvial mud and silt,"[30] McCrink falls victim to the influence of yet another interpretation: his own. His attempts to understand the actions of Gamble's killer are affected by his own experiences,[31] and he finds himself concocting an alternate story about McGladdery's behavior on the night of the murder.[32]

McNamee employs McCrink and other truth seekers in the novels as authorial surrogates, using their investigations to provide insights into his own procedure of researching and assessing the cases. Alongside discussions of the steps taken by McConnell, McCrink, and eventually Ferguson and Capstick, McNamee describes the process through which he examines case files, media reports, and other archival evidence, seemingly instructing his readers about methods they, in turn, might use to gain a better understanding of the past.

Like the trilogy's investigators, McNamee clearly feels the lure of fictional tropes and personal interpretation. He erases the third Curran sibling, Michael, from his account of the family, presumably because Michael was away at the time of Patricia's murder and possibly because he did not share the idiosyncrasies of his family members. The outspoken, gender-nonconforming, and ultimately doomed Patricia; the powerful, corrupt, and enigmatic Lance; the institutionalized Doris; and the fanatically religious Desmond—who, after the murder of his sister, abandoned his Protestant upbringing to become a Catholic priest, battling apartheid in South Africa—all contribute to the impression of a family plagued by its own dark secrets, an apposite basis for an atmospheric noir. Similarly, McNamee shares Ferguson's tendency to envision detectives in search of justice as the clichéd characters of crime fiction; he describes McConnell's growing agitation about the Gordon case as appropriate to the progress of an anticipated plotline: "There was a recognizable choreography involving the detective in charge of an unsolved murder. . . . The neglect of family and personal appearance . . . mood swings, morose solitary drinking . . . [s]piritual doubts. . . . It was part of a progression of failure and they [his colleagues] felt that McConnell had been dependable in his observance of it and they could comfortably await the next stage. An assault on a junior colleague. A transparent and doomed attempt to manipulate evidence or suborn a witness."[33]

This reliance on narrative standards is highly deliberate. McNamee repeatedly emphasizes to his readers that no amount of research can uncover the whole truth when it has been obscured by both calculated concealment and the deficiencies of memory and perspective. He describes poring over photographs of Patricia Curran, looking for clues in the full knowledge that "her memory remains devoid of hope of retribution or indemnity. The narrator's voice falls away into conjecture. Her slaughter has been told but not the motive for it, and the face of her killer remains hidden. The narrator's voice falls away into hypothesis and surmise."[34] Even in the more straightforward Taylor case, in which the guilt of the accused and the reason he was acquitted are easily discernible, McNamee suggests that a clear understanding of the events of the day of the murder and the motives for Taylor's excessive brutality—Mrs. McGowan was strangled, stabbed, beaten, and burned—is impossible to achieve: "No matter how often it is presented, the witnessed day comes to you in fragments, drummed out in policeman's argot, legalities, coroner's reports, the talk of neighbours, the day's deep pathologies left in the details."[35]

McNamee's assertions about the elusiveness of factual specifics do not constitute a resignation to the impracticability of truth seeking; rather, as is common in noir fiction, they lead readers to the conclusion that the most significant truths are situated less in these specifics than in more holistic considerations of the societies in which crime and injustice occur. As author Laura Lippman notes in a contribution to *Vulture*, the utility of true-crime stories—as opposed to traditional crime fiction—does not lie in the pacification of an audience through the construction of comfortable and complete narratives; instead, true crime offers an alternative approach to confronting fear—one that acknowledges the social, legal, and political sources of criminality and corruption in an attempt to better understand and address them: "A violent crime lays bare things that a community is trying to hide: Race, class, sexism, income inequality. . . . Crime fiction has long been . . . made up of stories in which a dogged investigator . . . makes the world safe again. But what if the world's not worth putting back together? At a time when it's increasingly difficult to feel safe anywhere—public spaces, workplaces, our own homes—a mystery story based on true events can be a gentle and respectful way to examine our culture's pathologies."[36]

Fittingly, then, while the cases of Gordon, McGladdery, and Taylor provide plotlines for the Blue trilogy, one has the impression that McNamee is more intent on unearthing the story of a region brought to the brink of civil war by political maneuvering, obfuscation, and bigotry. This sentiment is most plainly expressed through the investigative process in *Orchid Blue*, as McCrink and the other detectives examine letters by anonymous authors purporting to have information about the McGladdery case. Filled with fearful references to homosexuality and to religious and supernatural forces, the letters are nevertheless deemed worthy of study because they contain valuable information about the society in which the murder and subsequent inquiry take place, reminding the investigators "that there were other contexts to their investigation. It was felt that the detectives needed access to the psychic undertow of the town."[37] Indeed, the trilogy's summoning of the "psychic undertow" of pre-Troubles Northern Ireland, replete with misogyny, homophobia, xenophobia, and sectarianism, provides both a frame of reference for the individual cases and an exposition for the climactic outbreak of violence that is to follow. The specter of the Troubles looms large in the trilogy, providing the sense of foreboding that is missing from the photos of the murder victims.

It is perhaps not an accident that all of the cases McNamee chooses to examine involve female victims who were subject to superfluous violence: in addition to the excesses of the attack on Mrs. McGowan, Patricia Curran was stabbed thirty-seven times, and Pearl Gamble was beaten, stabbed, and strangled. Through these three murders and the public reaction to them, McNamee reflects on the historic abuse and oppression of women in Northern Irish society. Particularly telling is the refrain, in the cases of both of the young women, that the murders were somehow less onerous because the victims had not been sexually assaulted. A clear picture emerges of prioritizations of concern in a society that seemingly values women's chastity more than their lives.

Not surprisingly, the efforts of the public to come to terms with these killings involve characterizing Patricia Curran and Pearl Gamble as loose women, whose fates were sealed through their immoral behavior. The women of Newry frame Patricia as "a menace to the married man, a slut, a bad end waiting to happen"[38]; the men consider that "she might be better off as a victim of murder," since her death "rescued her femininity" in the face of her masculine will-fulness and purported promiscuity;[39] children are encouraged to view her as the lapsed heroine of a fairy tale: "a fabled figure . . . subject to a dark enchantment. The drugged apple. The poisoned needle. They understood from what they heard from adults that it was something she had brought upon herself, that she had somehow transgressed and wandered off the path."[40] Even Patricia's own family and the detectives assigned to her case are inclined to view her in this negative light: her brother Desmond regards her as a sinner with "blemishes that would be removed by no earthly ablution";[41] her mother refuses to accept a psychologist's assessment that her daughter's sexual curiosity is healthy, seeking a second opinion from a minister, who suggests that Patricia is possessed.[42] Capstick, too, condescendingly describes Patricia in terms of her sexual appetite and lack of control: a fact that is particularly noteworthy considering the inspector's own propensity for seducing and exploiting the wives of his colleagues. Ironically, Gordon is the only principal character who seems capable of acknowledging that Patricia was a normal, spirited, and kindhearted young woman, rather than "the lascivious figure that she had become, the gaunt and sex-haunted woman that had been created through the press."[43] Witnessing a trial in which a man is given a shockingly light sentence for assaulting his adulterous wife, while the wife is shamed for her infidelity, Gordon immediately recognizes a parallel with the public treatment of Patricia.[44]

Nor does chastity serve to safeguard a woman's security or reputation. While there is no evidence to suggest that Pearl Gamble was sexually active or even incautious with men, the general consensus is that she must have flirted with McGladdery and then refused his advances. She is thus construed as responsible for her own death by misleading her attacker and failing to submit to his desires. As he pursues his investigation into Gamble's death, McCrink discovers that single women—even the ones who conduct themselves according to social norms—are inevitably viewed with suspicion; after a certain age, they are regarded as spinsters, incapable of securing the love or attention of a man.[45]

The obsessive impulse to control standards of gender and sexuality belied by the treatment of women translates into homophobia as well. McNamee notes that the fear of homosexuality in the North was so extreme that "there were calls for the civil service to be vetted. In internal documents, police talked about the possibility of blackmail. People were alert for well-dressed men behaving with studied casualness in public parks."[46] The presumption that gay men can be identified by certain defining characteristics leads to calculated persecution; taken to its extremes, it enables Capstick to delineate Gordon as a gay man based solely on his appearance in a photograph,[47] and to thereby contrive a means of extorting his confession.

The public fear of otherness is frequently exploited in pursuit of a legal or political agenda in the trilogy. McNamee describes the local populace as a bigoted lynch mob, intent on reasserting control in the face of danger by scapegoating outsiders; this prejudice applies to immigrants, people of color, and anyone else perceived as nonhomogenous as easily as to homosexual men: "It was something that all itinerant workers, gypsies, migrant workers had to attune themselves to. The fear of persecution, the need to carry blame when harvests failed and daughters of marriageable age fell prey to a sudden inexplicable restlessness. . . . Townsfolk turning fearful and dangerous, seeking safety in numbers. You became aware of an angry murmuring, a torchlit mob in the middle distance."[48] In *Blue Tango*, Capstick limits his suspect pool to people with mental disabilities, gay men, and foreigners, in the knowledge that accusations against any such people will be unlikely to come under scrutiny. He eventually focuses on gay men exclusively because foreigners inevitably require interpreters, providing witnesses that impose restrictions on his coercive tactics.[49] This is something of a disappointment to others involved in the investigation, however, since pinning the crime on a Polish immigrant in particular would have allowed them to draw on xenophobic tendencies and fuel the flames of sectarianism at the same time. Sir Richard Pim, inspector general of the RUC, consents to abandon the quest for a Polish scapegoat with some regret, asserting that, since immigrants from Poland are "in the main Roman Catholics," there is some concern "that large numbers of Polish men settling in the Province might upset delicate balances."[50] For Pim, deflecting attention from the Curran family's possible involvement in Patricia's murder is not enough; he would prefer to use the case to strengthen the Protestant political stronghold in the region.

Although neither of the crimes is ultimately pinned on a Catholic, then, anti-Catholic sentiment informs both media and investigative discourse in the cases of Patricia Curran and Pearl Gamble. The press is inclined to blame the IRA for Patricia's murder, although there is nothing to suggest such involvement,[51] while McCrink understands that his handlers at Stormont would like to find a way to use the Gamble case to stoke sectarian sentiment, noting that they are "hoping the killer was a Catholic. The miscreant underclass sunk in the perversion of their faith."[52] Again, incriminating a Catholic proves impossible, since Gamble was attending a dance in an Orange hall on the night of her murder, but these moments in the texts offer insight into the political benefits of tribalism and suggest the possibility of other cases—perhaps many other cases—in which Catholic suspects may have been framed for crimes they did not commit.

By the same token, the outcome of the Taylor case makes it clear that these social and legal inequities also apply to situations in which Catholics are the victims of crime. One of the jurors in Taylor's trial asserts that, while "a child could see that Taylor killed the woman [Mrs. McGowan]," he is willing to work against a conviction because, as far as he is concerned, "Taylor done us all a favour. One less [Catholic] to reckon with."[53] As an older, married woman who maintains an immaculate household and has never been the subject of scandal or gossip, Mrs. McGowan is immune to the sort of sexual defamation directed at Patricia and Pearl after their deaths. Instead, during Taylor's trial, her reputation for chastity and religiosity is turned against her; when the defense lawyer emphasizes that she was "a generous large-hearted type of woman and a good devout practising Catholic," Ferguson notes that the aim is not "to make them [the jury] sympathise. The opposite. He was reminding them that she was a Fenian."[54] In order to emphasize his point to readers outside of Ireland, McNamee draws a clear parallel between the treatment of Catholics by the legal system in the North and systemic racism in America, offering a flashback to the arrest of a Black American soldier in Northern Ireland, who contends that he will not get a fair trial because the inequity of structural justice is the "same as the place I came from. Exact same." When explaining why Taylor will not be held accountable for his crime, Ferguson remarks that, in some parts of America, the murder of a Black person by a white person is considered a misdemeanor,[55] insinuating that, while such discriminatory practices are not on the books in the North, public pressure ensures that a Protestant responsible for killing a Catholic will be entitled to similar leniency.

Like sectarianism in the work of Adrian McKinty, Gerard Brennan, and Stuart Neville, in all of its incarnations in the Blue trilogy, bigotry is depicted as a tool that can be used to manipulate and distract the public in order to advance and mask corruption. While Brian Cliff describes corruption as the "signal crime" of Irish crime fiction,[56] author Niamh O'Connor notes that people are also particularly intrigued by true crime "that shows the gap between justice and the law, and makes the blood of middle Ireland boil." By way of example, she examines responses to the victim impact statement given by Majella Holohan, the mother of an eleven-year-old boy who was murdered by a neighbor in County Cork in 2005. Holohan made it clear that she was dissatisfied by the process of the trial and the emphasis on her son's ADHD and dyslexia, which, like the supposed promiscuity and flirtatiousness of Patricia Curran and Pearl Gamble, respectively, were interpreted as driving forces behind her son's murder: "The fact that trashing the victim's reputation is what is required in criminal law when proving provocation was cold comfort to her. . . . Having corrected the record as to who her son was, she listed the questions raised, not solved, by the criminal justice system. . . . She was accused of subverting the trial process. She was pilloried by the lawyers. How dare she criticise the system? So hers became a story of a mother against the system. David and Goliath."[57] The Blue trilogy might be read as a series of such David-and-Goliath tales, with the caveat that adversaries of the system in some circum-stances are enablers of it in others. This formula takes a step beyond the black-and-white posturing of individual ethics in opposition to systemic injustice to demonstrate how the former ultimately also contributes to the latter.

While certain themes—police and lawyers creating statements for witnesses, coerced confessions, and political motives—span the course of the three books, each examines corruption in the legal sys-tem from a different angle, offering a glimpse at the many and varied factors that combine to engender it. In *Blue Tango*, the goal of the deception is to protect the power and reputation of an individual, Lance Curran. Procedure is disrupted as the police neglect to search the Currans's house for more than a week following Patricia's murder and base their investigation on the timeline established by the Cur-rans. Likewise, evidence that contradicts the Currans's story about the night of the murder is systemically discounted. The positioning of Patricia's body and the lack of blood at the scene suggest that her body has been moved; her books and cap, discovered the day after the murder, are dry, indicating that they were added to the scene fol-lowing the rain of the night before; the judge himself appears to have placed a call to Patricia's friend inquiring after her whereabouts sub-sequent to the time he claimed to have discovered her body. Because he is vigilant in noting these discrepancies, McConnell is replaced by Capstick as lead investigator on the case, and the phone records that support his suspicions about the Curran family are made to dis-appear. In turn, Capstick is ordered to ignore his own misgivings about the Currans, and Ferguson, who also expresses doubts about the investigation, is blackmailed into silence.

In *Orchid Blue*, the McGladdery trial is portrayed as a means of maintaining public support for capital punishment in Northern Ireland. Already banned in England, the death penalty remained intact in the North as a means of discouraging and responding to IRA activity. To counter growing concern about the ethics of capital punishment, McNamee suggests, the pressure to put forth a criminal worthy of a death sentence was high. Viewed from this perspective,

McGladdery is an ideal culprit because his arrogance and previous run-ins with the law make him appear remorseless and irredeemable. Similarly, Curran is allowed to preside over the trial not in spite of the obvious conflict of interest, but because of it: if he was not complicit in the murder of his daughter, he will get retribution for Gordon's release by ensuring that McGladdery hangs; if he was complicit, he will follow the same course in order to keep up appearances. Either way, the notoriety of the case will override concern about Curran's eccentric family in his bid for Privy Council; with Curran on the bench, then, "McGladdery's well and truly fucked whether he done it or not."[58] Indeed, McGladdery's fate is sealed in part by Curran— who shuts down all possible avenues of appeal and delivers a charge to the jury that undermines the case of the defense[59]—and in part by the commutation of sentencing in another capital case, which makes McGladdery the only viable poster boy for the cause.

While *Blue Tango* offers an instance of an outsider brought in to obey orders rejected by a local detective, *Orchid Blue* follows an inverse scenario, suggesting that outside intervention is a tool, rather than a root cause, of corruption. McCrink, who was raised in Belfast and worked in London, is able to look at the McGladdery case objectively; alarmed by the intimidating and coercive tactics of local authorities, he is repeatedly informed that the town will pursue its own path to justice, regardless of his efforts to uncover the truth, because "that's the way it is around here."[60] When McCrink turns his attention to the case of Patricia Curran, unearthing the same phone records collected by McConnell, he is likewise prohibited from pursuing the lead. Thus, the possibility exists that the McGladdery trial involves "a guilty man hanging an innocent man,"[61] the implications of which are ironically underscored in a statement by the judge himself: "To equate law with equity is a mistake. Justice is a by-product of our system of law, not an end."[62]

While the treatment of the Taylor case certainly supports Curran's conclusions about the distance between law and equity, the corruption in *Blue Is the Night* is of a decidedly partisan nature.

The conviction of a Protestant for the murder of a Catholic would undermine unionist power; foreshadowing the eventual prominence of paramilitary groups over the government during the Troubles, legal officials are also willing to capitulate to sectarian pressure to prevent increased rioting in the region. We again see Pim in the role of puppeteer, allowing the mob to pursue Curran in order to teach him a lesson for arguing the case fairly.[63] Pim is supported by Ellis Harvey, the election officer for the city ward, who instructs Ferguson to talk sense into Curran, indicating that he recognizes that civil war is coming and wishes to stave it off for as long as possible by placating militant Protestants.[64] Convincing himself that he is doing Curran a favor by preventing him from destroying his career, Ferguson tampers with the jury, insisting that it is better for them to "leave justice to God. He's got plenty to go around. It's in short supply in this town."[65] The message is clear: what little justice is available for distribution in Northern Ireland should not be squandered on Catholics—and particularly not at the expense of keeping the peace.

There is a singular irony to the fact that, since the charges against Taylor are dismissed, the grave that has been dug for him is eventually used for McGladdery instead: having already established that McGladdery might have been an innocent man sentenced to death by a judge who was complicit in his own daughter's murder, McNamee further suggests that the same innocent man may have been buried in a murderer's grave after the same judge, in his role as prosecuting attorney, failed to convict that murderer. However, McNamee does not pretend to have an easy solution to this tangled web of injustice; on the contrary, it is noteworthy that, concerning the one case in which Curran prioritizes fairness and impartiality over potentially negative consequences,[66] McNamee theorizes that his actions may have helped to set the stage for the two other cases and the injustices that accompany them. The book concludes with a flash-forward to 1963, when Ferguson receives a call from Taylor, who claims to have murdered Patricia in an act of vengeance against her father. Certainly, this theory is one of many hypotheses about Patricia's death that is raised in the trilogy—Doris Curran, in particular, is examined at length as a viable culprit—but its situation at the end of the trilogy gives it a special significance.

In an article for the *Irish Times*, Brian Cliff emphasizes a "profound uncertainty" in Irish crime fiction that sometimes "takes the form of unanswered questions," adding that "such uncertainty is not a temporary problem to be resolved by the novel's end, but something rather more fundamental through which Irish crime fiction can reflect the experience of unresolved lives."[67] McNamee's true-crime trilogy adheres to this pattern, concluding on a note that not only underscores the impossibility of getting to the bottom of what happened in the three central cases, but also implies that the pursuit of truth and justice in general is ultimately quixotic. Taylor's call to Ferguson in the final pages of *Blue Is the Night* casts doubt on a fundamental premise of the series—the Curran family's involvement in Patricia's murder—and introduces a new and unsettling question: If Taylor is in fact Patricia's killer, is her death attributable to the corruption of the legal system that exonerated him or to Curran's attempt to subvert it?

As a true-crime researcher and writer, McNamee obviously understands the essentially human drive to uncover the truth by reconstructing the past better than most. However, in "The Judge," an article about the enigmatic Curran family and his process in writing the Blue trilogy, he betrays a certain fascination with the conflicting stories and gossip he encounters, hinting at the seductive powers of noirish, unsolvable mysteries. Such mysteries, he implies, present avenues for reflection on history, social inequities and injustice, and the appeal of narratives to impose a sense of order on chaotic surroundings. For McNamee, although these narratives may obscure certain facts, they also have the potential to bring significant truths to light. Like the peculiar anonymous letters received by McCrink and his team as they investigate the McGladdery case, stories can provide critical information about the society in which they are created—its fears, its biases, and the contributions its citizens can make to further discourse about justice. While he remarks that, in Ireland, narratives about crime in particular frequently depart from the standards of noir fiction to take on elements of folklore, McNamee also hints that mythologizing crime stories is not inappropriate, since extensive examination of real-life perpetrators of torture or murder inevitably challenges secular doubts about "the existence of pure evil."[68] More broadly, McNamee's work suggests that narratives about crime can tell us much about human experiences of justice and inequity: the treatment of bigotry, colonialism, and political maneuvering in the trilogy includes frequent references to the ubiquitous nature of these phenomena.

Similarly, the noir hero in crime fiction is a valuable reflection of the human condition and, in particular, of the individual's relationship with social protocols and structural justice. McNamee highlights the Curran family's unusual crossing of sectarian boundaries—apart from Desmond's conversion to Catholicism, it has been speculated that Lance Curran was the product of a mixed Protestant and Catholic background[69]—in order to underscore their subversion of established norms. If Lance was indeed the child of interfaith parents, he "would have been seen as going against nature, the natural God-given order of things. Defying, in the great sin of noir, [his] pre-ordained fate,"[70] providing context for his resistance against the institutionalized prejudice and corruption that highjacked the investigation and trial of Robert Taylor.

Like Adrian McKinty's Sean Duffy, who equates his struggles for fairness and equity with "sticking up a middle finger to the darkness closing in,"[71] McNamee stresses that, though the accomplishment of justice is often unlikely or impossible, its pursuit is an end game in itself: one that promotes dignity and hope and encourages us to be better—or, at the very least, to remember that we should be. By accepting that "the universe. . . . is weighted against you. There is a hand on the scales,"[72] the noir hero prioritizes human agency above anticipated outcomes, suggesting that our drive toward justice and truth allows us to retain our individualism and humanity in overwhelming circumstances. In this sense, McNamee appears to reflect not only on the heroes of the trilogy—McCrink, McConnell,

Ferguson, and even Curran—but also on his own role as a researcher and writer of true crime. The knowledge that we will never arrive at clear and factual narratives about historical crimes and injustice, McNamee implies, does not absolve us of the responsibility to try.

Of course, Curran adheres to this prescription only in *Blue Is the Night*; by abandoning his principles after the Taylor case, he not only ceases to be heroic in any sense of the word, but actually becomes part of the problem of systemic injustice: "If the heroes of noir know that their fate is sealed but turn and shake a fist it at [*sic*] in the name of humanity," McNamee remarks, "then the villains are guilty of the negative. Like Judge Curran they become the agent of fate."[73] Curran's shifting personae emphasize the innate malleability and unreliability of human perception; like the distorted witness accounts in the three cases examined in the trilogy, they underscore the way in which personal perspective and the inevitable construction of narratives that conform to it engender inequity and pervert the course of justice. Just the same, by using speculation and deduction to contribute to the case narratives himself, McNamee ultimately concedes that, whatever their shortcomings, stories might be all we have to prevent ourselves from despairing at the chaos of the universe and our powerlessness in the face of systemic corruption: "In this faithless city," he concludes, "the story [is] all."[74]

Conclusion

In the introduction to this text, I noted my decision to conclude with Eoin McNamee's Blue trilogy, owing to its emphasis on the cognitive and emotional significance of stories, and especially stories about crime and justice. McNamee's suggestion that "the story is all" says much about the weight of language and narrative in our understanding of history, politics, and social interactions. McNamee's own narratives evade classification: part true crime, part fiction, part reflection on the processes of research and writing, they offer a hybrid of perspectives. The thoughts and voices of historical persons, woven together from documents and imagination, zoom out to a kind of Faulknerian communal perspective and zoom in again to consider the writer's self-consciousness about his own subjectivity.

While McNamee's trilogy utilizes metatextuality to draw attention to perspective as a construct, all of the writers in this study make use of a similar process of magnification and panorama. Their narratives reflect the perspectives of individual characters, situate the characters' experiences in a broader cultural context, and hint at more ubiquitous applications and interpretations of social, personal, and political conflicts. At times, as in McNamee's work, we get something of a live authorial voice, emphasizing that the work is also the product of a singular perspective: Ken Bruen's characters make references to his life and critics; John Connolly includes an introduction addressing his incorporation of the supernatural; Adrian McKinty offers a first-person authorial interjection; Claire McGowan uses fictional excerpts of journal articles, supposedly written by one of her characters, to comment on the peace process in Northern Ireland.

Obviously, fiction by nature uses the personal to engage readers' empathy in situations that are unfamiliar to them, but in these
works, the fluidity of perspective, coupled with the undermining of
genre tropes, also calls attention to the fluidity of subjectivity, the
randomness of socially assigned identity, and the reductiveness of
attempts to categorize people and their stories. The zoom-in-zoom-
out effect enables readers to interpret the works as both situated in
and transcendent of a particular time and place. On the one hand,
most of the novels are set in Ireland, and even in the cases of the two
that are not—John Connolly's *Every Dead Thing* and Steve Cavanagh's *The Defense*—the authors are clear about the ways in which
their specifically Irish background and experiences inform their writing. On the other hand, all of the authors take pains to demonstrate
how these specific experiences are reflective of more global social
and political patterns. In this way, they suggest that their concerns
are equally applicable *outside* of Ireland.

In Connolly and Cavanagh, this applicability is demonstrated by
situating these concerns in an American context. Alex Barclay uses
an inverse strategy in *Darkhouse*, exploring the links between disenfranchisement and criminality in the United States and using this examination to reflect on the rise of violent crime in Ireland. However,
this pattern is equally evident in works with uniquely Irish settings,
where it ranges in scope from the specific to the comprehensive: Mc-
Namee compares the civil rights inequities of pre-Troubles Northern Ireland with systemic racism in the United States; McKinty asks
readers to consider that the conditions that gave rise to the Troubles
also exist on a global scale; McGilloway takes McKinty's suggestion
a step further, conflating Northern Ireland's sectarian history with
both the prejudices of individuals and other types of tribalist social
attitudes, such as racism and nationalist anti-immigration ideologies.
More generally, the novels in this study address issues common to
crime fiction—corruption, institutional shortcomings, and imperfect
justice—whose precise manifestations in Ireland are also vehicles for
exploring them as ubiquitous problematics. The authors thus make
a case for the value of Irish perspectives in global discourses about

justice, while reminding readers that each of these perspectives is uniquely informed by individual experiences.

This case for the unique contribution of Irish voices is reinforced not only through the subversion of genre tropes and the use of shifting perspective, but also through the interrogation of terms central to crime fiction and to both fiction and discourse about justice more broadly. While stressing the importance of narratives, the authors challenge the very definitions of words we use in constructing these narratives, examining how these definitions might be reductive and might vary depending on point of view. Further, they explore the ways in which our reliance on terms while failing to flesh out their meaning and substance leads to a complex web of interdependent ambiguities: signifiers that are used to inform and define each other, without ever fully defining themselves.

In "Walking the Tightrope: The Border in Irish Fiction," Brian McGilloway compellingly conflates disparate literal and allegorical interpretations of the border in works by Irish authors with ambiguity surrounding the terms "border" and "borderlands." A "border," McGilloway suggests, is a place where distinctions and dichotomies are both emphasized and undermined. "Borderlands" are areas of overlap between multifarious definitions, perspectives, cultures, and identities:

> It is perhaps this idea of a tightrope which best symbolises the border: walking between counties, countries, traditions, religions, police forces, political allegiances. For [Shane] Connaughton, the border is adolescence; the area between youth and adulthood, a time of rebellion. For [Colm] Tóibín, it represents bad blood, with the requisite letting of that blood on both sides; for [Spike] Milligan it is the absurdity of the personal and the political; for [Vincent] Woods' [sic] the repetitive rituals of violence that allow no prospect for progress or peace; for [Eugene] McCabe the secretive nature of relationships and the inability to trust even those closest to you.
>
> None of these ideas would be out of place in any work of crime fiction.[1]

It might be this sophisticated understanding of borderlands, developed through decades of reckoning with the enormous shadow of Ireland's border and correspondingly enormous discrepancies in its meaning for different people, that enables Irish authors to appreciate the complexity and nuance of terms that are generally taken for granted. In this study, I have explored some of the ways that Irish crime writers interrogate three of these terms—"justice," "faith," and "identity"—in particular. Specifically, I have examined their unique approaches to common themes in crime fiction, which address problematics of these themes partially in terms of the fluidity of terminology and the relationship of this fluidity to socially codified identity. Additionally, I have considered new questions the authors raise about justice, faith, and identity, which are specifically informed by their Irish perspectives.

Ambiguity about the meaning of "justice" has always played a central role in crime fiction. Early amateur detective stories shone a light on shortcomings of criminal justice—embodied by police who failed to solve crimes without the assistance of uniquely talented private citizens—while hard-boiled authors went a step further, suggesting that the legal justice system was mired in corruption and possibly irrevocably broken. The code of the hard-boiled detective, outlined by Raymond Chandler in "The Simple Art of Murder," amounts to a parallel definition of justice, as much as a parallel method of pursuing it, in that it is rooted in a system of ethics that is unconstrained by organizational standards and is implicitly posited as superior to the legal system.

The authors in this study respond to hard-boiled tropes by unpacking the complications of this assumption, underscoring that adherence to individual—as opposed to collective—decisions about what constitutes justice is a type of vigilantism and that vigilantism necessarily blurs the boundaries between justice and criminality. Bruen, in particular, emphasizes that the line between the detective's code and sociopathic, self-serving behavior is largely a matter of perspective. His very hard-boiled investigator, Jack Taylor, is self-loathing precisely because he understands that the violence and rule breaking he employs in the pursuit of justice, while sometimes allowing him to operate more efficiently than the police, also give him much in common with the very criminals who provoke his drive for justice in the first place. Taylor's nemeses include people who present or self-identify as vigilante justice seekers themselves. *In the Galway Silence* (2018), for example, pits Taylor against a killer who begins as a vigilante, but whose need to cover his tracks leads him to murder innocents and, ultimately, to embrace murder as a kind of sport. In this way, Bruen portrays individual justice as a slippery slope to criminality, even while acknowledging his protagonist's reliance on it.

For authors from the North, concerns about vigilantism are more than speculation. While it would be reductive to frame their discussions of vigilante justice as mere allegory, the shadow of the Troubles is always present, a reminder of what can happen when individuals, buoyed by the shortcomings of a legal justice system, attempt to nullify that system without popular consensus. In these novels, vigilantism is often viewed as a dangerous tool that, in its efforts to subvert ineffective or corrupt institutions, might ironically open the door to other unethical and exploitative systems of governance.

Ultimately, many of the authors in this study arrive, to varying degrees, at the conclusion that "justice" is by nature elusive owing to our inability to collectively agree on what "justice" entails—or, indeed, to fully acknowledge and address this disagreement. The problematic nature of vigilantism does nothing to make corrupt or discriminatory legal institutions more palatable as alternatives, and even when the law works with full transparency, limited considerations of context ensure that justice is also inevitably limited. The idea that a greater good might sometimes be achieved by not applying penalties mandated by the law is also not new to crime fiction—indeed, it is the cornerstone of seminal works such as Agatha Christie's *Murder on the Orient Express*. In Irish crime fiction, however, this question of context is explored not only as it applies to exceptional circumstances, such as the early release clause of the Good Friday Agreement, but also more broadly: Gerard Brennan,

Alex Barclay, and Tana French, for example, examine at length the role that poverty and systemic failures play in creating a prison pipeline. Though all stop short of implying that such circumstances entirely negate criminal responsibility, their work underscores an added layer of complexity in the pursuit of justice.

Perhaps surprisingly, then, justice is rarely conceived as completely unattainable in these works. On the one hand, the hero disgruntled by the illusory nature of justice—a standard noir trope—is central to many of the texts in this study; on the other, these heroes are inevitably driven to continue their efforts by the force of personal faith. While Irish crime fiction posits "justice" as obfuscated by heterogeneous definitions, it suggests that, by contrast, "faith" is too often reductively defined in terms of religion. Although religious faith does play a role in all of the works in this study, the notion of *goodness* that transcends visible and measurable effects—commonly associated with religion—is also more broadly applied to political, social, and personal issues. Such faith in the unseen is evidenced, for example, in the conviction that the suspension of immediate justice associated with the early release clause of the Good Friday Agreement will further peace and justice for future generations. While faith in these texts exists on a spectrum—Brennan, for example, fully embraces the possibilities of police reform, while Neville's characters are consigned to brief fantasies of hope and redemption—it is reflective of a larger tendency to resist discounting the potential of systems, institutions, and people to do better, despite their current flaws. The idea that such faith is imperative to the pursuit of justice is implicit in many of the works in this study.

Notably, of course, this faith in potential is not limited to the criminal justice system, but is also applied to religious institutions, and particularly the Catholic Church. This divergence from the secular roots of crime fiction is doubtless affected by culture and history: in a region where religious affiliation was a central factor in oppression, an emphasis on religious freedom becomes part and parcel of the pursuit of justice. I would suggest, however, that the rejection of secularism also follows a particular line of logic: that is, if early crime fiction filled the void created by diminished religiosity by emphasizing secular logic and legal justice, this dichotomy is undermined by increased cynicism about criminal justice systems. If we accept that criminal justice can be reformed, since the ideology on which it is based is more benevolent than its manifestations, it stands to reason that religious institutions can be ameliorated as well.

Furthermore, all of the major characters discussed in this study—even the ones who proclaim that justice is unattainable and that their actions in pursuit of it will thus undoubtedly come to nothing—reflect extensively on their own behavior, emphasize the importance of ethics, and believe there is value in doing good, even when positive results are not immediately apparent. This emphasis on personal commitment to justice corresponds to another type of faith—a faith in self—that enables even the most self-effacing of characters, such as Bruen's Jack Taylor, to conclude that they have a contribution to make in the long and complex process of actualizing justice. As in the cases of legal and religious institutions, the self is imperfect, and characters' faith in themselves is far from unwavering. Nevertheless, the implication is that the redeeming qualities of legal and religious institutions, combined with self-reliance and personal ethics, might eventually effect a hybrid system of justice that is more than the sum of its parts. Such an outlook allows authors to reconcile the elusiveness of justice with the value of its continued pursuit: through faith, justice can simultaneously be apparently unattainable and something we trust might eventually be attained.

In Ireland, faith—particularly religious faith—has historically been inextricably linked with identity, and identity has been inextricably linked with both conflict and the problematics of justice. Naturally, then, an interrogation of how identity is framed—and by whom—becomes central to discourse about justice in Irish crime fiction. The authors in this study consider ways in which identity is ideated through social and political dynamics, familial idiosyncrasies, and the tropes of literature and folklore. Moreover, they examine social constructions of identity as frequently reductive and damaging, both in terms of limiting options for and understanding of the self and in terms of heightening tendencies toward tribalism and othering. It thus feels somewhat contradictory to discuss "Irish crime fiction" without addressing the problematics inherent in that categorization.

In the introduction to this text, I considered aspects of justice, faith, and identity in Ken Bruen's Jack Taylor series, drawing parallels to the work of Colin Dexter, which provided intertextual references for Bruen. When I interviewed Dexter in 2015, he expressed admiration for the work of Bruen and other Irish crime writers and seemed flattered by Bruen's references to the Inspector Morse series. Nevertheless, he was surprised at the suggestion that Morse had had an impact on the development of the detective character in particular, remarking, "I was never interested—I know I should have been—in characterization. All I wanted was a good plot." His singular way of defining "characterization" became clearer when he expounded on the reason for this insouciance: "I was very jealous, especially of other people. . . . I don't know what characterization is; it seems to me that you just have to write about yourself."[2]

It would be difficult to argue that Dexter did not, in the most literal sense, write about himself through the character of Inspector Morse; the author and character shared distinctive traits, such as a love of real ale, opera—particularly by Wagner—and crossword puzzles. Less frequently noted, but perhaps even more significant, is the fact that both Dexter and Morse were the sons of taxi drivers and devoted themselves at various points in their lives to the armed forces and to the study of classics. The character, like Dexter himself, defied stereotypes about class, culture, and career. Both men seemed concurrently to be searching for their place in the prescribed social order and to be the better for not having found it.

It was of primary importance to Dexter that the actors who play Morse in television adaptations also share some of these characteristics; he took the unusual step of adding a clause to his will forbidding anyone but the late John Thaw and Shaun Evans from assuming the role.[3] In light of Dexter's dismissal of the art of characterization, it is tempting to view the clause as a desire to control the image reflected by his self-constructed mirror. Regarding the choice of Evans for *Endeavour*, the prequel to *Inspector Morse*, Dexter told me he recognized that the series' creators might have initially preferred a more recognizable face for the role, but he nevertheless intuitively fixated on Evans: "I didn't know anything about him or his acting abilities, and I said, 'I know you're going to be furious, but I just like the look of him.' Because I just think he looks interesting. . . . Shaun has one marvelous quality, and that is that he doesn't have to act."[4]

I would suggest that the reasons Dexter's Inspector Morse series resonated with Bruen, and with other Irish crime writers such as McKinty, whose *Gun Street Girl* is essentially a noirish—if sometimes satiric—homage to Morse, are twofold. First, Dexter was extremely concerned with the collapse of faith in institutions, expressing frustration both with the corruption that has tainted the very systems that were designed to enforce justice, equity, and empathy and with the dehumanizing powers of contemporary communication and media. Echoing McKinty's unease about anaesthetization through overexposure to violence and pain, Dexter emphasized:

> There are terrible disasters and tragedies and miseries all over the place. . . . So many of them have been brought to our notice by television that we've almost become inured to cruelty and disasters and hopelessness in the world. . . . I think part of it is that we've lost faith in the honour or honourability of our leaders. We read so much about incompetence and corruption. . . . Almost everywhere there seems to me to be an increase in incompetence and general dishonesty. This is what I mean about democracy—you feel that you've got the ability to arrange things and influence matters and it's not quite so easy as that, I'm afraid.[5]

Second, Dexter's remarks here, and his Morse series, identify an associated question that is at the heart of Irish crime fiction—that is, how does one understand one's identity when the social markers that define it fall away and when the systems and narratives one has been taught to depend on prove unjust and unreliable? In broader terms, what does this conundrum tell us about the fragility and shortcomings of perceptions of identity that are dependent on social constructs and unreliable institutions?

Dexter's urgent emphasis on not "[having] to act" when discussing or interpreting the self—and the relationship of the self to justice—speaks to a problem addressed by several of the authors in this study. As I note in chapter 1, authors such as John Connolly and Ingrid Black have discussed at length the pressure placed on Irish writers to construct their fiction around the notion of defining Irishness—and, in particular, to participate in discourse about what a distinct, postcolonial Irish identity should look like. Authors of color in the United States and Canada have complained about a pervasive expectation that they should write about the traumas of racism, which they feel has subjugated their individual perspectives; likewise, Irish writers have, to a certain extent, felt limited by the Revivalist mentality that implies that their primary responsibility as authors is to define and promote Irishness.

Many have speculated about the recent boom in Irish crime fiction, theorizing that it is a new path for embracing Revivalism, that it exposes a fear of social change or otherness engendered by the Celtic Tiger, or that it is a means of contending with the traumas of Ireland's past: colonialism, the Troubles, or the inequitable distribution of wealth. But perhaps it has more to do with an essentially human desire: the desire to not "have to act." By working in a traditionally non-Irish genre, authors are freed from Revivalist expectations; by operating from an outsider's perspective, they are freed from the prescriptions of genre. As a result, the authors in this study are able to consider structural justice—in both legal and religious forms—and its alternatives subjectively and objectively, deciding individually which elements of the old systems are worth preserving and which fall short of the mark. They are also able to explore their identities and perspectives in a way that allows them to acknowledge the effects of nationality and history on these perspectives, while concurrently asserting that nationality and history are not the only defining factors of identity. As Dexter suggested through Morse's transcendence of stereotypes about class, career paths, and religious beliefs, our backgrounds certainly play a role in how we view the world and how we perceive justice, but to suggest that they play the *only* role— or that we should pretend that they do—is ultimately reductive and limiting.

Like all literature, then, Irish crime fiction has undoubtedly been informed by issues unique to the society and political environment from which its authors emerged. It is difficult to imagine that the dramatic social and economic changes engendered by the Celtic Tiger, the rootlessness that resulted from abuses of power in the Catholic Church, and the fears, inequities, and frustration of the violent paramilitary struggles in Northern Ireland have not had a formative influence on the genre in Ireland. Indeed, these issues provide context and content for many of the works in this study. But, as Eoin McNamee argues in the Blue trilogy, there are many stories to be told about any context or content, even from the same perspective. When I interviewed them, both Brian McGilloway and Claire McGowan emphasized their personal stakes in their narratives: McGilloway told me that his treatment of gender discrimination in the Lucy Black series was born of concern for his daughter,[6] while McGowan noted that Paula Maguire's feeling of being caught between two cultures was an expression of her own sense of disorientation after leaving Northern Ireland to attend college in London.[7] Gerard Brennan remarked that *Disorder* allowed him a means to express his discomfort with global political developments;[8] Steve Cavanagh stressed that the Eddie Flynn series enabled him to explore the atmosphere of New York, which he considers "the greatest city in the world";[9] and Adrian McKinty explained his method of listening to various tracks of Tom Waits songs to create the sense of atmosphere he deemed appropriate for his Sean Duffy series.[10] McNamee referred me to his research interests and the theories he espouses in "The Judge" as a counterpoint to other interpretations of his work. The narratives of Irish identity and history are only a few of the many stories these authors have to tell. Wherever possible, then, I have relegated background information to footnotes and appendixes, giving them the space to elaborate on these narratives in their own words: the words of Irish crime writers, certainly, but also the words of individuals.

If, as I noted in the introduction, these writers implicitly ask contemplative readers to assume the role of detective, such a role might include looking beyond allegories of colonialism and the Troubles to examine what the texts can tell us about the elusiveness of truth, the self, and society; the difficulty of establishing standard definitions for discourse about justice, faith, and identity; and the possibility that some conflicts are exacerbated by our inability—or our unwillingness—to recognize that, in the pursuit of justice, we might be using the same signifiers to refer to a broad, and often subjective, range of concepts. As McNamee suggests, allowing for a variety of multifaceted perspectives—and their associated, fallible memories—necessarily blurs traditional narrative, so resistance to acknowledging discrepancies in discourse and perspective might reflect a drive to delineate complex problems and experiences in manageable ways. However, as McKinty's references to other crime fiction texts and to popular interpretations of the Troubles indicate, reliance on these more manageable narratives can prevent us from adequately recognizing obstacles in the pursuit of justice. To break the central trope of noir fiction—the perpetual pursuit of a justice as unattainable as it is invaluable—might, these authors imply, necessitate becoming *finders* in the comprehensive sense exhibited in accounts of Saint Anthony of Padua: that is, not only finders of lost things but also refurbishers of fallen, imperfect institutions; elucidators of previously unrecognized perspectives; and creators of new, more equitable, humanized, and inclusive systems.

Appendixes

Notes

Bibliography

Index

Timeline of Abuses of Power in Church-Run Institutions in Ireland

1767   The first Magdalene laundry opens in Dublin.

1993   The bodies of 155 women are exhumed from an unmarked grave at the former Donnybrook laundry.

1994   Brendan Smyth pleads guilty to seventeen counts of child sexual abuse. The case sheds light on both the church's involvement in covering allegations of abuse and the Irish government's protection of abusers. The coalition government in Ireland collapses owing to suspicions of collusion in delaying Smyth's extradition to Northern Ireland. Micháel Ledwith resigns as president of Saint Patrick's Seminary of Maynooth after allegations that he abused seminarians in the 1980s.

1995   Andrew Madden speaks publicly about being abused by Ivan Payne, prompting civil suits against the church by victims across the country.

1996   The last Magdalene laundry in Ireland closes. Bishops are instructed by the church to report all cases of suspected clerical abuse.

1997   Smyth is extradited from prison in Northern Ireland to the Republic, where he pleads guilty to seventy-four counts of child sexual abuse.

1998   Payne is convicted of fourteen counts of child sexual abuse.

1999   Seán Fortune commits suicide after being arraigned on sixty-six charges of child sexual abuse. Prime Minister Bertie Ahern apologizes to victims of abuse in church institutions.

2000	The Irish Commission to Inquire into Child Abuse is given the power to investigate abuses in church-run institutions.
2001	The Catholic Church Commission on Child Sexual Abuse is established.
2002	Bishop Brendan Comiskey resigns after admitting he failed to address issues of child abuse at the Diocese of Ferns. The Irish government announces a compensation package for victims of clerical abuse.
2002–2005	Allegations continue about church and government collusion in covering accusations of child sexual abuse.
2005	The Ferns Report concludes that multiple instances of child sexual abuse occurred at the Diocese of Ferns and were not adequately addressed by church officials or police prior to 1990.
2007	The Health Service Executive (HSE) publishes a report alleging that eighteen members of staff, including eleven members of clergy, abused at least twenty-one intellectually disabled children in residential care.
2009	The Commission to Inquire into Child Abuse releases a report revealing that physical, psychological, and sexual abuse were chronic in church-run institutions for decades, and alleging that accused abusers were transferred to other facilities rather than dismissed from service.
2010	Patrick Hughes is convicted on four counts of child sexual assault. Pope Benedict XVI apologizes to victims of church abuse, but is widely criticized for his failure to take direct action or to address the report made by the Commission to Inquire into Child Abuse in 2009.
2012	The HSE recommends an investigation into the trafficking of children of unwed mothers for adoption in the United States.
2013	Taoiseach Enda Kenny apologizes to Magdalene survivors on behalf of the government and announces a compensation package.
2014	The United Nations demands an investigation into abuse at Magdalene laundries, compensation for victims, dismissal of

clergy suspected of abuse, and access to church archives on sexual abuse.

2015   The *Irish Examiner* publishes the HSE memo on child trafficking.

2017   A mass grave of babies and toddlers is discovered in a septic tank at Bon Secours Mother and Baby Home for unwed mothers in Tuam.

2018   The Irish Council for Civil Liberties calls for more extensive investigations into illegal adoptions and abuses at homes for unwed mothers and Magdalene laundries. A report is published on governmental facilitation of abuses at Magdalene laundries. A Dublin event honors Magdalene survivors, and President Michael Higgins apologizes on behalf of the government. Pope Francis announces a summit meeting at the Vatican in 2019 on "the protection of minors," summoning presidents of all bishops' conferences worldwide.

Compiled from the following sources: Dan Barry, "The Lost Children of Tuam," *New York Times*, Oct. 28, 2017, https://www.nytimes.com/interactive /2017/10/28/world/europe/tuam-ireland-babies-children.html; Erin Blakemore, "How Ireland Turned 'Fallen Women' into Slaves"; Glenn Frankel and *Washington Post*, "Dead Priest Left Trail of Victim Boys," *Chicago Tribune*, Aug. 15, 2002, https://www.chicagotribune.com/news/ct-xpm-2002-08-15-0208150275-story .html; "Magdalene Survivors: An Emotional Week," RTÉ, June 9, 2018, https:// www.rte.ie/news/ireland/2018/0607/968854-magdalene-survivors/; Denis Mc-Cullough, "Inquiry into Certain Matters Relating to Maynooth College"; Kevin McCoy, "Western Health Board Inquiry into Brothers of Charity Services in Galway"; Marese McDonagh, "Comiskey Set to Officiate at Funeral of Fr Fortune," *Independent*, Sept. 12, 2018, https://www.independent.ie/irish-news/comiskey-set-to -officiate-at-funeral-of-fr-fortune-26156660.html; Henry McDonald, "'Endemic' Rape and Abuse of Irish Children in Catholic Care, Study Finds," *Guardian*, May 20, 2009, https://www.theguardian.com/world/2009/may/20/irish-catholic-schools -child-abuse-claims; Henry McDonald, "Magdalene Laundries: Ireland Accepts State Guilt in Scandal," *Guardian*, Feb. 5, 2013, https://www.theguardian.com /world/2013/feb/05/magdalene-laundries-ireland-state-guilt; Patsy McGarry, "Magdalene Laundries: A Brief History of the Institutions," *Irish Times*, June 11, 2011, https://www.irishtimes.com/news/magdalen-laundries-a-brief-history-of-the

-institutions-1.878079#; Gerard O'Connell, "Pope Francis Summons the World's Top Bishops for Sexual Abuse Prevention Summit"; "Profile of Father Brendan Smyth," *BBC News*, Mar. 15, 2010, http://news.bbc.co.uk/2/hi/uk_news/northern _ireland/8567868.stm; Carrol Ryan, "Irish Church's Forgotten Victims Take Case to U.N.," *New York Times*, May 25, 2011, https://www.nytimes.com/2011/05/25 /world/europe/25iht-abuse25.html; Associated Press, "Timeline: Investigations into Child Abuse in the Irish Catholic Church," *Guardian*, May 20, 2009, https:// www.theguardian.com/world/2009/may/20/irish-catholic-church-child-abuse; "UN Calls for Magdalene Laundries Investigation, Demands Vatican Turn over Child Abusers to Police," RTÉ, Feb. 5, 2014, https://www.rte.ie/news/2014/0205 /502368-vatican-abuse/.

Timeline of the Troubles in Northern Ireland

1920	The Government of Ireland Act partitions the six northeastern counties from the rest of the country for the purpose of creating distinct home-rule institutions.
1921	The Anglo-Irish Treaty allows for the creation of the Irish Free State and gives Northern Ireland the option to separate from the rest of the country.
1922	The Northern Irish Parliament announces its intent to opt out of the Irish Free State.
1968	The civil rights movement in Northern Ireland begins. Protesters complain that Catholics face discrimination in housing, employment, the criminal justice system, and voting rights. The RUC is heavily criticized for restricting the routes of marches and injuring protestors. Rioting ensues. Marches are banned, and the Nationalist Party adopts a position of civil disobedience.
1969	Extensive rioting, known as the Battle of the Bogside, erupts in Derry. British troops arrive in Northern Ireland in an attempt to restore order. Loyalist paramilitaries begin a bombing campaign.
1971	Internment begins: thousands of suspected paramilitary members are detained without trial.
1972	On Bloody Sunday, British soldiers open fire on a civil rights march in Derry, killing fourteen protesters. The government at Stormont is dissolved, and the British government imposes direct rule over Northern Ireland.

1974   The IRA extends its bombing campaign into Britain.

1980–1981   Hunger strikes begin in the Maze prison, in protest of the British government's withdrawal of Special Category Status for paramilitary prisoners. Ten protesters, including Bobby Sands, die in the 1981 strike.

1984   A Provisional IRA bomb explodes at the Grand Hotel in Brighton during a failed attempt to assassinate Prime Minister Margaret Thatcher.

1985   The Anglo-Irish Agreement sets up an intergovernmental conference between the British and Irish governments, acknowledging that the Republic of Ireland should have some input regarding the management of Northern Ireland.

1988   In the Milltown Cemetery attack, a member of the Ulster Defence Association kills three people and wounds sixty others at the funeral of three Provisional IRA members. Three days later, two British army corporals are shot at a funeral procession by the Provisional IRA, who mistakenly believe that the corporals are intent on staging a second attack. Both events are filmed and shown on television news reports.

1994   The IRA and Protestant paramilitaries agree to a cease-fire, with the aim of commencing negotiations toward peace.

1996   The IRA withdraws from the cease-fire, refusing to consent to decommissioning weapons as a condition of the peace talks.

1997   A second cease-fire paves the way for peace negotiations.

1998   The Good Friday Agreement is approved by referenda in Northern Ireland and the Republic of Ireland. It includes clauses to establish a power-sharing government at Stormont, to uphold the equity and civil rights of all Northern Irish citizens, to decommission paramilitary weapons, and to provide early release to paramilitary prisoners whose organizations agree to maintain the ceasefire. A dissident IRA group, the Real Irish Republican Army, carries out the deadliest attack in the history of the Troubles, planting a car bomb in Omagh that kills 29 people and injures approximately 220 others.

2002–2007   Because of sporadic ongoing violence, direct rule is reinstated.

2005   The IRA completes the weapons-decommissioning process.

2007   Sinn Féin and the Democratic Unionist Party enter into a historic power-sharing government at Stormont.

Compiled from the following sources: Sean Clarke et al., "Timeline: Northern Ireland," *Guardian*, Mar. 10, 2009, https://www.theguardian.com/uk/2009/mar/08/northern-ireland-timeline; Martin Melaugh, "A Chronology of the Conflict—1968 to the Present," CAIN Web Service, accessed Aug. 18, 2018, http://www.cain.ulst.ac.uk/othelem/chron.htm; Tom Rowley, "Timeline of the Northern Ireland Troubles: From Conflict to Peace Process," *Telegraph*, May 19, 2015, https://www.telegraph.co.uk/news/uknews/northernireland/11610345/Timeline-of-Northern-Ireland-Troubles-from-conflict-to-peace-process.html; "The Troubles: Thirty Years of Conflict in Northern Ireland, 1968–1998," BBC, accessed Aug. 18, 2018, http://www.bbc.co.uk/history/troubles.

Notes

Introduction

1. Ken Bruen, *The Guards*, 5.
2. Bill Phillips, "Religious Belief in Recent Detective Fiction," 139.
3. Bruen, *The Guards*, 54.
4. Bruen, *The Guards*, 54.
5. Mabel Adelaide Farnum, *Saint Anthony of Padua: His Life and Miracles*, 106–8.
6. "The Beloved Saint Anthony," n.p.
7. Farnum, *Saint Anthony of Padua*, 106–8.
8. Alban Butler and Kathleen Jones, *Butler's Lives of the Saints: June*, 102–3.
9. "A Saint of Many Miracles," n.p.
10. Butler and Jones, *Butler's Lives of the Saints*, 103.
11. Butler and Jones, *Butler's Lives of the Saints*, 102.
12. Colin Dexter, *The Remorseful Day*, 146–47, 158.
13. Rafael Alvarez, *The Wire*, "One Arrest."
14. Graham Yost, *Justified*, "The Collection."
15. Ken Bruen, *The Magdalen Martyrs*, 113.
16. Yost, *Justified*, "The Collection." Saint Anthony has been referenced in many other crime fiction texts and television shows in recent years, including the *Dexter* episode "Practically Perfect" and *Grantchester*, season 6, episode 5.
17. Ken Bruen, *The Killing of the Tinkers*, 104.
18. For a detailed analysis of the roots and development of crime fiction in Ireland, see Ian Campbell Ross's introduction to *Down These Green Streets: Irish Crime Writing in the 21st Century*, ed. Declan Burke.
19. Brian Cliff, *Irish Crime Fiction*, 27.
20. Paula Murphy, "Murderous Mayhem: Ken Bruen and the New Ireland," 5.
21. Bruen, *The Magdalen Martyrs*, 147–48.
22. Phillips, "Religious Belief," 146.
23. Bruen, *Killing of the Tinkers*, 179.

24. Ken Bruen, *Priest*, 189.

25. Bruen, *The Magdalen Martyrs*, 9.

26. Bruen, *Killing of the Tinkers*, 166.

27. The exposure of multiple instances of physical and sexual abuse in the Catholic Church has had a particular significance in an Irish context, owing to both the association of Catholicism with Irish identity during the colonial period and the church's long-standing political and social power in the Republic of Ireland. For a timeline of abuses of power in church-run institutions in Ireland, see Appendix A.

28. Phillips, "Religious Belief," 147.

29. Ken Bruen, *Headstone*, 11–13.

30. Bruen, *The Magdalen Martyrs*, 26, 83, 122.

31. Bruen, *Green Hell*, pt. 2, chaps. 2, 4, 5.

32. Bruen, *The Emerald Lie*, 124.

33. Declan Burke, "The Black Stuff: A Conversation with John Banville," 220.

34. John Banville, "John Banville, the Art of Fiction, no. 200," 150–51.

35. Mark Billingham, "Murder Most Foul: Poirot Would Never Survive the Psychopaths and Serial Killers Who Populate Modern Literature," *Independent*, July 23, 2004, https://www.independent.co.uk/arts-entertainment/books/features/murder-most-foul-554091.html.

36. Robert Murphy, *DCI Banks*, "Cold Is the Grave: Part 2."

37. Jay Stringer, email interview with the author, Aug. 15, 2016.

38. Shaun Evans, "Endeavour: Shaun Evans Video Chat."

39. Eric Rawson, "To Hell with Ya: *Katabasis* in Hard-Boiled Detective Fiction," 292–94.

40. Colin Davis, "Psychoanalysis, Detection, and Fiction: Julia Kristeva's Detective Novels," 296.

41. Billingham, "Murder Most Foul," n.p.

42. Fintan O'Toole, *The Ex-Isle of Erin: Images of a Global Ireland*, 13–16.

43. Peadar Kirby, Luke Gibbons, and Michael Cronin, eds., *Reinventing Ireland: Culture, Society and the Global Economy*, 197.

44. David Cregan, "Divided Subjectivities and Modern Irish Masculinities: 'The Makings of a Man,'" 166.

45. Banville, "Banville, the Art of Fiction," 151.

46. These foundational texts, along with numerous articles, also provide a context for close readings of individual texts. In the cases of some series that have already resulted in significant scholarship—John Connolly's Charlie Parker series, Tana French's Dublin Murder Squad series, Stuart Neville's Jack Lennon series, and Steve Cavanagh's Eddie Flynn series—I have focused largely on the first novels of the series.

47. For a timeline of the Troubles, the thirty-year paramilitary conflict in Northern Ireland, see Appendix B.

48. Signed on April 10, 1998, the Good Friday Agreement (or Belfast Agreement) was an agreement among the governments of Great Britain and Ireland and a majority of political parties in Northern Ireland. It established terms for the decommissioning of weapons by paramilitaries and for the future governance of Northern Ireland, creating a power-sharing system among unionist and nationalist parties. It also emphasized a commitment to diversity and civil rights. It is considered a crucial and effective step in the peace process that ultimately concluded the Troubles.

Part One. Finders of Lost Things

1. Ken Bruen, *The Ghosts of Galway*, 250, 191.

1. The System, Changed

1. Raymond Chandler, "The Simple Art of Murder," 219.

2. Maureen T. Reddy, "Contradictions in the Irish Hardboiled: Detective Fiction's Uneasy Portrayal of a New Ireland," 127; Ingrid Black, "Escaping Irishness," 212, 214, 218–19; John Connolly, "No Blacks, No Dogs, No Irish: Ireland and the Mystery Genre," 41–42, 47. In *Irish Crime Fiction*, Brian Cliff also notes that the use of American hard-boiled standards by Irish crime writers might reflect a preference for detectives who offer "an *ad hoc* justice for those left behind by official law and order" owing to cultural mistrust in the legal justice system (143). This suggestion aligns with my arguments about Irish protagonists' hesitance to refer to themselves as detectives or investigators, in the introduction and this chapter.

3. Reddy, "Contradictions in the Irish Hardboiled," 132.

4. Connolly, "No Blacks, No Dogs, No Irish," 44. Connolly's reference is to lyrics from Cohen's song "First We Take Manhattan."

5. Declan Hughes's "Irish Hard-Boiled Crime: A 51st State of Mind" expresses a sentiment similar to Connolly's. After outlining the impact of American culture in Ireland, his frustration with the limiting task of defining Irish identity, and his admiration for American hard-boiled authors, Hughes describes his approach to writing crime fiction as a merging of traditions: "The task was to employ the American model but to imbue it with a distinctive Irish feel. Perhaps a good analogy would be with jazz—a distinctively American music that, of course, was created using European instruments. When a European musician plays jazz, he negotiates a tradition that is at once alien but his own; he pays homage to Louis and Dizzy and Miles, but he must transcend mere pastiche; no matter whose shoulders he first stands on, he must eventually walk on his own two feet" (167). In *Irish*

Crime Fiction, Brian Cliff describes Hughes's Ed Loy series as a stellar example of the way in which Irish crime writers adapt, alter, and refine American hard-boiled standards (76–77).

6. For further reading on the ways in which Irish crime writers have used transnational contexts, both to escape the pressures of writing about Irish identity and to contribute to the evolution of the genre, see Brian Cliff, *Irish Crime Fiction*, chap. 5.

7. Andrew Kincaid, "Detecting Hope: Ken Bruen's Disenchanted P.I.," 67.

8. Bruen, *Killing of the Tinkers*, 145.

9. The Magdalene laundries were Catholic (or, less frequently, Protestant) institutions for women deemed to be "fallen" for a broad variety of reasons, from prostitution to pregnancy, petty crime, mental illness, or being the victim of a sexual assault. The women were subjected to hard labor, and widespread reports of additional abuse have been documented. For more on the history of Magdalene laundries in Ireland, see Appendix A.

10. Bruen, *Green Hell*, pt. 1, chap. 4.

11. Bruen, *Killing of the Tinkers*, 142.

12. In "Negotiating Borders: Inspector Devlin and Shadows of the Past," Carol Baraniuk outlines similar sentiments in Brian McGilloway's Inspector Devlin series. While more religious than Taylor, Devlin also "exercises his critical faculties to question orthodoxies," embracing the church's teachings on forgiveness and assisting the vulnerable, while rejecting those of its practices that he deems contrary to such values (80).

13. Ken Bruen, *Cross*, 16–17 (first ellipsis in the original).

14. Bruen, *The Emerald Lie*, 12.

15. Bruen, *Cross*, 29.

16. Ken Bruen, *Purgatory*, chap. 3.

17. Bruen, *Priest*, 131.

18. Bruen, *Cross*, 252.

19. Ken Bruen, *Sanctuary*, 23.

20. Bruen, *Headstone*, 252.

21. Kincaid, "Detecting Hope," 68.

22. Ken Bruen, *The Devil*, 112.

23. Ken Bruen, *The Dramatist*, 21.

24. Bruen, *Cross*, 77.

25. Bruen, *The Dramatist*, 8.

26. Bruen, *Sanctuary*, 38.

27. Bruen, *Purgatory*, chap. 33.

28. Bruen, *The Magdalen Martyrs*, 223.

29. John Connolly, *Every Dead Thing*, chaps. 6, 15, 13, 15.

30. Connolly, *Every Dead Thing*, chaps. 2, 17, 28, 45, 10.

31. Connolly, *Every Dead Thing*, chaps. 16, 30.

32. Connolly, *Every Dead Thing*, chaps. 9, 17.

33. Connolly, *Every Dead Thing*, chaps. 1, 17, 6, 9, 12, 46, 32, 33, 4.

34. Connolly, *Every Dead Thing*, chaps. 17, 33, 20.

35. In *Irish Crime Fiction*, Brian Cliff makes note of a similar theme of oppressed people and societies emulating their oppressors in Declan Hughes's Ed Loy series (72).

36. Connolly, *Every Dead Thing*, chap. 3.

37. Connolly, *Every Dead Thing*, introduction, chaps. 14, 13, 11, 28, 40, 33, 39, 40.

38. Connolly, *Every Dead*, chaps. 11, 15, 28, 23, 38.

39. Brian Cliff, "A 'Honeycomb World': John Connolly's Charlie Parker Series," 39–40. See also Cliff's discussion of the Charlie Parker series in *Irish Crime Fiction*, in which he expands on this point, concluding that "Connolly's work models . . . both what crime fiction can reveal about Irish culture and what Irish writing can bring to crime fiction" (174).

40. Connolly, *Every Dead Thing*, chaps. 29, 30.

41. Connolly, *Every Dead Thing*, chaps. 23, 24, 28.

42. In *Irish Crime Fiction*, Cliff describes Parker as "an outsider who imagines his way into connection through . . . supernatural empathy" (169).

43. Connolly, *Every Dead Thing*, chaps. 16, 28.

44. Alex Barclay, *Darkhouse*, 17, 67, 66, 47, 333, 214, 144, 227.

45. Barclay, *Darkhouse*, 105.

46. Declan Hughes, in "Irish Hard-Boiled Crime: A 51st State of Mind," notes that he has tried to convey a similar sentiment in his Ed Loy series, with specific emphasis on the seeming dichotomy between modernity and tradition: "The American Dream no more guarantees personal reinvention or flight from the burden of history than the Irish tradition ensures a firm sense of community, solidarity or identity" (168).

47. Barclay, *Darkhouse*, 86, 224, 349 (ellipsis in the original).

48. Barclay, *Darkhouse*, 125–26.

49. Barclay, *Darkhouse*, 432.

50. As Cliff notes in *Irish Crime Fiction*, Brian McGilloway's Inspector Devlin is likewise more hopeful than most detectives in Irish crime fiction owing, at least in part, to his strong religious faith and his clear-minded assessment of it (52–53).

51. Barclay, *Darkhouse*, 205, 175–76.

52. Barclay, *Darkhouse*, 384, 458.

53. Barclay, *Darkhouse*, 166.

54. Barclay, *Darkhouse*, 211, 296–97, 456, 446.

55. Barclay, *Darkhouse*, 231, 305, 242, 232.

56. Barclay, *Darkhouse*, 453.

57. Shirley Peterson, "Voicing the Unspeakable: Tana French's Dublin Murder Squad," 108.

58. Mimosa Summers Stephenson, "Liminality in the Novels of Tana French," 52; Tana French, *In the Woods*, 593.

59. Shirley Peterson, "Homicide and Home-icide: Exhuming Ireland's Past in the Detective Novels of Tana French," 99.

60. French, *In the Woods*, 20, 31.

61. Peterson, "Homicide and Home-icide," 98.

62. Peterson, "Voicing the Unspeakable," 110.

63. French, *In the Woods*, 5, 425, 433–35, 564–65.

64. French, *In the Woods*, 45, 112, 44, 60.

65. French, *In the Woods*, 339, 362–63, 381, 416.

66. French, *In the Woods*, 60, 355–56, 391.

67. Peterson, "Voicing the Unspeakable," 114; Rachel Schaffer, "Mystery, Memory, Metaphor, and Metonymy *In the Woods*," 100.

68. French, *In the Woods*, 13, 14, 300.

69. Moira E. Casey, "'Built on Nothing but Bullshit and Good PR': Crime, Class Mobility, and the Irish Economy in the Novels of Tana French," 95.

70. French, *In the Woods*, 113–14, 79, 110.

71. French, *In the Woods*, 218, 225, 93–94, 312, 57, 196–97.

72. French, *In the Woods*, 105.

73. John Teel, "Blurring the Genre Borderlines: Tana French's Haunted Detectives," 16.

74. Peterson, "Voicing the Unspeakable," 110–13; Casey, "'Built on Nothing but Bullshit and Good PR,'" 101.

75. French, *In the Woods*, 25–26, 457, 100–102, 446.

76. French, *In the Woods*, 198, 207, 493–94, 182.

77. French, *In the Woods*, 230, 434–35.

78. French, *In the Woods*, 323–24, 541–42, 555–57, 579.

79. Andrew Kincaid, "'Down These Mean Streets': The City and Critique in Contemporary Irish Noir," 45–50.

80. Fintan O'Toole, in the afterword to *Down These Green Streets*, makes a similar claim, noting, "Boom-time Ireland reproduced the social conditions that created crime fiction as a mass genre," but adding that disappointing postboom conditions increased pessimism about authority and the potential for change—and thereby improved realism—in some works of the subgenre, notably by Gene Kerrigan and Alan Glynn. O'Toole, "From Chandler and the 'Playboy' to the Contemporary Crime Wave," 360–61.

2. "A Middle Finger to the Darkness"

1. Adrian McKinty, *Gun Street Girl*, 10.

2. McKinty, *Gun Street Girl*, 293.

3. Adrian McKinty, *Rain Dogs*, 228.

4. Adrian McKinty, *Police at the Station and They Don't Look Friendly*, 10.

5. McKinty, *Police at the Station*, 222.

6. McKinty, *Police at the Station*, 24.

7. McKinty, *Gun Street Girl*, 288.

8. Adrian McKinty, interview with the author, Belfast, Oct. 28, 2017.

9. Adrian McKinty, *I Hear the Sirens in the Street*, 98.

10. Adrian McKinty, *The Cold Cold Ground*, 156. For more on Bloody Sunday and the hunger strikes, see Appendix B.

11. McKinty, *Police at the Station*, 248.

12. McKinty, interview with the author.

13. McKinty, *I Hear the Sirens*, 113.

14. McKinty, *The Cold Cold Ground*, 175–76.

15. The UDA was among the most active loyalist paramilitary groups during the Troubles.

16. McKinty, *Police at the Station*, 33.

17. Adrian McKinty, *In the Morning I'll Be Gone*, 199.

18. McKinty, *In the Morning*, 46.

19. McKinty, *In the Morning*, 307.

20. McKinty, interview with the author.

21. McKinty, *Rain Dogs*, 319.

22. McKinty, *Rain Dogs*, 290–91.

23. McKinty, interview with the author.

24. McKinty, *In the Morning*, 216.

25. McKinty, *The Cold Cold Ground*, 286. For more on McKinty's intertextual use of Tom Waits's lyrics, see my article "'This Isn't Fucking *Miss Marple*, Mate': Intertextuality in Adrian McKinty's Sean Duffy Series," in *Guilt Rules All: Irish Mystery, Detective, and Crime Fiction*, ed. Elizabeth Mannion and Brian Cliff.

26. McKinty, *Gun Street Girl*, 90.

27. McKinty, *The Cold Cold Ground*, 24.

28. McKinty, *The Cold Cold Ground*, 304–5.

29. McKinty, *Police at the Station*, 94.

30. McKinty, *Gun Street Girl*, 151.

31. McKinty, *Gun Street Girl*, 296.

32. McKinty, *The Cold Cold Ground*, 292.

33. McKinty, *I Hear the Sirens*, 191.

34. McKinty, interview with the author.

35. McKinty, *Rain Dogs*, 95.

36. McKinty, *Gun Street Girl*, 229.

37. McKinty, *Gun Street Girl*, 141.

38. McKinty, *Rain Dogs*, 117.

39. McKinty, *Rain Dogs*, 251.

40. McKinty, interview with the author.

41. McKinty, *The Cold Cold Ground*, 55.

42. McKinty, *In the Morning*, 101.

43. McKinty, *Rain Dogs*, 307.

44. McKinty, *I Hear the Sirens*, 307.

45. McKinty, *Police at the Station*, 312.

46. McKinty, *Police at the Station*, 181.

47. McKinty, *Police at the Station*, 299–302.

48. The UVF was another loyalist paramilitary group during the Troubles.

49. McKinty, *The Cold Cold Ground*, 31.

50. McKinty, *I Hear the Sirens*, 258.

51. McKinty, *In the Morning*, 88.

52. McKinty, *In the Morning*, 274.

53. McKinty, *In the Morning*, 306.

54. McKinty, *In the Morning*, 258.

55. McKinty, *Rain Dogs*, 307.

56. McKinty, *Gun Street Girl*, 130.

57. McKinty, *The Cold Cold Ground*, 178–79.

58. McKinty, *The Cold Cold Ground*, 190.

59. McKinty, *The Cold Cold Ground*, 152.

60. McKinty, *The Cold Cold Ground*, 146.

61. McKinty, *The Cold Cold Ground*, 130.

62. McKinty, *I Hear the Sirens*, 186.

63. McKinty, *Rain Dogs*, 212.

64. McKinty, *Rain Dogs*, 274.

65. McKinty, *Rain Dogs*, 280–81.

66. McKinty, *Gun Street Girl*, 130.

67. McKinty, *Gun Street Girl*, 295.

68. McKinty, *Police at the Station*, 219.

69. McKinty, *Police at the Station*, 226.

70. McKinty, *I Hear the Sirens*, 259–60.

71. McKinty, *Rain Dogs*, 39.

72. McKinty, *Rain Dogs*, 94.

73. McKinty, *The Cold Cold Ground*, 94–95.

74. McKinty, *In the Morning*, 145.

75. McKinty, *In the Morning*, 184.

76. McKinty, *In the Morning*, 185.

77. McKinty, *Police at the Station*, 275–76, 288.

78. McKinty, *I Hear the Sirens*, 149.

79. McKinty, *In the Morning*, 36.

80. McKinty, *In the Morning*, 313–14.

81. McKinty, *Rain Dogs*, 234–35.

82. McKinty, *Police at the Station*, 61.

83. McKinty, *In the Morning*, 139.

84. McKinty, *Gun Street Girl*, 36.

85. McKinty, *Gun Street Girl*, 91.

86. McKinty, *Gun Street Girl*, 265.

87. McKinty, *Gun Street Girl*, 309.

88. McKinty, *Rain Dogs*, 36.

89. McKinty, *Rain Dogs*, 271.

90. McKinty, *Police at the Station*, 11.

91. McKinty, *Police at the Station*, 92.

92. McKinty, *Police at the Station*, 196.

93. McKinty, *Police at the Station*, 242.

94. McKinty, *Police at the Station*, 185.

95. McKinty, *Police at the Station*, 302 (ellipsis in the original).

96. McKinty, interview with the author.

97. McKinty, interview with the author.

98. McKinty, *Rain Dogs*, 251.

99. McKinty, interview with the author.

100. Brian Cliff, "Subversive Series Shows 80s Belfast as Shape of Things to Come," *Irish Times*, Oct. 27, 2017, https://www.irishtimes.com/culture/books /subversive-series-shows-80s-belfast-as-shape-of-things-to-come-1.3271167. For more on the treatment of clichés—both about the North and about crime fiction— in the Duffy series, see my article "'This Isn't Fucking *Miss Marple*, Mate'"; and Cliff, *Irish Crime Fiction*, 38–39.

101. McKinty, *I Hear the Sirens*, 133.

102. McKinty, *Police at the Station*, 272–73.

103. McKinty, *I Hear the Sirens*, 265.

104. McKinty, *I Hear the Sirens*, 262, 265.

105. McKinty, *Gun Street Girl*, 11. For more on the incorporation of satire and dark humor in the Duffy series, see my article "'This Isn't Fucking *Miss Marple*, Mate.'" For more on the tradition of satire in Northern Irish crime fiction,

particularly in the works of Colin Bateman, see Connolly, "No Blacks, No Dogs, No Irish," 51–52; and Cliff, *Irish Crime Fiction*, 33.

106. McKinty, *The Cold Cold Ground*, 130.

107. McKinty, *Police at the Station*, 205.

108. Sinn Féin, an Irish republican political party, was widely considered to have strong associations with the IRA, particularly during the Troubles.

109. McKinty, *In the Morning*, 191.

110. McKinty, *Gun Street Girl*, 22.

111. McKinty, *Gun Street Girl*, 212.

112. McKinty, *Gun Street Girl*, 255.

113. McKinty, *Gun Street Girl*, 257.

114. McKinty, *Gun Street Girl*, 295–96.

115. McKinty, *Gun Street Girl*, 308.

116. McKinty, *Gun Street Girl*, 308–9.

117. McKinty, *In the Morning*, 61.

118. McKinty, *In the Morning*, 276.

119. McKinty, interview with the author. McKinty makes a similar argument when discussing themes in Brian Moore's *Lies of Silence* (1990): "How easy it is to be a Catholic living in the Republic of Ireland surrounded by confirmations of one's identity in church, in government, even in the colour of the post boxes? How much more interesting to be in the north where identities are confused, muddled occasions for angst?" Adrian McKinty, "Odd Men Out," 102.

3. Borders

1. The title of McGilloway's fourth Lucy Black novel is a reference to Colm Tóibín's *Bad Blood: A Walk along the Irish Border* (1994, originally published as *Walking along the Border* in 1987), which details the author's summer walking the Irish border from Derry to Newry immediately following the Anglo-Irish Agreement, recording the fears, poverty, and prejudices of residents of the borderlands. For more on the Anglo-Irish Agreement, see Appendix B.

2. Brian McGilloway, "Walking the Tightrope: Brexit, Books and the Border," *Irish Times*, Nov. 3, 2018, https://www.irishtimes.com/culture/books/walking-the-tightrope-brexit-books-and-the-border-1.3675777.

3. McGilloway, "Walking the Tightrope: Brexit, Books and the Border."

4. Brian McGilloway, *Little Girl Lost*, 32.

5. McGilloway, *Little Girl Lost*, 24.

6. Brian McGilloway, *Someone You Know*, 36, 39.

7. McGilloway, *Someone You Know*, 57.

8. McGilloway, *Little Girl Lost*, 93.

9. McGilloway, *Someone You Know*, 160.

10. McGilloway, *Someone You Know*, 359.

11. McKinty, *Gun Street Girl*, 130.

12. McGilloway, *Someone You Know*, 360.

13. McGilloway, *Someone You Know*, 359.

14. McGilloway, *Someone You Know*, 211.

15. Brian McGilloway, *Bad Blood*, 142.

16. McGilloway, *Bad Blood*, 146.

17. McGilloway, *Someone You Know*, 212.

18. Brian McGilloway, *The Forgotten Ones*, chaps. 18, 61.

19. McGilloway, *Someone You Know*, 74–75.

20. McGilloway, *The Forgotten Ones*, chap. 27.

21. McGilloway, *The Forgotten Ones*, chap. 17.

22. McGilloway, *Little Girl Lost*, 78.

23. McGilloway, *Little Girl Lost*, 85.

24. McGilloway, *Little Girl Lost*, 149.

25. McGilloway, *Little Girl Lost*, 267.

26. McGilloway, *Little Girl Lost*, 272.

27. Brian McGilloway, email interview with the author, Jan. 25, 2018.

28. McGilloway, *Bad Blood*, 34.

29. McGilloway, *Bad Blood*, 29. "Provos" is an informal term for the Provisional IRA.

30. McGilloway, *Bad Blood*, 311.

31. McGilloway, *Bad Blood*, 211.

32. McGilloway, *Bad Blood*, 39.

33. McGilloway, *Bad Blood*, 253.

34. McGilloway, *Bad Blood*, 301.

35. McGilloway, *Bad Blood*, 348.

36. McGilloway, *Bad Blood*, 346.

37. McGilloway, *Bad Blood*, 59.

38. McGilloway, *Bad Blood*, 132.

39. McGilloway, *Bad Blood*, 138.

40. McGilloway, *Bad Blood*, 318.

41. McGilloway, *Bad Blood*, 291–92.

42. McGilloway, *Bad Blood*, 295.

43. These considerations, though often tangential to the plots of the books and early episodes of *Inspector Morse*, become increasingly central as the series progress: both the *Lewis* episode "Life Born of Fire" (2008) and the *Endeavour* episode "Canticle" (2017)—which first aired shortly after the publication of *Bad Blood*—focus on homophobic attitudes in relation to religious extremism.

44. McGilloway, *Bad Blood*, 338–39.

45. McGilloway, "Walking the Tightrope: The Border in Irish Fiction," 303.

46. Baraniuk, "Negotiating Borders," 81–82.

47. McGilloway, *Little Girl Lost*, 218.

48. McGilloway, *Little Girl Lost*, 327.

49. McGilloway, *Little Girl Lost*, 259, 261.

50. McGilloway, *Little Girl Lost*, 209.

51. McGilloway, *Someone You Know*, 49.

52. McGilloway, *Someone You Know*, 246.

53. McGilloway, *Someone You Know*, 245.

54. McGilloway, *Little Girl Lost*, 177.

55. McGilloway, *Little Girl Lost*, 27.

56. McGilloway, email interview with the author.

57. McGilloway, *Little Girl Lost*, 269.

58. McGilloway, *Bad Blood*, 249.

59. McGilloway, *Someone You Know*, 25.

60. McGilloway, *Bad Blood*, 336.

61. McGilloway, *Bad Blood*, 338.

62. McGilloway, *Bad Blood*, 344.

63. McGilloway, *Little Girl Lost*, 337.

64. McGilloway, *Little Girl Lost*, 108.

65. McGilloway, *Little Girl Lost*, 211.

66. Caroline Reitz, "Nancy Drew, *Dragon Tattoo*: Female Detective Fiction and the Ethics of Care," 21, 30–31.

67. McGilloway, *Little Girl Lost*, 295.

68. McGilloway, *Little Girl Lost*, 307.

69. McGilloway, *The Forgotten Ones*, chap. 60.

70. McGilloway, *The Forgotten Ones*, chap. 68.

71. McGilloway, *Bad Blood*, 349.

72. McGilloway, *Bad Blood*, 350.

73. McGilloway, *Bad Blood*, 352.

74. McGilloway, *Someone You Know*, 37.

75. McGilloway, *Someone You Know*, 136.

76. McGilloway, *Someone You Know*, 310.

77. McGilloway, *Someone You Know*, 366.

78. McGilloway, *Someone You Know*, 368.

79. McGilloway, *Bad Blood*, 176–77.

80. McGilloway, *The Forgotten Ones*, chap. 29.

81. McGilloway, *Someone You Know*, 261.

82. McGilloway, *Someone You Know*, 262.

83. McGilloway, *Someone You Know*, 174.

84. McGilloway, *Little Girl Lost*, 310–11.

85. McGilloway, email interview with the author.

86. McGilloway, *Bad Blood*, 154.

87. McGilloway, *Bad Blood*, 339.

88. McGilloway, *Bad Blood*, 340.

89. McGilloway, *Bad Blood*, 258.

90. McGilloway, *Bad Blood*, 333–37.

91. McGilloway, *Bad Blood*, 350.

92. McGilloway, *Bad Blood*, 350.

4. Bridges

1. Claire McGowan, email interview with the author, Mar. 18, 2018.

2. Claire McGowan, *The Lost*, 369.

3. Claire McGowan, *The Dead Ground*, 207–8.

4. McGowan, *The Dead Ground*, 212.

5. Brian Cliff, *Irish Crime Fiction*, 59.

6. Brian Cliff makes a parallel point in *Irish Crime Fiction*, arguing that McGowan's inclusion of both a former Magdalene laundry and present-day misogynistic attitudes in the plotline of *The Lost* "[ties] the crimes inflicted by the laundries very much to long-enduring patterns that persist in the present, where they continue to generate further suffering, through official policies and less official social conventions alike. It is through such juxtapositions, anchored as they are in the central narratives rather than merely providing window dressing, that Irish crime novels with female protagonists take an issue in crime fiction in general— violence against women, whether fetishized *à la* Mike Hammer, or examined by more progressive authors—and tie it to particular Irish experiences" (132).

7. McGowan, *The Lost*, 311.

8. In *Little Girl Lost*, we learn that Lucy "sometimes . . . wasn't even sure she wanted to be in the police at all, but couldn't think of anything else to do" (108–9).

9. McGowan, *The Lost*, 12.

10. McGowan, *The Lost*, 82.

11. McGowan, *The Lost*, 10.

12. McGowan, email interview with the author.

13. McGowan, *The Lost*, 73.

14. McGowan, *The Lost*, 78.

15. McGowan, *The Lost*, 166–67.

16. McGowan, *The Lost*, 161.

17. McGowan, *The Dead Ground*, 306 (second ellipsis in the original).

18. McGowan, email interview with the author.

19. McGowan, *The Dead Ground*, 134.

20. Claire McGowan, *Blood Tide*, chap. 31.

21. Chapter 4 of Brian Cliff's *Irish Crime Fiction* offers a detailed, nuanced discussion of similarly complex, imperfect women characters across a spectrum of Irish crime novels.

22. McGowan, email interview with the author.

23. Claire McGowan, *The Silent Dead*, chap. 28.

24. McGowan, *The Silent Dead*, chap. 24.

25. McGowan, *The Silent Dead*, chap. 24.

26. McGowan, *The Silent Dead*, chap. 26.

27. McGowan, *Blood Tide*, chap. 39.

28. McGowan, *The Silent Dead*, chap. 32.

29. Claire McGowan, *A Savage Hunger*, chap. 25.

30. McGowan, *The Lost*, 26 (ellipsis in the original).

31. McGowan, *The Lost*, 25.

32. McGowan, *The Silent Dead*, chap. 2.

33. McGowan, *The Silent Dead*, chap. 9.

34. McGowan, *A Savage Hunger*, chap. 33.

35. In *Irish Crime Fiction*, Brian Cliff suggests that Brian McGilloway's Inspector Devlin series grapples with the compromises of the Good Friday Agreement more indirectly through plotlines: "So often in the series, Devlin ends with at best a qualified justice and a partial resolution, which may never be enough but which may be all we may receive. . . . [I]t is hard not to see . . . a ripple moving out from the Good Friday Agreement, with all the varieties of compromise it required, the laying aside of revenge and sometimes justice in the interests of a broader peace" (56).

36. McGowan, *The Silent Dead*, chap. 18.

37. McGowan, *The Silent Dead*, chap. 17.

38. McGowan, *The Lost*, 121.

39. McGowan, *The Dead Ground*, 226.

40. McGowan, *Blood Tide*, chap. 3.

41. McGowan, *The Lost*, 248.

42. McGowan, *The Dead Ground*, 377.

43. McGowan, *Blood Tide*, chap. 15.

44. McGowan, *The Silent Dead*, chap. 19.

45. McGowan, *The Silent Dead*, chap. 2.

46. McGowan, *The Silent Dead*, chap. 22.

47. McGowan, *A Savage Hunger*, chap. 29.

48. McGowan, *The Dead Ground*, 130.

49. McGowan, *The Dead Ground*, 224–25.

50. McGowan, *The Silent Dead*, chap. 9.

51. McGowan, *The Lost*, 263–64.

52. McGowan, *The Silent Dead*, chap. 2.

53. McGowan, *The Lost*, 119.

54. McGowan, *The Lost*, 197.

55. McGowan, *The Lost*, 203.

56. McGowan, *A Savage Hunger*, chap. 40.

57. McGowan, *A Savage Hunger*, chap. 15.

58. McGowan, *A Savage Hunger*, chap. 15 (ellipsis in the original).

59. McGowan, *The Lost*, 312.

60. McGowan, *The Silent Dead*, chap. 9.

61. McGowan, *The Silent Dead*, chap. 21.

62. McGowan, *A Savage Hunger*, chap. 25.

63. McGowan, *The Lost*, 344.

64. McGowan, *A Savage Hunger*, chap. 16.

65. McGowan, *The Silent Dead*, chap. 10.

66. McGowan, *The Silent Dead*, chap. 19.

67. McGowan, *The Silent Dead*, chap. 32.

68. In *Irish Crime Fiction*, Brian Cliff emphasizes the extent to which Paula's own past gives rise to complicated feelings about the vigilantes' actions in this novel: "Paula's narration . . . expresses both a deep horror at the violence and an equally deep empathy with the survivors' rage. . . . Hers is more than a passing empathy, for it persists despite Paula being subjected to her captors' horrifying rage as the book attempts to navigate a thin line between revenge and justice" (42).

69. McGowan, *The Silent Dead*, chap. 9 (second ellipsis in the original).

70. McGowan, *The Silent Dead*, author's note.

71. Claire McGowan, *The Killing House*, chap. 23.

72. McGowan, *The Killing House*, chap. 1.

Part Three. Saint Christopher

1. While this section focuses on works by Gerard Brennan, Stuart Neville, Steve Cavanagh, and Eoin McNamee, Adrian McKinty has announced that an upcoming book in the Sean Duffy series will be titled *Hang on St. Christopher*, another reference to a song by Tom Waits.

2. Fintan O'Toole, "From Chandler and the 'Playboy,'" 361.

5. A Disordered World

1. Gerard Brennan, *Disorder*, 7.

2. Brennan, *Disorder*, 18.

3. Brennan, *Disorder*, 121.

4. Brennan, *Disorder*, 24.

5. Brennan, *Disorder*, 38.

6. Gerard Brennan, email interview with the author, Apr. 17, 2018 (second ellipsis in the original).

7. Brennan, *Disorder*, 47.

8. Brennan, *Disorder*, 80.

9. Brennan, *Disorder*, 44.

10. Brennan, *Disorder*, 62.

11. Brennan, *Disorder*, 22 (ellipsis in the original).

12. Brennan, *Disorder*, 60.

13. In the introduction to *Belfast Noir*, Adrian McKinty and Stuart Neville underscore the ways in which economic disparity in contemporary Belfast masks the continued struggles of the working class and associated sectarian resentment from middle-class areas that are not immediately affected by these issues: "For all the shimmer and shine of the new Belfast, you can still walk a mile or two in almost any direction and find some of the worst deprivation in Western Europe. Those parts of the city have not moved on. While the middle class has enjoyed the spoils of the peace dividend, working-class areas have seen little improvement. The sectarian and paramilitary murals are still there: crude memorials . . . to heroes and martyrs still revered. . . . [D]enizens have trained themselves not to see these scars of the past. . . . [U]nderneath the fragile peace darker forces still lurk" (18–20).

14. Brennan, *Disorder*, 15.

15. Brennan, *Disorder*, 14.

16. Brennan, email interview with the author.

17. Brennan, *Disorder*, 48.

18. Brennan, *Disorder*, 42.

19. Brennan, *Disorder*, 125.

20. Brennan, *Disorder*, 123.

21. Brennan, *Disorder*, 101–2.

22. Brennan, *Disorder*, 124.

23. Brennan, email interview with the author.

24. Brennan, *Disorder*, 238.

25. Brennan, *Disorder*, 133–34.

26. Brennan, *Disorder*, 278.

27. Brennan, email interview with the author.

28. Brennan, *Disorder*, 282.

29. Brennan, *Disorder*, 112.

30. Brennan, *Disorder*, 113.

31. Brennan, *Disorder*, 111.

32. Brennan, *Disorder*, 147.

33. Brennan, *Disorder*, 166.

34. Brennan, *Disorder*, 167.

35. Brennan, *Disorder*, 268.

36. Brennan, email interview with the author.

37. Brennan, email interview with the author.

38. Brennan, *Disorder*, 247.

39. Neville's representation of the twelve has been interpreted in various ways; in "'The Place You Don't Belong': Stuart Neville's Belfast," Fiona Coffey asserts that "the ghosts are not represented as the symptoms of a psychotic mind, but as the real tortured souls of Troubles victims demanding justice from beyond the grave" (98). Brian Cliff, in *Irish Crime Fiction*, concurs with Coffey, offering that "it is essential to note . . . that these ghosts are in fact ghosts: they are not Fegan's feverish imaginations, not his guilt taking the form of the Freudian uncanny returned, and not just madness" (40). Gerard Brennan is less committal, writing in "The Truth Commissioners" that "whether the ghosts in *The Twelve* are metaphorical or actual manifestations is a moot point" (206). My sense is that Neville deliberately provides evidence that the twelve are actual ghosts (especially in that Fegan is not the only person who sees them) and contrasting evidence that leaves room for doubt, particularly through Fegan's internal confession that the information given to him by the twelve may in fact be a repressed part of his own understanding, as I discuss later in this chapter. In a way, this calculated obfuscation challenges readers to interrogate perceptions of trauma as anything less than a physical reality.

40. Stuart Neville, *The Ghosts of Belfast*, 8.

41. Neville, *The Ghosts of Belfast*, 27.

42. Neville, *The Ghosts of Belfast*, 122.

43. Neville, *The Ghosts of Belfast*, 57.

44. Neville, *The Ghosts of Belfast*, 35.

45. Neville, *The Ghosts of Belfast*, 124.

46. Neville, *The Ghosts of Belfast*, 213.

47. In "'The Place You Don't Belong,'" Fiona Coffey draws a connection between Neville's depiction of the North—a place where the boundaries between both peace and war and progress and corruption are blurred—and the compromises involved in the Good Friday Agreement: "Indeed, the very premise of *The Twelve* is that the victims of Troubles violence have not received justice since the Agreement. They are now forced to pursue individual retribution in order to achieve a sense of peace. This inherent contradiction—that justice can only be achieved outside of the law—along with the conflation of justice with retribution reflects how unstable Neville views the current peace process" (95). While raising similar concerns as other authors from the North, particularly Claire McGowan, Neville's outlook is

considerably bleaker, framing the early release clause less as the "price of peace" than as a solution so contradictory to the human drive for justice and closure that it is likely untenable. Coffey's phrasing is also interesting in its implication that Fegan, the central pursuer of "individual retribution" in *The Twelve*, can be viewed as a type of victim of the Troubles—a point that I touch on later in this chapter.

48. Neville, *The Ghosts of Belfast*, 6.

49. Neville, *The Ghosts of Belfast*, 166.

50. Neville, *The Ghosts of Belfast*, 61.

51. Neville, *The Ghosts of Belfast*, 164.

52. Neville, *The Ghosts of Belfast*, 97.

53. Neville, *The Ghosts of Belfast*, 257.

54. Neville, *The Ghosts of Belfast*, 91.

55. Neville, *The Ghosts of Belfast*, 106–7.

56. Neville, *The Ghosts of Belfast*, 165–66.

57. Neville, *The Ghosts of Belfast*, 324.

58. As Coffey notes, setting up indistinct boundaries between right and wrong, good and evil, and paramilitaries and government is one of the ways in which Neville breaks stereotypes and binaries associated with Troubles trash novels ("'The Place You Don't Belong,'" 104).

59. Neville, *The Ghosts of Belfast*, 141–42.

60. Neville, *The Ghosts of Belfast*, 166.

61. In "Walking the Tightrope: The Border in Irish Fiction," Brian McGilloway describes Fegan's position as both avenger and agent of injustice as akin to habitation of a kind of borderlands, not unlike the complex Irish border: "It seems wholly appropriate that the book [*The Twelve*] should end on the border, for the protagonist, Gerry Fegan, inhabits a number of borderlands of his own, both moral and psychological" (304–5). Interestingly, in *Irish Crime Fiction*, Brian Cliff makes a similar contention about uncertainty of ethical position in McGilloway's Inspector Devlin series, arguing that Devlin's empathy often creates "a seemingly irresolvable conflict" wherein no clearly just or moral stance can be defined (87).

62. Neville, *The Ghosts of Belfast*, 101.

63. In *Irish Crime Fiction*, Brian Cliff comes to a different conclusion on this point, drawing a distinction between forgiveness and mercy, and arguing that the latter "is of its nature bestowed rather than earned" (43). In either reading, however, Fegan is differentiated from the other targets of the twelve's revenge, who are not spared. In "The Truth Commissioners," Gerard Brennan explains the difference between Fegan's perception of himself and of the other targets in terms of conscious intent: "Fegan figures that the ghosts see him as an extension of the guns or bombs that killed them. He's a machine of death, bred to kill. But the ghosts want the blood of the men who pulled the triggers" (206).

64. Neville, *The Ghosts of Belfast*, 198.

65. Neville, *The Ghosts of Belfast*, 309.

66. Neville, *The Ghosts of Belfast*, 54.

67. Neville, *The Ghosts of Belfast*, 206.

68. Neville, *The Ghosts of Belfast*, 103–4.

69. Even Coffey's reading of the text, in "'The Place You Don't Belong,'" which maintains that the twelve are literal ghosts, also acknowledges allegorical connotations to the spirits. Specifically, Coffey indicates that Fegan's situation plays a role in defining Neville's larger argument "that Troubles trauma and violence continue to define and shape the peace process . . . that the history of the North will never be fully escaped," and "that the peace process is defined by a marked haunting of the past that must be fully recognized" (99, 105).

70. Neville, *The Ghosts of Belfast*, 84.

71. Neville, *The Ghosts of Belfast*, 83–84.

72. Neville, *The Ghosts of Belfast*, 70.

73. Neville, *The Ghosts of Belfast*, 254.

74. Neville, *The Ghosts of Belfast*, 175.

75. Neville, *The Ghosts of Belfast*, 175.

76. Neville, *The Ghosts of Belfast*, 297–98.

77. Neville, *The Ghosts of Belfast*, 83.

78. Neville, *The Ghosts of Belfast*, 137.

79. Neville, *The Ghosts of Belfast*, 167.

80. Neville, *The Ghosts of Belfast*, 195.

81. Neville, *The Ghosts of Belfast*, 198.

82. Steve Cavanagh, email interview with the author, May 15, 2018.

83. Brian McGilloway, "Top Ten Northern Irish Crime Novels," n.p.

84. Cavanagh, email interview with the author.

85. Steve Cavanagh, *The Defense*, 117.

86. Cavanagh, *The Defense*, 125.

87. Cavanagh, *The Defense*, 251.

88. Cavanagh, *The Defense*, 8–9.

89. Cavanagh, *The Defense*, 17.

90. Cavanagh, *The Defense*, 101–3.

91. Cavanagh, *The Defense*, 1.

92. Cavanagh, *The Defense*, 10.

93. Cavanagh, *The Defense*, 143–44.

94. Cavanagh, *The Defense*, 122.

95. Cavanagh, *The Defense*, 203–4.

96. Cavanagh, email interview with the author.

97. Cavanagh, *The Defense*, 197.

98. Cavanagh, *The Defense*, 281.

99. Cavanagh, *The Defense*, 120.

100. Cavanagh, *The Defense*, 306.

6. The Stories We Tell

1. "The Boy Who Fitted the Bill," *Herald Scotland*, Mar. 10, 1995, http://www.heraldscotland.com/news/12541447.The_boy_who_fitted_the_bill/.

2. Eoin McNamee, *The Blue Tango*, vii.

3. McNamee, *The Blue Tango*, 71.

4. "Boy Who Fitted the Bill."

5. "Last Man Hanged in Ireland 50 Years Ago," *South Belfast News*, Dec. 5, 2011, http://belfastmediagroup.com/last-man-hanged-in-ireland-50-years-ago/.

6. Tom McAlindon, "Robert the Painter: An Ulster Parable," n.p. (ellipsis in the original).

7. Eoin McNamee, *Orchid Blue*, 30.

8. McNamee, *Orchid Blue*, 153.

9. McNamee, *The Blue Tango*, 188–89.

10. McNamee, *Orchid Blue*, 184.

11. McNamee, *Orchid Blue*, 176.

12. McNamee, *Orchid Blue*, 239.

13. McNamee, *The Blue Tango*, 16.

14. McNamee, *Orchid Blue*, 224.

15. McNamee, *The Blue Tango*, 36.

16. McNamee, *The Blue Tango*, 18.

17. McNamee, *Orchid Blue*, 76.

18. Eoin McNamee, *Blue Is the Night*, chap. 16.

19. McNamee, *Orchid Blue*, 261.

20. McNamee, *Blue Is the Night*, chap. 8.

21. McNamee, *Blue Is the Night*, chap. 9.

22. McNamee, *Orchid Blue*, 166.

23. McNamee, *The Blue Tango*, 205.

24. McNamee, *Orchid Blue*, 246.

25. McNamee, *Orchid Blue*, 248.

26. McNamee, *Orchid Blue*, 246.

27. McNamee, *Blue Is the Night*, chap. 12.

28. McNamee, *Orchid Blue*, 127.

29. McNamee, *Orchid Blue*, 192.

30. McNamee, *Orchid Blue*, 242.

31. McNamee, *Orchid Blue*, 11.

32. McNamee, *Orchid Blue*, 227.

33. McNamee, *The Blue Tango*, 152–53.

34. McNamee, *The Blue Tango*, viii–ix.

35. McNamee, *Blue Is the Night*, chap. 5.

36. Laura Lippman, "When Crime Comes for the Crime Writer," n.p.

37. McNamee, *Orchid Blue*, 168.

38. McNamee, *The Blue Tango*, 36.

39. McNamee, *The Blue Tango*, 195.

40. McNamee, *The Blue Tango*, 132.

41. McNamee, *The Blue Tango*, 38.

42. McNamee, *The Blue Tango*, 42.

43. McNamee, *The Blue Tango*, 67.

44. McNamee, *The Blue Tango*, 48.

45. McNamee, *Orchid Blue*, 47.

46. McNamee, *The Blue Tango*, 124.

47. McNamee, *The Blue Tango*, 8.

48. McNamee, *The Blue Tango*, 225–26.

49. McNamee, *The Blue Tango*, 193.

50. McNamee, *The Blue Tango*, 127.

51. McNamee, *The Blue Tango*, 126.

52. McNamee, *Orchid Blue*, 8.

53. McNamee, *Blue Is the Night*, chap. 5.

54. McNamee, *Blue Is the Night*, chap. 7.

55. McNamee, *Blue Is the Night*, chap. 3.

56. Brian Cliff, "Why Irish Crime Fiction Is in Murderously Good Health," *Irish Times*, July 25, 2018, https://www.irishtimes.com/culture/books/why-irish-crime-fiction-is-in-murderously-good-health-1.3569128?mode=amp.

57. Niamh O'Connor, "The Executioners' Songs," 197–98.

58. McNamee, *Orchid Blue*, 174.

59. McNamee, *Orchid Blue*, 3–4.

60. McNamee, *Orchid Blue*, 274.

61. McNamee, *Orchid Blue*, 174.

62. McNamee, *Orchid Blue*, 167.

63. McNamee, *Blue Is the Night*, chap. 17.

64. McNamee, *Blue Is the Night*, chap. 11.

65. McNamee, *Blue Is the Night*, chap. 9.

66. McNamee, *Blue Is the Night*, chap. 13.

67. Cliff, "Why Irish Crime Fiction."

68. Eoin McNamee, "The Judge," 132.

69. McNamee, "The Judge," 132.

70. McNamee, "The Judge," 133.
71. McKinty, *Police at the Station*, 302.
72. McNamee, "The Judge," 137.
73. McNamee, "The Judge," 137–38.
74. McNamee, *Blue Is the Night*, chap. 24.

Conclusion

1. Brian McGilloway, "Walking the Tightrope: The Border in Irish Fiction," 312–13.
2. Colin Dexter, interview with the author, Oxford, July 21, 2015.
3. Nick Clark, "The Morse Code: No Other Actors Will Be Allowed to Play Colin Dexter's Detective after the Late John Thaw," *Independent*, Mar. 25, 2014, https://www.independent.co.uk/arts-entertainment/tv/news/the-morse-code-no-other-actors-will-be-allowed-to-play-colin-dexter-s-detective-after-the-late-john-thaw-9213246.html.
4. Dexter, interview with the author.
5. Colin Dexter, interview by Andrew Gulli, n.p.
6. Brian McGilloway, email interview with the author, Jan. 25, 2018.
7. Claire McGowan, email interview with the author, Mar. 18, 2018.
8. Gerard Brennan, email interview with the author, Apr. 17, 2018.
9. Steve Cavanagh, email interview with the author, May 15, 2018.
10. Adrian McKinty, interview with the author, Belfast, Oct. 28, 2017.

Bibliography

Alvarez, Rafael (adapted from the story by David Simon and Ed Burns). *The Wire*. Season 1, episode 7, "One Arrest." Directed by Joe Chappelle. Aired July 21, 2002, on HBO. https://www.amazon.com/The-Wire/dp /B006GLLTL6/.

Banville, John. "John Banville, the Art of Fiction, no. 200." Interview by Belinda McKeon. *Paris Review*, no. 188 (2009): 132–53.

Baraniuk, Carol. "Negotiating Borders: Inspector Devlin and Shadows of the Past." In *The Contemporary Irish Detective Novel*, edited by Elizabeth Mannion, 73–90. London: Palgrave Macmillan, 2016.

Barclay, Alex. *Darkhouse*. New York: Delacourte Press, 2007. Kindle.

"The Beloved Saint Anthony." Irish Franciscans. Accessed July 7, 2017. www.franciscans.ie/the-beloved-saint-anthony.

Black, Ingrid. "Escaping Irishness." In *Down These Green Streets: Irish Crime Writing in the 21st Century*, edited by Declan Burke, 211–18. Dublin: Liberties Press, 2013. Kindle.

Blakemore, Erin. "How Ireland Turned 'Fallen Women' into Slaves." *History*, Mar. 12, 2018. https://www.history.com/news/magdalene-laundry -ireland-asylum-abuse.

Brennan, Gerard. *Disorder*. Belfast: No Alibis Press, 2018.

———. "The Truth Commissioners." In *Down These Green Streets: Irish Crime Writing in the 21st Century*, edited by Declan Burke, 201–10. Dublin: Liberties Press, 2013. Kindle.

Bruen, Ken. *Cross*. New York: Minotaur Books, 2007.

———. *The Devil*. New York: Minotaur Books, 2010.

———. *The Dramatist*. New York: Minotaur Books, 2004.

———. *The Emerald Lie*. New York: Mysterious Press, 2016.

———. *The Ghosts of Galway*. New York: Mysterious Press, 2017. Kindle.

———. *Green Hell*. New York: Mysterious Press, 2015. Kindle.

———. *The Guards*. New York: Minotaur Books, 2001.

———. *Headstone*. New York: Mysterious Press, 2016.

———. *In the Galway Silence*. New York: Mysterious Press, 2018. Kindle.

———. *The Killing of the Tinkers*. New York: Minotaur Books, 2002.

———. *The Magdalen Martyrs*. New York: Minotaur Books, 2003.

———. *Priest*. New York: Minotaur Books, 2006.

———. *Purgatory*. New York: Mysterious Press, 2013. Kindle.

———. *Sanctuary*. New York: Minotaur Books, 2008.

Burke, Declan. "The Black Stuff: A Conversation with John Banville." In *Down These Green Streets: Irish Crime Writing in the 21st Century*, edited by Declan Burke, 220–32. Dublin: Liberties Press, 2013. Kindle.

———, ed. *Down These Green Streets: Irish Crime Writing in the 21st Century*. Dublin: Liberties Press, 2013. Kindle.

Butler, Alban, and Kathleen Jones. *Butler's Lives of the Saints: June*. Edited by Paul Burns. London: Bloomsbury, 1997.

Casey, Moira E. "'Built on Nothing but Bullshit and Good PR': Crime, Class Mobility, and the Irish Economy in the Novels of Tana French." *Clues* 32, no. 1 (2014): 92–102.

Cavanagh, Steve. *The Defense*. New York: Flatiron Books, 2016. Kindle.

Chandler, Raymond. "The Simple Art of Murder." In *The Longman Anthology of Detective Fiction*, edited by Deane Mansfield-Kelley and Lois Marchino, 208–19. New York: Pearson Longman, 2005.

Cliff, Brian. "A 'Honeycomb World': John Connolly's Charlie Parker Series." In *The Contemporary Irish Detective Novel*, edited by Elizabeth Mannion, 31–44. London: Palgrave Macmillan, 2016.

———. *Irish Crime Fiction*. London: Palgrave Macmillan, 2018.

Coffey, Fiona. "'The Place You Don't Belong': Stuart Neville's Belfast." In *The Contemporary Irish Detective Novel*, edited by Elizabeth Mannion, 91–106. London: Palgrave Macmillan, 2016.

Connolly, John. *Every Dead Thing*. New York: Atria Books, 2000. Kindle.

———. "No Blacks, No Dogs, No Crime Writers: Ireland and the Mystery Genre." In *Down These Green Streets: Irish Crime Writing in the 21st Century*, edited by Declan Burke, 39–57. Dublin: Liberties Press, 2013. Kindle.

Cregan, David. "Divided Subjectivities and Modern Irish Masculinities: 'The Makings of a Man.'" In *Redefinitions of Irish Identity: A*

Postnationalist Approach, edited by Irene Gilsenan Nordin and Carmen Zamorano Llena, 159–79. Oxford: Peter Lang, 2010.

Davis, Colin. "Psychoanalysis, Detection, and Fiction: Julia Kristeva's Detective Novels." *Sites: The Journal of Twentieth-Century/Contemporary French Studies* 6, no. 2 (2002): 294–305.

Dexter, Colin. Interview by Andrew F. Gulli. Excerpts from *Strand Magazine* 19 (2006). https://strandmag.com/the-magazine/interviews/colin -dexter/.

———. *The Remorseful Day*. New York: Ballantine Books, 1999. Kindle.

Evans, Shaun. "Endeavour: Shaun Evans Video Chat." Interview by Erin Delaney. *Masterpiece*, PBS, 2014. Video, 30:47. https://www.youtube .com/watch?v=THJON6QcS-w.

Farnum, Mabel Adelaide. *Saint Anthony of Padua: His Life and Miracles*. London: Didier, 1948.

French, Tana. *In the Woods*. New York: Penguin Books, 2007. Kindle.

Hughes, Declan. "Irish Hard-Boiled Crime: A 51st State of Mind." In *Down These Green Streets: Irish Crime Writing in the 21st Century*, edited by Declan Burke, 161–68. Dublin: Liberties Press, 2013. Kindle.

Kincaid, Andrew. "Detecting Hope: Ken Bruen's Disenchanted P.I." In *The Contemporary Irish Detective Novel*, edited by Elizabeth Mannion, 57–71. London: Palgrave Macmillan, 2016.

———. "'Down These Mean Streets': The City and Critique in Contemporary Irish Noir." *Éire-Ireland* 45, nos. 1–2 (2010): 39–55.

Kirby, Peadar, Luke Gibbons, and Michael Cronin, eds. *Reinventing Ireland: Culture, Society and the Global Economy*. London: Pluto Press, 2002.

Lippman, Laura. "When Crime Comes for the Crime Writer." *Vulture*, July 31, 2018. http://www.vulture.com/2018/07/when-crime-comes-for-the -crime-writer.html.

Mannion, Elizabeth, ed. *The Contemporary Irish Detective Novel*. London: Palgrave Macmillan, 2016.

Mannion, Elizabeth, and Brian Cliff, eds. *Guilt Rules All: Irish Mystery, Detective, and Crime Fiction*. Syracuse, NY: Syracuse Univ. Press, 2020.

McAlindon, Tom. "Robert the Painter: An Ulster Parable." *History Ireland* 8, no. 2 (2000). https://www.historyireland.com/troubles-in-ni/ni -1920-present/robert-the-painter-an-ulster-parable/.

McCoy, Kevin. "Western Health Board Inquiry into Brothers of Charity Services in Galway." Health Service Executive. Accessed Aug. 15, 2018. https://www.hse.ie/eng/services/publications/disability/mcoy-boc.pdf.

McCullough, Denis. "Inquiry into Certain Matters Relating to Maynooth College." Wayback Machine Internet Archive. Accessed Aug. 15, 2018. https://web.archive.org/web/20110721125511/http://www.maynooth college.ie/news/documents/McCulloughReport.pdf.

McGilloway, Brian. *Bad Blood*. New York: Witness Impulse, 2017. Kindle.

———. *The Forgotten Ones*. New York: Witness Impulse, 2015. Kindle.

———. *Little Girl Lost*. New York: Witness Impulse, 2014. Kindle.

———. *Someone You Know*. New York: Witness Impulse, 2014. Kindle.

———. "Top Ten Northern Irish Crime Novels." *Strand Magazine*, June 19, 2017. https://strandmag.com/top-ten-northern-irish-crime-novels/.

———. "Walking the Tightrope: The Border in Irish Fiction." In *Down These Green Streets: Irish Crime Writing in the 21st Century*, edited by Declan Burke, 302–13. Dublin: Liberties Press, 2013. Kindle.

McGowan, Claire. *Blood Tide*. London: Headline, 2017. Kindle.

———. *The Dead Ground*. London: Headline, 2014.

———. *The Killing House*. London, Headline, 2018. Kindle.

———. *The Lost*. London: Headline, 2013.

———. *A Savage Hunger*. London: Headline, 2016. Kindle.

———. *The Silent Dead*. London: Headline, 2015. Kindle.

McKinty, Adrian. *The Cold Ground*. Amherst, NY: Seventh Street Books, 2012. Kindle.

———. *Gun Street Girl*. Amherst, NY: Seventh Street Books, 2015. Kindle.

———. *I Hear the Sirens in the Street*. Amherst, NY: Seventh Street Books, 2013. Kindle.

———. *In the Morning I'll Be Gone*. Ashland, OR: Blackstone, 2019.

———. "Odd Men Out." In *Down These Green Streets: Irish Crime Writing in the 21st Century*, edited by Declan Burke, 96–105. Dublin: Liberties Press, 2013. Kindle.

———. *Police at the Station and They Don't Look Friendly*. Amherst, NY: Seventh Street Books, 2017. Kindle.

———. *Rain Dogs*. Amherst, NY: Seventh Street Books, 2016. Kindle.

McKinty, Adrian, and Stuart Neville. Introduction to *Belfast Noir*, edited by Adrian McKinty and Stuart Neville, 13–20. New York: Akashic Books, 2014. Kindle.

McNamee, Eoin. *Blue Is the Night*. London: Faber and Faber, 2014. Kindle.

———. *The Blue Tango*. London: Faber and Faber, 2001.

———. "The Judge." In *Down These Green Streets: Irish Crime Writing in the 21st Century*, edited by Declan Burke, 130–38. Dublin: Liberties Press, 2013. Kindle.

———. *Orchid Blue*. London: Faber and Faber, 2010. Kindle.

Murphy, Paula. "Murderous Mayhem: Ken Bruen and the New Ireland." *Clues* 24, no. 2 (2006): 3–16.

Murphy, Robert (adapted from the novel by Peter Robinson). *DCI Banks*. Season 1, episode 8, "Cold Is the Grave: Part 2." Directed by Marek Losey. Aired Oct. 21, 2011, on ITV. https://www.amazon.com/Aftermath -Part-One/dp/B07CJSGDK8/.

Neville, Stuart. *The Ghosts of Belfast*. New York: Soho Press, 2009. Kindle.

O'Connell, Gerard. "Pope Francis Summons the World's Top Bishops for Sexual Abuse Prevention Summit." *America: The Jesuit Review*, Sept. 12, 2018, https://www.americamagazine.org/faith/2018/09/12/pope -francis-summons-worlds-top-bishops-sexual-abuse-prevention-summit.

O'Connor, Niamh. "The Executioners' Songs." In *Down These Green Streets: Irish Crime Writing in the 21st Century*, edited by Declan Burke, 195–200. Dublin: Liberties Press, 2013. Kindle.

O'Toole, Fintan. *The Ex-Isle of Erin: Images of a Global Ireland*. Dublin: New Island Books, 1997.

———. "From Chandler and the 'Playboy' to the Contemporary Crime Wave." In *Down These Green Streets: Irish Crime Writing in the 21st Century*, edited by Declan Burke, 358–61. Dublin: Liberties Press, 2013. Kindle.

Peterson, Shirley. "Homicide and Home-icide: Exhuming Ireland's Past in the Detective Novels of Tana French." *Clues* 30, no. 2 (2012): 97–108.

———. "Voicing the Unspeakable: Tana French's Dublin Murder Squad." In *The Contemporary Irish Detective Novel*, edited by Elizabeth Mannion, 107–20. London: Palgrave Macmillan, 2016.

Phillips, Bill. "Religious Belief in Recent Detective Fiction." *Atlantis: Journal of the Spanish Association of Anglo-American Studies* 36, no. 1 (2014): 139–51.

Rawson, Eric. "To Hell with Ya: *Katabasis* in Hard-Boiled Detective Fiction." *Journal of Popular Culture* 42, no. 2 (2009): 291–303.

Reddy, Maureen T. "Contradictions in the Irish Hardboiled: Detective Fiction's Uneasy Portrayal of a New Ireland." *New Hibernia Review* 19, no. 4 (2015): 126–40.

Reitz, Caroline. "Nancy Drew, Dragon Tattoo: Female Detective Fiction and the Ethics of Care." *Textus* 27, no. 2 (2014): 19–46.

"A Saint of Many Miracles." *Irish Catholic*, June 9, 2016. https://www.irishcatholic.com/a-saint-of-many-miracles/.

Schaffer, Rachel. "Mystery, Memory, Metaphor, and Metonymy *In the Woods*." *Clues* 35, no. 1 (2017): 93–102.

Summers Stephenson, Mimosa. "Liminality in the Novels of Tana French." *Clues* 32, no. 1 (2014): 51–60.

Teel, John. "Blurring the Genre Borderlines: Tana French's Haunted Detectives." *Clues* 32, no. 1 (2014): 13–21.

Yost, Graham (adapted from the story by Elmore Leonard). *Justified*. Season 1, episode 6, "The Collection." Directed by Rod Holcomb. Aired Apr. 20, 2010, on FX. https://www.amazon.com/Pilot/dp/B003AYU23I/.

Index

257

Photograph by Jaytee Van Stean, 2021. https://fotoinitiative.de/.

Anjili Babbar has a PhD from the University of Rochester and MAs from the University of Rochester and McGill University. She is a scholar of Irish and British literature, with a particular focus on crime fiction and criminality, including literary forgery and deception. She has published on topics ranging from Irish crime fiction to representations of Irish folklore in popular culture.

CPSIA information can be obtained
at www.ICGtesting.com
Printed in the USA
LVHW010903150723
752409LV00003B/292

9 780815 611578